SHADOW HUNT

Gabriel knew he'd found the lair.

He took a few cautious steps forward and the dirt beneath his feet gave way. His right foot disappeared into nothingness, but he managed to catch himself. The lantern, thankfully, had not gone out. He picked it up and held it out in front of him.

Below him was a deep pit, a hole, at least fifteen feet deep, perhaps much deeper, and easily as wide. At first his mind rebelled against identifying what his lantern revealed down inside this hole. Then his eyes settled on a pattern of yellow daisies on white just below him. And then every form below defined itself in the gloom.

The pit was filled with rotting human corpses. . . .

Praise for Jane Jensen's first
***Gabriel Knight*® interactive adventure**
***Sins of the Father*™**

"Stands as a pinnacle in the annals of interactive fiction."   —*Computer Gaming World*

"Every aspect of this neo-Gothic psycho-thriller is designed to raise the hackles of even the most seasoned of gamers . . . a not-to-be-missed experience."   —*INTERACTION* magazine

"Has the pacing of a spine-tingling horror novel."
          —*PC Gamer*

THE
BEAST
WITHIN

A GABRIEL KNIGHT™ MYSTERY

Jane Jensen

A ROC BOOK

ROC
Published by the Penguin Group
Penguin Putnam Inc., 375 Hudson Street,
New York, New York 10014, U.S.A.
Penguin Books Ltd, 27 Wrights Lane,
London W8 5TZ, England
Penguin Books Australia Ltd, Ringwood,
Victoria, Australia
Penguin Books Canada Ltd, 10 Alcorn Avenue,
Toronto, Ontario, Canada M4V 3B2
Penguin Books (N.Z.) Ltd, 182–190 Wairau Road,
Auckland 10, New Zealand

Penguin Books Ltd, Registered Offices:
Harmondsworth, Middlesex, England

First published by Roc, an imprint of Dutton NAL,
a member of Penguin Putnam Inc.

First Printing, December, 1998
10 9 8 7 6 5 4 3 2 1

 REGISTERED TRADEMARK—MARCA REGISTRADA

Printed in the United States of America

To my husband and confidant,
Robert Holmes

ACKNOWLEDGMENTS

Thanks to Sabine Duvall, Nathan and Darlou Gams, Will Binder, Dean Erickson, Joanne Takahashi, Peter Lucas, Richard Raynesford, Wolf Muser, Russell Mitchell, Clabe Hartley, Clement v. Frankenstein, Edmund Shaff, Andrea Martin, Kay Kuter, Nicholas Worth, Frederick Solmes, Judith Drake, Bruce Morrow, Brad Greenquist, and the many other members of the Beast cast, crew, and production staff for making the filmed version of this story so rewarding, and for their influences on this retelling, both subtle and overt.

I'd also like to thank several of Ludwig's excellent biographers including Desmond Chapman-Huston and Anton Sailer for their work, and to acknowledge my primary werewolf sources including Charlotte F. Otten's wonderful "A Lycanthropic Reader" and Richard Nolls' "Vampires, Werewolves & Demons."

Prologue

Rittersberg, Bavaria
1750

The jailer's name was Aug. It had once been Augustus, but the boy had none of his mother's pretensions, and no one still living knew the longer appellation that made sense of the shorter—not even the jailer's wife.

Right now Aug wished he'd taken the higher road his mother'd urged and had ended up an officer in the army perhaps, or a local magistrate or solicitor. For that matter, he would gratefully trade places with the merchants or farmers, the ones sent to destroy the Beast's family. Even being the executioner would be better, for *his* duty would be carried out tomorrow in the sane light of day and amidst the fear-salving crowd at the scaffold. He'd rather be *anyone* and *anywhere* other than the village jailer sitting where he was sitting at this moment—alone, at night.

Which was at the wooden table outside the dungeon door. Aug rooted himself to the spot by sheer force of will, not because he was brave (although he'd seen battle with the French and was brave enough) but because it was his job, and to refuse would mean not only the loss of it but loss of face in the village as well. He told himself that the door was made of massive oak planks chosen expressly for the purpose of confinement, and that the iron bar that lay across it was the finest chastity belt ever given that seductress,

Escape. But both the bar and the door had been invented for the worst that a *man* could do. Who knew what the Beast was capable of?

Helllllpppppppppppppppppppppppmeeeeeeeeeeeeeeeeee-eeeeeeeeeeeeeepleeeeeeeeeeeeeeeeeeeeeeseinGoooooooo-oooooooooooooodsnaaaaaaaaaaaaame!

The pleas went far beyond shrieks of pain. He knew a man's scream well enough. This was not a human body in pain; it was a soul's anguish. It was the sound of the act of damnation.

Aug clutched the rough table in front of him as desperately as he would grip an assailant's neck. His tanned and weathered face was the shade of palest coffee, like the cast of fresh cream in a brown wooden bucket. His eyes were fixed on the dungeon door. His brain stopped reassuring itself about locks and hinges and began reciting the rosary.

And still the cries went on. The screams became deeper and gruffer; the words were taken over by snarls. . . .

Hail Mary, full of grace, have mercy on us poor sinners now and in our hour of need . . .

And then stopped abruptly.

For what seemed like an eternity, there was only the sound of Aug's own terrified heartbeat.

Then there was a snuffling sound, very close by, a low, huffing grunt, like a pig in the dirt but darker, *larger.*

And something began to scratch at the door.

Chapter 1

Spring, 1995
Schloss Ritter, Rittersberg, Germany

UNTITLED *Blake Backlash* adventure
by Gabriel Knight
chapter 1, page 1

More than a year since his last big case, Blake Backlash found himself stuck in a dilapidated castle. He's supposed to be some kind of hero, having inherited late Uncle Daemon's role of "Guardian of Truth and Light" along with this wreck of a family fortress. What Uncle D. didn't explain was what the hell that meant. The most exciting developments of the past year involved building plaster and a lot of hammering. It was enough to drive a scion to seek out the highest ramparts and throw himself over. Still, he reasoned, things could be worse. If it wasn't for all the money he'd stolen from the voodoo *hounfour* before it went up into flames, he'd still be reading by candlelight and freezing his balls off in this Bavarian refrigerator.

Fortunately, Blake was about to be rescued from the ordeal of self-reflection. Brunhilde brings in the mail one chilly spring morning and he finds a mysterious package—postmark: India. Curious, he rips open the thick brown wrapper and out falls

"Out falls . . ." Gabriel Knight muttered, staring at the page in the typewriter with knotted brow. His fingers thrummed on the desk.

There followed a long and ultimately unproductive pause.

"Damn it!"

He struck his hand on the table in frustration and ripped the page from the typewriter's grasp. The opening wasn't bad—it was what came next that sucked. He'd had a brief glimmer about a haunted ashram last night, but in the glare of the waiting page, Blake Backlash in a sari revealed itself as worse than unbelievable; it was self-parody. He wadded up the sheet of paper and sent it sailing to the floor, where it was happily reunited with a few dozen of its closest relatives.

For the tenth time since dinner he got up and paced over to the window. Down below, the town of Rittersberg should have been asleep, disappearing as its lights were put out, one by one. But the lights in many of the homes still shone, the village floating on the darkness. For this reason Gabriel mistakenly deduced that it was earlier than it actually was, and his self-recrimination eased just a bit.

Still time to come up with something before bedtime, or at least assuage the recalcitrant muses with a show of faith.

Were those flashlights down below?

He'd just put a fresh sheet in the typewriter when a knock came at the library door. Not surprisingly, it was Gerde Hull, the only other human being living at Schloss Ritter. Gerde had served great-uncle Wolfgang as housekeeper too—for years, it seemed. Still, she was a quite attractive blonde, despite her air of having walked these halls for eons.

Not that he'd noticed.

"Herr Knight? Some people are downstairs to see you."

"What, *now*?" The natives had not exactly beaten a path to his door, even in the light of day.

But Gerde had that serious look on her face. "Yes, Herr Knight. Will you please come down?"

He leaned back in his chair and studied her. "What's up? You've been actin' weird all day."

She had, in fact, been gone most of the day, and when she'd finally served him dinner, her surreptitious glances had been heavier than the *hackbraten*.

"Just come downstairs, please. And don't forget your talisman." She observed its position on the desk critically. "You should wear it. *Always.*"

"Damn thing's heavy," Gabriel muttered defensively as he slipped the chain over his head. But Gerde was already gone, pointedly leaving the door open behind her.

Gerde was waiting for him at the castle's front doors. He joined her at one of the massive handles, and together they pulled.

He was blinded by the glare of flashlights—a lot of flashlights. He stole a glance at Gerde as the beams were being politely redirected. The Determined One did not look back.

Ah! It overcame him with a wave of déjà vu. The image he was recalling was not an experience of his own; it was the imprint left by watching too many 1950s Hammer films.

He smiled satirically. "Shouldn't those be torches?"

Werner Huber stepped forward. The tall old man was Gerde's uncle and the owner of the local *gasthof*; a man so traditional he made *The Sound of Music* look like counterculture. He was clearly spokesman of this group, as one of the few English speakers in the village. And he was not amused.

"Herr Knight, we have come for the *Schattenjäger.*"

He used the formal title—*Schattenjäger,* Shadow Hunter. It was as dramatic a gesture as the midnight visit, but for some reason, perhaps it was the old man's expression, Gabriel suddenly found the situation not at all funny. "Really? What seems to be the trouble?"

Werner put his hand on the shoulder of a small, plain-looking man. "This is my cousin, the Huber

Sepp. He has a farm up north, just outside of Munich.''

Huber gazed up at Gabriel with red, swollen eyes.

''Two nights ago his daughter Toni was outside playing in the grass. There is a forest along his property, yes? And the child liked to play close to the trees.''

Gabriel's stomach began to tighten. No, this was definitely not amusing.

''It was getting dark, and the mother goes to the door to call in the child. She sees Toni at the edge of the woods. Then she sees something else—a wolf, she thinks. It is huge, and it is moving toward the child!''

Sepp Huber was looking at the ground.

''She screams to Toni a warning and begins to run toward her. Sepp is in the barn. He hears his wife screaming and knows that something is terribly wrong. He grabs his gun and comes out, but by now it is already too late.''

Werner glanced at Sepp, past Sepp, and Gabriel realized that the woman was here, the mother. She was a tiny, round thing. She stepped out from her husband's side so that Gabriel could see her better or, perhaps, so that she could see him. Her eyes were gray and long-lashed. There was something dire in them.

''They say she died quickly,'' Werner concluded.

''She did,'' the mother said in a thick but firm voice.

Gabriel felt a terrible weight press on him. It seemed to come through her eyes.

''It was dragging her away,'' she said. ''I didn't know if she was dead, but I was not about to let that . . . that *thing* . . . I grabbed for her foot, but her boot . . .''

The night fell silent except for the sound of crickets. Her mouth remained open for a moment, as though she would go on, but it slowly closed.

Gabriel glanced at Werner. The old man shook his head solemnly. ''They buried the remains of Toni yesterday.'' He took out a handkerchief and wiped his brow. ''It was a very small box, Herr Knight.''

"I'm . . . sorry," Gabriel said. He felt a sick dread at the story's images.

"You can help them," Gerde replied.

Gabriel shot her a glance. What did she expect him to do?

"Haven't you notified the police?" he asked gently.

"*Ja, natürlich!*" Werner replied disdainfully. "The police believe it is wolves escaped from a zoo! This is not the first such killing, Herr Knight. There have been others, all near Munich. And the police, they find nothing!"

Gabriel blinked at the old man, startled. "There have been *other* wolf attacks?"

"Other attacks, yes. All in the past few weeks. But the killer is not a *wolf,* Herr Knight." Werner was looking at him as though he were stupid.

"But you just said . . ."

"I *saw* it." The quiet words came from the mother, and it silenced all others effortlessly.

"*What* did you see, Frau Huber?"

She stared at Gabriel unswervingly. "It was *not* a wolf, Herr Knight. It was a *beast*—something bad, something terrible. And its eyes . . . its eyes were *human.*"

Her own beautiful and dreadful eyes sent a chill through him as she said this. His mind conjured up a wolf's howl to chase the goose bumps on his spine. It would almost be funny if it wasn't so goddamn awful, if these people weren't *serious,* and if he wasn't suddenly so creeped out.

"Are you saying it was a . . . a . . ."

"*Werewolf,*" Werner said.

"Christ!"

"I have told them that you are the new *Schatten-jäger,*" Gerde interjected helpfully. "Wolfgang said it was meant to be before he died."

"I know, I—"

But Gerde and Werner had obviously worked out a tag-team approach in advance, for Werner did not let him speak. "*Are* you the *Schattenjäger,* Herr Knight? Or are you not?"

You had to hand it to the old guy, he was blunt. Werner's bushy eyebrows furrowed at him in the battery-operated brightness, and Gabriel understood that his choice in this matter would mean a lot more than whether or not he'd be hanging out in Munich for a few weeks. After all, he'd come to this tiny German village a family heir, bearer of the blood that had named the town, the Ritters. He'd been chosen successor to a strange priestly tradition these people took as seriously as they took their lederhosen. This might be a forgotten part of the world, but the villagers themselves knew damn well who they were and what they believed in.

But it was *his* heritage, after all, not *theirs.*

Gabriel crossed his arms stubbornly. "Of course I am."

Werner grunted. "Then you will do it? You will find the werewolf and kill it?"

"Well, I'd be happy to look into it for you. See what I can find out, but . . ."

"Yes! Good!" Werner clapped his hands together. "Sepp and Christa go to Regensburg to be with her mother. Their farm will be empty for a while—you can stay there. Meet us at the *gasthof* in one hour."

Before Gabriel could even speak, Werner and the others were walking away.

"I'll go pack your things," Gerde said. She actually smiled at him for a change.

"Great. Thanks," Gabriel deadpanned. He opened his mouth to have it out with her, but she was already slipping inside.

He was not at all surprised to find a bag packed and waiting for him when he reached his room sixty seconds later. He supposed she'd figured he'd need it either way—whether he took the case or not.

It was a stiff neck that woke him well before noon. He was up from the couch where he'd slept in an instant, excited about being on a new case, though he told himself it might well lead nowhere. He'd noticed little about the Huber farmhouse when he'd arrived last night; he was too tired and it was too dark. In the light of day the traditional plaster-and-frame home was clean and uncluttered. One room done in oak furniture and country prints served as kitchen, dining, and living rooms. A doorway led to a hall, the bedrooms, and a bath. It was a bit too cutesy for his taste, and the sense of Toni Huber rested on everything like invisible sheets.

He opened his suitcase, anxious to be on his way. Right on top was yesterday's unopened mail—a letter from Grace—stuck in there by a certain meddling hausfrau. He frowned as he pulled out a clear pair of jeans and a white T-shirt. A new case. He should call Grace. He ripped open the letter with a sigh.

St. George's Books, New Orleans
Gabriel:
   I have an amazing new preternatural phenomenon to tell you about—sales have actually been picking up around the shop. I know it's too bizarre to be true, but I swear I've seen it with my own eyes. In other fortean shockers, that Blake Backlash epic, *The Voodoo Murders,* is up to #20 on the *New York Times* paperback best-seller list. Avonly has deposited a couple more checks, and your U.S. bank account is blossoming—not unlike the desert after a fluke storm.
   So have you made your decision yet? I know I'm bugging you about it, but—look, I can still register for classes next fall if I hurry. If you decide to sell the shop and move to Germany, that's fine, but I really need to know. Okay?
   Anyway, I've been reading up on a little German as well as anything occult I can find. I've also been getting three major newspapers. Haven't seen anything that looks like a case so far. Have you?
   Write soon. Grace

"Gaaaaaaaad!' Gabriel tossed the letter down and rubbed his eyes.

Grace Nakimura had been preying on his mind for a while now. This was not the first letter of its kind, and it made him feel . . . well, guilty. After the Voodoo Murders case she'd asked to stay on at the shop, excited by some Chandler-esque vision, wanting to help out with this whole *Schattenjäger* business. It had seemed like a fine idea at first. She'd practically taken over the grunt work of the shop that summer, and she'd done a lot of research for the case as well. Besides, he liked her. She had a funny, sarcastic kind of charm that suited him, a New York bluntness that made him laugh. She wasn't hard on the eyes either. Sweet kid, really, though she had a crust on her that could bruise a lesser man, and her brain was more trouble than it was worth.

Rather like Gerde, now that he thought about it.

But on the strength of his unthought-out agreement she'd dropped her plans for her Ph.D. and taken up shopkeeping for him full-time, something that had to be dead boring to a girl like her. And there hadn't *been* any more cases for over a year. It was precisely this sort of dependency and responsibility that he dreaded, the reason he avoided like the plague any meaningful relationship with a woman. And the stupidest part was—he wasn't even sleeping with her!

He'd been planning for months to write to her and urge her to go back to school, but he hadn't yet. He didn't know why he hadn't, except . . .

He read the letter again and sighed. What a nut. He did kinda miss her.

"All right," Gabriel muttered. "Okay."

He sat down and began to write, but his writer's block had seemingly transferred itself to simple correspondence. He made several attempts, then realized, with some surprise, what his hand already knew; he didn't *want* Gracie here.

He leaned back, thought about it. It probably wasn't

a real case anyway, he told himself. Nothing supernatural, that was; it would turn out to be some kind of normal animal or other—had to be. And by the time she got over here from the States it would all be over, anyway.

That's what he told himself.

He looked at his watch and did some quick, halting math. If he called now, there was no way she'd be at the shop—he could just leave a message. He made the call, grabbed his black leather jacket, and walked outside.

The morning was crisp, cold, and cloudless. The forest was just as Werner described it: a dense bank of trees edging a long, sloping lawn, and then the fields that marched away over the rolling landscape. To the right were a stone barn and the driveway that led to the road. Gabriel began at the house and walked slowly toward the woods on a path his mind conjured for Frau Huber. He studied the grass beneath his feet, soggy from spring rain.

He reached the woods and saw nothing at the spot he had chosen. But twenty feet away there were footsteps and trampled grass, even the marks of narrow wheels. The police had been here and the coroner probably. This was the site. He stood still and looked around.

The birds were warbling unconcernedly, the grass was sending up new green shoots, and the farm had a crisp, earthy texture, like biting into an apple, that painted an idyllic moment straight out of *State Fair*. How could anything ever go bad in a place like this? But something had gone bad, very bad indeed. The knowledge of what had happened was made even more tragic in this setting.

He studied the footprints, the invasive and eradicating marks of the investigators, and tried to look beyond them. He found the edge of the prints corresponded with a matted section of grass. He trod carefully,

leaned in, and found a trace of blood, flattened grass—
a paw print in the soft earth.

He took a step back, feeling queasy. He'd not recognized the print at first. His eyes had insisted it was yet
another footprint a bit beyond the others. The thing
was enormous, easily the size of a small man's shoe,
and as large as Gabriel's own outstretched hand. The
pad was narrow and arrow-shaped, and topped by four
oval indentations.

Did wolf paws really get that big?

He walked back to the barn and pulled open the
sliding wooden door. It was neat inside, with bags of
fertilizer, grain, and power equipment arranged
against the walls and in bins. He found what he was
looking for—a half-used bag of cement. He mixed a
small dose of the stuff in a metal pitcher and walked
back to the site of the attack, poured the cement into
the print indentation.

It would take a while to set.

He left the pitcher at the site and moved back
around through the trees. The woods brought the
abrupt chill of shade and dampness, and his jacket got
wet as he pushed past piney limbs. He glanced back
toward the pitcher on the ground, threading his way
along until he could barely see it.

From which direction had the wolf come?

If he were a woodsman, he could read the snapping
of twigs and disturbance of leaves, but to a French
Quarter boy everything out here looked the same—
wet, cold, and green. So he tried to use his writer's
instinct instead. He circled through the trees, eyeing
the pitcher, trying to see a little girl where it stood. It
was not a pleasant visualization, for he knew what
came next. He kept glancing at the ground, hoping for
another print, but the floor of the woods was coated
with pine needles, dead leaves, and berry vines, making it a less impressionable surface than the wet sod.

When he was as far south of the house as he could
go and still keep the pitcher in his line of sight, he

felt he'd found the vantage point. He didn't know how he felt it, but he did. He stood, breathing hard in the chilly silence, staring through the woods at the grass. He succeeded so well in placing the wolf here in his mind that he began to feel eyes on his back. He turned nervously—and saw nothing but the trees.

He began moving toward the pitcher on a sharp diagonal. He crouched, slunk.

And broke into a small clearing. It was not a clearing exactly, just a break in the trees only six feet or so across, but the ground was even here, a natural high point, and the vines cleared way for moss. He stopped and looked down, certain that the wolf had stood here. Wasn't it a perfect spot for reconnaissance? He didn't see any prints; the moss was spongy and hard.

He bent down and peered at the forest floor from mere inches away, scanning the moss with his hands as well as his eyes. Something stuck to his fingers.

He was certain it was only a leaf or moss fuzz, but he was wrong. It was hair, several strands of coarse hair, each an inch or so long. He bent down again, and this time his eyes knew what to look for. He found another clump of strands and a few singles near the edge. He gathered them carefully with his wet fingers and placed them in his palm. They were reddish-brown in color, the color of a light cherry stain, and the tips of them, the last quarter inch or so, were white.

They're its *hairs. The beast's. It sat right here and watched Toni Huber, maybe even* waited *for her; which meant that it had been here before, was* stalking *her*.

He knew he was jumping to conclusions, but damn if it didn't feel like the truth, especially squatting here like this with those hairs against the skin of his hand.

There had to be some way to find out if he was right.

He found nothing else in the woods. He was standing in the yard, considering his next move, when he noticed the newspaper and mailboxes out on the main road. He walked down the driveway and found that he was in luck. There was a feature article on the wolf killings on the front page of the *Freistaat Bayern Zeitung*. Unfortunately, he'd spent more time in the castle this past year than out of it, and he'd further discovered that his natural ear for language was apparently deaf. Still, he could make out a few things. The headline on the article, "*Zwei Killerwölfe aus dem Zoo immer noch auf freiemfuß,*" was legible enough to his American eyes to pick up the fact that the Munich papers considered the case to be about two killer wolves from the zoo. It had a photo of wolves at the zoo, though probably not the ones that had escaped, and it had another picture of a bald, heavyset man at a press conference. The man was identified as "*Kriminalkommisar Leber aus dem Polizeirevier am Prinzregentenplatz.*" And the name of the zoo was given— "*Tierpark Hellabrunn.*"

Christa Huber had advised against driving in the city. There was an U-Bahn stop just up the road in Lockham, she'd said; park the car and take the subway from there. Gabriel took her advice, grabbing his German-English pocket dictionary and his hand-held tape recorder from the car before locking it. He'd recorded most of his conversations on the last case— even before he'd known it *was* a case. The idea had originally been to make the construction of a novel easier, but the tapes proved critical to unraveling the heart of the Voodoo Murders. It was one of the few things he'd done right.

The subway map showed a stop for Prinzregentenplatz up the U4 line from downtown. The zoo was listed too, at the Thalkirchen stop on the U3. Gabriel headed downtown.

He'd been to Munich three times in the past year— twice on his own when bored to tears and once last December when Gerde dragged him up here for the

Christkindlmarkt. He'd come to Germany a few months after the death of Malia and the destruction of the voodoo *hounfour*. Part of it had been to settle Wolfgang's estate, but mostly he'd wanted to get away from New Orleans, from the memory of the dark-skinned woman who had been the first true love of his life, the woman he'd pretty much murdered. He never dreamed he'd stay this long. He found he needed to be in Schloss Ritter, to be surrounded by the very real evidence of the *Schattenjäger* past in order for him to retain any belief in it at all. So he'd stayed at the castle and worked (or tried to)—yet another form of catharsis.

He hadn't gotten out much.

The stop at Prinzregentenplatz was a bust. Gabriel found the *polizei* sign without too much trouble, but getting past the bloodhound at the desk was another matter. The officer cum receptionist set his stare to stun even before the words "Kriminalkommisar Leber" came out of Gabriel's mouth. Once they had, well, a rotweiler with hemorrhoids would have been more gracious. Leber, Gabriel managed to gather from the officer's indecipherable German, was either off bounds, inaccessible, or just plain not there.

He was not invited to return.

The zoo was considerably more congenial. "The *Tierpark* is a natural habitat zoo," the English brochure informed him. That further translated into a lot of walking.

He located the wolves twenty minutes from the gate. A sign showed a picture of a wolf and read CANIS LUPUS LUPUS, EUROPEAN WOLF in several languages. Beyond it was a ditch, then a wood and wire fence, then a broad, park-like setting. The wolves themselves were inactive. A half dozen were visible from the main path, all lying around under the trees, where they were sheltered a bit from prying eyes. They were slight and gray. They did not look particularly ferocious.

Gabriel heard the squeak of wheels and turned to see a slight, dark-haired young man coming down the path. He was pushing a cart, and he wore brown coveralls with the park's logo. The young man took a hitherto unnoticed path back into a chain-link kennel structure that was mostly hidden by brush. He poured the contents of a sack into a steel trough. A few of the wolves glanced up, but none of them moved. Whatever the pellets were, they weren't exactly high on the wolves' priority list.

The young man returned to the cart and said something briefly into a walkie-talkie. Gabriel strolled over.

"Hey! Do you speak English?"

"Yes. Do you have a question?"

"Yeah, actually." Gabriel gave the boy his most winning smile. "My name's Gabriel Knight."

The boy nodded with little interest.

"Hey, I saw you walk into that kennel . . . um . . ."

"Thomas."

"Thomas. Nice to meet ya. Weren't you scared at all, Thomas?"

Thomas slouched in a display of bored machismo. "No! I go in there all the time."

"Really? That takes some balls—especially with the recent killin's. The two wolves got out of here, right?"

The boy looked uneasy. "Yes."

"When was that exactly?"

"About a month ago. Are you a reporter?"

Gabriel gave him an innocent smile. "No, novelist. I'm just curious about wolves. Do you know what happened? Did they get over the fence or what?"

Thomas nodded toward the kennel door. "Doktor Klingmann thinks the night attendant left the door open." Thomas rolled his eyes to indicate how very large an error this was—akin, perhaps, to wearing one's pajamas to school or knocking one's wedding ring down the kitchen drain.

Gabriel whistled. "That sucks. *You* weren't on duty that night, were ya?"

Thomas shook his head. "I work days only. The guy who *was* working, he was . . . you know." Thomas made a throat-slitting gesture.

"Fired?"

Thomas nodded grimly.

"Hmmm. What about the wolves—there were two that got out, right?"

"Hilda and Parsival."

Gabriel arched a sardonic brow. "Oh, yeah? What did Hilda and Parsival look like?"

Thomas pointed toward the habitat. "Like that."

Gabriel bit back a sarcastic remark. "I know, but were they the same color? These guys look kinda gray from here."

"*Ja*, gray. Hilda was young still—only about a year old. She was light gray with white at her chest. Parsival was a male, older, maybe five years. He was darker gray. They get darker when they get older."

"Not . . . *reddish* at all?"

Thomas looked perplexed and shook his head. He brushed his coveralls self-consciously, as if wondering why Gabriel kept staring at them.

Gabriel switched his gaze to the wolves. "What about temperament? Did you ever think those two could do something like this?"

For the first time Thomas seemed to have a real opinion. "No. Not possible." He wagged his head angrily.

"Not possible? They are *carnivores,* right?"

But Thomas just repeated his opinionated gesture. "I know the wolves. They can be dangerous. Maybe even bite if you move too fast. But kill and eat *people*? *Nein*. Not these wolves. Hilda was still a puppy, and Parsival, he was okay, a little slow maybe. He was not so mean, like some of the other males."

Gabriel thought about this for a moment.

Thomas grew restless. "Well, I must . . ."

"Thomas, is there any way at all . . ." He gave the boy a sheepish grin. "I'd really love to get a good look at one of the wolves. For a book I'm workin' on. Just for a *second*."

Thomas chuckled low and ironic. "Not possible!"

Gabriel sighed. "Yeah. All right. Who's this Dr. Klingmann you mentioned?"

"Herr Doktor Klingmann is in charge of the mammal division."

"So he'd be the man to talk to about seeing one of the wolves up close?"

Thomas smirked. "Sure. Yes. Why don't you go ask him?"

Dr. Klingmann's office was in the administration building at the other end of the park. Gabriel sat on a bench outside, contemplating his next move. Of course, Thomas was having him on. Besides the smirk there was the fact that anyone who would require the park employees to call him "Herr Doktor" had to have a stick up his butt the size of Wyoming. No matter what cover story Gabriel thought up, the scene played out the same way. Klingmann would never grant him access to see one of the wolves. He couldn't pretend to be a veterinarian; the park would have their own. An animal-rights activist would be thrown out on his ear, and "health inspector" wouldn't wash either—he was too obviously a non-native. He couldn't even fake a good accent.

This case was going to be a lot tougher than his last one, when such deceptions had not only been possible, they'd worked and had paid big dividends.

Could he get around the wolf thing? Gabriel shook his head in answer. There was only one way to determine if the beast that had been at the Huber farm was one of the escaped zoo wolves, and that was pretty much what this entire case hinged on, wasn't it? Unfortunately, he hadn't seen any of what he needed on Thomas's coveralls.

What about the police? Wouldn't they have the answer right there in their files?

Gabriel sighed. Presumably. They might not have found what *he* found in the woods at the Huber farm, but chances were good that they'd found it at *one* of the crime scenes. Unfortunately, the police weren't talking to Gabriel Knight.

And that was when he got an idea.

Gabriel's knock was answered by a reedy male voice.

"Kommen Sie!"

He entered a sterile-looking office. The room was of decent size, but the plain cream walls, blue carpeting, and bonded wood desk made it look like a rental. The only human touches in the room were, oddly, non-human. A large print of wolves was the only art, and below it was a cheap display case that contained an animal skull, what looked like pelts, and various anatomical models of wolves, foxes, and other carnivores.

The man behind the desk was looking up at him blankly. *"Kann ich Ihnen helfen?"*

"Dr. Klingmann? My name is Gabriel Knight." Gabriel walked forward and stretched out his hand. The man accepted it coolly.

"What can I do for you, Mr. Knight?"

Klingmann was a thin, loose-skinned man. His light brown hair was on its way south, and wire-rimmed glasses gave a scholarly pensiveness to a thin, intense face that might otherwise have looked peevish.

"I was hopin' I could do a quick interview with ya, Doctor," Gabriel said, laying on the twang. (For some reason, people seemed to associate the Southern accent with honesty and harmlessness, if not actual stupidity.) "Ya see, I'm workin' on a novel about wolves? I have a few books on the market in the U.S."

"Yes?"

"Well, I read about this situation here in Munich,

with the zoo wolves escapin' and all? And I thought to myself, well, innit that unusual? You don't get a chance to see what captivity-raised wolves'll do in an urban setting very often."

Klingmann dropped his pen and leaned back. "No. That's true. I do not have much time, unfortunately . . ."

"Just a few *real* quick questions. 'Course, I'll give you credit in the acknowledgments. Send ya a copy. I do appreciate the help of experts like yourself."

Klingmann drummed his fingers on his chair arm for a moment, then waved reluctantly at a visitor's chair. "Sit down. Mr. Knight."

"Thanks." Gabriel sat down and pulled out his tape recorder. "Ya don't mind, do ya? My memory leaves somethin' to be desired."

Klingmann made an uninterested acquiescence.

"I was out lookin' at the wolves just now, and I ran into one of your feeders, a young boy. Uh . . . Frank was it?"

Klingmann looked at him blankly.

"Or, uh, Todd?"

"Thomas?" Klingmann asked, as if he could hardly see the relevance.

Gabriel taped his forehead in a duh gesture. "Thomas! Right! Aren't ya worried about sendin' people into the kennels now that it's been proven that the wolves are man eaters?"

Klingmann smiled indulgently. "The park employees are in no danger as long as they follow the safety guidelines that I myself have laid out."

"Uh-huh. But you *do* think these killin's are the work of the two escaped wolves?"

Klingmann's smile faded. "I don't know what else it could be." The tenseness in his voice was painful.

"Wild wolves?"

"There haven't been wild wolves in Germany for centuries. There might be a few small packs left in the Alps, but otherwise . . ." Klingmann glared at him dully. "Surely you know *something* about wolves if you're to write about them?"

It took an effort, but Gabriel tried to appear grateful. "Yeah, Doc, I sure do, thanks for askin'. But I'm less familiar with Germany's situation *specifically*."

Klingmann made a dismissive gesture. "What happened to wolves happened here first, in Europe. The farmers wanted to protect their livestock so they put a price on the wolves' heads. Money hunters killed entire species. It happened the same way in America in the eighteen hundreds."

"That's true, but I was thinkin' that with all the new animal-protection laws, a few of those packs maybe moved back in? It has to be somethin' the police have considered. Right, Doc?"

Klingmann heaved an impatient sigh. "People refer to me as *Herr Doktor Klingmann* here."

"Of course, Herr Doktor. I do apologize."

"And the police *have* considered it. I told them what I tell you—there *are* no wild wolves anywhere near here."

"Right. Thanks. I suppose, knowin' wolves as you do, you have some idea of why these two wolves would behave like this?"

Klingmann frowned. As before, Gabriel sensed it was a reaction to the question itself, not the deliverer. It was hardly surprising. This man was in charge of the wolves, and two of them had escaped and were now mutilating little girls. He was obviously a priggish ass, but he still had to feel the public pressure, if not actual personal liability.

"As much as we might like to compare wolves to dogs, they are not domesticated creatures, Mr. Knight. Even those that are raised as pets from birth are unpredictable. They're *wild animals*."

"Yes, Herr Doktor," Gabriel said meekly. He felt like he should have a pencil in his hand.

"Morality—that is *our* invention. It has nothing to do with the wild, with *nature*."

Gabriel blinked in surprise—both at the idea and the enthusiasm of the delivery—but he nodded agreeably.

"A wolf would have no moral compunction about killing a human versus, say, a *deer*. It makes no distinction between the two."

"Even though these wolves are raised *among* humans?" Gabriel asked.

"Their comfort with humans only makes things worse." Klingmann smiled tightly. "Wild wolves might avoid our homes, our cities, because of their strangeness. Zoo wolves would do the opposite. They're used to relating *food* with *humans*."

Gabriel nodded his head humbly. "Well, that sure makes sense to me. So, assumin' they *would* eat a human being, how would the wolves go about *choosin'* a victim? Would they be capable of, say, returnin' to a spot where they'd seen a potential victim? Of *stalking*?"

"Oh, yes!" Klingmann said, eyes shining. "As for choosing a victim . . . Have you heard about the Language of Death?"

"No."

"Ever since Darwin it has been accepted that predators like wolves participate in natural selection; that they choose the old, the sick, or the very young and thus 'cull the herd.'" Klingmann leaned forward intently. "At first glance that *appears* to be the case, but for the past few decades researchers have been camping out with wolf packs, and they've been finding anomalies."

"Such as?"

"For example, a pack of wolves surround a sick moose cow. She can barely stand, but she does stand, and she glares back at the wolves that surround her. The wolves break up, back away."

The cow must have been related to Grace, he thought. He muttered an articulate "Huh."

"Recently one of the researchers proposed a new

theory—the Language of Death. It says that predator and prey have a kind of agreement whose rules have been handed down genetically. The wolf's chase says, 'I am Death. Are you ready to go?' And the individual members of the herd, by their action or inaction say, 'No, I am not ready,' or 'Yes, take me.' "

Gabriel arched a light brown eyebrow quizzically. "Doesn't the herd pretty much just . . . *run*?"

Klingmann chuckled. "It may look that way to the untrained eye, but there are *patterns*. Maybe one doesn't run, or maybe one runs in a direction apart from the herd, making themselves an easy target."

Gabriel rubbed his chin. "That's very interestin', Herr Docktor, but how does it explain the recent killin's?"

"The Language of Death explains many things! First, the extinction of the wolves. Why did the farmer hunt the wolf? Not because the wolf took a cow or goat now and then, but because a wolf in a domestic herd went on a killing *frenzy*. And why? Because the stupid cattle do not know the language!"

"So . . . as far as this case goes, maybe *humans* don't know the Language? Is that what you're sayin'?"

Klingmann looked at Gabriel in surprise. And there was something else on his face, something fearful. "Yes," he said simply. He neatened the book on his desk. "This is not the first time wolves have eaten human beings, Mr. Knight. Lions do it, tigers do it. When wolves and humans coexisted, they did it too. The Language of Death simply explains why they might do it in a particularly brutal and senseless fashion."

Klingmann glanced at his watch. "Now I'm afraid I really must get back to work."

Gabriel rose reluctantly and gave Klingmann a lopsided grin. "Well, I really appreciate your time. One more thing, though. I was wonderin' if it might be possible for you to show me one of the wolves up close? For my work?"

Klingmann gave him a frozen, put-upon smile. "We don't 'show' our wolves to anyone, Mr. Knight. You may look as long as you'd like—from the *path*."

Gabriel headed back to the Huber farm. He picked up the paw print, which had dried. He cleaned it off in the barn's sink. The impression was a good one.

Then he went inside and rummaged through the Hubers' kitchen drawers. He found what he was looking for—another tape recorder. The Hubers' model was an older, clunky one. On it was a recording of Toni Huber singing "Silent Night" in German. He played it twice, just because it ripped his heart out. The flip side was blank.

He sat down at the kitchen table and reviewed his taped conversation with Klingmann, taking notes. Then he made the new tape.

It took him an hour of skulking around the zoo for the right opportunity to arise. It came at the kangaroo habitat. A perky teenage *fräulein* was giving a tour to a group of schoolchildren. She wore a brown T-shirt with the park logo, and next to her was a small pushcart. On the cart was a walkie-talkie.

Gabriel sat and watched the group for about ten minutes, until his break came. One little girl wandered down the fence. She began yelling and pointing excitedly at a mother whose baby was sticking its head out of her pouch. The girl in the park shirt ushered the children down the fence to see the wonders of marsupial motherhood.

She left the cart behind.

Gabriel walked over as quickly as he could without being obvious. He grabbed the walkie-talkie, held down the Send button, and played the first few seconds of the tape in his tape recorder. Klingmann's voice said, "Thomas?"

He waited, holding his breath. The walkie-talkie beeped and came on in his hand. "Thomas here."

Gabriel suppressed a giggle and played the rest of the message.

"Herr Doktor Klingmann here. Show our wolves to Mr. Knight."

Thomas's voice came back genuinely amazed. "*Ja,* Herr Doktor. I go to the wolf habitat right away."

Thomas was waiting for him. "Hello Mr. Knight. I was asked to show you one of the wolves. Please stay close to me and remain calm. Don't make any quick moves."

"Sure," Gabriel said, his smile fading. Maybe this wasn't such a hot idea after all.

The two went down the path to the kennel, and Thomas unlocked the door.

The kennel enclosure was roughly ten by twenty feet with the door on one end and the other end open to the habitat. Thomas paused inside the door.

"Stay here," he said nervously. He walked over to the habitat opening and took what looked like a dog biscuit out of his pocket. *"Margarite? Schau mal was ich hier hab! Na komm' mal her!"*

He squatted down and called out softly, as though hoping to avoid summoning all of the wolves. He seemed to be addressing a smallish wolf that was under a tree not far from the kennel. Several of the larger wolves glanced in their direction, including, Gabriel noticed, one large, dark wolf that was obviously a male. He cocked his head as though to see past Thomas, and when his eyes found Gabriel, they locked on. The animal's ear stood to attention, but he didn't rise.

Yes, this had made a lot more sense from *outside* the kennel.

"Margarite! Komm' her! Komm' mal her Mädchen!" Thomas cajoled.

The slight female rose with a yawn, as if barely

interested. She padded over to the kennel. Gabriel was amazed at the length and delicacy of her legs. The large paws only accentuated this thinness and gave the wolf a puppyish air. Gabriel thought Margarite must look like Hilda as Thomas described her.

Thomas gave Margarite the biscuit, which she daintily ate. He moved to one side so that Gabriel could get a better look.

"Margarite's about fourteen months old," Thomas explained in a low voice. He seemed calmer now that things were going smoothly. "She came to us from a zoo in Amsterdam when she was very little still."

While Thomas was busy watching Margarite, Gabriel was taking careful steps forward. He held his breath, desperate not to startle Margarite away before he'd gotten what he came for.

"Get back!" Thomas hissed as Gabriel approached his left side.

But Margarite was not alarmed. She looked up at Gabriel with clear, curious eyes. She made a low whining noise and dipped her head at him, sat on her haunches, and walked her front paws forward a bit. She dipped her head again.

"That's strange," Thomas said, dumbfounded. "She likes you."

"I have a way with women," Gabriel quipped. He squatted down next to Thomas.

"I don't think it's a good idea . . ."

But Gabriel was already reaching out a hand. He stroked Margarite's head. She panted, looking at him with large brown eyes.

"Mr. Knight, please don't touch her!" Thomas hissed angrily.

"She's fine," Gabriel replied, which was perfectly true. He dug his fingers into her fur and tugged gently, pulled his hand back, and stuck it in his coat pocket.

"That's enough!" Thomas put a hand on Gabriel's arm.

It was just about then that something explosive

struck the chain-link wall to their left. They felt and heard the impact a split second before the cacophony that followed told them *what* it was.

It was a large gray wolf, the male that had spotted Gabriel earlier. He was standing on his hind legs, his front paws up against the fence. He was snarling and snapping his teeth, growling in rage, his eyes a frenzy of attack lust.

Gabriel uttered a cry of surprise and lost his balance. He fell back onto the ground, reached out to scramble to his feet, lost his footing, and went down again on one knee. Thomas grabbed his arm and yanked him upright, pulled him to the kennel door.

It took six seconds to get out of the wolf kennel, and they were the longest six seconds of Gabriel's life. The two men *ran* down the path to the cart.

"I told you not to touch her!" Thomas panted angrily when he'd regained his breath enough to speak.

"I'm sorry. She was just so cute, and she did that head thing. I thought she *wanted* me to pet her." It wasn't the truth. No matter how cute she was, he'd never have dared it, not unless he'd had to.

Thomas glared at him, his breathing slowing down. He walked toward the habitat fence and looked inside. A few of the wolves were pacing nervously, and the one who'd attacked was trotting back and forth in the kennel in an agitated manner. But the worst of the crisis seemed to have passed.

"It will take days to get them back to normal," Thomas complained.

Yeah? Tell that to the ulcer I just sprouted. "I'm really sorry. Does that kind of thing happen a lot?"

Thomas wiped his brow on his sleeve. "I've never seen a wolf do that before, not even when we introduced new handlers. But then, we don't go around petting the wolves, not unless we know them *very* well. That one, he was just being territorial. Maybe he likes Margarite. Or maybe he does not like *you*."

Thomas glared at Gabriel, plainly on the wolf's side.

"Huh. Well, thanks for your help. I'll, uh, I'll put in a good word for you with Klingmann."

The mention of Klingmann's name only evoked new horrors. Thomas paled, *"Don't* tell Herr Doktor what happened. *Please."*

"Son, I won't mention it if you won't," Gabriel said, giving Thomas an avuncular pat on the shoulder.

Back on the U-Bahn, Gabriel carefully collected the gray hairs from his pocket and studied them in the train's fluorescent light. He brought out the red ones from the farm and laid them next to the grays in his palm. The red hairs were coarser than Margarite's, perhaps twice as large in diameter but shorter in length. Both had white tips.

Gabriel put them away. He needed a better analysis than his own untrained eye. For one thing, it was possible that the red hair from the farm didn't even belong to the animal that killed Toni Huber. It could be anything—dog hair, fox, even raccoon.

Were there such things as red German raccoons?

Anyway, if the hair he'd found at the farm was something other than wolf hair, then all the trouble he'd gone to with Thomas would count for diddly squat.

Gabriel thought about it, then realized that he knew someone who just might be able to help.

The law offices of Übergrau, Höffen and Schnell were housed at a prestigious address on the Marienplatz and had been for the past hundred years. The firm itself had represented the Ritter family for even longer. The tradition between the two was so old, in fact, that for the past decade of Great-Uncle Wolfgang's life the firm tended what family business there was free of charge. That business consisted mainly of trying to keep the German government from confiscating Schloss Ritter for unpaid property taxes.

Fortunately, the money Gabriel had stolen from the

hounfour on his last case had enabled him to clear up all that and to put the firm back on retainer. Their genuine pleasure at the family's resurgence had been apparent in their letters, even if the heir *was* an American who chose to keep his Anglicized name. They'd even gone to the effort of obtaining Gabriel's birth certificate and his grandfather's, Heinz Ritter's, immigration forms and legalizing Gabriel's status as official descendant of the Ritter line. (They insisted it wasn't because the firm itself had any doubts about his story.)

Being officially registered as heir didn't seem relevant to Gabriel, since the family had no official titles or duties, at least not these days. But it mattered to Übergrau, Höffen and Schnell, and it helped ease the deed transfer for the castle.

They had offered their every assistance after that. It was about time to call that pony home.

There was a bit of confusion in the lobby, mostly because the receptionist didn't think Gabriel looked like the firm's typical clientele. But eventually Gabriel was ushered in, with great apology, to the office of Herr Harold Übergrau.

Harold Übergrau was not what Gabriel expected. He'd pictured a gray-haired, elderly gentleman, officious and obsessively proper. Übergrau was barely thirty, blond, and fair, with a kind of boyish self-consciousness. He struck Gabriel as someone who'd just been promoted from mail boy and was still getting used to wearing suits.

"Mr. Knight! Very glad to meet you! So glad! Please, please! Come in! Sit down!"

Gabriel took a seat. "Nice to meet you too, Herr Übergrau. Are you the one who's been writin' to me?"

Übergrau blushed. "Yes, actually. I mean, my secretary types the letter, but I, um, yes, I compose them. My uncle assigned me to your account because I have the best English. I took my law degree at Harvard."

"Really? Well, nice job. On the grammar and all."

Übergrau looked at Gabriel as if trying to gauge if he was kidding. "Er . . . thank you. Well! I'd be happy to be of service to you, Mr. Knight. Of course, if you'd prefer to speak with my uncle or Herr Schnell . . ."

"Heck, no!" Gabriel made a *pshah* sound. "I'm okay if you're okay."

Übergrau's official smile faltered again. "Er . . . okay."

"Look, Harry," Gabriel said, leaning forward, "you don't mind if I call you Harry, do you?"

Übergrau reddened. "No. That is, if you . . ."

"I actually came by because I could use some help."

"Anything, Mr. Knight."

"Gabriel."

"Okay."

"I need an introduction to an animal biologist. I was thinkin' maybe someone at the university."

Übergrau looked perplexed. "I'm sorry?"

"You know, someone who'd be able to look at a couple of hair samples for me, give me an analysis on species, that sort of thing."

For a moment Übergrau stared at him blankly; then his eyes widened. *"Mein Gott!* This is about those wolf killings, isn't it? Are you working on a new book?"

Gabriel clenched his jaw in mild irritation. He hadn't anticipated the lawyer doing his homework quite so thoroughly. "Not really," he hedged, determined to avoid a long explanation of the samples and the case.

But Übergrau paid no attention. "I read your last book, Mr. Knight! *The Voodoo Murders*? I really enjoyed it! Especially because it was based on true life. That makes it so much more frightening, doesn't it? Do people tell you that a lot? It *was* based on a real case in New Orleans, wasn't it? That is what the back of the book said."

"Yeah, but I'm not really here on—"

"Have we been worried about these wolf killings!

Some of the secretaries are afraid to go down in the U-Bahn alone at night. They haven't attacked anyone in the city, of course. The wolves, that is, not the secretaries." Übergrau tittered. "How would they even get into the city with all the traffic? No, it's all been out in the countryside, but even so—"

"*Harry!*" Gabriel waved his arms to get the man's attention.

"What?"

"Can you just get me that name?"

"Oh! Oh. Yes. Let's see." He thought for a moment, tapping his foot nervously. "I have a client at the university, but he is in mathematics."

"Maybe he knows someone in biology."

"Let me try."

Übergrau opened his desk and brought out a Rolodex. These Germans kept absolutely *nothing* on their desktops, Gabriel thought irritably (neatness not being a trait he himself possessed). Übergrau found the number and picked up the phone. The conversation was unintelligible, but Harry looked brightly optimistic by the time he rung off.

"*Ja! Gut!* He says you can go right over. He will meet you in the Lichthof. That is just off Ludwigstraβe. He will take you to the lab himself."

"That's terrific. Thanks, Harry."

Übergrau looked very pleased with himself. "If you have anything else for the case, you will let me know, yes, Mr. Knight?"

Gabriel sighed. "You bet."

For a lone wolf, he sure had a knack for picking up overly enthusiastic sidekicks.

Übergrau's client not only took Gabriel to the biology lab, but he'd arranged for a graduate student, Michael Hessel, to meet them there and do any work Gabriel required. Hessel took Gabriel over to a set of microscopes and laid out his samples one by one on white blotting paper. He made neat little labels for each, questioning Gabriel carefully about their origin.

Naturally, Gabriel lied. He hastily concocted an uninspired story involving dead chickens, neighbor's dogs, and civil suits.

This seemed to give Hessel the direction he needed, for he began to hum happily. He rolled his seat around, collecting materials to make slide samples. When the two types of hair were enclosed in glass to Hessel's satisfaction, he rolled over to the microscopes and put them into side-by-side machines.

"Let's just see . . ." he muttered between refrains.

He studied the slides for some time, adjusting knobs here and there. Then he looked at Gabriel with a mystified expression. He stopped humming and went over and got a thick reference volume off a bookshelf. He brought it back and began leafing through pages.

Gabriel anxiously twirled a long lock of his dirty blond hair.

"Mr. Knight," Hessel said, his eyes still attached to the microscope, "neither one of these samples is dog hair."

"Oh?" Gabriel said innocently. His heart began to beat a little faster.

"No. You said you found them both near a chicken coop?"

"Yeah."

"On a farm?"

"Uh-huh."

Michael looked up. His face was concerned. "Where exactly is this farm?"

Gabriel realized, blankly, that he knew none of the local names. "Um . . . about half an hour south? What is it? Can you tell what the red hair is?"

But Hessel didn't answer right away. He was chewing on his lip worriedly. He turned back to the microscope and looked again, now turning pages in the book, now looking in the viewer, and so on back and forth. Gabriel noticed that the right-hand scope, the one with the gray hair, went untouched this time around.

Surely if the red hair was raccoon or fox hair, Hessel would have known it right away. Wouldn't he?

Hessel leaned back once more. "Mr. Knight, I think you should notify the police."

"What?" Gabriel said, blushing.

"First, the gray hair. It's *wolf* hair—European wolf, *canis lupus lupus*. According to the newspapers, that's the same species that escaped from the zoo." Hessel said this in a grim, this-is-some-trouble voice.

"Wow," said Gabriel, acting surprised.

"So it looks like the missing wolves have been past this farm of yours. You say they took some chickens?"

"Yup."

Michael nodded, one eyebrow arched. "The police would want to know about this. Also, you should warn—is it *your* farm?"

"No, a friend of mine's."

"Then you should warn your friend. These wolves are very dangerous."

Gabriel didn't have to feign a look of concern. "Yeah, I know. I mean, I've been following the story about the killin's. Wow. I'll have to tell my friend."

"And call the police," Hessel added.

"Right. We'll get them out there right away. So . . . um . . . what about the red hair?" Why was his heart racing? Surely, Hessel's concern was for the Margarite sample.

But now Hessel's frown deepened. He spun back around and looked in the viewer again. He looked for several long minutes, then said: "Mr. Knight, I have no idea what this hair is."

Gabriel felt a thrill of fear stab him right in the solar plexus. "You don't? I mean, it's not dog hair or raccoon or . . . or even *human*?" Gabriel walked over the microscope, though he'd be clueless as to what he was looking at even if Hessel offered.

Hessel shook his head. He pulled his book over so Gabriel could take a look.

"No. It's not dog hair—they don't have the same kind of undercoat as a wolf—you see this flat white tip? It's closer to wolf, but it has some odd characteristics. It's too short and it's thicker than wolf hair—much thicker. Wolf hair tends to be fine. This is . . . this is almost, what is the word, rubber-like, coarse, like maybe sea mammal hair or something."

"*Sea* mammal?"

"No, it's *not* sea mammal hair. I'm just trying to explain."

Gabriel had a brief vision of a seal bounding out of the woods to chase Toni Huber and almost laughed out loud, though it really wasn't funny at all. He was losing it.

"So it's not dog hair and it's not wolf hair. You're *sure*?"

Hessel nodded. "Yes. It's closer to wolf than anything else as far as I can tell. But it's not matching any species in the book, and some of the characterizations . . . Well, if it's a wolf, it's a very *strange* wolf."

Hessel suddenly remembered that there was further evidence to examine. "Let me look at that paw print."

He grabbed a tape measure and rolled over to the cement cast. He measured it, jotted the results on a piece of paper, rolled back to the book, and flipped more pages.

"Ah! I thought it looked too large when you put it down. It *is* too large."

This time Hessel's expression when he looked up at Gabriel was on the seen-a-ghost side. "This print was taken closer to which hair sample, the red or the gray?"

"Um . . . the red."

Hessel did a hurried calculation on the paper. "The print is definitely a wolf print. It looks normal to me, except for the size. This print was made by a wolf around sixty-eight, seventy kilograms."

Gabriel had to do a quick conversion in his head. That was something like a hundred thirty-five pounds. "That's large for a wolf?" he asked.

Hessel stared at him. "Mr. Knight, that is *huge*. *Canis lupus lupus,* for example, the one that matches the gray hair sample? Biggest they get is about forty kilograms."

"No shit."

"The biggest wolf species is the Alaskan timber wolf. Even for that species, seventy kilograms would be huge—a *huge* male, maybe one in a thousand. *Huge.*"

"Yeah, I'm gettin' your drift on that one."

"We should call the police right now." Hessel put both hands on his knees as if preparing to rise and waited for Gabriel's permission. He looked awfully pale, just about the shade of his white coat, and a jittering index finger, like a white worm, further betrayed his perturbation.

"Look, I'd rather tell my friend and let him do it. It's his farm after all," Gabriel backpedaled. "He's the one who found the stuff. He just asked me to have it analyzed."

Hessel looked unconvinced. "I can understand that, Mr. Knight, but this is very serious. If one or both of the zoo wolves is traveling with something like this— some huge wolf hybrid—it may explain these attacks."

Gabriel shook his head as if to clear his ears. "A *hybrid*? You think the red hair belongs to a *wolf hybrid*?"

Hessel made a fifty-fifty gesture with his hand. "I can't say for certain, naturally. But the print is too large for the gray-haired wolf. It had to have been made by something else, and I would guess it was whatever left that red hair. It may be a wolf-dog hybrid, or a wolf and something else? They couldn't breed with anything outside the canine family, but perhaps a coyote or . . . No, these are not existing in Germany. A fox would explain the color but not the size." He shrugged. "It is probably a wolf-dog hybrid. But it is large and may be vicious. It may be the true killer."

Okay. You walked right into this one. Now get yourself out.

"Wow! All right, I'll tell you what. If you just write up somethin' for me explainin' your analysis, and *sign* it, then I'll take it over to my friend right now and we'll call the police. I'm sure they'll want to interview you, so write down your phone number and address."

Hessell looked undecided.

"I really think my friend should be the one to report it," Gabriel pressed. "If you don't hear from the police in a few days, you can give them a call. All right?"

And wait for them to sort you out from all the cranks they're no doubt getting.

Hessel agreed. He organized a new stack of forms and a few pencils under a table lamp and set out to document his findings in neat, legible handwriting. And Gabriel waited through it all, staring out the window at the rain that had begun to fall and thinking, *Oh shit, oh shit, oh shit.*

It was the only lead he had, and it was pretty damn sorry. His instinct told him Klingmann was lying, or at least not telling the whole truth. What a scoop—break out the search warrant, Dano.

So he went back to the zoo and scouted out the closest exit to the administration building. He found it—a gated exit requiring card access that was only a few yards away. On the other side of the wrought iron fence was a parking lot. Gabriel studied the configuration of cars, then went outside the zoo and walked its tree-lined perimeter. He found the lot. It was employee parking.

And there he sat, discreetly shielded behind a bush. Darkness was falling by the time he settled in, and he was glad to have his coat. The sun had warmed the day, despite the brief March shower, but the air forgot Sol's kiss the instant it said good night, like some heartless and petulant teenage girl, and took on a frigid bite before the last of the sunset had faded on the horizon.

He waited several hours in that cold air, and his discomfort made him crotchety. Probably the man had left before Gabriel even got here. And even if he did come out, how could Gabriel follow him if he got in a car?

But Klingmann did come out, at 7:32 P.M., and he didn't get into a car. He walked down the footpath to the road and took a left. He walked right past Gabriel and his bush, and he didn't even glance in their direction.

Klingmann descended down into the U-Bahn at the Thalkirchen station, and Gabriel followed him, trying to keep behind a group of punkish adolescents. The zoo official went directly to the platform for the train heading north. Gabriel stepped into the car just behind the one Klingmann chose when the train arrived.

The man certainly was making this easy. Gabriel could have been wearing purple sequins and a feather boa, and the scientist would've been none the wiser. From the brief glances Gabriel got of his face, he looked extremely preoccupied.

They both got off at the Marienplatz exit.

The tail was even easier in the crowded downtown station. Indeed, the challenge was keeping Klingmann in sight at all with the milling masses moving up and down the steep escalators. Klingmann headed for the Dienerstrasse exit and up into the night air. Dienerstrasse ran in a straight shot between the Marienplatz—ground zero of Munich—and the Residenz, the palace where the kings and queens of Bavaria once lived. Gabriel followed him past the closed shops and the brightly lit *kellars* on either side of the cobblestone street. Just before Max Joseph Platz, his target entered an old stone building with a plain facade. He did not come back out.

After a bit, Gabriel wandered over to the building and read the small brass plaque next to the door. It said DIE KÖNIGLICH-BAYRISCHE HOFJAGDLOGE. There were no windows.

Gabriel entered a small coffee shop a few doors down. He took a seat near the window and decided to order—he hadn't eaten all day. The bratwurst came, along with a coffee that was consumed lovingly, with rhapsodic delight.

He kept an eye on the door.

His dictionary got him as far as *Die Königlich Bayerische*—it meant "the Royal Bavarian," which he more or less already knew. It was the kind of descriptive precursor one could see on lots of titles in Munich. "Royal Bavarian Opera House" and "Royal Bavarian Museum," for example, not to mention the infamous "Royal Bavarian House of Schnitzel." But *Hofjagdloge* was one of those run-on conglomerates Germans were wont to invent that made the dictionary next to useless.

"It means Royal Bavarian Hunting Lodge," his waitress informed him after he showed her the words written on his notepad. He hadn't bothered trying to pronounce it.

"Really? A huntin' lodge? Are you sure?"

The girl, a pretty thing that was just a little too gawky and potato-fed and was (in any event) *way* too young, smiled at him giddily, a hormonal glint in her eye.

"Yes. Hunting lodge. It's across the street, yes?"

"That's right." Gabriel gave her an encouraging smile. "You wouldn't know anythin' about it, would you?"

The girl looked as though she wished to God that she did. "No. But sometimes you see someone go in or come out. Not many people. They never come over here. It's one of those . . . you know, places with much money."

"Like a private club?"

The girl nodded, bobbing her head energetically. "Yes. In Germany there used to be many such clubs— we call them *logen*."

"*Logen*? Like lodges?"

"I think so. Not all for hunting. The *logen* are for men, mostly."

"Huh."

The girl's hands trembled a little as she poured him more coffee, her eyes taking the opportunity to steal another glance at his chiseled face.

But he'd forgotten her already. He had eyes for only one thing, and that was the door across the street. What would a zoo official, not to mention an animal behaviorist like Klingmann, be doing at a hunting lodge?

He sighed. There was only one way to find out.

The club's concierge stared at Gabriel with unmasked horror. "I beg your pardon?"

"Yeah, I saw your *sign*? Out *front*?" the American twanged. "Me 'n' the boys back home were always out huntin' up some bucks. Boy, I've missed it! I was hopin' you could maybe squeeze me in on your next trip. I'd love to take a crack at some of the local wildlife." Gabriel pointed his index finger and checked the sight down his arm. *Bing*, his arm recoiled.

"*Sir,*" came the shuddering response, "this is a *private* establishment."

Gabriel began patting his coat pockets. "What, 're you talkin' about membership? Hell, I don't mind. What is it, a couple thou a year? D-marks, that is to say? You name it, I can write you a check right now."

The concierge's panic deepened. "No, we—"

"*Ah-ah*! Munich bank!" Gabriel grinned, wagging his finger.

The concierge's jowls quivered. "I don't care if it's

underwritten by God Himself, membership here is by invitation only!"

"So invite me. I don't bite."

"That's not how it works! Now, if you please . . ."

The concierge pointed fiercely toward the front door, but Gabriel was more interested in the other side of the room, where dark wood paneling surrounded an archway that led to an equally dark-paneled hall. There was a glimpse of a larger room beyond, and he heard the low rumble of male voices. He stalled for time.

"How does it work, then?"

The concierge *humphed.* "This club is for men from the very *best* German families." He gave Gabriel a look that was meant to be withering.

"Is that all? Heck, I'm from a *great* German family."

"I seriously doubt it."

"I am! The Ritters, ever heard of 'em? We have this castle down south? Nice place—Schloss Ritter in Rittersberg?" Gabriel leaned forward conspiratorially. "Bet not many of your members have a whole *town* named after 'em or a family castle. Am I right?"

Now the man's eyes narrowed, and he stared at Gabriel blankly as his ears pinkened. He had a constipated look as though he was certain Gabriel was putting him on and yet . . . what if he wasn't?

"Xavier?"

Gabriel had been so intrigued by the mental battle raging on the concierge's face that he hadn't noticed that they were no longer alone. The voice was deep and exotically accented. Gabriel found its owner in the shadow of the archway.

He was a tall man, at least six-two. He was extravagantly handsome with dark hair that curled on the shoulders of his immaculate gray suit and a strong, rugged yet boyish face. As he stepped forward, the breadth of his shoulders and the long, angular lines they narrowed to struck a chord of envy in the shorter

American. The man's face was curious and not unfriendly.

Xavier fell over himself trying to apologize; that intent was clear even if the words were indecipherable. But the man stepped past the concierge, his eyes never leaving Gabriel's. "Did I hear you mention the Ritters?"

"Yes."

"Of Rittersberg, Bavaria?"

Gabriel was surprised. Not many people had heard of the tiny village—it was barely on the map. "Yeah! Well, it *used* to be Bavaria. It's Germany now."

The man smiled slightly as though he found this distinction naive. "You don't sound German, Herr Ritter."

"I'm not. My grandfather immigrated to the States. As a matter of fact, he even changed his name. I go by Knight. Gabriel Knight."

Gabriel reached out a hand, hoping the man was as friendly as he looked. The man took it.

"Gabriel. Like the angel," the man said, looking with bemused curiosity into Gabriel's eyes. "My own name is Baron Friedrich von Glower. Friedrich will do."

"Thanks," Gabriel said, feeling a rush of victory. He was definitely in.

"Rittersberg is a beautiful spot." Von Glower put a hand on Gabriel's back and began to escort him toward the archway.

"Oh, it's great, what with the Alps right there."

"Yes, magnificent. You do . . . *hunt,* don't you, Mr. Knight?"

Von Glower paused, as though he wanted no distractions from the answer. He waited politely, his dark brown eyes gazing earnestly into Gabriel's.

Gabriel's neck burned. The concierge had been a lark, a shot in the dark, but there was something about this man's open stare that made the subterfuge much more serious. Fortunately, he found he didn't have to lie.

"Sure, I hunt. You might say it's a family tradition." He returned von Glower's gaze calmly and without blinking.

"Very well," said von Glower, breaking into a slow smile. "Let me introduce you to the others."

Down the hall was a large, high-ceilinged great room. The carpeting was expensive and old, and the walls were decked out with enough antlers and glazed eyes to have made some taxidermist a very rich man.

Gabriel's nervousness resurfaced when he saw Klingmann. The doctor was engaged in what looked like an intense and very private conversation with a blond, arrogant-looking young man. The blonde's cashmere jacket and Italian loafers bespoke a silver spoon crammed well and truly down his throat. The only other occupants of the room were three older men who were drinking at a long, polished wooden bar.

"Gentlemen!" von Glower said as they entered. All eyes turned their way. "I'd like to introduce Herr Knight, a hunting enthusiast from America. I've invited him to join us for a while. How long are you in Munich, Herr Knight?"

"Just a couple of weeks."

Von Glower turned back to the others. "Then, for a few weeks Herr Knight will be my guest, so let me introduce you. By the fireplace is Baron von Zell."

Von Zell, the blonde that had been speaking to Klingmann, was scowling irritably at von Glower as if wondering why the hell he would bring in such a ragamuffin. He gave Gabriel a begrudging nod.

"And Doktor Klingmann . . ."

Klingmann had an expression of befuddlement that was about to become suspicion. Gabriel rushed into the void.

"Wow, this is amazin'!" he gushed. "I'm doin' some

research for a novel while I'm in town, and I met Dr. Klingmann at the zoo. I guess we have more in common than we thought, hey, Doktor?"

The words fell like lead on the room, and Gabriel could feel his fair skin reddening, an obvious betrayal of the smile plastered on his face.

"Yes, quite a coincidence," Klingmann said, frowning. He appeared to be about to say more, but he cast a surreptitious glance at von Zell and closed his mouth.

Gabriel had hoped the missing wolves screw-up at the zoo wasn't something Klingmann would want to bring up in front of this crowd. It looked like he was right.

"A novelist too? How interesting," von Glower said, breaking the awkward pause. "Over by the bar, the large one is Herr von Aigner . . ."

Von Glower was being polite; Von Aigner was both tall and enormously fat. He raised a glass cheerfully in Gabriel's direction.

"Prost!"

". . . Herr Hennemann . . ."

A smaller gray-haired man waved his hand. *"Guten Abend,* Herr Knight."

"English, please, Hennemann!" von Glower cajoled. He turned to Gabriel, "Or am I underestimating you?"

" 'Fraid not," Gabriel said sheepishly.

"What about me?" said the third and final man at the bar. He'd been staring at Gabriel since he and von Glower walked in. There was a predatory look in his eye that Gabriel didn't quite know what to make of. The man sauntered over.

"This is our own Herr Preiss," von Glower said.

Preiss crossed the room and stopped uncomfortably close to Gabriel He was an odd mix of brutishness and style, like a boxer in a tuxedo. He had a patterned velvet evening coat on, and there was nothing at all on his head except for a healthy glow. His face was fleshy with broad, enlarged features that looked almost swollen. Preiss reached for and took Gabriel's hand, pressing it warmly between his own.

"A pleasure, Herr Knight," Preiss rumbled in a low, liquid rush.

For an insane moment Gabriel was sure Preiss was going to kiss his hand. He snuck a glance at von Glower, more to escape Preiss's gaze than anything else. Von Glower looked amused. He dropped a graceful hand on Preiss's shoulders.

"Thank you for being so *friendly,* Preiss," von Glower said in a low, laughing voice.

Preiss reluctantly let go and strolled back to the bar.

"I'm, uh, real happy to meet all of you," Gabriel managed.

"Then have a drink!" von Aigner bellowed. Hennemann nodded lollingly. Gabriel realized they were both drunk off their asses.

"Good idea!" Von Glower placed his hand once again at Gabriel's back, urging him toward the bar. "We have beer on tap, or wine if you prefer."

"Anythin's fine, Baron."

"Friedrich."

"Friedrich. Anythin's fine."

Yes, anything, anything, anything at all. Gabriel had the feeling it was going to be a *very* long night.

What the hell had he gotten himself into this time?

Chapter 2

"Mom, I'm not a salesclerk." As usual when talking to her mother, the New York edge on Grace Naki-mura's voice was exaggerated into a nasal whine.

A man walked up to the counter with a Dorothy Parker paperback. Grace punched in the numbers on the register.

"That'll be $6.20," she whispered, covering up the phone. He fished in his pockets.

"Mom, I *have* looked into it—registration closes at the end of next month. Okay, the fifteenth, how did you . . . ?"

She gave the man his change and managed a smile before he walked away. With her mother squawking in her ear, smiling posed the same technical challenge as rubbing your stomach and patting your head at the same time.

"Mom, I'm *not* ruining my life, and I don't care if Mark Kobayashi's gotten engaged—*you* liked him, not me."

A middle-aged woman came to the counter. That she was a middle-aged woman was evident from her hands and her swinging purse; her face was hidden behind a stack of *The Voodoo Murders* hardbacks.

"I gotta go, I'll call you later," Grace insisted. "I gotta *go*.

"Sorry," she said to the woman as she hung up. The

stack of books had been delicately balanced on the counter, and now the woman's enthusiastic round face was visible.

"I'm a *huge* Blake Backlash fan," the woman admitted with a giggle.

"I never would have guessed."

"Oh, these are for my *friends. I've* already read it three times!"

"Won't your friends be thrilled!" Grace managed to keep the sarcasm from her tone.

"I hope so. Mr. Knight has quite a way with words, and I just love the character—Blake? He's so masculine, so *take-charge!*" The woman's face glowed.

"That's the miracle of fiction."

"I'm sorry?"

"I mean, they don't make men like that anymore." Grace tried not to sound relieved.

"Don't I know it!" the woman agreed with a demeanor of sisterly bonding. "That scene in chapter twenty with his sidekick, Fujitsu? The way he swept her off her feet and carried her to his bedroom? I thought I would just die! Just lay down and die!"

"I had exactly the same reaction," said Grace, reddening. "That'll be $123.21."

"But then, Mr. Knight himself is pretty cute, isn't he? At least his picture." The woman ripped off her check and handed it to Grace. "I read in the *Picayune* review that he, um, *owns* this bookstore?"

The hope in the woman's voice was painful.

"He does, but he hasn't been here in months. I'm sorry." Grace dug up a sympathetic smile.

"That's all right. I didn't really expect to . . . you know." The woman got very flustered. She took her purchases and left.

Something about the encounter made Grace upset, or perhaps it was a residue from the phone call with her mother. She looked at the clock, but it was still hours from lunchtime. She decided to go back into the studio and check the answering machine. It used to be the first thing she did every morning, but there were never any messages on it and she'd gradually stopped expecting there to be. But checking it was still a distraction she allowed herself several times a day, and at the moment she needed one.

It turned out to be more of a distraction than she'd bargained for. The little box blinked its indication of a message, an event so rare as to deserve an entry on the astronomical calendar. Grace hit the button, glad for once that the shop was empty. Gabriel's voice came on.

"Hey, Gracie. Um, somethin's come up. It *might* be a new case, but I'm not sure yet. I'm on location so, um, don't bother tryin' to reach me at the castle. I'll call you if this thing looks like it's goin' anywhere. Okay? Until we know for sure, Gerde can handle any research I need. We'll talk about the shop just as soon as I get back to Rittersberg. I promise. Give my love to Gran."

Click.

Grace replayed the message. Then she replayed it again.

For a long, suspended moment there was nothing but incredulity. When that faded, what remained was not what she would have expected of herself—anger and indignation at being left out of a potential case, at being replaced as research assistant by Gerde, the alleged housekeeper of Schloss Ritter. Those emotions would come, but they would be aftershocks, not her immediate, gut reaction. Her gut reaction was a wave of certainty and direction as unquestionable as her own name.

It was time to go to Germany.

Schloss Ritter
Rittersberg, Bavaria

By the time Grace landed in Munich, she'd had time to digest the voice message fully—the message and, along with it, every remotely feasible implication and subtext a human mind could possibly come up with in response to the words left on the recorder. The words, and her own fairly ripe experience of Mr. Knight, hair gel and all.

The pretty twenty-seven-year-old had inherited this unique capacity, this paranoia-tilted well of imagination, from her Japanese mother. It went with her current, long-suffering situation with Knight the way that nitroglycerine went with gunpowder.

So that by the time the door of Schloss Ritter opened in response to her knock, and the tall, blond, and attractive (if somewhat severe) figure of Gerde came into view, the sight was received as the final confirmation of what was already a foregone conclusion—that Gerde was stoking more than the castle's furnace. There was no way a womanizer like Gabriel could spend a winter alone with such a woman and not try *something,* and to Gerde, surely the handsome young family heir was a dream come true?

"Is Gabriel here?" Grace asked tersely, not even trusting his message on that regard.

"No, he's away on business. You must be Grace." Gerde held out her hand, a surprised but welcoming smile on her face.

Grace accepted neither the hand nor the smile, picking up her luggage to avoid the former. "May I come in? I can get a room in the village if that's not acceptable."

Gerde cocked her head to one side and studied Grace with confusion.

"Of course you can stay here," she said slowly. She reached over and took one of Grace's bags, leading the way inside.

"It's one of the few comfortable bedrooms," Gerde explained as she switched on the light in Gabriel's room. "We're still making repairs. There's a fireplace in here, and it gets very cold at night."

Grace looked around the room. She'd had a hard time imagining Schloss Ritter. To suddenly be here was very surreal.

"Don't worry," Gerde said with a smile when Grace's eyes fixed on the bed. "I just changed the sheets."

Grace tried not to scream. She took her suitcase over to the bed and opened it.

"You must be tired. Did you—did you have a bad flight?" Gerde asked, pausing at the door.

"No," Grace said stiffly. "Where *is* Gabriel, by the way?"

"He's on a case."

Grace felt her face burn. *A case.* The louse. She stole a glance at Gerde and thought the blonde looked pleased with herself. Probably she was feeling triumphant about having booted Grace so easily out of the way.

She closed her suitcase and sat on the bed. "Where?"

Gerde hesitated. "North of here."

"Really? Do you have an address and phone number?"

Gerde looked extremely uncomfortable. "I'm sorry, but I don't think it's my place to talk about Gabriel's case with you. When he calls, he can tell you himself."

Grace nodded, her temper rising. "His message mentioned research for the case."

"He gave you instructions, then?" Gerde sounded relieved.

Grace could just kill her. "Actually, he mentioned that *you* would be doing some research."

"Oh. Yes, I suppose he did ask me to check the library."

"For what?"

Gerde sighed and gripped the handle of the door. "Grace, this is between Gabriel and the people who needed his help. I'm very sorry."

Grace sucked in her cheeks and glared at the blonde.

"Would you maybe like some dinner before you go to sleep? Or some coffee?" Gerde offered.

Grace declined. She went to bed with a repast of hot, frustrated tears instead.

The morning brought relief. Grace awoke to the sun shining in the window. When she sat up in bed, the full panorama of the snow-peaked Alps came into view. The window had been left slightly ajar in the night, and the air was brisk and as rich as newly milked cream. She was in Germany at last, and it was a beautiful day! How bad could things be?

She dressed and went downstairs, a renewed sense of purpose cheering her. She gave a curt good morning to Gerde, who was seated in the front hall surrounded by what looked like remodeling plans, and grabbed her coat. Without further conversation, she slipped out to explore Rittersberg.

The town dated from the 1200s. An old stone wall surrounded the heart of it, forming curious and beguiling archways and secret passages. On the main square the *Rathaus* and its glockenspiel were bursting with the kind of charm Disney spent a fortune replicating. And across from the square was a perfect little church with a stone pathway and a bell tower. She walked the village byways several times, past houses with Bavarian murals painted on the white stucco walls, a tiny grocery shop, and an equally small school. She greeted everyone she saw, delighting in practicing the German greetings she'd been studying. Then, when her hunger became insistent, she headed for the *gasthof* on the main square.

The interior of the Goldener Löwe was all lacquered pine and ceiling beams. One old gentleman was the only person in attendance, and he brought *frühstück*—breakfast—consisting of coffee, a hard-boiled egg, and a plate of rolls and meats. It was not exactly what Grace was used to eating this early, but it tasted great after the fresh air.

"Are you on your way to Austria?" Werner asked as he refilled her cup.

"No. I'm staying at the castle."

Werner raised a fuzzy gray eyebrow. "You are?"

"Yes," Grace said around her toast. "I'm a friend of Gabriel Knight's. Do you know him?"

Werner nodded grimly. "I know him. My niece, Gerde, she works at the castle. You have met Gerde?"

"Oh, yes," Grace said neutrally. It occurred to her that Werner might know something. She looked around, but there was no one else in the pub. She spoke confidentially. "I'm Grace Nakimura, Gabriel's research assistant. I came to help out on his new case."

The spark of interest in Werner's eyes grew. "Ah, so! Good for you."

"I didn't catch your name."

"Werner Huber."

"What do you think about this case, Herr Huber?" Grace asked, giving him a concerned smile.

Werner put the coffeepot on the table and sat down on the bench across from her. He leaned his large, weathered arms on the planks and spoke in a low voice.

"It was I who brought him the case. For our cousin. Poor Sepp!"

Grace's pulse quickened. "Really?"

"*Ja.*"

"And . . . do, um, do you think the case will be a difficult one?"

Werner glowered ominously. "Oh, yes! Very bad, I think. There have already been many deaths."

Grace's stomach did a slow roll. She had a very

visceral, very vivid recollection of the moments of sheer terror she'd had over the Voodoo murders in New Orleans. The idea that Gabriel actually was on a new case, a *real* case, struck home for the first time.

"What's he up against?" she asked, edging forward in her chair.

Werner shrugged enigmatically. "It may be one. It may be more than one. It's very smart, I can tell you that." He tapped his temple.

Grace shook her head, confused. "More than one . . . what?"

Werner sat back, a look of vague suspicion dawning.

"Um, Gabriel called me and told me to get here, pronto," Grace explained quickly. "I just flew in last night, and I haven't had a chance to speak to him yet."

Werner considered this and seemed to find it reasonable—or maybe the old man just couldn't resist the temptation to talk about it. In any case, he hunched forward, his light gray eyes filled with conspiratorial grimness.

"Werewolf," he whispered.

Grace's jaw ended up somewhere around her breastbone. She didn't have the first idea what to make of it—whether to laugh or scream. She didn't know what she'd expected, but this was not it. Her expression was fuel to Werner's fire. He filled Grace in on the story of Toni Huber, embellishing it considerably.

"Oh, my God," Grace said when he was done. "Oh, my *God*."

"Yes, you see? Very dangerous. We had a werewolf right here in Rittersberg many years ago. People still talk about it. It was a devil—pure *evil*."

Werner's long face was pulled into a grimace, and he nodded knowingly as if he were keeper of some dark secret.

"You had a *werewolf*? Here? When was that?"

"Long ago. I heard stories about it when I was a child."

Grace sat silent for a moment, her mind racing. "If he . . . if Gabriel took the case for your cousin, you probably know where he is."

Werner nodded solemnly. Grace felt a sense of relief flush her. "Well . . . where?"

Werner looked at her oddly, as if considering, then shook his great, gray-bearded head. "*Ne*. If he wants you to know, he must tell you himself. When it comes to matters of good and evil, one must be careful, you see? I have maybe said too much as it is."

Werner got up and went back to his duties. It was the first time Grace noticed the family resemblance between the old man and his niece. She took another bite of toast and chewed determinedly.

Grace looked from room to room back at the castle—those not boarded over or nailed shut—and finally located the *Schattenjäger* library near Gabriel's bedroom. Gerde was in it, scanning the shelves. She flushed a bit when Grace entered.

"You reminded me that I had some things to do for Gabriel," Gerde said, trying to sound pleasant.

Grace tossed down her purse and headed to the shelves. Just one glance at the old volumes got her excitement flowing, even if Gerde's presence dampened the moment.

"Stuff on werewolves, I know," Grace said with a hint of satisfaction. "What did you find?" She spied a small stack of books accumulating on the table. She went over and picked up the top one. It looked ancient. The cover said *Werewolfs: An Inquisitor's Gyde*.

"Grace . . ." Gerde began firmly, "I know you will get angry again, but I'm afraid the *Schattenjäger* library is off limits to anyone but—"

Grace lost it. Her candle of restraint had burned to the quick with all of this nonsense. She slammed the book down on the desk and turned, fury in her eyes. "No way. You *can't* be serious."

Gerde recoiled a little but held firm. "I know it must be difficult for you to understand traditions like—"

"No, *you* don't understand," Grace interrupted, her voice rising. "I've got a *master's* degree, and I've been tending a stupid bookshop for Gabriel for over a year, waiting for a case to come up. So I don't care what your personal issues are, *Ms.* Hull! I don't care if you're sleeping with him, I don't care if you want to play Queen of the Castle, I don't care if you think women shouldn't mess with the manly business of being a *Schattenjäger,* I just don't care! I'm working on this case, because *I'm due.* And I'm not going to sit around and watch someone else take what *I've* earned just because he . . . just because . . ."

She stopped. Something inside her could not bear to voice the words, as if reluctant to subject her own ears to them. And then there was the look on Gerde's face. The blonde, the much larger of the two, stood there as though she'd been slapped. Tears defied gravity on the edge of her lashes.

"Fine. Do whatever you wish," she said in a quiet voice. She turned and marched from the room, shutting the library door softly behind her.

Grace took a long, quavering breath. *"Shit."* She had the bitter aftertaste of a nasty blow-up, an inward wincing at her own actions. She'd meant what she'd said, at least the part about the work, but the delivery had been brutally raw.

Well, it was done now, and she couldn't take it back. And if she'd made her point and could now work in peace, perhaps it was for the best.

Werewolfs: An Inquisitor's Gyde

There are two kindes of werewolfs the Inquisitor may confronte in his doutes: the firste is the "false" werewolf, and the seconde is the "true" werewolf. The false werewolf is a man or womman who cannot chaunge his or her forme, but whose bedeveled minde beleves otherwyse. The false werewolf may run nayked in the night, and may een kille and ayt humankinde, alle the while convynced that he or she is a wolf. In these cases, the Inquisitor wil finde no evydence of an animal in fact or in witnesses, and the bodyes may also be shewn to baar the markes of human attack only, howere wilde.

The cause of the false werewolf is possessyn by an evyl spirit. Contact with the devel may also had ben made, for the devel can cause swich delusyns and can so use a sinner for his owne mordrous purpose. In swich cases, the Inquisitor is fortunayt, for the tounfolke may alredy know who is the werewolf. Swich behavyr is impossyble to hyde.

It is muche haarder with true werewolfs. A true werewolf shyfts forme from human to wolf and back agayn. Swich creatyres can hunte their victyms with human kunning and animal ferocyte. They can be haarde to finde, for unlike the false werewolfs ther minde is sane and ther behavyr is otherwyse normal. In severyl cases, swich a creatyre has killed for many yeers without captyre. Indeed, swich crimes as these creatyres commit might een be blamed on a reel wolf and nere be solved, more so if the werewolf moves from toun to toun.

These thyngs han ben set doun by Inquisitors who han faced swich beasties:

The true werewolf may shyft forme at wil, but the Chaunge may be forced upon them by certeyn sounds swich as the howling of a wolf or the presence of a ful moon.

A true werewolf ne dooth grow old. Aske the tounfolk about kinsmen and neigheboures who staye yonge.

A true werewolf heels swiftly when wounded. One werewolf in Lyons loost a paw in a trape lyd for him. The paw chaunged to a foote, but when the Inquisitor wente to the werewolf's hoose, though there was freshe blood on the floor and a pyle of bloody linens under the hoose, the man himself was ne wounded. Where the paw han ben rypped away was a foote, pure and whyte and softe like newe skin, and ne matchyng the age and waar of the older foote.

A true werewolf can be killed only be destroying his or her brayn or herte. Also, death by elementales: Fire, Earth, Water, Ayr, is sayd to be effectyf. Alle executyns sholde ende with removing the brayn and herte from the body or burning the body as precautyns agaynst the werewolf's returne.

A true werewolf is one of the moste mysteryes and cursed creatyres of darkness. The curse is a curse of the blood, and in swich creatyres the blood is tainted. The true werewolf is fashyned in these maneres:

If a man or womman be borne to a true werewolf, they han the tainted blood.

If a man or womman be byten by a true werewolf and lyve, they han the tainted blood.

If a man or womman be cursed by one with the power to lay swich evyl, their blood becomes tainted.

If a witche or a sorcerer makes swich concoctyns as can force the Chaunge, or gaynes a magikal wolfskin, salve, or belte from the devel, they can effeck the Chaunge without the tainted blood at firste. But with muche use the Chaunge wil infecte the blood til the witche or sorcerer becomes controlled by the Curse and the Curse becomes irreversyble.

Werewolf packes

A true werewolf han it in his wolf nature to desyre a packe. In this manere mighte a clever Inquisitor spote his werewolf. Looke for those who lyv in unnatural groupes. When swich a packe is formed, the firste werewolf, he or she with the blood tainted through byrth, curse, or sorcery, is the Alpha werewolf. The others who are converted by the Alpha werewolf's byte are called Beta werewolfs after the Greek fashyn. There is usually only one Alpha werewolf, but there may be many Beta werewolfs in a packe. A Beta werewolf is easyr to detect than an Alpha, for many Betas go madd from the blood. Looke for increysed aggressyn, unprovoked rage, sleeplessness, and chaunges in physikal appeyrance.

A victym who is byten by a true werewolf for this purpoose—for the purpoose of making a Beta werewolf—is doomed to the werewolf curse unless they, by some actyn of their own hande or minde, cause the destructyn of the Alpha werewolf. They are by swich a meyns cured and the tainte lifted. In contraryness, if a Beta is haarmed the Alpha shal suffer pangs by the power of blood sympathee, but if the Alpha commit the haarm the suffering shal be one for one. For swich raysons an Alpha wil ne haarm a Beta of its owne making with its owne hande.

Alle creatyres who dye with the tainted blood are doomed to Helle with the rest of the devel's minyns. But for swich a victym that becomes a true werewolf through no act of his or her owne, their soule may remayn in Purgatory if they han committed no grievyse sin—that is, if they han ne taken human lyf or ayten of human flessh or blood. Even for swich a one as this, they can in no way enter Heven with the curse on their soule.

Grace was putting the book down when something slipped inside the cover and a trace of cream peeked out. She carefully opened the back of the book and saw an envelope with a red seal.

The envelope looked old, but not as old as the book itself. It was addressed to König Ludwig II vom Bavaria and was dated March 4, 1864.

She had to break the seal to open it. The letter was written in German, but between her own studies and her dictionary she was able to get a rough translation together quickly, for it was a short and pointed missive.

> To the benevolent and beloved King of Bavaria:
> I have had the honor of meeting your highness only twice, but you may depend upon me as your most loyal subject and one who holds your life more dearly than his own. It is my profession to seek out certain kinds of criminal behavior, and I am currently on an investigation which I fear comes too close to Your Highness. I am investigating the one who calls himself "the Black Wolf," and I have learned that he is extremely dangerous for reasons which I cannot fully express to you by such means as this letter. Please, I beg you, do not see this man alone and guard your person at all times with the highest diligence. I hope to finish my proofs soon, and then I will be happy to explain everything to you. In the meantime, take this as a most serious warning from one who loves you.
> Your servant, Baron Christian von Ritter of Rittersberg, Bavaria

"The Black Wolf?" Grace mused, her curiosity pushing all thoughts of Gerde or, indeed, of anything else from her head. "It must have been a werewolf case, or why would the letter be in this book?"

She'd seen a chapel on the first floor, and now she returned to it, drawn by a large Bible she'd glimpsed on the altar. The Bible, old and heavy, did indeed contain a family history scribbled among the branches of an illuminated tree. Christian von Ritter was born in 1820, ordained as *Schattenjäger* in 1838 and died . . . March 4, 1864—the exact date on the letter! According to the log, he broke his neck in a fall from his horse. He was succeeded by his son, Stephan, who was not ordained for two years, being only been sixteen at the time of his father's death.

So it was likely that Christian's investigation had

died with him. Had Christian been riding off to deliver the letter when he had his fatal fall? To track the Black Wolf? In any case, the letter to the king had obviously never been sent, for its seal was intact and, well, it was still here.

Grace returned to the library and located the journals of the *Schattenjägers* in a glass-enclosed bookcase. Some of the older journals were fragile, falling apart. She had a deep urge to begin cataloguing this treasure trove, to get a computer in here and begin typing before all of this history was lost to disintegration. But that would have to wait.

Christian von Ritter's journal was easily found by the dates written on the spine: 1838–1864. Curiously, as with the journal of Gunter Ritter that Werner had sent to New Orleans, the handwritten entries were in English. Could the family have originated in the Green Isles? Their patron saint, St. George, was England's own. Such a history was undoubtedly in these journals somewhere, but she'd have to take one mystery at a time.

3 January, 1883. I am now in Prussia. The beast that brought me here has so far bested me. He is secretive and skillful. He has much self-control, unlike what I'd been led to expect. He seems to know almost before I do where and when I will be stalking him. He turns up his nose at my lures. Three more disappearances have occurred, and I'm no closer to learning his identity or finding his lair. I can't even prove *he* took them. Not a single corpse has been found.

And the last entry.

3 March, 1864. I have had a break at last. The key was in front of me all the time. The Black Wolf, he so daringly calls himself, for all to hear and none to truly see. It is worse than I could ever have suspected. He is not just a beast, but a monster! His jaws are already around some of the best throats in Europe. I

am so very fearful. I return to Rittersberg tonight. I
must warn those in danger and get someone to assist
me. I dare not attempt to take him alone.

Grace checked the journal of Stefan von Ritter,
Christian's son, but there was only a brief mention
that he had not been able to follow his father's trail,
and that he thought that the suspect in question had
long since left the area.

So what had happened to King Ludwig II? Although a history major, Grace's specialty had never
been European monarchy. Still, she knew vaguely
who the man was. He was a Wittelsbach and, as the
date on the letter reminded her, he was probably
one of the last Wittelsbach monarchs. The Prussian
kaisers took over when the common German country was formed.

Did the Black Wolf have anything to do with the
downfall of the Wittelsbachs? Did this story have any
bearing on Gabriel's case at all? Grace sighed. Probably not.

She began to go through the other journals carefully, pulling each out gingerly and leafing through
them. It was time-consuming and tedious, and she had
to keep stopping herself from getting interested in entries that obviously were not about werewolves.

She was about to take a break when she found
something. It was in a journal dated 1720–1753.

   20 April, 1750
   Numerous deaths at the hands of a marauding wolf
being recorded in a neighboring county, I set out to
see if I could determine the cause. There had been
rumors of a werewolf, and the dark signs did indeed
seem to be present.
   The deaths had all occurred within a forty-kilometer
range of woods, and at the heart was the village of
Alfing. My assistant and I set a trap a short distance
from the village. Though the beast had shewn a pro-
pensity for human flesh, livestock has also been taken,

and it was a newling lamb we loosed in the thicket as a lure.

We awaited downwind. For two nights the lamb bleated to no purpose, and once we had to fend off a hungry fox. On the third night the beast himself took the bait. I might have missed him, for the night was so dark and the wolf itself was black, but my son saw the light of its eyes and I heard the lamb's cries turn fearful.

It had the poor dumb lamb by the throat when we sprang. It was swift and might have escaped, but its fatal mistake was to attack rather than run. My dagger struck through its chest and into its right lung.

As I had agreed, we bound the wolf and tied shut his jaws. We brought it home to Rittersberg, still breathing. It was turned over to the magistrate.

I pray for the man's unfortunate soul. May the law be swift and merciful. God be praised for aiding his servant. From his hand came the strength and the wisdom to end the killing.

Victor von Ritter, Schattenjäger.

The Rittersberg *Rathaus* had a quaint old interior with a weathered counter and lots of wooden chairs lined up as though they were expecting a crowd. This seemed a tad optimistic, particularly since an older gentleman and a woman at a decrepit typewriter were the only signs of life. The man came over immediately and introduced himself as the town mayor, Herr Habermas. Grace gave him the same story she'd given Herr Huber at the *gasthof,* and as soon as he realized she was an American, he superceded her faltering German with heavily accented English.

"Herr Huber mentioned a werewolf in Rittersberg many years ago," she told him, "and I found a mention of it in the *Schattenjäger* archives. I was hoping . . . do you keep old town records here?"

Habermas was a pleasant-faced, plump man with magnificently groomed white hair in a pompadoured style. He smiled proudly, revealing stained teeth. "Miss Nakimura, our archives are some of the best in

Germany. We were too small to be bombed in the war, and Rittersberg has been very careful about making records. Some records date back to 1223, when the town was founded."

Grace's eyes shone with anticipation. "Would you check the archives for me, then? The *Schattenjäger* journal mentioned a trial for the werewolf with a date of April 1750."

Habermas wrote it down and disappeared through an archway in the rear. The woman at the typewriter turned and gave Grace a rosy smile from a plain, large face. Grace couldn't help but smile back.

When Habermas returned, he was carrying a file. "What do you think I did?" he asked.

"You found it?"

"I found it!" he beamed.

"What's it say?" Grace leaned over the counter eagerly, but the scrawled German was indecipherable.

"20 April, *siebzehn hundert fünfzig*. A werewolf was brought to town by the *Schattenjäger*. It was put in the dungeon . . . There was a trial three days later. The werewolf, by the name of Baron Claus von Ralick of Alfing, was executed here, in the town square."

"Baron Claus von Ralick? How'd they know? I mean, it was a wolf when the *Schattenjäger* brought it in, right?"

Habermas turned back a few pages. "Ja, *Fräulein*. It says a large black wolf was brought to town and put in the dungeon . . . Oh! Here. The morning after the wolf was brought to town, they found a man in the cell. How interesting!"

"Wow. But how'd they figure out his name?"

Habermas looked through the notes and shook his head. "It is not written. Maybe someone knew the man or maybe he told them his name. He would have been . . . *questioned* most strongly."

Habermas gave Grace a knowing look, but she didn't notice. She was thinking it through. "How'd they execute him?"

"It says his head was cut off; then he was, uh, cut into four pieces; then they burned him at the stake."

"All three?" Grace's face scrunched in disgust.

Habermas smiled sympathetically. "In that time people *believed* in evil. Not like now. Such a thing as this beast . . . they would take no chances."

"He couldn't have escaped, then," Grace muttered to herself.

"Oh, no! Not his family either."

Grace looked up sharply. "What about his family?"

"Did I not say? It was written down. . . ." He turned pages. "Here it is. The day the werewolf changed back into a man, a group of villagers was sent to Alfing, his hometown."

"To do *what*?"

Habermas blinked his large watery blue eyes as if befuddled at her question. "Miss, his wife and children would have been burned alive also. People believed that such a thing ran in the blood."

"Oh." Grace tried to dismiss the ghastly images that came into her head. "Uh, thanks very much for your help, Herr Habermas."

Habermas closed the file. "*Kein problem, Fräulein.* Do you want to see the dungeon also?"

"*The* dungeon? The one von Ralick was in?"

"*Ja.* It is just beneath our feet. Downstairs."

The door that accessed the staircase was on the central courtyard, separated from the public spaces of the Rathaus. They descended down into a dank stone corridor. There was only one cell, and its door was made of massive old wood.

Herr Habermas brought out a set of keys. He had to unlock a padlock, then lift a heavy iron bar. They went inside.

The room was made of stone, and it had a chill that nipped at Grace's bones. The only window was small and high up on the wall. It was open to the air but closed to escape by means of vertical bars. The morning air was cool, but the room itself was colder still. It was completely empty.

Grace stood quietly, taking in the place. She knew it was her imagination, but she sensed something tangible in the room, something wild, something enraged, something panicky.

"Von Ralick wouldn't have wanted to change back," she said, surprised at the clarity of this thought.

"Wie bitte?" Habermas asked, confused.

She walked around the room slowly. She could picture the beast here, that odd feeling she often got at historical sites. It was pure fantasy, yet sometimes it offered interesting insights. "They put the creature in here. They were waiting for it to change back. If it hadn't, they probably would have decided it was just a wolf. Maybe shot it."

Habermas was watching her curiously.

"If he changed back, it was probably because he didn't have a choice." Grace turned to look at her companion. "I wouldn't have wanted to change. Would you?"

"I don't know."

"Especially if he knew . . . He *would* have known, wouldn't he? That they'd go after his family once he was recognized?"

"If he was a baron, he would know the law well enough."

"Hmmm . . ." Grace went over to the window and looked out. Across the square a bit of the church was visible.

"What would his last few days have been like? Would he have seen a priest?"

"Probably. There would be a last meal also."

"And the execution took place where?"

The mayor came to the window and pointed. "In the center of the square, *there*. You see?"

Grace's dark eyes stared out, narrowing. "He would have seen them preparing for it."

"Ja, Fräulein."

Whoosh. Thwack! She could almost see the practice swings of the axman. She lowered herself from her tiptoes and suddenly felt claustrophobic.

"Can we go now?"

Habermas must have seen something on her face, for he helped her out with an urgency he had not yet displayed. By the time they reached the courtyard, Grace was on the verge of either vomiting or passing out. She sat down on the steps until the fresh air and sunlight banished the heebie-jeebies.

The church was called St. Georg's. *Of course,* Grace thought, *after the patron saint of the Schattenjägers.*

But if St. George was the patron saint of the *Schattenjägers,* it was clear that the *Schattenjägers* were patron saints of the town. On the front of the church was a plaque noting that Martin Ritter had erected the church in 1231. And just inside the doorway a staircase led downward. A small sign said *gruft*—crypt.

Although she was hardly anxious to visit another underground hole, she couldn't resist the temptation to descend the stairway. Fortunately, the area beneath the church was not a small, dank space. Quite the opposite. Below the main nave was a secondary, smaller chapel with pews and stones in the floors marking the burial places of the townsfolk. There were Ritters here along with other town names. But those buried beneath the chapel floor were all women or Ritters who had died young. The dates were amazing: Johann Ritter, beloved son, 1633–1636, Halla Rittersberg, wife and mother, 1582–1617. Some were not legible at all, worn smooth with centuries of footsteps.

Beyond the chapel she found the *Schattenjägers* themselves. They were in a long, broad hall made of stone, but well lit, with casement windows lining the upper spaces of the walls and modern lights aiding the balance against the shadows. And here were stone sarcophagi, row upon row, some ancient, some newer, all with coffin-shaped boxes four feet high, and on top of them were knights in full armor carved in stone, each holding a sword.

The names were carved below the knights: *Claus Ritter, Michael Ritter, Johann Ritter, Hans Ritter, Wolfgang Ritter* . . .

Grace paused at the last, a pure white sarcophagus. Yes, it did look new, and there was a bouquet of wildflowers on the casket that was only a few days old. Her eyes searched for a date. . . . Died 1993. It was Gabriel's great-uncle.

She reached out a hand slowly and touched the hand of the stone knight.

"Guten Morgan, Fräulein."

Grace turned to see a priest approaching her with a warm smile. "Are you interested in our history?" he asked in German.

"Yes," she answered in kind. "Very much."

"What can I help you with?"

It took Grace a few minutes to communicate the request—her vocabulary was limited and her pronunciation was not always on track. It took her even longer to persuade the priest that he would not be violating some divine guideline by complying. The records were very old, Grace argued, and the interested parties long dead. Father Getz agreed to go look to see if there even was such a record, probably because, Grace thought, it was a bit silly to argue over something that might not exist.

He led Grace upstairs to his office. He planted her in the chair at his desk and disappeared again. When he returned, he had a file in his hands. He did not resume their argument about the sanctity of confession, to Grace's surprise. He only put the file on the desk, gave her an unreadable look, and left.

Grace opened the file eagerly. It contained the notes of a Father Beidermann outlining the last confession of "Baron Claus von Ralick, a convicted werewolf." Using her pocket dictionary, she worked out a translation.

The von Ralick family crest has long (featured?) the image of a black wolf, for the family prided itself on its skill in the hunt and on physical strength and speed. Claus von Ralick admits that he was reckless in his youth—a "devil"—and that he lived up to the crest so well that he gained the (nickname?) "the Black Wolf" from his friends. He had a terrible temper, loved violence and fighting, and was particularly violent with women. As caretaker of his family's lands, he felt that the women on it were his property, and he took many against their will. His (demeanor/attitude?) as he spoke of these things showed great remorse.

One day a party of gypsies camped on his land. He rode out with his men to (oust?) them, and he saw a young girl who was very beautiful. He kidnapped her against the pleas of her family and took her back to his estate. The girl committed suicide that very night by jumping from his bedroom window down to the yard, where the dogs were out.

The next day, an old gypsy woman came to the house and demanded to see him. She cursed him, saying that his heart was so foul and (bestial?) that he had earned the form of a beast as well. At the time he laughed with his men and had the woman thrown out. But less than a month later, the curse came true—he began changing into a wolf in the night. He has lived with the curse ever since, often killing humans, particularly children, and eating their flesh.

He begs God's mercy for his wife and son, that they be spared both the stake and the curse.

I record this for the education of those who come after me. May they be saved by God's mercy from such hellish creatures. Father Beidermann.

"The *Black Wolf*?" Grace said aloud. Could it be possible? Was this werewolf case of 1750 somehow linked to Christian von Ritter's werewolf pursuit in 1864?

"That's not possible," Grace spoke again. Von Ralick, the Black Wolf, had been executed right there in Rittersberg. According to the werewolf lore book, beheading, drawing and quartering, and then burning at the stake would have been overkill—even for a werewolf.

But there was something else in the file. A letter. Grace pulled it out.

It was dated 1764, and it was from a lawyer in Buenos Aires. He was requesting information about the trial and death of Baron Claus von Ralick "for the family." What family? Surely von Ralick's own offspring had perished in Alfing. Distant relatives perhaps? Grace looked at the broken wax seal on the back of the envelope. It was black, and the image pressed into the wax was of a wolf.

She shuddered with a sudden chill. She dropped the envelope and rose from the desk. The priest must have heard her chair leg squeal, for he came in immediately.

"*Haben Sie etwas gefunden?*" he asked her anxiously. Find anything?

Grace pulled herself out of her thoughts and gave him a smile. "*Ja. Sehr gut. Schönen Dank.*"

"Gerde?" Grace said as she took off her coat. "I have some information for Gabriel. Where can I send it?"

Gerde, who was still messing with all the remodeling paperwork, refused even to look Grace's way. "I told him I would send any mail to his lawyer's office in Munich."

"Can I get the address?"

Without a word Gerde picked up a notepad and jotted the address down. She ripped off the page and held it out. She did not look up.

Grace typed out the letter on an old typewriter in the library. It was Gabriel's—she'd sent it over from New Orleans herself. He had this superstitious writer's thing about the ancient hacker. Give her a Pentium anytime.

She put the werewolf manual and the two journals in a package and ran down to the post office to mail it. She paid for overnight delivery.

It had been a long day and the sun was fading. She grabbed a yogurt and some crackers from the grocery store and took them up to Gabriel's room. Gerde did not offer her dinner, which was just fine. Grace started a fire and settled onto the bed with her groceries and a few *Schattenjäger* journals to spend a quiet evening.

From downstairs came a loud, booming knock.

She knew immediately that it was the iron knocker on the front door. She'd heard the noise herself when she arrived, though it had sounded less hollow and reverberating from the other side of the door. She was up in a flash.

"Gabriel!" she muttered as she ran downstairs.

She reached the door just as Gerde was opening it. It was not Gabriel. It wasn't even close. Out on the stoop was a middle-aged couple—the man in a bad polyester maroon suit and slicked, dyed black hair; the woman in a similar jumpsuit (only in hot pink) and a light brown beehive straight out of *The Simpsons*.

"Can I help you?" Gerde asked, bewildered.

"Someone's home. How *thrilling*!" The woman sounded ecstatic.

"We're the Smiths, from Merrimac, Pennsylvania," the man explained.

"Of course you are," Grace said blankly.

"I'm Meryl and this big lug is my husband, Emil!"

"Nice to meet you," Gerde said, still looking confused.

"Is the *Schattenjäger* home?" Mrs. Smith asked the question as though she couldn't keep it buttoned up behind her lips another moment. Only she pronounced the word "Shootin' Jogger" as though the role involved Winchesters and Nikes.

Grace and Gerde exchanged a look.

"No," said Gerde, "I'm afraid he's out of town."

Mrs. Smith's chubby face fell. "Oh, *darn*! And I was *so* hoping to talk shop!" She leaned forward conspiratorially. "We fighters of darkness are so rare these days."

"Tell me about it," Grace said dryly.

"How did you hear of the *Schattenjäger*?" Gerde asked. She stepped back, fighting a smile. The Smiths were more than ready to take the plunge through the doorway. Grace could have kicked her.

"Meryl is a psychic and occultist scholar," Mr. Smith said proudly. "She knows all sorts of things. Don't you, Mother?"

Mrs. Smith flushed with pleasure. "Well, I suppose. I was reading about an old witch trial last spring, and I came across the *Schattenjägers*. I was on a scent then, I can tell you! You all have an *amazing* family tree!"

She looked from Gerde to Grace and back again, and obviously decided Gerde looked more like the family tree she'd expected. She beamed at Gerde and patted her hand.

"I told you we should have called first, Mother," Mr. Smith muttered. To Gerde and Grace he said, "You don't just cross the Atlantic and expect to find people at home. Not these days—it's just go, go, go."

"Private phone numbers are the dickens to get from overseas, and you know it, Em!"

"Well!" Grace looked at her watch. "Nice to meet you, but since the *Schattenjäger* isn't here right now . . . Maybe you could leave your name and address?"

"Oh, we're staying right in town at that cute little *gasthof*," Mrs. Smith giggled. "We just got in! 'Course, I had to get up here right away. That's how I am!"

"The *gasthof* is a very nice place," said Gerde, amusement still evident in her arched brow. Apparently, this particular breed of American was one she didn't run into very often.

"Yes, um, well, if he comes back anytime soon, we'll let him know you're down there." Grace took a step forward, holding the door open plaintively. She was dying to get back to those journals.

Mrs. Smith looked confused. "But, my dear, you two must know *something* about the *Schattenjäger* business, don't you? Will you come by? Tomorrow perhaps? You can tell us more about the family."

Grace shot Gerde a look. *Don't you dare.*

Gerde smiled sweetly. "I must be very busy tomorrow, but Grace knows more than I do anyway. She's the *Schattenjäger's* assistant!"

"*Really?*" Mrs. Smith looked terribly impressed. "Then we *must* talk!"

She reached out her hand to pat Grace, but Grace shied away.

"Actually, I'll be very busy tomorrow myself, but, um, we'll see," Grace fumbled, not wanting to be completely rude.

Mr. Smith got the message. He frowned and tugged Mrs. Smith's arm. "Come on, now, Mother. These ladies look real tired. We'd best be getting back down to our room."

"But, *Em*," Mrs. Smith whined. She shot an envious glance up the staircase.

"Come on, now. Tomorrow's another day."

These words of wisdom managed to get her out on the stoop. Grace was just about to close the doors when a pale and pudgy hand snaked back inside and grabbed her wrist. It startled her, for there was something off about it, something altogether too quick and too cagey. The grip of the fingers on her wrist bone was aching and cold.

Mrs. Smith pushed the door slowly open.

"Please . . ." Grace said nervously.

"Mother?" Mr. Smith said.

But as Mrs. Smith took a step back into the light of the room, there was something on her face that made them all fall silent. Her head was tilted back, and her eyes were looking straight upward and yet somehow didn't seem to be seeing anything at all. Her mouth was stretched in an unnatural O, and her skin had a greenish glow under her rouge.

"*Tell him . . .*" she whispered in a soft voice. "*Tell him . . . beware the Black Wolf!*"

Chapter 3

Munich

He was sitting on the banks of a lake. He knew he was dreaming, but the sensation was so pleasant he hung on to it willfully. It was an alpine lake, he thought, for the grass that he lay upon ran down to the water's edge and the lake itself was sweetly blue and clear. Snow-capped peaks marched away on the horizon.

He wondered half-incoherently if there was such a place near Rittersberg, and wouldn't he love to find it? Someone would know, maybe Werner or . . .

A large white swan was flying in over the lake, and now it flew straight at him over the water's surface, feet down, wings ballooned, poised to land. What a large creature—how magnificent, and how close it was getting.

It landed only twenty feet from the bank. Gabriel stayed absolutely still so as not to startle the bird. Its blue eyes were looking right at him, right through him.

How odd. He was mesmerized.

In a heartbeat the bucolic scene around him dissolved. It was nighttime and it was raining. He was in some German village square, and an old-fashioned carriage was at a standstill directly in front of him. A woman in a black knit shawl approached the carriage. The window pushed open and a man leaned forward. The man had an amazing face—pale with a thick black mustache. It was a proud and terrible face, full of such sorrow and anguish, so *haunted*. The woman offered the man a glass of water with a deep curtsy and a trembling of her hand and . . .

He was back at the lake. It was so sudden, the sunlight hurt his eyes. The swan was still swimming at him, its eyes so intent it was a bit disconcerting and the . . .

The carriage. He was at the carriage and he was closer now. The woman handed the black-mustachioed man a glass of water, and he glanced around, then motioned her forward. He reached into his coat breast and passed her a roll of paper. His mouth opened and he said something to her, something whispery Gabriel couldn't make out.

Like falling down a tunnel, he was slammed back to the lake. The swan was almost at the bank now. Did swans really have such blue, blue eyes?

And then he felt a change—a malignant presence in the bushes to his right. He *felt* it, then he saw it. It crept forward from the brush, hunched low on all fours in a feral crouch, its teeth bared. It was a wolf; a wolf so black it was almost a hole in reality.

The beast rushed into the water. The swan screamed and flapped its wings. The water was spraying . . .

Gabriel uttered a cry and sat up on the couch. He remained still for a moment, chest heaving.

He wandered back to the mailbox on bare feet, enjoying the icy bite of the gravel. By the time he got back inside, his toes were as wet and cold as ice cubes. He drew on a pair of white cotton socks and sat down to read the paper.

The moment of relaxation was not to last. The cover story screamed up at him spitefully. There had been another wolf killing, and this one had taken place *inside* Munich—right downtown.

It wasn't difficult to find the crime scene. The paper had said Filserbergstrasse, and that street, though unpronounceable, was short and not hard to find on his city map. It was exactly three blocks away from the hunt club on Dienerstrasse.

Doing anything useful once he got there, however, was a harder nut to crack. Filserbergstrasse was a dead-end alley, and the police had cordoned off the entrance. Official vehicles crowded the street, and a TV news crew took up what space might have been left with a van and lights. Even the gathered pedestrians—wide-eyed and grim—were holding their ground with good old-fashioned German stubbornness.

Gabriel couldn't see a damn thing.

But he *heard* something. He heard the female news reporter call out a name in a bid for attention that obviously failed. The name was Kommissar Leber— the man from the paper.

He pushed his way through the crowd like an infant making its way down the birth canal. His target was no longer the cordon's edge but the reporter. He caught a glimpse of Leber as he went. The *kommissar* was down the alley along with a half dozen other men. He was a large man in a worn brown suit—tall and heavy with a bald head and a fat neck. He was easily recognizable from his photograph.

Gabriel didn't bother trying to get the man's attention. Leber hadn't even acknowledged the reporter. But that was all right. There was more than one way to skin a cat.

He reached the van, and one of the news crew tried to push him back. Gabriel yelled out to the woman with the microphone.

"Excuse me? Miss? I have some information you might find . . . *interestin'*."

The reporter glanced his way. She looked highly doubtful that he had anything at all she'd find interesting. She was attractive (weren't they all), but she had that I-can't-be-bothered look coating her like the skin on a sausage.

"I *really* think you'll want to hear this," he pressed.

He gave her his best it's-your-loss-not-mine look and wished he had a cigarette to light just to look like he didn't give a crap.

"Nun gut, was soll's." The reporter nodded to the man who had a hold of Gabriel's arm, and let him go. Gabriel pushed his way forward.

"You're an American?" the reporter asked.

"That's right."

"What makes you think you have new information about these killings?"

"Well, funny thing," Gabriel began, speaking loudly. He was close to the yellow tape now, and Leber was some twenty feet away with his back turned. "I've been doin' some investigatin' of my own. I tried to see Kommissar Leber over there, but he was busy. It's too bad, actually, because I have some real important questions that the police have never answered."

The woman looked mildly curious, especial since Gabriel was addressing this more at Leber than at her. She motioned to the cameraman. *"Dreh schon, Dieter."*

The tape began to roll. The lights switched on, nearly blinding Gabriel in the process. The woman spoke into the microphone and gave a brief introduction to the camera. Gabriel didn't understand a word of it, but Leber did, for he turned slightly and looked suspiciously at Gabriel. It was an insect-appraisal kind of stare.

"Can you tell us what you think you know?" The reporter tilted the microphone in Gabriel's direction.

"Sure." He smiled rakishly at the camera. "I was gonna ask Kommissar Leber how come animal hair found at the crime scene is *reddish* in color when the escaped zoo wolves were *gray*?"

The woman looked impressed and repeated his question in German for the camera.

". . . And why paw prints found at the scene indi-cate an animal much *larger* than the zoo wolves species, *canis lupus lupus*," Gabriel continued, speaking as loud as he could without actually shouting. He was gratified to see Leber's face turn a quivering purple.

"Und er fragt wieso die Pfotenabdrücke am Tatort viel großer sind als die der Zoowölfe."

The reporter turned back to him, looking pleased with herself. "Can you tell us how you got this information, S—?"

Hands gripped Gabriel's shoulders and lifted him up. The yellow tape of the cordon flew by beneath his feet, and then a brick wall slammed into his back. When the dark dots cleared, Leber was in his face, all two hundred sixty pounds of him. His little pig-like eyes, swollen from lack of sleep, were inches from Gabriel's own.

"Who the hell are you, and what do you think you are doing?"

"Nice to meet you, Kommissar Leber," Gabriel gasped.

"Answer my question!"

"You asked *two* questions, actually, which I'd be happy to answer if I had some air."

Leber took a begrudging step back and let go of Gabriel's jacket. Gabriel slumped a good foot down the wall before his heels touched the ground.

"That's better." He smiled gamely. "The name's Gabriel Knight. I've stopped by the station to see you for two days runnin', but the man at the desk was kinda rude."

"Good! Now, how did you know about the—"

"Do you really want to discuss this *here,* Kommissar?" Gabriel nodded toward the news crew, which had lights and cameras aimed their direction.

Leber scowled. "I could have you arrested!" he hissed.

"For what? Wouldn't it be nicer if you and I got together and had a little chat?"

Leber considered it. "I can't have you talking to reporters."

"If you'll meet me at your office later, I won't say another word. Scout's honor."

Leber's eyes got even smaller as he did a squint-eyed examination of this unexpected interloper. He must have bought something on Gabriel's face, for he said, "All right. I'll be back at the station in an hour. *Don't* be late."

It had been fun, but more important, it was progress. After yesterday's fruitlessness, it made Gabriel feel immeasurably better. Not only had he *not* gotten in to see Leber yesterday, but he'd learned nothing new at the zoo, and the club had been deserted last night. Xavier, the concierge, informed him that Wednesdays were slow nights, while managing to convey the impression that Gabriel himself was the reason that none of the others had shown up. Gabriel had had a drink and left. He honestly wasn't sure if he was disappointed or relieved to have been spared the company of the night before.

But the evening had not been a total waste. Xavier had reluctantly handed over von Glower's personal card before he left, saying the baron had called to apologize for his absence and had invited Gabriel to call on him at home.

Yet an hour wasn't long enough to hit von Glower's, and Leber would not appreciate it if he was late. He headed for the Marienplatz. Perhaps Übergrau had some news from Gerde.

At the offices of Übergrau, Höffen & Schnell, Gabriel had to ring the bell for the receptionist several times. He could hear an animated conversation going on somewhere beyond the etched-glass screen, but he couldn't make out a single word of it.

It was clear, however, that Übergrau had been participating, for he appeared in the lobby the minute Gabriel said his name. The young lawyer looked excited and nervous.

"Good morning, Herr Knight! Come back to my office, please!"

"Gabriel."

"What? Oh, yes, Gabriel."

Gabriel followed him past ergonomic cubicles and curious stares. The office was definitely not running efficiently today.

"This is so amazing!" Übergrau said as soon as he shut the door. "Did you hear about this new killing?"

"Yeah. I was just over there, actually."

"*Verlich*? What did you see?"

"A lot of police cars."

"Yes. Of course. This is most horrible!" Übergrau was all a-flutter.

"Have you heard who the victim was?"

Übergrau picked up a newspaper from a nearby cabinet. "They have not announced this yet. They only say it was a male in his fifties. They must notify first the family and so forth."

"Right."

"But how could this happen here?" Übergrau asked, still amazed. "How could the wolves get so far into town? With all the traffic and streets and lights? It is not as though they could take the *Untergrund*!"

"Not on all fours, anyway," Gabriel muttered. He had a mental flash of an odd furry figure dressed in a trench coat and a low-riding hat. It was a kind of anthropomorphic character, like something from Aesop, but there was nothing cute about it.

Fortunately, Übergrau didn't hear him. He was still expressing dismay over the invasion of the murders into the city's inner sanctum. Gabriel interrupted him.

"Harry, did you get any mail for me?"

The lawyer looked abashed. "Oh! Yes! I'm so sorry!"

He buzzed his secretary, and she brought in a brown-paper-wrapped parcel. "Here I am talking on and on, and you have business to do."

"It's okay, Bud."

Gabriel opened the package, hoping for something illuminating. Inside were two journals and a book about werewolves. He tried to shield the title from Übergrau with the wrapping. The kid was already too riled up. Reminded him of Grace.

There was also a letter. He had to read the first paragraph twice because he could simply not comprehend what he was seeing at first.

Gabriel:

Guess where I am? It begins with an R, ends with 'erg' and rhymes with YOU PIG. Actually, it doesn't rhyme with YOU PIG, but I had to get that in there somewhere. I feel much better now.

So what's the deal? You finally get a new case and I'm supposed to sit in New Orleans and rot? Sorry, but methinks not. I'll be happy to go back to New York once this case is over if you want to let Gerde handle things, but this one I earned. Yes? So I'll give you the benefit of the doubt and assume you really *weren't* sure it was a real case.

Here's what I've found out. 1. There was a werewolf trial here in Rittersberg in 1750. The werewolf was a Baron Claus von Ralick, a.k.a. the Black Wolf. Executed in a big way right here in town. Read all about it in Victor Ritter's journal. 2. I found another case in 1864. See journal of Christian Ritter. He was also tracking a werewolf and had a suspect whose nickname was the Black Wolf. He never caught him— Christian died in a fall from his horse while on the case. (Suspicious? Of course.)

I don't see how these two cases could involve the *same* werewolf, since von Ralick was definitely reduced to ashes in 1750. Could "The Black Wolf" be common? The lycanthropic equivalent of "Bubba"?

Here's my only other lead. Christian Ritter had written a letter to King Ludwig II of Bavaria, warning him about the 1864 Black Wolf. Perhaps there's more to be learned in Ludwig's story?

So let me know if you want me to join you there or stay here and look into it. Hope you're safe.

Grace

Gabriel let the letter fall into his lap.

"Bad news, Herr—Gabriel?"

The American's brow was pursed in a frown. "Not sure."

Was it? Why had his pulse suddenly jack-hammered when he'd read those opening lines? She'd seen right through his stupid phone message, obviously, and had come at once. Now she was here, in Rittersberg. Everything else in the letter fell away in the face of that one fact. She was here. Of course, he'd never intended to keep her off a case should one appear, never would have dreamed of such a thing, but that was then and this was now. Now he was sitting in this office in Munich, and he was staring at the newspaper headline on the desk, and he knew that, come what may, he did not want Grace in Munich, not anywhere near *that thing*.

"What do you know about King Ludwig II?" Gabriel asked abruptly.

Übergrau looked surprised. "Ludwig II? The mad king? He built several castles and now they're *huge* tourist attractions. He was crazy, eccentric . . . He's the Bavarian enigma—like your JFK or Elvis. Do you know, I went to Graceland once. It was—"

"Where are these castles?"

Übergrau cleared his throat. "They're marked on all of the German maps. Herrenchiemsee is an hour and a half southeast. Neuschwanstein and Linderhof are southwest—two, three hours, depending on traffic and sight-seeing stops. Do you want me to have my secretary make you a map?"

Gabriel shook his head, pondering. "I wasn't thinkin' of goin' myself."

"They're really quite nice if you haven't been," Übergrau put in helpfully.

"Hmmm. Would your secretary post something if I write it up now? I need to overnight it to Rittersberg."

There was no putting it off. The wily creature had crossed the ocean, done research, and written to him all in the forty-eight hours or so since he'd called her. If he let this go, she'd be at the Huber farm by noon tomorrow.

"Of course! Anything at all, H—Gabriel."

"Ah! See? You *are* gettin' good."

Übergrau blushed with pleasure.

The reception at the police station was more cordial this time, if not the actual receptionist. Gabriel was buzzed in and taken back through the corridor. The desk officer knocked on Leber's door and didn't abandon his charge until the *kommissar* had bid them enter.

"Hey!" Gabriel grinned broadly as the door closed behind him. He almost expected to hear the sound of a key in the lock.

Leber looked at his watch. "You're ten minutes late."

"I'll just go, then," Gabriel said, reaching for the knob.

"Sit down!" Leber jabbed one knobby finger at the visitor's chair in front of his desk.

Gabriel sat, trying not to smirk. "So what's up?" He put his right boot up on his left knee with great deliberation and let out a contented sigh.

" 'What's up?' Let me tell you: I have a stupid American in my office who's about to tell me what the hell he's up to or face thirty days in the klink."

"I'm sure you'll sweet-talk it out of—him," Gabriel said dryly.

Leber drummed his fingers on his desk. "Open your mouth, Mr. Knight, and *speak*."

This guy was wound tighter then the local glockenspiel. He had more bugs up his ass than a decaying bear in the woods. He was stuffed tighter than bratwurst on a summer's . . .

"Speak!"

" 'Kay. I'll tell you where I got my info, but I have just a few *teensy-weensy* questions first."

"They'd better be 'Where do you want me to start?' and 'How much do you want to know?' "

Gabriel smiled appreciatively. "You're focused, I'll give you that. No, what I want is just a few small facts about the case."

Leber snorted. "Never."

"Wait a minute! Here's the deal—*Ich nicht spreche Deutsch*. Which means I can't even read the goddamn newspapers. All I want is the basics. Press-release stuff."

Leber's tongue was searching out some edible in the hidden folds of his cheek. Either that or it was trying to get loose and attack. "All right," he said slowly.

"Great! You're a pal." Gabriel pulled out his notepad and pen. "So how many deaths have been pinned on the wolves so far?"

"Five, if you count the one downtown."

Gabriel jotted this down. "Could there be bodies you haven't found yet?"

Leber didn't look happy with the thought. "Maybe. But the victims were killed in broad daylight. Body parts left lying like a trail of *Brotkrümel*. If there are other bodies out there, someone would have seen them, I think."

"And when did this start exactly?"

Leber glanced at the wall near the door. There was a bulletin board there with pictures and a large map of the area. Gabriel cast an envious glance at it, realizing what it was: a case board. There were things up there he wanted to know.

"Thirty-two days ago was the first," Leber said.

"The zoo wolves escaped right around then, didn't they?"

"They escaped thirty-four days ago."

Gabriel scribbled this down. Of course, he'd turned on his pocket tape recorder as always before entering the room, but Leber didn't need to know that.

"So what was the first attack like?"

Leber took a deep breath. His skin was slowly losing

its redness, and he seemed to be calming down a bit. Perhaps it was just that the questions gave him bigger things to worry about than the American seated across from him.

"A young husband and wife were taking a picnic. North near Eching. He walks away to get some wood in the forest. When he comes back he finds her body—some of it."

Gabriel swallowed. "Did you link it to the zoo wolves right away?"

The policeman rubbed his forehead with a middle finger. "We knew it was an animal attack. No one thought about the zoo wolves for a day or two."

"And the second attack?"

Leber leaned back, sighing. "Two teenage boys. They were climbing rocks to the east at Feldkirchen."

"Two at once?" Gabriel asked, surprised.

"Yes." Leber nodded grimly. "And they were strong boys. They had come down from the climb and were walking to the car. A park employee heard screams. When he got there, the boys were dead. He didn't see the animal."

Gabriel stroked his lip with the pen thoughtfully. "That's three."

"Fourth was a young girl. She was killed on her parents' farm to the southwest at Lochham. The mother saw the attack."

"What about this latest one?"

"Male. Fifty-two. He was a furrier." Leber gave a huff. "Ironic, isn't it?"

"A *furrier*? That is odd. What was his name?"

Leber pursed his lips and studied Gabriel suspiciously. "We have not released that information, Mr. Knight."

Gabriel tried to look innocent. "Oh. Okay. What's the exact cause of death, by the way?"

Leber gestured with an open hand to his neck. "Throats crushed."

"Asphyxiation?"

"*Ja.*"

"Is that the way wolves kill in the wild?"

Leber shrugged. "So the experts tell me."

"Hmmm." Gabriel considered that for a moment. "What else does forensics say about the killer?"

"I have told you enough, Mr. Knight. All I can say is that it *is* an animal."

"*An* animal? As in *one*?"

Leber flushed. He said nothing.

"Forensics have found signs of only *one* animal? Not *two*?" Gabriel insisted.

Leber sucked in his cheeks and did not reply. He thrummed his pudgy fingertips on the desk. It sounded like a military drum roll.

"*Jesus,*" Gabriel said softly. But was he really all that surprised? Yes. For some reason he was. "What about the animal's bite mark? Saliva? Are they normal?"

Leber stopped thrumming and looked at Gabriel, his brow knit. "Normal for what?" he thundered.

"They're *not* normal, are they? Lemme guess. Forensics says the bite marks and/or saliva are canine and closer to wolf than dog, but beyond that they can't pin it down—nothing like it on the records. Probably some weird hybrid."

Leber just glared at him, the spidery veins on his cheeks flushing purple.

"Or is the saliva *canine at all*?" Gabriel said, suddenly feeling cold.

Leber slammed his hand down on his desk with a loud crack. "*Enough*! You know something, Mr. Knight. Do you want to tell me now, or do you want us to extract it the hard way?"

The Kommissar rolled the *r* in *extract* threateningly. He had his hands poised on the desktop as though preparing to spring.

"All right! Don't get excited! I'm a private investigator. I'm lookin' into the death of Toni Huber."

Leber didn't exactly relax, but he looked less prepared to leap and conquer. He stared at Gabriel with those beady eyes. "Who hired you?"

"I'm a friend of the Hubers' cousins. They asked me to look into it."

Leber stood up. He jingled some loose change in his pocket. "They don't believe it was the zoo wolves, then," he muttered. Before Gabriel could even begin to answer, Leber did it for him. "No. Of course not. The mother saw it."

Leber turned to Gabriel. "So you know the animal was red—the mother told you that. How did you know about the size? She couldn't judge such a thing."

"I found some evidence at the Huber farm—a paw print and some hair. I took it over to the university for analysis."

Leber nodded. "Very well. I *want* that evidence. I want you to bring it here." He pointed at the floor beneath his feet.

"Sure. So why are you lettin' everyone believe it's the zoo wolves when you know it's not?"

Leber sat back down. He straightened his tie. "First, it's none of your business. Second, we don't know for *certain* that it was not one of the escaped wolves—"

"But the killer is nothing like the zoo wolves!"

Leber made a moronic you-never-know expression. "Two wolves escaped from the zoo. We don't *know* that they were like the ones that did *not* escape."

Gabriel blew a *pshah* sound. "I think the zoo would have known if it had a huge, reddish-brown wolf hybrid in the kennel."

Leber made the face again. "I only said it is possible. Third, if we tell the newspapers we do not know what it is, this is much worse for the public than being afraid of the zoo wolves. You see?"

Gabriel thought about it. "In other words, people might panic if you admit you haven't the first freakin' clue what's goin' on."

Leber sucked in his cheeks. The man was stiffer than a new pair of lederhosen on a washline in Jan—

"That is the decision of men who outrank myself. As for you, Mr. Knight, it is none of your damn business."

"Plus, I bet it also helps to keep the public outrage focused on the zoo. Right now it's *their* fault as much as yours. Am I right?"

"So you will say nothing to the newspapers," Leber continued. "When we have caught something—even one of the zoo wolves, then . . ."

"Why *haven't* you caught the zoo wolves?" Gabriel asked abruptly. He leaned forward, curious. "I mean, they're just two *wolves,* right?"

Leber ignored him. ". . . and if you *do* say anything to the papers or television, you will be arrested. Is that clear?"

Gabriel sighed. Clearly, the interview was over. "Yeah. Whatever." He rose and stretched, turning casually toward the case board. He held the yawn for a moment, his eyes searching feverishly until he found the information he sought. He made a mental note of the name, suppressed a grin, and turned. "I do have one more thing before I go. I mean, it's probably nothing."

"What?"

"Is there any connection to this case and a *black* wolf?"

Leber grunted. "No! You said yourself, the zoo wolves are gray and the killer is *rot.*"

"All right. Never mind." Gabriel went over to the door. "Thanks for the chat, Kommissar."

But Leber had an odd look on his face. "Wait." He got up and went over to a filing cabinet. He sorted through it for a moment, then brought a file back to his desk.

"What is it?"

"A missing-persons case. It happened in a town called Kirchl in the Naturpark Schwabisch-Frankischer Wald ten years ago." Leber flipped through the file.

"It was sad—a teenage girl, very pretty. We thought she had run from home, but we never found her."

"And this has somethin' to do with a black wolf?"

"*Ja.* I just remembered. There was an old woman who lived in the forest. She told the police that 'the wolf' killed the girl. She was always complaining about a huge black wolf in the forest. The townspeople looked into it, but they found nothing. They decided she was *verrückt*—crazy."

Gabriel frowned. "And there was no blood in the woods? Nothin'?"

Leber shook his head. "Nothing. There *were* no wolves in the Schwabisch-Frankischer Wald—then or now. Never heard of such a thing as wolf attacks—not until this case."

"Well . . . it's probably not related," Gabriel said slowly.

"Probably not."

It was noon by the time Gabriel left the police station. He was close to the Marienplatz and he had something new to run by the Kid, so he went back to Übergrau's office. Unfortunately, Harry was at lunch. Gabriel didn't have any better luck with the baron. When he called the phone number on von Glower's card, a polite male informed him that von Glower had been out of town last night and had not yet returned home. Would the gentleman call back in another hour or so?

He was glad he hadn't wasted all the U-Bahn connections getting over there. He'd looked up the address last night. The baron lived south at the edge of Munich near a park called Perlacher Wald and the U.S. base. It was not a short trip. Gabriel headed back to the club instead, hoping to sniff out something useful.

The truth was, he hadn't bothered to look around the club last night for several reasons. For one thing, nobody else was there, and that had been both disappointing and boring (yes, they were weird, but then, he'd been alone in a castle with Gerde for the past year). For another, he'd more or less reached the opinion that the club had very little to do with the killings. The lodge was a stuck-up, self-important, and eccentric group, that much was obvious. But what use were they on the case other than providing an opportunity to watch Klingmann, maybe learn some background data on him that would prove incriminating? Even at that, what kind of incriminating evidence was there to find? Klingmann's relationship to the real killer was getting more tenuous by the moment. If the real killer was not one of the zoo wolves, then Klingmann probably had nothing to do with the case at all.

Or so he'd thought last night. Today things looked a little different. What did Klingmann and the latest killing have in common besides the zoo wolves? *The club*. The latest attack was only three blocks from the club.

Yes, it was definitely time to get a bit nosier at the ol' huntin' lodge.

Xavier looked as pleased to see him as ever. "Don't you have anything *else* to do in Munich, Herr Knight?"

"I could go stand in the middle of the road or jump off the *Rathaus* tower," Gabriel said sweetly. "But I dunno. I'd rather talk to you. Call me a masochist."

Xavier expelled a short breath from his nostrils in what would have been a sniff, had it been going the other way. "The gentleman is hilarious."

"Really? I'll tell him when I see him."

"What do you *want,* Herr Knight? If you've come for a free drink, the bar is in the back, I'm sure."

"I'd *hope* you'd be sure. How long've you been here anyway?"

It was the opening he'd been hoping for, though the segue was weak. Gabriel strolled over and leaned on Xavier's desk. It was the sort of pulpit-style work-center at which one stood, not sat, so leaning was very tempting. Besides, it would no doubt irritate the concierge intensely.

"Since 1970," Xavier said. He was proud of the fact, poor sod.

"Is that when the club started?"

"Die Königlich-Bayrische Hofjagdloge is practically ancient. However, it was *revitalized* in the seventies."

"How's that?"

"Baron von Glower joined. He brought a new vision." Xavier had that adoring/toadying expression again.

"Huh," Gabriel said. He tried to look bored.

Xavier grew irritated. "He *did*. The lodge had nearly died out before he came. Hunting is not as popular as it used to be."

"No kiddin'? Can't imagine why. So what did von Glower do exactly?"

"He brought . . . *enthusiasm*." He pronounced it 'in-twosie-azim.' "You wouldn't understand."

"Maybe. This place still isn't exactly burstin' at the seams, though. Is it?"

Xavier flushed. "*Quantity* of members is not our priority. The baron chooses *quality*." He looked at Gabriel pointedly. "With the rare exception, of course."

Gabriel smiled and batted his eyes. "Is that so? How many members are there anyway?"

Xavier had to think about it for a moment. "Five now. Not including you."

"Have you lost someone recently?"

"Of course not."

"You had to add it up just now."

Xavier sighed. "Besides yourself, we've had another recent addition."

"Klingmann," Gabriel guessed.

"Yes, Herr Doktor joined us a few weeks ago."

"Uh-huh. Did von Glower pick him out too?"

Xavier snorted. "Really, I don't gossip about club

members! How Klingmann was chosen for membership is his own affair. Now please move along."

But Gabriel only leaned in further and smiled lazily. "In a sec. I have one more question. Have you ever heard of 'the black wolf'?"

"What kind of a black wolf?" Xavier said, annoyed.

"Oh, any kind."

"No." Xavier made a shooing gesture. "Now run along. Go get yourself a drink or leave or . . . something."

Gabriel went to go get a damned drink.

He wandered around, a short mug of beer in one hand. Over here was a fireplace, a moose head, and lots of deer antlers. Over there, the bar, a couple of leather chairs, sofa, coat rack, wood paneling run amok.

At the back of the great room was a hallway. It lead to a back-street exit, this one (as Gabriel saw when he poked his head out) leading to an alley behind the building. It locked heavily when he pulled it shut.

Besides this door at the back of the hall, there were two other doors here, both on the left-hand wall. The first led to bathroom facilities done in a manly style. No women broached this domain, that was evident. The second door was locked.

Gabriel poked his head back into the great room to make sure no one was about, then gave up a silent prayer for the health of Xavier's bladder and went back to the locked door. It was an old door, not originally fitted with a lock. A modern dead bolt had been installed some years ago above the knob. This would certainly not be the first time Gabriel had picked a dead bolt. He used to lock himself out of St. George's at least once a month. Fortunately, the thieves on Bourbon Street were no more interested in his wares than the tourists, so he was the only one ever to bust the useless thing.

He took his Louisiana driver's license from his wallet and slid it into the crack in the door jamb. He wiggled it, worked it up. The door popped open.

Inside was a flight of stairs that led down to a basement. Gabriel flicked on the light and closed the door softly behind him.

How now, little logen *cow?* he thought as he descended the stairs. The ceiling was cut off low, and he had to stoop as he went. Despite the overhead bulb somewhere down below, there was a strong feeling of darkness to the place that made him nervous. He clutched the railing. He told himself it was because the stairs were steep.

When he cleared the overhang and got his first shot of the basement, he expelled a short gasp of alarm. The first thing that caught his eye were the heads, huge heads; lions and tigers, alligators and cheetahs, a black panther.

"*Christ,*" he muttered.

They were stuffed, of course, but there was nevertheless an immediate fleeing response, ingrained in the species from more vulnerable days. He took a deep breath and tried to slow his hammering pulse. The sense of something lurking remained long after his brain told the fear impulse it was being idiotic. Perhaps it was the faint scent of decay that filled the room like cotton in a chloroform bottle, a determined insistence upon death that nothing in the taxidermist's bag of tricks could completely camouflage. But there was something else in the air too. Gabriel's brain sought to sort and identify it—*incense*. Odd.

He descended the rest of the way down the stairs. The trophy heads each bore a plaque with a name and a date. Von Zell, 27/6/91; Von Glower, 3/4/87; Preiss, 17/8/83. He frowned. Where were they hunting these things, anyway? And why keep *these* trophies down here while the less impressive ones—the deer and the elk—were displayed in the great room?

Because it's probably fuckin' illegal that's why.

Yes. Good point. It ought to be, at any rate. He moved from trophy to trophy, reading the names of the hunters. He found no names he didn't recognize, and Klingmann was not on any of them. Xavier had told the truth, then; Klingmann had just joined. What Xavier hadn't mentioned was how von Glower and von Zell dominated the club. Hennemann, Preiss, and von Aigner had only a few trophies apiece while Von Zell and von Glower each had a dozen or more.

The feeling of being someplace very unpleasant did not dissipate as he moved around the room. A glass-enclosed rack of polished teak and gleaming metal firearms didn't help. There was even a lethal bow and arrow set in the case. The smell of incense continued to grow until he found the source. Against the wall opposite the stairs was a table covered with a red cloth. On the table were two candelabra and an incense bowl. Several necklaces made from what looked like claws were laid out, and a wolf's skull took center place like an idol.

Gabriel stared at the tableau, baffled. What the hell were these guys playing at? *Tarzan, Lord of the Apes* meets Masonic Lodge 357?

I've got a better one for you: if they don't draw the line at hunting down and slaughtering an endangered species now and then, where do they draw it . . . hmmm?

He shook his head. He was getting paranoid. What use would a werewolf have for rifles and taxidermists? Whatever these men's sins were, they were entirely human ones so far. Then his eyes fell on something else on the table—a black book. It was a slim appointment book, the kind that businessmen carry. He picked it up and opened it to a tabbed page at the back.

Preiss—100,000
Aigner—~~1 m.~~ 700,000
Hennemann—30,000

Gabriel whistled. "Holy alimony. Either the club dues is *way* outta hand, or—"

The door at the top of the stairs opened. Gabriel froze. Xavier, no doubt, looking for the missing wanderer.

He put the book down hurriedly and took a few steps from the table. Someone was coming down the stairs. He looked around, panicked. There was absolutely *no* place to hide. He gave up and tried to look natural—and stupid.

When the stair descender's upper torso appeared, Gabriel saw that it was not Xavier at all but Baron von Zell. Gabriel cringed—it could hardly be any worse. He tried to dumb down his dumb look. Von Zell glanced up and saw Gabriel. He stopped instantly, completely thrown off guard. His eyes were huge.

"What are you doing down here, Mr. Knight?" It was a reasonable enough question, but the tone in which it was spoken was hubris personified.

"Hey, Baron von Zell!" Gabriel tried, waving an awkward hand. "I was just lookin' around the club. Nice room, huh?"

"The basement is for members only!" Von Zell said scathingly.

"Oh? Really?" Gabriel thought the blush, at least, had to be convincing. "I *am* sorry. My word! I'll go right up."

Gabriel crossed to the bottom of the stairs and waited for von Zell to move. He didn't. He was glaring at Gabriel suspiciously. "The door was not locked?"

"Huh? Oh, huh-uh." Gabriel tried to look virtuous. "It just *op*ened."

Von Zell uttered a low growl of irritation. "All right. Go upstairs. Now."

Von Zell pushed past Gabriel—with a bit more shove than was necessary—and finished his descent. Gabriel started up the stairs slowly, watching what von Zell was up to. The man went directly to the table and picked up the black book. He walked back to the stairs and practically pushed Gabriel up the rest of the way.

When they reached the upstairs hall, von Zell shut the door firmly and tried the handle. It was locked. He gave Gabriel another doubtful look, then walked away. Gabriel heard him cross the great room and then scream at Xavier in German in the lobby.

Gabriel felt a tad guilty, but not much.

He wandered into the great room and poured himself another drink. Von Zell came back carrying a newspaper. He seated himself near the fire.

"Can I get you a drink, Baron von Zell?"

"No," von Zell said sharply. "I only have a few minutes between appointments." He opened the paper.

"Kay." Gabriel brought his drink over to the fireplace and sat down in a chair. Von Zell lifted his newspaper higher.

"So you work downtown, huh? What is it that you do, Baron?"

Von Zell did not lower the paper. "My family is in *banking*. If you were German, you would know that."

"Ah!" Gabriel gave a deep, bored sigh.

Von Zell turned a page and said nothing.

"I, uh, I noticed you're a darn good hunter," the American drawled. "I saw your name on lots of those trophies downstairs? Very impressive."

Von Zell lowered the paper and peered at Gabriel with narrowed eyes. He seemed to be considering the hidden agenda in this remark.

"Yes," he said briefly. "Von Glower and I are the best." He went back to his paper.

" 'Course, huntin's like anythin' else, I guess. Ya need lots of practice. I don't get to hit the woods as often as I'd like."

Von Zell lowered the newspaper with a crash into his lap. "*Hunting*," he said with great enunciation, "is a matter of the *will,* of the *soul.* It is *not* about target practice."

Gabriel shrugged. "Oh, I dunno. It always helps my game to spend some time in the arcades. Maybe it doesn't seem that way to you because you do it so often—I mean, it doesn't seem like *practicin'* cause you're actually just *doin'* it." He laughed in a forced way. "How often do ya'll go huntin', anyway?"

Von Zell scowled, obviously not at all sure how to deal with Gabriel and not interested, truth be told, in dealing with him at all. "Once a month the lodge hunts together." He paused. "It is true that von Glower and I go more often than the others, I suppose."

He smirked a bit and lifted the paper.

"You and von Glower go every week*end*?"

"We used to," came the muffled response.

"Ya see? No *wonder* you two are so damned good!"

Von Zell said nothing.

"Hey, ya'll musta been tight goin' out every weekend together. How come ya don't go out that often anymore?"

Von Zell glared at him over the page. He appeared unsure of a response. "I suppose I have simply . . . outgrown his methods. As, I'm sure, he will outgrow you. *Imminently.*"

Gabriel's smile curled up a bit. He forced his lip down. "Speakin' of huntin', ya ever heard of the Black Wolf?"

"No." Von Zell sounded bored and annoyed. He stood up and tossed the paper down. He had clearly decided to go spend his lunchtime elsewhere—anywhere more quiet.

"Huh. Bet ya'll go on a lot of huntin' trips abroad, though, right? What, like to the Orient or somethin'?"

"No."

"But . . . far as I know, they don't have panthers in Germany. Or tigers." Gabriel grinned lopsidedly.

Von Zell exploded. There was no other way to describe it. One moment he was patronizing. The next he was livid. He crossed the distance between them and had Gabriel pinned up against the back of his chair before Gabriel even knew what hit him.

"Listen, you ignorant little pig! You don't know anything about this club, and what you don't know is none of your business! The trophies in the basement are none of your business! *Where* we hunt and *how* we hunt and *what* we hunt are none of your business! And you'd better keep your nose *out* of our business and keep your damn mouth shut. Because if you *don't,* I will hunt you down myself. Is that clear?"

The man's once handsome face was twisted with rage. His eyes were positively insane.

"Sure. I'm sorry. No problem," Gabriel said in a small voice.

Von Zell backed off. He tore himself away (Gabriel swore later that he had not mistaken this) like an alcoholic passing a liquor store window. Without another word he turned and left the room. Gabriel saw Xavier's scared face peeking in from the front hall for just a second before it dodged away. He reached down and checked. He had *not* peed his pants.

He left the club and walked back down Dienerstrasse to the Marienplatz and Harry's office. This time Harry was in.

"*Ja,* here it is," Übergrau said, returning from the hall and his most recent errand. "Herr Heffel Grossberg, furrier. Business office, 172 Silberhornstraße."

He handed Gabriel a piece of paper with the address on it.

"Thanks."

"It was very considerate of Kriminalkommissar Leber to give you this name. It hasn't been in the newspapers yet."

"We bonded, what can I say?" Gabriel tucked the paper in the pocket of his jeans. Harry didn't need to know that he'd stolen the name of the most recent victim from Leber's case board.

Übergrau sat back down and studied Gabriel with bright eyes. "Have I told you how much I like P. D. James? I just finished the one about the nuclear power plant."

"Um, no. When I'm in the mood for that British stuff, I go right for the jugular: A.C."

"A.C.?"

"Agatha Christie."

"Ah!" Übergrau's face lit. "There was this one set on a train, you know? And this man—"

"Harry," Gabriel interrupted gently, "there *was* one more thing."

"I'm sorry. Yes?"

"I need a newspaper search done."

"No problem! What are you looking for?"

"Missing-persons cases. I'm only interested in ones that occurred near medium to large-sized forests."

Übergrau took a pad of paper and a pen from his upper drawer and wrote it down. His ears—so prominent with his short-clipped haircut—tinged pink with excitement.

"Medium to large-sized forests. Yes. How far back do you want to look?"

Gabriel drummed his fingers on the arm of his chair. "Well . . . I could really use it back twenty years, I guess, but I hate to put you out."

"No problem! My secretary can start this afternoon. The main library, it has the newspapers archived on microfiche, and there exists an index for the major stories. With the index such a search would not be unreasonable. I can have it for you by tomorrow."

"Harry, you *are* a wonder."

He took the U6 train south and then U1 east to Silberhornstraße. Fortunately, it was on the way to von Glower's, so he wouldn't waste much time

Number 172 was five blocks from the U-Bahn station. The area went from congested and commercial to seedy as he walked. The building itself was an old high-rise. Grossberg's name was all that was listed near the buzzer out front.

The interior of the office was even seedier than the exterior. The rug was threadbare and the furniture was cheap. A chunky blonde sat at the lone desk in the outer office. She wore a sweater as threadbare as the rug and a short brown wool skirt that was natty and clumped with wear. She'd been crying. She looked up as Gabriel entered.

"Hi, I'm an American associate of Grossberg's?" Gabriel tried to look serious and businesslike.

The secretary threw her tissue in the trash can and grabbed another.

"Herr Grossberg is dead," she said bluntly. "I was going to close the office."

This provoked a fresh round of tears. Gabriel waited awkwardly.

"That's terrible news about Grossberg. Won't someone be comin' in to take over?"

"I don't know. I don't know even if Herr Grossberg has family."

"He didn't have any business partners, then?"

"No."

"What exactly did Herr Grossberg do?"

The secretary looked up at him with baffled, red-rimmed eyes.

"I mean . . . I know what he did for *me,* but, um, what else did you do here in the office?"

"Imports and exports. I never saw the furs myself. Herr Grossberg, he has a warehouse on the other side of town."

"Ah!" Gabriel said lamely. He wondered what the hell he was doing here. "Did Herr Grossberg belong to a club, by any chance? A men's huntin' club?"

The secretary took a deep sniff and frowned. "I never heard him say so." She considered it. "No, I don't think he would go to something like that."

No, Gabriel thought, glancing around the office. Herr Grossberg wasn't quite in the same league as the boys from the Hofjagdloge, was he?

The secretary opened a Rolodex. "Would you give me your name, please? I was going to make a letter to everyone in the file telling them about Herr Grossberg's death. I can take you from the list."

She looked up tiredly. Her hair was black at the roots and unwashed. He realized that beneath her makeup she was quite young—perhaps no more than nineteen. And newly unemployed. Gabriel felt sorry for her.

"Um, Knight. Herr Knight."

She flipped through the cards. Most of them, Gabriel noted, were blank.

"No, I'm not finding you. There is nothing under K."

"Try under 'von,' 'von Knight,' " Gabriel said, bargaining for time. He was trying to think of what else he could ask her, with little success.

The secretary looked impressed. She spun the Rolodex in a remarkable imitation of Vanna White. Her fingers caught the roller at the V's with great deftness and began walking through the cards.

"Von Aigner, von Dussen, von Stein . . . No, I'm not finding you."

Gabriel stared at her wordlessly, so flummoxed he was unable to get his tongue to work. "Excuse me, did you say *von Aigner*?"

"Yes."

"Is he a really big guy? Laughs a lot?"

The secretary sighed. "I never met him. I have met only a few of Herr Grossberg's associates. Mostly they ring on the phone."

"Oh. Well, thanks anyway."

The secretary pushed the Rolodex away. "If this is about money, you will be disappointed."

"How's that?"

"I know that Herr Grossberg owed many people

money. They ring here all the time. Sometimes they come to the office. But Herr Grossberg, he was much behind on his debts, and I don't think there was anything in the accounts when he died."

She stood up and fished a large handbag from beneath the desk. She opened it and put the Rolodex inside.

"As a matter of fact, he did owe me somethin'," Gabriel said quickly. "Is there any way I could look at his books? At least see if his accounts agree with my own? That way, if there's any estate, it will be easier for a lawyer to claim my share."

He smiled engagingly at the secretary, hoping his charm would win her over, but she only gave a bitter chuckle. "There is no *estate,* Herr von Knight. He liked the horses, you understand? Also, the police took all of Herr Grossberg's papers. They took everything this morning."

"Oh," Gabriel said, cursing his luck.

"I think I will go home now to write those letters. Let me walk you out."

Gabriel went over it in his mind during the bus ride from the U-Bahn station to von Glower's house. Grossberg was a furrier, a gambler with a seedy business that was barely hanging on. Imports and exports. Of what? Furs, the girl had said. Was that it? Grossberg certainly didn't appear to actually manufacture furs.

A middle man, then. A man who claimed to be a furrier, perhaps even had some training, but he was a salesman now, nothing more. And he knew von Aigner.

There was something there, Gabriel could feel it, but he couldn't quite tap what it was. Hell, he didn't even know what von Aigner did for a living or anything at all about him other than his presence as a member of the club.

It was time to try to remedy that.

*   *   *

Von Glower's house was a large residence painted the palest of yellows with a garden in front. It was across the street from a public park that looked more like a groomed forest, with walking paths that stretched away into the distance. A group of young school-children with backpacks were unloading from a van and preparing to embark on a hike.

Gabriel walked to the front door and rang the bell.

The door was answered by an older gentleman in a formal gray suit. Yes, the baron was home now. He took Gabriel's coat and showed him into a lush, mas-culine living room. Leather couches in soft tan and vibrant oriental throws created a warm interior. As Gabriel waited, he noticed a Frankfurt paper and car keys lying on an end table. The baron *had* been out of town, then.

"Gabriel!" Von Glower greeted him warmly as he entered. He grasped his guest's hand in one of his own and half embraced him with the other. His wel-come was so open-handed that Gabriel felt guilty.

"It was nice of you to invite me, Baron von Glower."

"Call me Friedrich, please! Gunter, *bringen Sie uns bitte ein zweites Glas Wien.*"

"Ja, Baron."

"Please, sit down." Von Glower motioned to the sofa. They both sat, one on each end.

"I suppose I should have waited a few days before stoppin' by, but I really am curious about the club."

"Not at all! My invitations are most earnest."

Gunter returned with two crystal glasses of red wine on a tray.

"Do you like wine?" Von Glower asked. "I got hooked on the grape myself when I lived in France."

"You lived in France?"

"Oh, yes. I've lived all over."

"Are you from Germany originally?"

Von Glower smiled and picked up his glass. "No, but my parents were. *Prost!*"

"Prost." Gabriel sipped the wine. "Good stuff."

"I like the best." Von Glower studied Gabriel appraisingly. "And you? Were you born and raised in America?"

"New Orleans."

Von Glower settled back into the sofa, his dark eyes never leaving Gabriel's face. "And what is it that you write?"

Gabriel cleared his throat. His books weren't exactly highbrow. Besides, he was supposed to ask the questions. "I'm sure there're more interestin' subjects," he said.

"I hope you will forgive my inquisitiveness. You see, I like few people, and when I do find someone I like, it's a pleasure getting to know them—new thoughts and impressions uncovered and examined one by one, like rare birds."

Gabriel wondered if the baron was quoting someone. Perhaps he was, but it was not done lightly—his eyes were personal and ingenuous. Gabriel leaned forward and put down his glass to have something to do. "That's inquisitive, all right."

He was losing his footing, and quickly too. He glanced up from under his lashes; sought for and found nothing predatory in his host, nothing manipulative or sarcastic—only sincere male camaraderie. It was so generously proffered that it truly bewildered Gabriel. Given his real purpose at the club . . . *here,* he was at a loss as to how to deal with it. Rudeness was an easier hurdle somehow.

Von Glower rumbled a low laugh. "On the other hand, perhaps it's mere boredom. When people get to know each other, well, there's nothing new to say. I dearly love my friends at the club, but we reached this stage long ago."

"How long have you known the men at the club?" Gabriel asked, breathing a sigh of relief.

"Hmmm. Most of the men have been with me at least ten or fifteen years. Is it not amazing how time flies?"

"You said it. What about Doktor Klingmann?"

"Oh! Yes, forgive me. Herr Doktor is very new, like yourself."

"Then you can't be as bored as you claim."

Von Glower made a dismissive gesture. "To tell you the truth, I don't know the man very well, nor have I made an effort to. There, you see? You caught me. I told you, I am very selective. Klingmann seems perfectly fine, but not in the least interesting. Am I a terrible ass?"

"You're entitled to your opinion," Gabriel said, but he was puzzled. If von Glower hadn't brought in Klingmann, who did?

"So how'd you end up in Munich, Friedrich?"

"I was just going to ask you the same question."

Gabriel smiled. "You first."

"All right. My circumstances are probably not much different than your own. I wanted to return to the land of my ancestors and so I did. And you? Or had I better ask how your family ended up in America in the first place?"

"My grandfather left the family and moved to New Orleans."

Von Glower gazed at him curiously. "But *you* chose to return. Why?"

Gabriel opened his mouth to speak some meaningless lie but found that he didn't have the heart for it. He sighed. "To tell you the truth, I didn't have a hell of a lot of choice."

He tried to add a lighthearted grin, but it fizzled out in a drenching bitterness that welled up from out of nowhere. He pushed it aside. What was *that* about?

Van Glower was nodding thoughtfully. "I understand. Are there other Ritters besides yourself?"

"Nope," Gabriel answered. He picked up a glass and held it to the light self-consciously.

"Well, it was your duty, then. Sometimes there's no escaping it. Have you produced your heir?"

Gabriel laughed. "God, no!"

Von Glower smiled. "No, you don't strike me as a family man. Ah, well. I suppose all trees eventually stop bearing fruit."

Von Glower refilled his glass, and Gabriel felt that confusion imbue him again. He was relating far too well to this magnetic man. He was more vulnerable than he'd realized, after his year alone and all the unanswered questions, all the changes. And why the bitterness? Was it from finding out he had a real family after all, but that the other members of it were dead by the time he'd arrived, leaving him with naught but some musty journals? Wolfgang had not lived long enough to answer the thousands of questions Gabriel had, to fill the hole that the death of his father and grandfather had left in an infant boy's life.

He got up as if to distance himself physically as well as mentally and wandered over to the fireplace to look at the objects d'art on the mantel. He resolved to be ruthless.

"I wanted to talk to you about the club, Friedrich. I was over there earlier, and I found this room downstairs when I was lookin' for the bathroom? I didn't mean to pry or anythin', but I noticed there was this kinda altar-and-candle business. You all are into somethin' a little heavier than marksmanship. Am I right?"

He turned and gave von Glower an innocent smile and braced himself for the explosion. None came. The baron was simply sitting on the couch. He crossed one long leg easily and looked back at Gabriel with a hint of amusement. "You're determined to know *our* secrets as well, aren't you?"

"No. I mean, the door was open and . . ."

"It doesn't matter. Yes, the men and I have a kind of philosophy. I don't mind sharing it with you at all.

But are you sure you want to know? I can get quite verbose on the subject."

"I want to know." Feeling more sure of himself now, Gabriel wandered back to the couch and sat down.

"All right. The basis of our philosophy is a desire to reconnect with our true physical nature."

Von Glower took a drink of wine and put his glass down carefully. He watched Gabriel as though waiting for a reaction.

"Go on."

"Think of it this way: what makes man different from every other species on this planet?"

Gabriel shook his head.

"Civilization! Don't get me wrong—I don't resent progress. I enjoy the finer things in life as much as any man. But I recognize that without supreme effort of will, luxury leads to laziness. Over the centuries since our ancestors stalked their daily food in the woods, we have gained much, but we have lost as well. We have lost certain skills, perhaps even certain physical traits. Modern man is like a dulled, rusty blade!"

"What kinds of traits?" Gabriel asked, his pulse quickening.

"Our sensory power, our instinct! Think of a beast in the woods. It sees, it smells, it *feels* everything around it. It knows from the scents on the wind whether another animal has passed days before and in which direction lies food and water. It can sense the most silent danger."

Gabriel had a brief flash of the beast stalking Toni Huber. He swallowed. "And man doesn't?"

"No! You put civilized man in the woods, and he might as well be deaf, dumb, and blind!"

Von Glower had warned Gabriel about his enthusiasm, and here it was. His words were pointed and sharp; his delivery impassioned.

"But we don't need the skills that, say, a wolf has,"

Gabriel said slowly, but von Glower didn't flinch. "And . . . maybe we never had them at all," he continued. "Weren't we given brain power instead?"

"Who says we never had them? Can a blind man not improve his sense of smell and hearing? Can Native Americans and other shamen not read the forest the way the white man cannot? We had those senses, that power! But as generations of city dwellers failed to use their more acute senses, genetically they began to fall away, the way limbs wither when not exercised!"

"And you hope to . . . to—"

"To reclaim them!" Von Glower's voice was zealous. "Not just to *halt* the degeneration but to *reawaken* that which was lost!"

Gabriel took a deliberately drawn-out drink of wine, his mind stunned by the implications of this speech on his case. Perhaps von Glower read this as doubt, for he leaned forward and spoke urgently. "Come, Gabriel! Think about the phenomenon of extrasensory perception. Now and then an individual *is* born who has true powers—to read minds or perhaps move small objects by thought alone. Have you ever wondered where this power comes from? There are those who say these so-called freaks are harbingers of the future. Not I! With our fax machines and modem lines, what need have we for ESP? Why would evolution award it to us? No! I say these powers are throwbacks to the past—mental equivalents of vestigial tails!"

Gabriel found that his mouth was hanging open. He abruptly shut it. "It's . . . um . . . it's an interestin' theory, Friedrich. Do you have any proof that such powers are recoverable?"

Von Glower's intensity faded into a frustrated pensiveness. "I have felt some things myself—sharper hearing, keener smell. But documentable proof? That is harder. To what extent we can recover our primal senses—or even what those senses might prove to be—that is what we still struggle to find out."

"I take it that huntin' is part of this recovery process?"

"Of course," von Glower said, brightening again. "Just reconnecting with nature is important, but hunting is even better. Hunting is the closest we can get to our ancestry."

"You could try gettin' eaten by a lion," Gabriel quipped.

Von Glower smiled. "True, but the benefits are short-lived."

They were both quiet for a moment, then Gabriel said, "There's somethin' I still don't understand. Where are you *goin'* with this? I can understand how these rejuvenated senses could be useful for huntin' itself, or even if you wanted to live in the woods or expected the apocalypse or somethin'. But . . . I don't get the feeling that's your angle."

Von Glower looked at him appreciatively. "You have a way of finding the heart of things, don't you?"

Gabriel shrugged, embarrassed. He had an odd sensation of being a pupil at the foot of his teacher.

"The application, yes, that is the question. No, we're not going to live in the woods. Look at us. You have seen something of our group. What *is* our angle?"

Von Glower studied him, waiting. Gabriel considered. "Money?"

"Yes," the baron said slowly.

"Prestige?"

"*Power* is a better word, but yes. So how does the philosophy apply?"

Gabriel thought about it. At last he shook his head. "I'm not sure."

Von Glower leaned forward. "The Germans have a word—*Übermann,* the super human. If we *can* regain these powers, why be anything less?"

"And if you can be the *Übermann,* you'll have an

advantage over those who are not," Gabriel said, finally getting it.

"Of course!"

"So you can use these sharpened instincts in the boardroom and against your competition, is that it?"

Von Glower smiled and leaned back contentedly. "Something like that. First, all of the men I chose for the club are excellent specimens—bright, strong, from excellent families, in good positions. The philosophy makes them more fully realized, yes? The men may each view their use of the philosophy in different ways, but to create a superior man, a man who brings the full physical and psychic skills of the wild to the modern world and dominates his setting, yes. That's about right."

It was an intriguing idea, and no doubt a seductive one to those chosen to participate. But it didn't exactly jive with what Gabriel had seen of the club members so far.

"How has it affected the men? It's been fifteen years for most of them, you said."

Von Glower flushed with pride. "They are all at the top of their fields. Von Aigner, for example, owns one of Germany's largest meat-butchering plants, and he runs an exclusive private brewery. It's true that he inherited the butchery from his father, but he's expanded it a great deal."

"A butchery?" Gabriel asked, thinking about Grossberg and the murder.

"Yes. This is much more prestigious in Germany than in America, believe me. Germany is known for her sausages and meats."

"Oh, I'm not . . . no, that's terrific. What about Preiss?"

"Preiss is one of Germany's top trial lawyers. He's charming and affectionate in person, but he can be absolutely vicious in the courtroom, I assure you."

Gabriel's green eyes stared, bemused, into von Glower's dark ones. "Go on."

"Herr Hennemann is a politician. He has a prominent position in the current government and is an acknowledged contender for higher office."

"How high?"

Von Glower smiled conspiratorially. "Just between you and I, I wouldn't be surprised if we had a prime minister in the club in the near future."

Gabriel whistled. "That would be convenient for his friends, wouldn't it?"

"All of the men are assets to each other."

"What about Baron von Zell?"

Von Glower's parental look faded. A slight frown creased his brow. "Von Zell's family owns the majority of stock in one of Munich's oldest banks."

"What about his own accomplishments?"

"Garr was—*is*—a promising young man. He was always top of his class—the best at everything he did."

"I keep pickin' up a past tense here," Gabriel joked lightly, but his eyes were watching von Glower intently.

"You haven't seen Garr at his best. He's been going through a dark period lately, I'm afraid."

"It happens to the best of us," Gabriel said, but it was only a polite response. Personally, he thought von Zell was a grade-A asshole.

Von Glower poured himself another glass of wine and held the glass up to the light. He sighed deeply. "Ah, Gabriel! How I hope you will join us. Speaking of the other men like this—it reminds me of what high hopes I have had for them and how they are . . ."

"Yes?"

"I don't know. They are all doing well, but we are none of us as close as we once were. I miss that." Von Glower shook off an air of sadness. He smiled. "Are you hungry? I'll have Gunter prepare us a meal."

"No. No, thank you. I should be goin', actually."

"All right. I'll be at the club this evening. Are you planning to come by?"

"I thought I would, yeah."

They were rising when Gabriel remembered Grace's letter. There was no way to slip it in cleverly now. Besides, he didn't really think it had anything to do with the case. He said, "Oh. By the way, have you ever heard of the Black Wolf?"

There was a tinkling crash, and Gabriel turned to see that von Glower, who was now standing, had broken his wineglass. Shards of crystal and the spill of red wine splashed the coffee table and the cream of the oriental carpet just below.

"How stupid of me," von Glower said blankly. "I was just putting it down so I could see you out, and I caught the edge. Gunter!"

Gunter appeared instantly. *"Ja, Baron?"*

"Würden Sie das bitte reinigen?" Gunter exited at once.

"Did you get any on you?" von Glower asked. He put a hand on Gabriel's arm and looked at his clothes with concern.

"No. I'm fine." Gabriel said, pulling away. Gunter returned with a tray and towel and began to clean up the spill. Gabriel watched the baron oddly throughout this procedure. Neither one of them spoke until Gunter left.

"There we are. It's only wine," von Glower said breathlessly. His face was still flushed. He seemed terribly embarrassed by his own clumsiness.

"Have you?" Gabriel asked. "Ever heard of the Black Wolf?"

"Oh!" von Glower said, as though he had forgotten all about it. "I'm sorry. You asked me that, didn't you? Perhaps that's why I missed the table. It must have reminded me of these killings in the papers. Have you read about them?"

"Yes."

"They've been very upsetting."

"Any particular reason?" Gabriel asked, trying to keep his voice neutral.

Von Glower looked surprised. "Any reason? People being slaughtered . . . *children* . . . in broad daylight. Do you think I am heartless because of my philosophy? Nature can be cruel, Gabriel, but it is orderly, it is *purposeful*. It does not waste or torture—not like this."

He spoke with punctuated ardor and gave Gabriel with an oddly pleading look. He was anxious for Gabriel to believe him, but why? Why did he care what Gabriel thought?

"I'm sure that's true," Gabriel said calmly.

Von Glower took a deep breath. The tenseness in his shoulders eased. "I'm sorry. I must sound like I'm badgering you. It's just that I'm afraid the club is not put in the best of light under these circumstances. Believe me, this is nothing like the nature we espouse. When a healthy beast kills, it takes only what it needs to survive and it does so respectfully. It's only man who is capable of such—such pointless slaughter!"

Gabriel stared at him. "But . . ." he said carefully. "The killer *isn't* a man."

Von Glower colored and looked away. "Of course not. But if it *is* a beast, it is a very *sick* beast. It happens sometimes. Even in the wild."

Gabriel barely registered the walk back to the bus stop or the ride back to the subway line. Even the U-Bahn station, with its warm, sulfurous blasts of air, did not dislodge his mind from its mooring. If he'd been confused before, he was positively bewildered now, wrapped in cords of thought as entangled as a Gordian knot.

Nothing about his interview with von Glower had gone as expected, and he was damned if he had the slightest idea what to make of it.

Was von Glower really as innocent as he seemed? Did he even *seem* innocent? The business about the philosophy, for instance. *To regain primal instincts and powers*. Might something like that not be taken too far? How far into the mind of predatory man did the club members go? And what would happen if they couldn't find their way back out? Then there was that bit with the glass. Von Glower wasn't exactly the clumsy type. But he seemed thoroughly genuine in his adamancy against the killings. Besides, the "black wolf" was some historical thing; it wasn't involved with this case anyway—so forensics told them; the killer was red. Besides, would someone who could transform into a wolf hybrid be bragging about achieving a "slightly keener" sense of hearing? No. In the wake of red fur and animal bite marks, von Glower looked like an underachiever.

Gabriel found that he was inclined to believe Friedrich, even that he *wanted* to believe him. The club's philosophy wasn't inherently bad, after all. Gabriel believed in following his instincts, and that stuff about ESP—he could use that in this line of work. You couldn't blame the man if *someone* or *something* had taken his ideas a wee bit too far.

Of if something with a healthy carnal appetite had been attracted to them. Gabriel narrowed his eyes and looked out over the buildings passing by. *Been attracted to them, perhaps even very recently.*

He arrived at the club at seven p.m. He was relieved to see that he was not the first—Preiss had just arrived and was pouring himself some beer. Gabriel joined him at the bar.

"Good evening, Herr Preiss."

"And to you, Herr Knight." Preiss was blotting the back of his neck with a handkerchief. His graying sandy hair was wet.

"Did you run into some rain?"

Preiss smiled. "No, I was visiting a friend nearby. Our play got a bit . . . aromatic, shall I say? So I took a quick shower."

The word *aromatic* was accompanied by a lazy, knowing wink.

"Oh." Gabriel's smile faded. "Huh."

Preiss took his glass of beer and walked over to the fireplace. Xavier had a pleasantly crackling fire going, and Preiss settled down in the chair with obvious contentment. But even contented, the man had the air of a stray dog keeping an eye out for its next meal.

Gabriel poured himself a beer and, with some effort of will, followed him. The man creeped him out.

"Baron von Glower mentioned that you're a lawyer," he said as he sat down.

"When I choose to be." Preiss's honeyed tone was the vocal equivalent of a rose's scent—a siren's call to the bees.

"I'm sorry?"

"I have enough money to work only when I choose, Herr Knight, which means I only take cases of special interest." The look on Preiss's face made it clear what he would consider interesting.

"How fortunate. Whaddya do with all your spare time?"

Preiss took a sip of beer. "I *entertain.*"

It was obviously an invitation to a territory that Gabriel did not want to explore, but to find the swallowed diamond you sometimes had to poke through a lot of manure.

"Really? And what sort of entertainin' is that?"

One corner of Preiss's mouth tipped upwards sardonically. "Do you like women, Herr Knight?"

"I've been known to," Gabriel said dryly.

"I *adore* them," Preiss rumbled. He leaned his head back on the chair, and his light blue eyes gazed in half-lidded rapture into Gabriel's own. "All kinds of women, all races—all beautiful, of course. I enjoy the hunt—the stalk, the approach, the seduction. It's a game I never tire of. It's a game I always win."

Gabriel had to make an effort to keep his surge of disgust hidden. Looking at Preiss was like looking into one of those fun-house mirrors that makes you larger; Gabriel had had more than his share of such "hunts," but surely he'd never been as obvious or as ruthless as this.

"Sounds . . . interestin'," he said.

"And *sometimes*"—Preiss's eyes widened mockingly—"I vary the game even further. A true gourmand appreciates all *kinds* of food, all *sorts* of textures."

Gabriel felt his face burning. "I'm more a meat and potatoes man myself."

Preiss laughed out loud. The sound was as lazy and suggestive as everything else about him. "You're not nearly as stupid as you like to appear, Herr Knight."

Gabriel sucked in his cheeks and willed his embarrassment away.

"But I'm not sure I believe you," Preiss continued, eyeing him frankly. "Unless I'm mistaken, you're quite the hedonist."

"You must be gettin' a whiff of the past," Gabriel said bitterly.

As Preiss continued to eye him (Gabriel had the feeling he knew very well that he was causing discomfort), Gabriel struggled to turn the tide. He forced a cold smile. "But your ideas intrigue me. Friedrich was telling me about the club philosophy earlier today."

Preiss's amusement faded at once. He looked away toward the fire. "Was he, now? Here?"

"No. At his home in Perlach."

"Ah! How fortunate for you."

"He's a very persuasive speaker."

"He is magnificent."

Gabriel studied Preiss. He was rolling his head on his neck in an athletic stretching gesture that was the kind of thing people did to show how relaxed they were when they were just the opposite. Gabriel wondered what exactly was bugging Preiss, that he'd been told about the club philosophy? Or that he'd been to the baron's house?

"So I was wondering what the other members of

the club thought of the philosophy. You, for example, Herr Preiss."

"I?" Preiss shrugged and took a drink. "It works, doesn't it?"

"How so?"

Preiss's blue eyes returned to Gabriel's. "We're all animals. Why fight it?"

Gabriel hesitated for a moment, wondering if Preiss was serious. He appeared to be. "Perhaps you and I heard different lectures on the subject," Gabriel said with a smile.

"No, Herr Knight. The baron doesn't put it quite that way, but that's the point, isn't it? 'Return to nature,' 'recall our primal instinct.' In other words, shake off the shackles of repressed human society and respond only to your gut desires."

Gabriel just watched him, saying nothing.

Preiss leaned forward lasciviously. "Our gut instinct is that of the unfettered beast, a purely physical, *sensory* creature."

"In other words . . . don't suppress your urges."

Preiss leaned back and grunted. "That's right. If your body wants something, it must be natural." A meaningful stare followed.

"Hmmm. What if you get a 'natural urge' to rip someone's throat out?"

Preiss's face clouded with confusion. It was clearly not the direction he'd anticipated. He responded delicately. "Fortunately, my own tastes run to pleasures of the equally sticky but less fatal variety." He smiled once again, pleased with having restated his point.

"But what if someone's natural instincts *are* that violent?" Gabriel pressed. "Shouldn't they suppress those urges?"

"Nature is about *sex,* Herr Knight. Every living creature has one primary urge—to reproduce. Not, fortunately, to *murder.*"

"And yet sometimes they do," Gabriel said darkly. "Sometimes they do murder—even their own kind."

For a moment Preiss said nothing, his slick amusement gone. He stared out into the room as if thinking of something else. When he answered it was in a disinterested tone. "I believe nature knows how to handle that kind of aberration. In the wild, when a member of the pack turns cannibalistic, it is hunted down and executed. End of mutant instinct—and its genetic bloodline."

He blinked and smiled, turning back to Gabriel. "But why dwell on such distasteful things? Surely, that is not your opinion of our philosophy? Have you no respect for the ways of nature? Believe me, civilized man is far more violent to his own kind than the beasts of the woods. And what does man fight about? Religion? Politics? Ownership? Morality? If we all lived like animals, there'd be no more war and we'd all be far happier, I assure you."

"Do the other club members share your views?"

"Of course."

"Really? Baron von Zell doesn't seem very happy to me."

Preiss gave a breathy dismissal. "Von Zell is an asshole these days. Ignore him."

"What's his problem?"

"Who knows? He used to be the baron's favorite. Oh, he was always arrogant, competitive on the hunts . . . We all are. But he was pleasant enough, even charming. I know it's hard to believe now."

"So what happened?"

Preiss shook his head, his face betraying his apathy. "I don't know. Maybe he has personal problems, who cares?"

"You've written him off, then."

"He's an asshole, as I've said."

"And I thought he was just that way to me," Gabriel said with a wry smile.

Preiss shook his head again; then he seemed to relive something, for he flushed with anger. "He offends *everyone*—even the baron himself! One day I heard them talking. Von Glower was telling von Zell that he'd acted stupidly about something—which, knowing von Zell, is not difficult to imagine. Von Zell was *furious*."

Preiss stopped, fuming but cautious. It was clear he was not planning to eludicate.

"So . . . von Zell insulted him?"

"He called the baron *weak,* a coward!" Preiss spewed this angrily, as though it was the ultimate insult. "Bastard! I can't believe the baron let him get away with it. He should have made him leave the club that moment! I would have done something myself, but . . ." He paused and swirled his beer. "Well, it was a *private* conversation."

Yeah, and you're scared shitless of von Zell. Gabriel couldn't say that he blamed Preiss much.

"Did this just happen? Maybe the baron hasn't gotten around to dumpin' von Zell yet."

"It was a month ago at least."

"Oh."

The two men drank their beers in silence for a while. The conversation had at least curbed Preiss's leering, which was some relief. Gabriel tried to sort through the facts in his head.

"It's too bad about von Zell," he mused. "Havin' a friend in bankin' would have been convenient."

Preiss chuckled bitterly. "If you're talking about borrowing money, take my advice: keep your head out of that lion's mouth."

"Some of you have already pumped that well, huh? But why would any of you need money? The baron says you're all models of success."

Preiss rubbed his overly large lips, his eyes sour. "*I* took less than some."

"Really? I suppose I can see how Herr Hennemann might have needed a friend like von Zell. Elections are awfully expensive."

"So are scandals," Preiss said darkly. He looked immediately regretful.

"Scandals?"

Preiss stood up. "Excuse me," he said coldly, and walked away. He wandered into the front hall, where Gabriel could hear a door open and voices raised in German greetings.

Gabriel put down his mug and wiped his hands on his jeans. He could feel a cool sweat coat him as if he'd just gone on a long run, and his pulse was beating just as rapidly.

God, he'd missed this. It was like walking on the blade of a razor, or riding his motorcycle on the rim of the Grand Canyon.

He wondered how close he was to the edge.

Von Aigner strolled in. He was ruddy and shining in his massive black overcoat, as bearded and towering as the ghost of Christmas past.

"Good evening and good cheer to you, Herr Knight!" He beamed. "Where's the beer?"

His words echoed through the building, and Hennemann, as if being called by the Pied Piper, hurried in from the front hall, still extracting himself awkwardly from his raincoat.

"Guten Abend," he nodded to Gabriel as he headed for the bar.

Gabriel went over to join them.

Von Aigner was still pulling beers when Klingmann entered. He was carrying a briefcase, and he looked terribly nerdy as he paused in the doorway. He sat his case down carefully to remove his coat and nodded to the others. "Good evening, gentlemen."

Von Zell entered, bumping into Klingmann and then glaring at him as though it were his fault. Klingmann hastily moved aside.

"Guten Abend, Baron von Zell," von Aigner called out cheerfully.

"Abend." Von Zell marched to the bar and took the beer von Aigner offered. He did not look at Gabriel.

"Meine kleine Familie! How are you all this eve-

ning?" Von Glower stood in the doorway in a gray wool cape, his frame impossibly tall and broad-shouldered in the garment's graceful lines. He swung it off like Errol Flynn.

"So glad you could join us, Gabriel." Von Glower smiled across the room as he hung up his cape. His double-breasted black suit and high-necked white shirt were impeccable and elegant. Gabriel wondered, should he ever abandon blue jeans, if he could look like that. He decided it would be too much work.

"Me too," he said.

Von Zell glared at him and went over to sit in front of the fireplace.

Preiss had reentered behind von Glower and now he hovered, trying to get the baron's attention.

"Könnte ich Sie für einen Moment sprechen, Baron?"

"Natürlich, Preiss.. Was ist los?" Von Glower put a hand on Preiss's shoulder, and the two stepped to one side.

Gabriel observed this worriedly. He'd been perhaps a bit heavy-handed with Preiss.

"So what have you been up to in Munich, Herr Knight?" von Aigner asked.

"Oh, just hangin' out."

Von Aigner shot Hennemann an amused glance. "I'd be happy to recommend a nightclub or a few good restaurants. Do you like good German food?"

"Sure."

"I know the best in town, don't I, Hennemann?"

"Ja." Hennemann nodded affably. "He knows about food, our von Aigner."

"There's a *kellar* near the Hauptbahnhof that has the most delectable *Rindfleish.*"

"Actually, it's kinda difficult to get interested in food with these killin's in the papers," Gabriel said with a shiver. He took a sip of beer.

"Ach! Terrible. Just terrible," Hennemann complained.

"Of course it's terrible," von Aigner said, offended. "But what has that got to do with food? A man has to eat, am I wrong?"

"And just last night there was a fatal attack only a few blocks from here," Gabriel added. Across the room, he noticed that Klingmann was still hovering undecidedly near the coat rack. He seemed to want to approach von Zell but was having a hard time getting up the nerve to do so.

". . . Herr Knight?"

"What?"

"I was just saying," Hennemann repeated with carefully elucidation, as though slurring had been the cause of the communication backfire, "that I spoke to the governor myself about the situation, and I told him that we must clear things up, and right away. The police! What do we pay them for? And I said, 'That's all one can do.' Isn't that right, Herr Knight?"

"All one can do. Hmmm. Let's see. Well, you guys could offer to hunt the thing down yourselves. Ya'll are supposed to be good at that, right?"

Von Aigner and Hennemann both looked at him as though he'd gone mad.

"But that's not the sort of thing we do at all!" Hennemann exclaimed.

"Isn't it? Why not?"

Von Aigner was glowering. "Herr Knight, the city is the business of the police. We hunt in the woods."

"Are you sure?" Gabriel hinted broadly. Von Aigner looked blank.

"Well, it *is* the duty of the police." Hennemann pouted. "What do we pay them for?"

"Did you know the latest victim was a local businessman—a furrier?" Gabriel finished his beer and put the mug down on the bar with a hardy bang. He pushed it toward von Aigner for a refill, but von Aigner was just looking at him, his brow pressed into a frown of uncertainty.

"I hadn't heard that," said Hennemann. "Very strange."

"Yep. Grossberg was the name."

Gabriel was watching von Aigner from the corner of his eye as he addressed Hennemann. He saw the color drain from the large man's face.

"I didn't even bother going into the office today!" Hennemann bitched. "I took one look at the newspaper and knew it would be a nightmare, and I was right. My secretary called this afternoon in tears, just in tears! People calling all day long—'what are we doing about it,' they want to know. I've done everything I could be expected to do and—"

"More beer, please, von Aigner?" Gabriel asked.

"Was? Oh. Yes."

Von Aigner took the glass and filled it from the tap behind the bar.

Hennemann's narrative trailed off at the sight. *"Ich auch, bitte shöen."* He gulped what was in his glass and pushed it forward.

"Did you know Herr Grossberg?" Gabriel asked von Aigner as he pushed back the full glass and their eyes met.

Von Aigner looked flustered. "Me? No. No. Why do you ask?"

"You look a little upset."

Von Aigner shook his head, as adamant as Peter before the cock crowed. "I never heard of him."

"Huh. I thought . . . since you're both in the business of processin' animals."

"I don't know him, Herr Knight!"

"Well, of course you don't. Why should you?" Hennemann said, deeply confused.

Gabriel and von Aigner looked into each other's eyes for a moment. Gabriel smiled apologetically. "Didn't mean anythin' by it."

Von Aigner muttered something about it being all right and finished off his beer. He poured himself another and glanced in the direction of von Zell anxiously. Gabriel followed his gaze and watched Klingmann make his approach and sit down across from von Zell at the fireplace.

Gabriel eyed the situation covetously for a moment, then spotted the periodicals on the end table near von Zell.

"Excuse me," he said, getting up from the stool. "I have to go drain the snake."

The expressions of bewilderment on his companion's faces were priceless. He went into the bathroom in the back hall, where he took his tape recorder out of his coat pocket and put in a new tape. He pressed the Record button and slipped the compact device up his right sleeve.

When he came out, he headed for the fireplace. Klingmann was speaking in hushed German as Gabriel walked up.

"Yes, Herr Knight?" Von Zell signaled Klingmann to pause with an upraised hand.

"Just wanted to grab a magazine."

Von Zell glared at him, waiting for him to complete said task and get the hell away.

Gabriel leafed through the stack of magazines as though looking for an appealing cover. He waited until the two men got bored enough to stop watching him. Then he let the tape recorder slip from his sleeve and onto the table behind the stack of magazines, a side that conveniently faced the wall.

"Got one. Thanks."

Gabriel took the magazine back over to the bar. He noted that von Glower and Preiss were still talking quietly. Von Glower spied him over Preiss's head and smiled at him. Gabriel nodded back.

"Ja, ich habe meine Nachmittagstermine abgesagt. Wir treffen uns hier um vier Uhr?" Von Aigner was saying to Hennemann.

"Soviel ich weiß."

"Hey." Gabriel put the magazine down on the bar. "Whatcha talkin' about?"

"Our monthly hunting trip," von Aigner said. "We're going to our lodge in Eppenberg tomorrow. It's in the Bavarian National Forest. Will you be joining us?"

"Um, I don't know." The idea was both unexpected and unpleasant, especially since he'd never actually gone game hunting in his life. "I don't think so. I need to have my gun cleaned."

"There are plenty of guns at the lodge," von Aigner offered expansively.

"Herr von Aigner," Hennemann urged circumspectly, "perhaps the baron didn't mean for Herr Knight to join us *quite* so soon."

Von Aigner shrugged. "Oh, hell. Let's ask him. Baron von Glower?" He called across the room, and the dark head swiveled towards them.

"Yes, von Aigner?"

"The trip tomorrow. Will our new American friend be joining us?"

Von Glower opened his mouth to speak, but someone got there first. Von Zell interjected bitterly from across the room.

"Of course not! He's not a club member!" Von Zell rose and took several steps toward von Glower. He paused there, in mid room, fists knotted at his side.

Von Glower turned toward him calmly. "He's my guest."

"I doubt he has even a hunting license!" Von Zell turned to Gabriel. "*Do* you? Do you have a permit from the *landratsamt*?"

Gabriel looked back at him and blinked slowly. He was really starting to hate this guy. "Darn. I knew I'd forgotten somethin'," he said dryly.

"See? He cannot go!"

"Nonsense, Garr," von Glower said smoothly. "The sooner we get to see his technique the better. He can register when we get back."

"But that's not legal!" von Zell sputtered.

Von Aigner guffawed. "Since when do *you* care

about what is legal? It's only a hunting license, for God's sake."

"Von Aigner's right," von Glower said in a firm but even tone. "No one will disturb us in Eppenberg, and I would enjoy Gabriel's presence very much."

"Well, we certainly wouldn't want to deny the baron anything he would enjoy!" von Zell spat out sarcastically. The room was silent as von Glower blinked lazily at the younger man, then looked back at Preiss as if dismissing him. Von Zell's eyes were large and glittering like two blue jewels. He glared at Gabriel as if it were all his fault. And then he must have seen something revealing on the American's face, for he suddenly smiled—a mocking, tight smile.

"Yes. I suppose it might be an *interesting* exercise at that."

The threat in the words was evident. He was to be outdone if not *un*done on the hunt. Gabriel's discomfort deepened, his skin telling the tale. This appeared to satisfy von Zell immensely, for his smirk broadened and he went back to his seat.

"Our lodge in Eppenberg is privately owned," von Aigner explained. "We have forty acres. We're rarely disturbed." He made an effort to sound pleasant.

"Does Klingmann have a license yet?" Gabriel asked. "He's new too, isn't he?"

"He asked me about it weeks ago," Hennemann said. "I am certain he filed for one. Whether or not it has come back, I couldn't say."

Someone brushed Gabriel's elbow. It was Klingmann himself. He mumbled an apology and asked von Aigner for a beer.

"Have you got your hunting license, Herr Doktor?" Hennemann asked.

"*Ja*. Last week it came in the mail."

As soon as von Aigner delivered Klingmann's beer, he excused himself. He had a pensive look on his face as he went over and bowed curtly to von Zell. Von

Zell waved him into the chair Klingmann had just occupied.

"Does von Zell always hold court like this?" Gabriel asked, nodding his head toward the banker.

Klingmann followed his gaze and frowned. He said nothing.

Hennemann shrugged. "I can't imagine."

Preiss and von Glower broke off and headed over.

"I'm sorry to have abandoned you, Gabriel," von Glower said. "Are you enjoying yourself?"

"Oh. Hey. Sure."

Von Glower smiled at the implicit sarcasm. "I'm glad you are coming with us on the trip. I was going to invite you myself."

"That's kind of you. I have to tell you, though, it's been a couple of years . . ."

Hennemann served the baron a beer.

"You'll be excellent, my friend. If you like we can go over the general layout of the weekend later tonight. We usually disperse here by ten on weeknights, and I'm quite the night owl. Would you join me for a late supper?"

"Where?"

"At my home. I have an excellent French cook."

The others at the bar were listening, though pretending not to. They all looked down at the bar or their drinks with great intent.

Gabriel hesitated. He ought to say no. He was on a case, after all, and he should review his tapes tonight, burn some little gray cells. Besides which, he really couldn't afford to get too personal with any of these men, not until the case was over. But the idea of going back to the cold, tragic heart of the Huber farm could not hold a candle to the warmth and luxury of von Glower's living room, a home-cooked meal, even the effortless charm of the man himself.

"I'd love to, thanks," he found himself saying.

Von Glower smiled broadly and tilted his head in a courtly bow.

The pleasant moment was not to last.

"Was?" Von Zell's voice boomed through the room. Gabriel felt his stomach clench up again. He turned to see von Zell rise from his conversation with von Aigner and storm toward him. Von Aigner peered around the large arm of his chair—he looked frightened behind his great dark beard.

Von Zell marched directly to Gabriel and pointed a shaking finger at him. "I demand to know what you are doing at this club!"

"Garr!" von Glower said, shocked.

Von Zell was shouting. "Did you know this 'guest' of yours has been sniffing around the club? I found him in the basement myself earlier today. And he is asking everyone questions! He must be a reporter, or the police!"

Gabriel felt the ground dip away beneath him. He darted a glance toward the front hall, but he was a good long dash from that exit, and von Zell was in the way. He'd have an easier time, he decided quickly, to make a run for the back exit and the alley.

At the bar, Preiss was leaning against the service counter with his arms folded. He watched the scene with half-lidded eyes. Klingmann stared into his beer, and von Aigner had disappeared into the chair. Only Hennemann looked confused.

Von Glower put his beer down and turned to face von Zell squarely. His hands were relaxed at his sides, but his eyes were livid.

"And what, exactly, do we have to fear from a reporter or the police?" Von Glower's words were spoken low, soft velvet-covered iron.

Von Zell's expression of triumphant rage faltered a bit. He looked from Gabriel to von Glower and back again. "You . . . you don't *care* that he's prying into our private business? Sniffing around the club? Our practices? What possible motive could he have?"

"Garr!" von Glower interrupted sharply. "Gabriel

is my guest. Of course he's curious about the club. *You're* the one who's turning this into an inquisition!"

Von Zell's face registered pure incredulity and incomprehension. He stared at von Glower as though he couldn't be serious. "You *don't* care," he said, almost to himself.

"Why should I? He's welcome to know anything he wishes to know about this club. I have nothing to hide." Von Glower turned his shoulder ever so slightly away from von Zell. It was a small gesture, but it said quite clearly that the conversation was over.

Von Zell blinked rapidly, his jaw working. "Then . . . then it is on *your* head!" he spat, almost in tears of rage and frustration. He turned on his heel and stormed from the room. The bang of the front hall door echoed loudly with his passing.

Gabriel turned to find Preiss's eyes upon him. Preiss stared, as expressionless as a shark. Gabriel turned away uneasily. His hands were shaking. He put down his glass.

"I'm sorry you had to put up with that," von Glower said, his voice still angry. "It's unforgivable."

"No, um, I should have . . . I do ask too many questions."

"Nonsense. What else is a good mind for?"

"But it's been upsetting people. I'm not exactly helpin' the harmony around here."

Von Glower uttered a bitter laugh. "The harmony was shattered a long time ago. Garr gets . . . territorial. I'm tired of it, frankly."

But Gabriel's heart was still hammering. His ears were hot and he knew they were bright red. God! His fair complexion really sucked in this line of work.

"I should get goin' anyway. I'd like to clean up before tonight. That is, if . . ."

"Of course!" Von Glower smiled reassuringly. "Don't fret about Garr. He won't be with us for long."

Gabriel gave von Glower a bewildered look but said nothing.

"I'll be home in about an hour. I'll see you then?"

"All right, Friedrich," Gabriel said numbly. He backed away and waved a hand toward the bar. "Good night, everyone."

The men at the bar responded to Gabriel's valedictory pleasantly enough, but it was clear they were all unnerved. That von Zell had lost favor, they'd known for some time. But how far from grace he'd fallen and who might replace him, those were different matters entirely.

They watched Gabriel leave with grim, invidious eyes.

The machine pulled into the driveway of the Huber farm. It was a dull, strange-smelling, cold gray blob. It did not appeal to the thing in the woods, but the thing knew that what would get out of the cold blob would—would appeal very, very much.

It licked its snout anxiously and permitted itself an impatient whine because the human had not yet emerged and wouldn't hear, couldn't hear, not from this distance. Humans were such pitiful, hapless, stupid creatures.

The human emerged from the machine. Its footsteps crunched loudly on the gravel, and it was making a strange sound, one that the thing in the woods could have identified as whistling if it had concentrated, but it chose not to. The sound was not important; it was just something that humans did. What was important was that the human was crossing the driveway and heading for the door.

The thing's hind legs danced in anxious delirium, then tensed down, prepared to bolt from its cover at the edge of the woods. It watched.

The human found its present. The man stumbled upon it in the dark, exactly as the thing had known it would. Its breath quickened into a pant of need as it watched the human stop and look down, bend over to see.

It began to creep forward on stealthy paws.

Yes, the human was examining its prize now, a gift from Death, the neighbor's cat with its entrails strewn across the lawn. The thing could see the human's bright yellow glow shift into a darker tone with disgust and a little fear too. Soon, oh soon, that same light would be awash in the primal red of terror—like ethereal blood staining the aura.

The human looked around, but didn't see the thing approaching in the dark, dark, dark. Oh, the man was so close now and he didn't see what stalked him in the dark! He couldn't even smell Death coming! The cat had been smarter! The thing pulled its lips back from its teeth, baring them for the delicious moment to come. Pleasure and excitement made it quiver.

The human bent over farther, picked at something in the grass. At that moment—the moment the thing was about to leap—something blinding swung free of the human's covering, something that seared the thing's brain with a light like fire.

The thing from the woods whimpered a cry of pain and began to back up.

The object—the blinding light—swung freely in the air, back and forth, hanging from the human's neck. It sent its torturous rays out to seek and pierce. The human looked up and tensed. Its aura blushed darker with fear.

But the thing was beyond enjoying or even caring about such things. The pain was excruciating. It was unbearable. It turned and fled back into the safety of the woods. When it had gotten far enough from the light for the pain to stop, it turned and peered back at the human through the trees.

The man stood up, looking at the woods now. It began backing toward the house, its aura and its body language a hideous enticement of fear, an invitation that could not be acted upon. The human spent some time fumbling at the door, then disappeared inside.

The thing in the woods lifted its head and howled its frustration and rage at the moon.

Chapter 4

Rittersberg

The cold, companionless silence of the castle had wrapped around Grace like a bitter blanket all evening, seeping into her heart and numbing her spirits. So it was no surprise that when sleep finally came it was a bitter sleep, with dreams as icy and sterile as the walls of the castle itself.

She dreamed of snow.

She was in a fir- and oak-strewn forest, and it was laden with arctic glitter in icy white crystals and rolling pearly beds. The forest was absolutely still; not even her footsteps made any sound. She seemed to be floating, or perhaps just walking, like a North Pole messiah, across the top of the downy drifts.

She wandered in this alien landscape for some time. The silence and the snow became oppressive, as if the frosty hand of Death itself was gathering around her for a good hard squeeze. She was cold, but despite the fact that she was wearing only a nightdress in her dream, the cold seemed to be coming from inside her, as if the scene was injecting the chill directly into her bones.

She moved about that silent, piney citadel looking for a way out—a cabin, perhaps, or a road. And after a while she realized she was being followed.

By wolves.

She didn't hear them—nothing broke the stillness of the woods. She happened upon her own footprints, a record of her confusion, and later she happened upon them again. The third time this happened, her mind (perhaps simply bored with the repetition) supplied something new—a set of footprints curving out of the trees to join her own. The tracks looked a little like dog tracks to her inexpert eyes, but they were large. Huge even. When she realized what they were, terror raced through her blood in an icy rush. She choked back a scream, afraid they would hear it and beset her. She began to run.

Now the dream changed entirely. Now it was a nightmare pure and unadulterated. She was running, running through the snow and the woods, and behind her were wolves, a pack of wolves, and yes, she could see them now, in flashes, when she looked behind. Three wolves, four, five, maybe more. They wove in and out of trees, fanning out and circling her—tireless hunters functioning with eager efficiency. She ran and they closed in. They grew so close she could feel the wet spittle of the snow kicked up by their churning paws.

She broke through the trees and found herself at the top of a snowy embankment. Below, an open field stretched into the horizon. She half tumbled, half ran down the bank, spilling into the valley, and now when she looked behind, her hunters were clearly visible, no longer glimpses of fur and fang from behind the trees. They sped toward her. She realized, fully, that she had only made their job easier.

Then something intruded upon the silence and the white like a trumpeted reprieve. It was the sound of bells, of something heavy moving across the snow. She turned from her pursuers and saw, miraculously, that a sleigh was up ahead and was speeding toward her down the valley. A sleigh!

And what a sleigh. It was like the drawings of Cinderella's coach she'd seen in picture books as a child. A team of four horses drew it, and their trappings and the sleigh itself were gilded and carved and bedecked with cherubs like some baroque gravy bowl enlarged and set on runners. The driver whipped the horses, swung toward her.

She cried out to the sleigh driver, an entreaty.

And then the sleigh was there. It didn't slow, she was simply able to grab the hand that reached down from the passenger seat and was swept upward with one strong pull. She landed on a velvet seat and stared up into the face of the man who had rescued her. He was a brilliant figure, more alarming and surreal than the sleigh itself. He was tall, with glittering black hair and mustache, crystal blue eyes and the palest skin. A heavy fur blanket covered him from the waist down and a thick black wool coat with ribbons emphasized the broadness of his shoulders, gave him an imperial air.

Grace recognized him from the picture she'd seen in the *gasthof*. It was King Ludwig II. She studied his face with amazement and wonder, struck and quickened by his beauty, by his iridescent blue eyes. Then he turned to look out the back of the sleigh, and she reluctantly tore her eyes from his face and followed his gaze. The wolves raced on, but they were already far away and falling back steadily, like snowflakes drifting across the surface of the icy field.

She was suffused with relief and gratitude and something else—a sense of anticipation and girlish awe about the man who sat next to her.

She turned to face him once more, her skin warm and blushing.

But the man who'd sat next to her had disappeared. In the seat beside her now was a huge silvery wolf. It bared its teeth.

Grace woke up screaming in the blackness of the Ritter bedroom.

No one came.

She had just come downstairs when the phone rang. Gerde was nowhere to be seen, so Grace answered it.

It was Frau Holstedder at the post office. There was a letter waiting from Herr Knight. Frau Holstedder sounded almost as excited as Grace.

She reached the town square in five minutes and (to the disappointment of Frau Holstedder) took the letter over to a bench in the town square to read.

> Gracie:
> You decided to come over. Great. Guten tag and all that. I'm sure you and Gerde are hitting it off.
> Thanks for finding the werewolf book and journals. They might come in handy. About Ludwig II—you know, I think you might have something there. Harry says there are two places you should check out. Ludwig had a castle called "New Swan" something or other, and there's a museum about him at . . . Herrenchiemsee (Harry helped me spell that). I really think you should look into it.
> As for me, never fear. Things are going smoothly. The case is being handled by a Kommissar Leber, and I've finally gotten the okay to go see him. My main suspect, a Doktor Klingmann (from the zoo), belongs to a hunt club run by a man named von Glower, and I think I've managed to get myself in there too. Whether it leads to actually learning anything is another matter.
> Gabriel

Grace lowered the letter and checked the envelope. There was nothing on it except the address of the lawyer—Übergrau. No phone number or hotel. She frowned.

And nothing about the Black Wolf either, not even a response to her warning. There was just this suspiciously eager encouragement about Ludwig II. Did Gabriel really think it was relevant to the case?

She thought about it, her cheeks hollowing vexedly. Probably not, not really.

The things was, she was pretty sure he was wrong.

*   *   *

The Smiths were just being served their breakfast when Grace entered the *gasthof*. She approached their table leerily.

"Mr. and Mrs. Smith? I'm Grace Nakimura from the castle."

"Yes, I know. How are you, dear?" Mrs. Smith was pleasant enough, but there was a restrained air about her.

"Miss Nakimura," Mr. Smith said. He stood up.

"Sit down, please. I just wanted to apologize for the other night, and for not coming by earlier. I suppose I was a bit thrown by what you said."

Mrs. Smith's round face spread into a generous smile. "You're forgiven, dear! Why don't you join us?"

"All right."

Werner brought her *frühstück*, and it was as good as she remembered it. Although the table manners of her companions left something to be desired, they were a welcome change from the silent reproach of Gerde. While they ate they chatted about the kinds of things Americans in Germany chat about—the weather, the quaintness of the villages, the sturdy meticulousness of the natives. Mrs. Smith was much savvier this time around. She did not breathe a word of the occult. Grace finally brought it up herself when Werner at last disappeared with their empty plates.

"At the castle you said something about the Black Wolf?"

"So Emil tells me."

"Where did you get that name? What did you mean?"

Mrs. Smith smiled regretfully. "I don't know, sugar pie. When these things come, I'm just like a telephone. I don't know who the message was from or what it meant. I've never heard of the Black Wolf myself. Have you?"

"Yes," Grace said after a moment's hesitation.

There was a heavy pause, but Grace said nothing more.

"Well!" Mrs. Smith sniffed. "The important thing is to answer exactly the questions you raised. *Who* was the sender and *what* did they mean for us to do?"

"But how can we answer those questions if you don't know?"

"I don't know *now,* but if we put our energies together and ask for the answers we may learn something."

Grace studied Mrs. Smith, confused. "You're not . . . you don't mean a séance, do you?"

"Of course not!" Mr. Smith interjected with a chuckle.

"Good, because I—"

"I'm much better at tarot cards," Mrs. Smith said cheerfully. She reached down to retrieve her enormous vinyl purse and rooted around in it until she pulled out a deck of cards.

"*Tarot* cards?"

"Just think of it as a language, dear. The spirits can't speak to us directly—not *usually* anyway—but through symbols they can get their point across."

Mrs. Smith merged the cards with an expert hand, rapped them on the table, separated and rejoined them. Satisfied, she clasped them between both hands, nearly hiding them from sight, and brought her hands to her bosom. She closed her eyes and prayed over them silently.

"There! Now, who shall we do the reading for: you or your *Schattenjäger?*"

"Um, I thought the idea was to learn about the Black Wolf?"

"Of course, but he's relevant to *one* of you—maybe both. I can't very well do a reading on the Black Wolf—I don't even know who or what he or it is."

There was a hurt tone carefully applied to that last remark.

"Hmmm . . ." Grace frowned skeptically. "Mine, I guess. I'm the one that got the message."

"Good!" Mrs. Smith held the deck out to Grace. "Now, I want you to take these cards and push your energies into them with all of your might."

Grace, feeling more than a little silly, did as asked. Fortunately, Werner was still back in the kitchen and was not on hand to watch this bizarre ritual. Grace handed the cards back. She was real close to deciding that she'd been right about the Smiths after all—they were kooks. Mrs. Smith might have an open channel somewhere, but the rest of her wiring was a mess. She glanced at her watch.

"We begin," said Mrs. Smith, "praise Jesus."

She very deliberately laid out four cards in a row, turning each over slowly and studying the faces with interest.

"Well? What's it say?" Grace asked, curious despite herself.

Mrs. Smith pointed at the first card on the left. "This is your soul card. It applies to all of your lifetimes. You've drawn the Empress, dear!"

"The Empress?"

"It means your soul's path is one of leadership—a kind of maternal or Amazonian leadership, if you prefer. It also means that your soul is essentially *feminine*. We incarnate in the opposite sex sometimes, you know, just to round out our natures. But you're definitely a woman at heart."

"That's a relief," Grace said dryly.

"This second card represents you in *this* lifetime. It's the Chariot. It represents self-discipline and control—victory over instincts and desires. You put on a mask of detachment to hide your emotional nature. The Chariot is very masculine—ambition, dominance. You will seek out great achievement, but you *will* pay a price."

"This doesn't sound anything like me," Grace pointed out.

"Yes, dear," Mrs. Smith soothed, patting her hand. "The third card represents the Other. You've drawn the Magician."

Mrs. Smith looked up at Grace slyly. "Who is he, dear?"

"I'm sorry?"

"The Magician, your Other! Oh, this is a very powerful card—major Arcana!"

Grace glanced at Mr. Smith but didn't see anything there to illuminate her. "You're whizzing right by me with this Other business," she said.

Mrs. Smith shook her head, making her extra chins jiggle. "*Everyone* has an Other! It's the soul who is most interwoven with your own at this moment. Sometimes it's someone you've been linked to in other lifetimes as well. It's the *Schattenjäger,* isn't it? What's his name, dear?"

Grace put on a "this is stupid" face, but her heart thudded painfully in her chest. "The *Schattenjäger?* Gabriel Knight."

"Gabriel Knight! A name of power! And he is powerful, this one!"

Mrs. Smith's face glowed and she pinned down the Magician card with one chubby finger. The card itself showed a robed man standing before an altar-shaped rock, one hand thrusting forward a wand. Grace looked at it distrustfully.

"The Magician is dexterous and cunning, mischievous and manipulating," Mrs. Smith said.

"That's Gabriel, all right," Grace quipped.

"And *very* strong with magical and occult powers. How interesting! Your chariot is all logic and reasoning while his Magician is spiritual and intuitive. Those are feminine qualities really."

Grace snorted. "Gabriel's about as feminine as a jock strap."

Mrs. Smith smiled patronizingly. "Yes, dear."

She unpinned the Magician and moved to the fourth card. "This last card shows us what you're trying to achieve at this moment. It's the Strength or Trial card."

Grace gave Mrs. Smith a confused look.

"A trial—a test, dear. The card represents finding the strength to continue some difficult task. It also represents the integration of conflicting energies to create some kind of explosive force—I wonder if that's your Chariot and his Magician energies."

Grace looked highly doubtful.

"What is the trial, do you know?" Mrs. Smith asked.

Grace shifted uncomfortably. "Um, we *are* on a case right now."

Mrs. Smith clasped her hands to her chest dramatically. "A *Schattenjäger* case? I knew it! What's it about?"

Grace began to speak, then thought better of it. "I'd . . . I'd rather not say."

Mrs. Smith smiled pityingly. "As you wish. But the case will be difficult. You must let your love give you power—*use* the positive energy of your union or you may not succeed."

"Look, Gabriel and I are just friends," Grace said impatiently. "There *is* no . . . like . . . *union.*"

Mrs. Smith exchanged a knowing glance with Mr. Smith, then said gently, "If I might suggest . . . This isn't the best of times for defenses, punkin'. When you face evil, positive emanations like love are powerful weapons."

"I'll try to remember that if I run across any," Grace said with a scowl.

"I hope *so,* dear." Mrs. Smith gathered up the cards. "Now, shall we do one for your *Schattenjäger* as well?"

Grace glanced at her watch again. "I don't think so. My reading didn't tell us anything about the Black Wolf, and I don't have much time."

She hadn't meant it as a reproach; it just came out that way.

"The spirit world works at its own pace and in its own ways," Mr. Smith said with a hint of censure.

Mrs. Smith patted his hand reassuringly. "Emil is right. I can't guarantee that Gabriel's reading will give us the answers we're looking for, but the message was a warning for him, wasn't it?" She looked at her husband. "Didn't I say, 'Tell *him*, beware the Black Wolf'?"

"That's right, Mother," Mr. Smith said. Grace sank back with a sigh into her chair.

After shuffling the cards again and having Grace think about Gabriel over them (this was even stupider than last time), Mrs. Smith laid out another line of four.

"Yes! His soul card is the Magician!" Mrs. Smith said as she turned it over. "You see, dear? It matches your Other exactly!"

Grace wondered how quick of hand Mrs. Smith *was* with those cards, but she smiled politely.

"And his lifetime card . . . Oh. The Lovers."

Grace snorted. "If that means what I *think* it means, you're starting to convince me. His bio does read like a porno version of Lewis and Clark."

"It's not a *sexual* card," Mrs. Smith said worriedly. "It's a *duality* card. The Lovers represent opposites—male versus female, but also good versus evil, altruism versus selfishness, hedonism versus saintliness. It tells me that Gabriel is someone with two very distinct faces and two conflicting sets of impulses."

Grace brought her thumbnail to her mouth worriedly.

"Gabriel's challenge in this lifetime is to integrate the conflicting sides of himself. Until he does, he will be a very troubled soul." Mrs. Smith shook her head sympathetically.

Grace said nothing.

"And *you* will find peace," Mrs. Smith said, reaching out to rescue Grace's hand from being munched, "when you learn to love the *worst* of him as well as you already love the *best*. When you can admit that the things that draw you about him and the things that repel you are all a part of the same man."

Grace pulled back her hand. "I told you, we're just friends!"

"*Mother,*" Mr. Smith warned.

Mrs. Smith made an I-call-'em-as-I-see-'em face. She moved to the second card. "His Other is the High Priestess."

"I suppose that's me," Grace said cynically.

"No, dear, it's not. The priestess represents psychic mysteries, deep wisdom, spiritual powers. No, this is a very different energy than that of your own earthy Empress."

Grace felt an unwelcome flash of jealousy and pictured the elegant Gerde, but Mrs. Smith was lost in her own ideas and didn't notice her discomfort. "The Other card can change from time to time, depending on the situation. I wonder if this is our connection to the voice? Perhaps the High Priestess represents the force that's trying to contact Gabriel right now."

"*That's* not much help," Grace said impatiently. "What about the Black Wolf?"

"But it *is* a help. The High Priestess is a spirit guide card if ever there was one! At least it tells us the voice is benevolent. Someone or some force—the High Priestess—is trying to warn Gabriel."

Grace huffed. "But . . . if Gabriel's this *Magician* and if he's so very psychic or whatever, why did this spirit guide talk to *me*?"

Mrs. Smith shrugged helplessly. "I don't know, sweetie. Perhaps Gabriel's blocked right now. And there *is* this duality business—perhaps Gabriel's blocking himself. Let me go on and see if things clear up."

Mrs. Smith laid down a new card, the fifth. Grace took one look at it and gave a bitter laugh. "Ha! Death! No worries, then."

"Now, you leave the card reading to me!" Mrs. Smith admonished. "The Death card is a *transforma-*

tion card. It doesn't usually mean *physical* death; it implies some kind of shift from one thing to another. The transition may be painful, but the new state isn't necessarily bad. I'm going on."

She laid out a sixth card. Grace sat forward to peer at it.

"Two of wands," said Mrs. Smith in a flat voice.

"Yeah? So?"

Mrs. Smith chewed her salmon pink lips. "Hmmm. Wands is Mars in Aries; that's a war card. And the two . . . I would say, in conjunction with the Death card, that there are *two* possible transformations."

Mr. Smith put his arm around the back of the bench and placed a firm hand on Mrs. Smith's shoulder. Grace did not mistake the gesture or its meaning. Mrs. Smith *was* turning a little peaked.

"What kind of transformations?"

Mrs. Smith began shaking her head to and fro in a jittery gesture. "It's a . . . I think it's a spiritual battle. He's confronting a very real challenge about his duality, perhaps one of many he will face, or perhaps *the* battle of his lifetime. As for a result—he could go . . . either way."

"Either way *what*?" Grace asked, caught between feeling exasperated and frightened.

"Mother . . ." Mr. Smith said softly.

"We're talking about a transformation." Mrs. Smith's voice was trembling audibly now. "Either he'll come out of this pushed more toward his good side or more toward his bad. It will not be a little push, either, it'll—it'll be a *big* push. The spirit guide has been sent, after all, to help him . . . help him choose."

Grace said nothing, watching Mrs. Smith with growing concern.

"Gabriel has inherent gifts, p—p—powers." Mrs. Smith was no longer even looking at Grace now but staring past her. "There is something he must d—d—do. If he goes wrong, it will be not a small hole. Not small."

Something in Mrs. Smith's face made all of this very real and very frightening, despite the bizarreness of the words themselves. So much New Age fluff and stuffing, so Grace would have thought, but Mrs. Smith's hands were shaking in a palsied manner and she seemed unable to put down the cards. She fell silent, her eyes fixed on the wall behind Grace's head. A fine sheen had appeared on her upper lip and cheeks.

Mr. Smith took the cards gently from his wife's hands and pushed them as far away from her as he could. He put both of his arms around her and held her tightly, his face grim.

"You'd better go now, miss. Come back later."

Grace nodded and stood reluctantly. She paused.

"She'll be all right," Mr. Smith said a bit sharply. "Just *go*."

The episode in the *gasthof* made Grace feel a bit guilty about leaving town. What exactly had happened? Had something been trying to prevent Mrs. Smith from speaking? Was it some kind of epileptic condition? Or was she putting on an act? Whatever it was, Mr. Smith would look after his wife, and Grace herself had still learned nothing about the Black Wolf. If Ludwig II knew the Black Wolf, as Christian Ritter implied, there might be a mention of him somewhere in some official archive or another. It was worth a look, despite Gabriel's obvious skepticism.

Besides, the truth was that she was more than a little interested in seeing the castles herself, particularly after her dream. She bought a southern Bavaria map at the grocery store and set out in her rental car. And as she drove the hour and a half to Neuschwanstein, Grace thought about what she'd learned the day before.

Ludwig II of Bavaria. That she had dreamed of the king and of wolves was no mystery—she'd gone to bed with her brain full of the stuff. Still, now that the terror of it was safely behind her, she recalled the dream with some interest. What emotional intensity it had evoked! She could still remember how compelled she was by the look in his eyes, the awe and desire she had felt in his presence.

The man in her dreams did not look like the king—or, rather, he looked like the pictures she'd seen of him in his early thirties. Werner was quite a fan, and yesterday he'd taken her on a tour of his Ludwig memorabilia—several pictures in the *gasthof* proper and more back in his living quarters. He'd given her a brief and obviously slanted summary of the king's life, but it was heartfelt for all that

Ludwig had been eighteen when crowned. His father had died unexpectedly, leaving the young heir little choice. The pictures from this time were of a very tall, still gawky boy. His black, naturally curly hair formed baby-doll ringlets around his thin, pale face. Enormous, black-lashed blue eyes stared out at the viewer, and the colorful, tight-fitting militia-style costumes he preferred finished off the romanticism with a flourish.

No wonder the entire country had fallen in love with him—called him the fairy tale king. No wonder Bavarians had not forgotten him even to this day. Werner had made that abundantly clear.

And there were other official portraits, portraits of a handsome man coming into his prime. In his late twenties Ludwig began sporting a mustache and goatee. In his late thirties, his hair was still thick and wavy and his bearing regal. His figure had gradually thickened to a staunch, solid paternalism.

But he had never been a father, or even married, or so Werner admitted briefly when she'd probed. He had built castles instead, and had died at the age of forty-one. *How*?, Grace had asked. *They drowned him in a lake,* Werner'd confided. When probed who "they" were, he gave her one of his knowing looks.

Naturally, the historian in her was aroused. She'd

even phoned her old Yale professor, Barclay, to see if he knew the name of a local Ludwig scholar. He'd promised to get back to her.

And today there were the castles. The road to Neuschwanstein roamed through countryside and farmland that was green and rolling. White Bavarian farmhouses with window boxes full of early spring daffodils dotted the landscape. The day was cold and rainy, but it was thrilling nonetheless to be in such a beautiful and foreign place, to wander the back roads of southern Germany for the first time in her life.

Then she rounded a bend and saw the castle. It took her breath away, floating above the green valley below like a vision of the Second Coming—a magnificent palace in white stone resplendent with towers and turrets, shining against the backdrop of the purple-blue mountains beyond.

Neuschwanstein.

She bought her ticket and rented an English audio tour headset. The gift shop was crammed with mugs and T-shirts and posters and steins, all with the image of the castle or Ludwig on them. There were books too, in several languages. She promised herself she'd be back and forged ahead into the castle itself.

She walked through the rooms slowly, marveling at the evident expense. Every wall was covered with hand-carved wood in a shining light cherry. Painted murals filled the upper six feet of the walls before coffered and carved ceilings capped the expanse. The furnishings were just as elaborate. The bed was a baroque carved masterpiece, like some altarpiece for a grand cathedral, covered with blue and gold hand-embroidered coverlets. The tour tape explained.

Ludwig was obsessed with building castles throughout his adult life. Neuschwanstein, his third and greatest, was built between 1869 and 1886. Another obsession was mythology, a taste he shared with the composer Richard Wagner. Ludwig adored Wagner's operas, and Neu-

schwanstein is filled with images from them. The entryway panels are from the Siegfried saga. The
bedroom murals depict scenes from the tragic love
story, Tristan and Isolde.

There were few visitors on this rainy March week-
day, and Grace paused at her leisure, taking in everything with wide eyes and filing it away as best she
could. It was odd, but she could feel a sense of Ludwig
here, a feeling not unlike the one he'd evoked in her
dream, but colder and more aloof. Something about
the excessiveness of the bedroom bespoke a soul who
loved beauty but who was also out of control. The
tape concurred.

*It took fourteen woodcarvers four and a half years
to create the bedroom. It was precisely this kind of
extravagance that bankrupted the king. In the years before his death, he found it increasingly difficult to find
money from any source. That is why this castle was
never fully completed and plans for a beloved fourth
castle, Falkenstein, were never begun.*

There was a doorway at the far end of the room
with red rope draped across it. From the entrance one
could look into a small chapel, no larger than a walk-
in closet. A stained-glass window let in colored light
through images of a black-haired monarch in angelic
garb. On the altar was a shining gold cross and an
image of the Madonna and child, both with black skin.

*The king was a devout Catholic, as were all of the
Wittelsbach rulers. They kept Bavaria true to the Holy
Roman Church even during the worse rampages of the
Protestant wars. The Madonna figure here is a repre-
sentation of the Black Madonna of AltÖtting, a favorite
pilgrimage site of the Bavarian monarchy.*

*The figure on the window is St. Louis, Louis IX of
France. Ludwig was fascinated by the French monarchy, which he admired for its absolute authority and
aristocratic rule. Besides Louis IX, whom he admired
for his saintly qualities, Ludwig also adored Louis
XIV, the Sun King, who is featured at his castle in*

Herrenchiemsee. The king's fickle obsession with these figures was legendary. For a period of about a year the king had all Louis images covered up with black cloth. No historian has ever satisfactorily explained why.

Grace sighed, her mind troubled by the picture that was forming. She moved on.

This is the king's living room. The tapestries and murals in this room depict scenes from the Lohengrin story. Note the swan images on the ceiling and on the fabrics throughout the room. Lohengrin was the first Wagner opera the king ever saw. He was only sixteen when he attended a performance in the Residence Theater in Munich, and it so affected him that he considered it a form of enlightenment.

Perhaps because of his early connection to Lohengrin, the swan became a favorite motif of the king's. To him the swan represented majesty and purity—the qualities of the Knights of the Grail with whom Ludwig identified.

Of course, the tragedy of Lohengrin was his essential loneliness. This, too, was the fate of the king.

Grace walked the large room carefully. It was indeed filled with swan images—in the woodwork, in the decorative embellishments on the walls, even in the embroidered cushions on the chairs. Here was an elaborate cabinet, carved from wood to look like a miniature castle; a broad, dark desk where the king conducted his affairs; the long sofa and chairs and table where he sat. Alone.

Why had he remained so solitary? Surely, he'd been the most handsome and eligible bachelor in Germany, perhaps in the world, for most of his adult life. Obviously, he had a heart. No soulless person could create this kind of art.

Beyond the living room the ceiling dropped, and Grace found herself stepping incongruously into a cave-like room carved from rock.

The grotto is a reproduction of a scene from the Tannhäuser opera. The king loved to create fantasy worlds and immerse himself in them. As the years went on, Ludwig became more and more reluctant to leave his fantasy playlands, and more removed from the duties of the state.

She reached a flight of stairs and took them up, winding in a circle around a massive stone pillar in what was clearly one of the towers. At the top was a huge, gilded hall.

This is the Singer's Hall. It was built for concerts and performances, though Ludwig himself never gave a public concert here. It is said that during the last few years of his life, Wagner would visit the king and the two men would shut themselves up in this room. The mystery is further compounded by the murals on the wall. Initially, they were from the Parsival saga, but in 1882 Ludwig had them all repainted, supplying the descriptions of the scenes himself. Unlike the other rooms in the castle, the scenes in the Singer's Hall are not from any identifiable opera or myth. It has fueled rumors of a "lost opera," particularly since the king wrote to the conductor of the Munich opera in 1883 telling him to "prepare for a new Wagner." Of course, no such piece ever appeared and the composer died the same year.

It is yet another of the many enigmas left by the life of the fairy-tale king.

Grace, by now familiar with the fantasy paintings of the castle, walked over to the first mural. The style was the same as those in the compartments below, a kind of Arthurian fantasy blended with realism that was really quite beautiful and appealing, rather like illustrations from a children's book.

On the first panel was a Valkyrie-type maiden with long, wavy gold hair. She stands in a modest dwelling with an older couple, surely her parents. They're all dressed in expensive but threadbare clothes. The parents hold out a picture to the young maiden beseechingly, a picture of an older man. The girl weeps.

The second panel. The rich older man, in a public

ceremony, gives the golden-haired girl a bracelet. The girl looks terribly sad, but her parents stand firmly behind her. A betrothal?

The third panel. The girl, alone in her room, casts the bracelet into the fire in a tearful rage.

The fourth panel. The girl, now draped in concealing robes, is at the blacksmith's. She speaks with a dirty, ragged apprentice, showing him the bent and ruined bracelet. Her face reflects her fear, and that of the youthful and handsome apprentice reflects loyalty and love.

The fifth panel. The maid sits in a garden glen. On the ground next to her is a newly opened burlap parcel with a mended bracelet inside, but the maid isn't paying it the slightest heed, for the apprentice is leaning over, kissing her. Her posture indicates that she is startled but not necessarily displeased.

Grace grinned.

The sixth panel. The maid and the apprentice fleeing in the dark woods. Dogs and men on horseback are almost upon them.

Grace crossed the room and began making her way up the opposite side of the hall.

The seventh panel. A legal proceeding. The maid and the apprentice stand bound while the rich fiancé pleads his case. He is pointing a finger at the apprentice, his face dark with thunder. Accusing? Condemning?

The eighth panel. Grace stopped in her tracks and stared. In the foreground is a white, shining wolf. It stands in front of a pair of terrified children, barring the way. A few feet down the painted path is a black wolf, growling carnivorously.

A black wolf. And a white wolf. A black wolf and a white wolf. Geez Louise.

The intent of the painting was clear—the white wolf was protecting the children from the black wolf. But what, if anything, did it have to do with the Black Wolf that Christian Ritter had warned Ludwig about?

For that matter, what did it have to do with the first seven panels?

The ninth panel. The golden-haired maid is confined in a sparsely furnished stone tower. She sits at the window, looking down. At the edge of the woods in the distance stands the white wolf. She is staring at the wolf, and the wolf at her.

The tenth panel. The wedding feast. The villagers are gathered in their finest clothes, and at the bridal table is the cruel-looking rich man, the maid dressed in white, and her parents. Everyone in the picture is in a state of alarm, for in the middle of the room stands the white wolf. Its snout is raised in a howl. At the head table the rich man is in the act of trying to rise. One hand clutches his throat.

Grace stared at the picture for a long time. What, exactly, was going on in the scene? She moved slowly to the eleventh panel, hoping for elucidation. It was the final, requisite tragic scene, reminiscent of so many of the Wagner operas or of the Shakespearean tragedies, for which the catchphrase was formulated "everyone dies."

Here lay the white wolf on its side, bloody from battle and clearly dying. Draped over the wolf in mourning is the maid with the golden hair. The wedding guests, now carrying torches and rough weapons, light the wooded scene. And the black wolf, its tongue hanging out, lies dead and conquered to one side. The look on the maid's face is tragedy personified.

Grace wondered how many times the artist had had to redo that look before Ludwig was satisfied. What had the solitary king meant by these paintings? Had he written the story himself? Perhaps even a libretto? And whatever happened to the apprentice? Was he linked somehow to the white wolf? *Was it a were-wolf story?*

With these questions chilling her, Grace wandered downstairs to the gift shop, barely conscious of the journey. She approached the girl behind the counter.

"Grüss Gott. Sprechen Sie English?"

"A little."

"Is there any more information about the paintings in the Singer's Hall?"

The girl smiled regretfully. "No. The tape has all the information."

Grace frowned. "But someone must have worked on the paintings. The artist perhaps? Didn't he leave a record of Ludwig's instructions?"

The girl looked at Grace blankly. "I don't know. We have slides and postcards."

Grace sighed and gave up. She bought a full series of the Singer's Hall paintings on postcards and an English biography of the king written by a Sir Richmond Chaphill, then took her package out into the courtyard.

The rain had stopped, and though the sky was still thick with gray clouds, the sun peeked through stubbornly. Grace found a wooden bench that was almost dry and tucked her raincoat carefully underneath her. She began to skim through the book.

Other than his long-standing friendships with his mother and the Empress Elizabeth of Austria, relationships were nearly always a disappointment for Ludwig and a bewilderment for his partners. He would become obsessed with someone—a singer, an artist, a nobleman, or peasant—and would bombard them with gifts and praise. When they would fail to return the depths of rapturous passion he required, he would get hurt and would cut himself off from them abruptly. The objects of his interests were occasionally women, usually ones he fell in love with after seeing them in idealized roles on the stage. But they were most often young men who fit his fantasies of the heroic sagas like Lohengrin and Parsival.

Grace's brows creased in a thoughtful frown. Was the author trying to say what she thought he was trying to say? She flipped through the pages and found a letter dated 1864 from Ludwig's manservant to a friend.

> The king has been in a high mood these days. The reason, of course, is a new interest. Thursday last the king attended a performance of *Lohengrin* in the Residenztheater. He returned in a fever and demanded that a man be found. The man, it was gathered, had been sitting in a box opposite the king's own, and had drawn the king's attention by his "beauty" and his "deep emotional response" to the performance. The king declared, "Here at last is a sensitive soul!"
>
> The man was tracked down and brought in for an audience. Upon my word, never have I seen any mind so in line with His Majesty's own! They discussed Wagner and France and Byron and all manner of things until well past dawn. The young man, beautiful indeed to look upon, met the king's enthusiasm and knowledge bit for bit! Well, His Majesty has been in the thick of it ever since and, while I welcome his good temper, I grow tired of fetching letters back and forth to "Louis" (so called by His Majesty—that should tell you who the young man looks like) at all hours of the night!

Grace read the letter twice, trying to absorb it. 1864! That was the same year Christian Ritter warned Ludwig about the Black Wolf. Could one thing be related to the other? Grace thought about it. Probably not. After all, many things happened in a single year—a fact easy to forget when that year was so long ago. And Christian Ritter's letter had only implied that the Black Wolf *knew* Ludwig—not that they were particularly close.

Grace found nothing else about "Louis," and once again the author had sidestepped the critical issue the letter raised—was Louis a lover? A friend? She checked the copyright page. The book had been written in 1958. No wonder.

Then, when she'd about given up on the writer, she

found it, in the very last chapter. It was discreet, but it was clear.

> The king, particularly later in his life, experienced a great deal of guilt about his sexual nature. His diaries are full of entries begging God for forgiveness and swearing to remain pure henceforth. The sheer number of these "oath entries" indicates that Ludwig was not very successful at resisting temptation. Yet those who would condemn him out of hand should note that Ludwig was clearly a God-fearing man and that, though his flesh might occasionally fall, he never surrendered his heart and his mind to sin.
> Indeed, it might well be this conflict between his Christian heart and his unnatural desires that led him down the path to reclusiveness, insanity, and, ultimately, destruction.

Grace put the book down slowly, feeling tempted to throw the author at the wall. Ludwig didn't deserve such prying eyes, such boorish, bigoted prying eyes. But her anger was only the tip of the emotional swell; the rest had no name. She'd connected with something about him in the dream—connected mentally and physically. Now the picture that she'd begun to form at this place, so inexplicably sad, so ignominiously personal, struck her to the quick.

She sat there in the courtyard for a very long time, staring at nothing.

The idea of the diary was uppermost in Grace's mind when she arrived at Herrenchiemsee. Like Neuschwanstein, Ludwig had picked the location for this castle based on pure scenic beauty and isolation. Practicality, it seemed, was not an important consideration for Ludwig. Where the workers on Neuschwanstein had lugged heavy rock and marble up the steep mountainside in horse-drawn carts, the workers of Herrenchiemsee had had to ferry it over a lake, then tote it another mile to the actual construction site. Grace took the same journey, her spirits buffeted by the rigorous March wind and the sloshing of the gray, restless lake.

The castle was based on Versailles—an elongated governmental palace, not a vertical phantasm like Neuschwanstein. Yellow stone and matching columns marched along the facade with a nod to the Greek, and a fountain and formal gardens bespoke of more logical minds than the king's. Did Ludwig really find such orderliness soothing? Or was this palace merely another set piece, a prop built to play French monarch, then abandoned soon after like a longed-for toy that does not deliver the joy it had plighted.

The impression of a set was deepened inside. Beyond the doors to the royal suite was the grand entrance hall. An enormous staircase bombarded the eye with brightly hued marbles in reds, golds, and blues. And here, as if welcoming the king home, or perhaps, more pertinently, as if heralding Act I, was a golden statue of the Sun King himself, Louis XIV, with his long, curling wig, hose, and pointy shoes, and no doubt idealized regal countenance.

"Louis", that should tell you who the young man looks like.

Grace studied the statue, as if the face would tell her something, but if it held any secrets it did not reveal them to her. She moved through the rooms quickly, feeling no compulsion to pause. The king had abandoned this place, as he had his third castle, Linderhof, an even smaller depiction of Versailles. He'd fallen out of love with them well before he died. His soul was not here.

His mature dreams had been of Neuschwanstein and the illusive Falkenstein, and it was easy to see why. Herrenchiemsee was all white walls with heavy, garish gilt cherubs and swirls in every nook and cranny. Its design was that of a baroque palace but, like a prop piece, it had been constructed with materials that could offer only the immediate illusion. The plaster was wearing on many walls, and the gilt that covered the swirls and cherubs was darkened with the dirt of time and, in some cases, worn away entirely, revealing cheap resin underneath. At its peak the palace would have been sterile and garish. Now it was a shabby curiosity piece and had the sort of appeal an old, elaborate dollhouse had; the power to evoke amazement that someone had once gone to so much trouble and expense for something so nonfunctional.

The last room on the tour was the hall of mirrors. At last Grace felt a sense of Ludwig. There was something in the endless procession of glass that had, perhaps, captured a piece of the elusive monarch's soul. At night, the tour guide said, hundreds of candles would be lit in this room, and Ludwig would walk here alone, watching his reflection in the glass.

Grace walked up to one of the mirrors and stared into it. She could picture Ludwig standing where she stood, doing the same thing.

The face in the glass was not a smiling one.

After the tour she hurried downstairs. There was something more important here than the palace itself. One wing had been converted to a Ludwig museum.

It did not disappoint. Clothing, furniture, and personal effects were housed here, letters and official documents bearing his signature and seal. His life story was told progressively on modern, opaque white signs that hung from wires amidst the displays.

Childhood portraits. A Victorian royal household; cruelly strict discipline and diet, structured, endless lessons in Greek and Latin, mathematics and science and all the other graces thought necessary for a crown prince. And a boy who loved art and poetry and daydreaming had to steal his pleasures the way another steals cookies from a shrewish maiden aunt. His younger brother, Otto, was his only companion.

At sixteen, the young man who had convinced his tutors to let him study the German legends finally gets permission to see *Lohengrin*. The opera is based on the saga of a Knight of the Holy Grail, a story painted on the walls of Ludwig's childhood castle Hohenschwangau. For hours as a child he would stand and stare at the romantic paintings of knights and swans and maidens. Now he stares, enthralled, as Wagner presents his virtuoso adaptation. Ludwig falls to Wagner like a teenage girl succumbing to Lennon and McCartney.

At eighteen his father dies and Ludwig is crowned. The people can scarcely believe the ephemeral beauty and romantic chivalry of their new king. The middle-aged parliament ministers cannot believe their luck at having such a naïve charge. Now the real regimentation begins: meetings, paperwork, hours and days in parliament. Sign this, sign that—no, don't bother to read it. Put on the robes and pose.

When she came to a large portrait of a beautiful woman, she stopped, curious. EMPRESS ELIZABETH OF AUSTRIA, a placard said, LIFELONG FRIEND OF LUDWIG II. Elizabeth, a cousin, had grown up in a royal house on Starnberger See, and she and her sister had played with Ludwig as children. But Elizabeth was eight years older than Ludwig, and she was married to the heir of the Austrian throne before Ludwig came of age. The two shared a lifelong bond, however, exchanging letters frequently. True to his tendency to playact, Ludwig called her "the Dove" and he was "the Eagle." Ludwig had been smitten with her ever since her romantic, storybook engagement and wedding, perhaps because he could not have her.

In a glass case was correspondence between the two cousins and their translations.

3 July, 1863

My Dove, You can have no idea, dear cousin, how happy you made me. The hours recently passed with you in the railway carriage I consider among the happiest in my life; never will their memory fade. You gave me permission to visit you at Ischl; if the time comes for this ardent hope to be fulfilled, I shall be of all men upon the earth the most blessed.

The feelings of sincere love and reverence and faithful attachment to you which I cherished in my heart even as a boy make me imagine heaven upon earth, and will be extinguished by death alone. I beg you with all my heart to forgive the contents of this letter—but I could not help myself. . . . Your Eagle

1 March, 1868
My dearest Eagle. You have not written me in a few months—I have missed you. I often try to imagine what you are doing. I hear tales that you have been on retreat and have not been seen in Munich for some time. I suspect it is this friend you write of so mysteriously that takes you away from home!

I hope you are enjoying yourself, my beloved, but I beg you to caution. The people need to see you on the throne. I also hesitate to suggest that what your officials do in your absence may not always be in your best interest. You have always been a true king, but you must let the people *see* you to ensure that they don't forget that.

E., your dove

14 June, 1878
My beloved Eagle. In your last letter you spoke so bitterly of your torment that I was moved to tears. What *is* this torment? Why won't you confess to me what is truly troubling you? You must know that I would never despise you, no matter how horrible you believe your sins to be. Please do not write such barbs to my heart by even suggesting such things. If you do not wish to confess to me, at least tell me how I can help. I am always your true one, your Dove.

Next to this letter was a placard which read, "It was obvious to his few close friends that Ludwig was struggling with his mental state near the end."

Grace frowned at this interpretation of the letter. Perhaps his torments were real enough. But whatever they were, not even Elizabeth had been allowed to share them.

In his twenties, it appeared that Ludwig had taken his role as king seriously. There were signed decrees and pictures and drawings of Ludwig in public processions, even a portrait of Ludwig in heavy blue velvet robes with the classic ermine, knighting a member of the gentry. Around him men in blue velvet watched.

Ludwig as Grand Master of the Knights of St. George. This was a hereditary role for the Bavarian monarchy and one Ludwig relished before his natural reclusiveness and dislike for public display caused him to give up such activities.

Knights of St. George? Could this be Ludwig's connection to Gabriel? To Christian Ritter? At the very least it was an odd coincidence. And yet something about the description did not ring true. The portrait, with the romantic pomp and circumstance and the costumes, seemed to reflect the kind of thing Ludwig would have loved. He was no doubt an introverted soul, but was it really that urge that had driven him away from this kind of ceremony or was it the restrictive hand of his ministers? Was it their vision of a figurehead he had rejected? Or was it something else altogether?

The turning point came in 1873, when Ludwig was twenty-eight. One of the displays depicted Ludwig being knocked from his horse in the woods.

Ludwig, while young, was in fine physical condition and loved to hike in the Alps and to ride horses. He had a hunting lodge, Schachen, built for this purpose. Unfortunately, in 1873 a rather traumatic accident befell the king at Schachen, and his leg was cruelly damaged. His physical health deteriorated from that time on, leading to stoutness in later years.

Grace paused nervously. The words *hunting accident* reminded her of Gabriel's letter and the "hunt club," but surely that was simple word association?

Beyond this display even the lighting grew dimmer, and the images themselves grew more disturbing. Displays of Neuschwanstein drawings and models were combined with tales of the king's obsessive demands. A workman falls from scaffolding due to exhaustion. The king has no idea how long things take or how much they cost and doesn't care. Warnings from parliament. Newspaper headings from underground printers blaming Ludwig and his extravagance for the country's financial woes.

1878. Ludwig's brother Otto, his childhood companion and only sibling, is declared insane after years of disfunction. The flaw is one inherited through his mother; his great-great-great uncle Friedrich the Great of Prussia and two sons of Wilhelm II had also been mentally afflicted. Ludwig is inconsolable. Was he perhaps afraid for his own sanity as well?

1881. Ludwig now rarely leaves his castle and does not receive visitors. He's abandoned all duties of state. His servants must wear elaborate costumes and are not allowed to look at his face; they are trained to enter bowed over in a painful posture. He communicates with them through notes passed under doors. Some of the notes are smuggled out of the castle and passed on to those who seek to discredit the king. A few of these instruments of betrayal have survived to be displayed here.

Dec. 14th–15th, 1881. Linderhof. Every day get up earlier, for certain. See to that VERY PARTICULARLY. WRITE IT DOWN. Remember that when the Great Friend arrives at Neuschwanstein and we retire to the hall we are not to be disturbed! I will not tolerate stupidity or insubordination!

Dec. 19th–20th, 1881. Linderhof. Order another work by Jennings on the occult. Write urgently to Klug say-

ing that I insist that the stoppages by the banks cease.
We must get a hundred glass cutters working on my
special project this very week. I WANT it and therefore it MUST be done. Write very urgently; he must
succeed AT ONCE and then must report to me
urgently.

If I give orders to clear my room, doing so must
not be postponed as has happened. Pencils must be
pointed without special orders. The day after tomorrow a thousand Marks. How is Louis now? I want to
know whether or not he looks unhappy. How often
have I said that the coffee must not come up boiling
hot so that it can be drunk only after standing an
hour. If any more correspondence from Louis come,
they are to be burned at once, but I am to be informed
of their arrival.

Grace had gotten so involved in the displays, she'd
almost forgotten her purpose in coming. She read the
note again, excited.

Louis. According to the Chaphill biography, Ludwig
met a Louis in 1864. Now, in 1881, Louis was definitely
out of favor and yet still clearly an obsession. Was
this a temporary feud? Was it even the *same* Louis,
or did Ludwig call all his paramours that? Had "the
Black Wolf" been a paramour too? She moved on,
her scholar's mind desperate to find answers instead
of more questions.

The mounting picture of irrationality so eloquently
exemplified in the king's notes was not ameliorated
by the rest of the displays. Ludwig is ordered by parliament to Munich—he refuses. His ministers arrive at
Linderhof to see him—he denies them entry. He
builds grottos and swan boats and plans a new castle
when the one currently under construction cannot be
finished for lack of funds.

And then, in what seemed to be presented as the
pinnacle of damning evidence, Grace found a reference to the diary.

Ludwig's Diary

Ludwig kept a diary from the time he was twenty-four years old until his death in 1886. The actual diaries themselves are kept in the Königlich Bayerische Archiven. The diaries reflect Ludwig's growing inner torment. Below are some sample entries.

26 July, 1870. By the power of the lily we shall have the strength to resist temptation throughout the whole year. L & R

21 August, 1878. Solemn oath before the picture of the Great King. "Refrain for three months from all excitement." This oath has its binding power, as well as its potency by De Par Le Roy. L & R, D P L R.

The actual photocopies of the entries showed grand flourishes and seals and what looked like magical symbols by the initials. Had the magic served him? Had it helped him keep his promises? Don't we all wish for such talismen at times—when the desires our logical mind abhors sneak in like serpents under the door? *If thine eye offend thee, pluck it out.*

But surely there were other things in the diary—notes about friends, events, other feelings. Why had the museum chosen *these* entries? To show how Ludwig's mind was failing? Or was this the museum's nod toward the theories of men like Chaphill? Certainly, they hadn't touched upon Ludwig's sexuality at all in this sad record of a life.

Grace approached a female guard standing not far away. The woman had a severe countenance. Grace tried her German, figuring the woman didn't look like she had much patience for tourists.

"Excuse me. Ludwig's diary . . . the diary is in the Königlich Bayrische Archiven? Do you know where that is?"

It seemed like a perfectly reasonable question, but the woman—who had blond hair pulled so tightly back from her face it slanted her eyes—scowled.

"Königlich Bayrische Archiven," she repronounced with greatly cut vowels. *"This is not for tourists."*

"Oh. But I'm doing some work—"

"No! No one sees the diary. No one."

Grace left the conversation not overly encouraged. She'd have to simply hope the woman was wrong and that the records could be accessed, perhaps with the aid of Professor Barclay.

Why would the diary be refused to historians? They're already saying he was insane. Chapbill claims he was gay. What could be more sensitive than that?

And now she had looped nearly to the front again. Here was the end, 1886. An account was told, in pictures and text, of the last few days of Ludwig's life. A case displayed the suit he'd been wearing when he'd drowned. In another was the pale plaster death mask of the sort popular with Victorians. Grace found the bloated, lifeless impression too poignant to look at.

June 7, 1886. A group of men arrive at Neuschwanstein castle demanding to take the king into custody. With them is Dr. Gudden, the doctor in charge of Otto, the king's mentally ill brother. The men are refused admittance by a brave group of farmers and local soldiers who have come to Ludwig's aid. They are forced to retreat to nearby Hohenschwangau. This is the first Ludwig hears of the conspiracy to take him into custody.

June 12, 1886. Ludwig knows the conspirators will return. He despairs. He asks his servant for the keys to the tower. The servant, fearing the king intends suicide, says the key is lost. The conspirators return to the castle. This time there is no one to stop them. Ludwig is lured from his bedroom to the entry hall of Neuschwanstein. There he is taken into custody.

Ludwig is driven by carriage from Neuschwanstein to Berg, place of his brother's imprisonment. On the way the group stops at Seeshaupt. Ludwig asks to see the postmistress, Frau Vogl. She brings him a glass of water, and he says something to her. She never reveals these last words to anyone.

June 14, 1886. At Berg, Ludwig seems cooperative and coherent. Dr. Gudden writes to the government that he has Ludwig well under control. The two men go out for a walk, and Dr. Gudden is so confident that he dismisses the guards. When Ludwig and the doctor do not return after several hours, a search is undertaken. The bodies of the two men are found in the lake, drowned. Circumstances unknown.

June 16, 1886. Ludwig's funeral procession marches through the streets of Munich, followed by enormous crowds of mourners. The service is held at a packed St. Michael's church. Lightning strikes the church during the service, but no one is harmed. Ludwig's body is entombed in the Wittelsbach crypt at St. Michael's. His heart is placed in an urn in the pilgrimage chapel at AltÖtting in the Wittelsbach tradition.

A picture showed Ludwig lying in state amongst a sea of candles and flowers. And there was an artist's rendering of Ludwig wading into the water fully dressed, the floating body of Dr. Gudden behind him. The painting suggested . . . murder/suicide? Had he been trying to escape? To end it all? Or was Werner right? Had "they" done him in? According to the displayed newspaper headings, rumors of murder, even of escape and a fake corpse, were rampant in Munich for years.

Grace rounded the corner and came face to face with a large painting—the museum's finale. For a moment she just stared at it, unable to comprehend.

It was an illustration all in blues of a night scene in the snow. The scene was dominated by a baroque gilded sleigh pulled by a team of horses and a masked driver. Ludwig sat in the sleigh underneath a lap robe.

The image was straight out of her dream.

She sought the explanatory note with a growing panic and found it. She traced it with her fingertips, not trusting her eyes alone.

The Midnight Sleigh Rides

In his later years Ludwig suffered from insomnia, restlessness, headaches, and toothaches. He often demanded to have his sleigh brought out in the middle of the night and would go on long drives through the countryside at breakneck speed. This romantic but bizarre vision frightened more than one peasant, and superstitious rumors abounded about the king and his midnight excursions.

Grace reluctantly raised her eyes to confront the painting again and was alarmed to recognize the red buttons depicted on the upholstery of the sleigh's backseat. She turned and ran from the museum, her heart thudding painfully in her chest.

Outside, the wind had accelerated into heavy gusts. It snatched at her thick black hair and the hem of her yellow raincoat so that she imagined, as she half stumbled, half ran the mile to the ferry, that something had exited Herrenchiemsee with her and was nipping at her soul—trying to snatch pieces of life, perhaps, or trying to pull her away, to whisk her off to some unknown place where the damned and the lonely have long been abandoned.

By the time Grace returned to Rittersberg, it was early evening and darkness had fallen. She was almost looking forward to seeing Gerde, she realized, as she drove up the hill to the castle. Seeing anyone at all would be a comfort.

But then she remembered—she *couldn't* talk to Gerde. Thoughts of why that was only increased her agitation and confusion. The knowledge of what it might be like later, when Gabriel got back, and he and Gerde . . . It made her stomach ache and her chest palpitate. She grew irritated at these feelings and scolded herself mercilessly. After all, the Gabriel Knight she'd known in New Orleans was not the sort of man any woman could count on. How many phone calls from one-night stands had she turned away at his insistence? It was true that he was a beautiful man, there was no denying it. And he had a cockiness and a sense of humor that was exasperatingly endearing. But she could acknowledge that stuff without allowing herself to fall for it, couldn't she? She was not some hormone-driven machine. She was determined not to be the kind of woman who fell for hopeless causes, not a "when good women fall for bad boys" basket case. He was funny, a good friend, a partner. Leave it at that.

But how could she even be *those* things to him with Gerde in the way?

The castle was dark and silent—no lights at the castle door, no lights in any of the windows. And when she entered the front door, no light or warmth greeted her. Silence. Dark.

Grace began to fret. How long had it been since she'd seen Gerde? Hadn't she screamed aloud in the night and no one had come? Had Gerde really been that cold-hearted? Or had she not been in the castle at all?

There was a message on the machine. Grace played it back, hoping it was Gerde or even Gabriel himself. It was Professor Barclay. He'd gotten a name and phone number for a Ludwig expert living in Salzburg—a Josef Dallmeier. Grace jotted the info down.

Then she went to the *gasthof* to see Werner.

Gerde's uncle was polishing glasses behind the bar. The Smiths were nowhere in sight, but their car was still in the lot outside. Werner gave her his grim, secretive nod.

"Have you seen Gerde?" Grace asked. "She hasn't been at the castle all day."

Werner looked at the calendar and grunted. "It's her anniversary. I forgot. I should make her something to eat. Probably she was there all day. Some *Spätzle* maybe."

Grace's dark brows knit in confusion. "Anniversary of what?"

Werner looked at her oddly. "The anniversary of Gerde and Wolfgang. I think it was the day they met."

Grace's jaw slipped open in a non-vocal O. A series of realizations played across her face. "Well . . . well, where *is* she?"

"At the *gruft,*" Werner answered, as though this should be obvious.

It was eight o'clock when the front hall doors creaked open and Gerde entered. She wore a long woollen coat and sturdy galoshes. In the shadows of the entryway she removed these things, slowly and heavily, as if each limb were weighed down by the same stone. She paused in her actions once or twice, her head lifting and sniffing the air.

"You've been cooking?" she asked, trying to sound disinterested. Her growling stomach betrayed her.

Grace put down her magazine and smiled. "Yup. You've had such an unpleasant visitor; I wanted to make it up to you."

She walked over and took Gerde's hand—it was an awkward gesture and one that was hedged by an expectation of rejection. But Gerde was too non-plussed to protest.

"Werner gave me the idea of making you dinner," Grace said as she pulled Gerde toward the kitchen. "I tried to do Japanese, but I have to warn you, the supply of ingredients in town is pretty damn grim."

Gerde stopped, pulling her hand away. Her eyes filled with tears. For a moment she just looked at Grace as though trying to judge this change of heart. Then she said, "Grace, Gabriel and I . . . we never . . ."

Grace blushed from her asymmetrical part to her toenails. "I know. I'm an idiot, okay? Gabriel, he's just the sort that would. . . . God, you must know that by now, even in this small a town!"

But Gerde just looked at Grace and shook her head, confused.

"Never mind," Grace said, her blush deepening further still. "Anyway, I'm sorry about before."

Gerde took a quavering breath and smiled tentatively. "Okay."

"Really?" Grace looked at Gerde hopefully. " 'Cause I was hoping you wouldn't mind talking over dinner—about the case, that is. Will you help me figure things out?"

Gerde pushed away her tears, her smile lighting up. "Yes. I would like that very much."

At nine o'clock Grace was sitting at the desk in the library, trying to decide whether it was too late to call Josef Dallmeier. She gave in to temptation and dialed. Dallmeier didn't seem at all bothered. He had a light, pleasant voice, and he cajoled Grace into telling him her impressions of the castles. For the second time that night Grace went over it—this time leaving out the sensitive parts like the sleigh.

"You've certainly picked up the feel of it," Dallmeier said, impressed. "But what they won't tell you at those places—because it doesn't make for happy tourists—is the political side."

"What political side?"

"Ludwig is the Bavarian monarch who gave away the Bavarian monarchy. He signed away our independence, our country. . . . It *should* be what history remembers him for, but that act has gotten lost in all the fluff about castles and sleigh bells."

"I knew the unification happened around then!" Grace said, remembering her initial impression of the Christian Ritter letter. "So Ludwig himself signed the treaty?"

"It was Ludwig, all right. We were just getting over the Hundred Years War. France was threatening to rise again. Prussia proposed that they and Bavaria unite into a common German state for strength. Ludwig resisted for a while, but he signed in 1870. He became a figurehead under the Prussian kaiser. Shortly after his death the Bavarian monarchy dissolved completely."

Grace frowned into the receiver. "That doesn't make sense. Everything I've seen implies that Ludwig wanted an absolute monarchy—just the opposite."

Dallmeier grunted. "I agree. Maybe he thought he wasn't a real king anyway. The parliament did have a great deal of power. And Prussia's push to unite the German peoples against France was logical. Still, he could have negotiated better terms for Bavaria. I'm convinced that Bismarck had a hand in there somewhere. He usually did."

Grace thought back, trying to remember her European history. "Bismarck was a Prussian chancellor, right?"

"*The* Prussian chancellor," Dallmeier said sourly. "He was in power before Ludwig came to the throne, and he outlived him, too. What a cagey son of a bitch he was."

"Did he know Ludwig?"

"Officially, yes, but they had no personal relations. No, Bismarck was subtler than that. He had a reputation for learning people's weaknesses and exploiting them from behind the scenes. It was a matter of record that Bismarck had spies on Ludwig's staff. And you can bet that he had a hand in the insanity conspiracy."

"Wow," Grace said, her mind racing with the possibilities. "What about Ludwig's diary? Have you seen it?"

"No. It's locked up like diamond-encrusted dirty laundry. There was an English biographer who got permission—he was some blue-blooded cousin of the family. That's about it."

Grace bit back a profanity at the disappointing news. "Was the biographer named Chaphill?"

Dallmeier sounded surprised. "Yes, actually! Have you read his book? I thought it was moronic myself. Imagine having access to that kind of material and wasting it. I suppose he was a product of his generation. Even so, that's no excuse."

Grace sighed. "God, I *really* need to see that diary."

"Why?"

Dallmeier sounded genuinely curious. Grace considered how much to tell him. She certainly had no desire to scare him off with talk of werewolves, but she wasn't going to learn anything without putting out some bait.

"Have you ever heard of anyone called the Black Wolf in association with Ludwig?"

There was a pause while Dallmeier went through his mental file. "No."

"I found a letter that was written to Ludwig warning him about 'the Black Wolf.' I'm desperate to find out more about it."

"This letter was written when?" Dallmeier's voice held the restrained excitement of a scholar smelling a new discovery.

"1864."

"I would like to see it."

"You're welcome to see it. So you've never heard of the Black Wolf? There was nothing at the castles except for a few paintings in the Singer's Hall."

"No . . . but I can do some research if you'd like. We have an impressive collection of German documents here at the university."

Grace sat up, sparked by hope. "Would you? That would be great."

"And there's so much more to tell you about Ludwig. Would you meet me in the morning? About an hour north of you is Starnberger See. We could rendezvous there at the chapel. Say about nine o'clock?"

Grace nodded eagerly at the receiver. "That sounds perfect. I'd really appreciate it."

"No problem. Maybe I can bring you some good news about the Black Wolf. I'll look into it tonight."

"Great. Thank you very much, Herr Dallmeier. Good night."

Grace hung up the phone and wrapped her robe tighter around her. *Good news about the Black Wolf.* Somehow that didn't seem likely. She padded back to the warmth of the bedroom and the fire she and Gerde had laid earlier.

She climbed onto the enormous antique bed and tucked her freezing toes underneath her. She pulled and prodded the blankets until they surrounded her like a shroud. Then she stared into the fire, the crackling fire, and shivered.

And she wondered what Gabriel was doing right now.

Chapter 5

Munich

When Gabriel awoke it took him several seconds to remember where the hell he was. He was lying on red satin sheets and the room around his bed was wallpapered in a deep burgundy fleur-de-lis print. This was definitely *not* the Huber farm.

Ah! Last night.

He'd decided to go to von Glower's. Though he was a little nervous after what had happened at the club, he was even less interested in staying at the farm alone—particularly after that nasty feeling he'd had in the yard.

But von Glower was neither angry nor suspicious of him. They'd sat on the couch telling stories and drinking wine for several hours. Friedrich really had traveled all over the world, and he had some great stories to tell.

And then the girl had shown up.

Gabriel couldn't even remember her name. He'd been about two and a half sheets gone when she'd arrived, and all he could remember was a tight red gown over an incredible body and shining gold hair.

She was on her way home from the opera, she'd said, or at least he thought he'd recognized the word *opera* in her German, though it was pronounced a little more like "Oprah." And then she was in Friedrich's lap and her lips locked with his and . . .

*   *   *

Gabriel stood up from the couch, feeling awkward. "I'd better get goin'."

Friedrich pushed the girl back gently. "You don't have to go."

"Nah, I should go."

"Wait."

His host whispered something in the girl's ear. She looked at Gabriel—a playful, appraising gleam in her eye—and nodded. She climbed off Friedrich's lap, grabbed Gabriel's hand, and pulled him back down into the sofa. Soft limbs and hands pushing him back—soft lips, warm tongue.

Gabriel felt his body move from zero to fifty in about two seconds flat. It had been a *long* stay in Rittersberg.

"I can't," he said when she finally released his lips. His voice held little conviction. The girl ignored him, nuzzling his neck.

"Why not? I didn't expect her tonight, and for some reason I don't find myself in that mood."

At Gabriel's expression, Friedrich smiled. "Don't worry, she doesn't speak English. Besides, she and I understand each other well enough."

"But . . . she's . . . she's *yours*."

Friedrich picked up his glass and laughed. "It's not an exclusive arrangement, I assure you. From what you've told me, you've been living like a monk down at that castle. Your body deserves some attention."

The baron smiled slowly as he leaned back. He seemed to find satisfaction in the spectacle before him and displayed not a trace of discomfort, but Gabriel felt awkward. He grabbed Detta's left hand, which was slowly unbuttoning his shirt.

"Detta, Zeige ihm sein Schlafzimmer," Friedrich said. It was amazing how commanding his voice could be, even when it was agreeably soft.

Detta stood and tugged on Gabriel's hand. He looked at Friedrich, questioning one last time. "Are you sure?"

"Enjoy your evening," Friedrich said. His eyes were warm and encouraging.

And Gabriel, who had protested as much as he could muster, went with Detta up the stairs and into oblivion.

Afterward, Detta dressed and left him. Between the wine and the physical release he felt heavier and more relaxed than he had in ages. He closed his eyes and seemed to be sinking deeper into the bed with every breath.

Then something on his chest moved, soft, like the brush of an insect's wings. He opened his eyes to see Friedrich sitting beside him. The dark-haired man was backlit in the glow from the hall as he looked down at the talisman in his hand. He raised his eyes from it slowly.

"It's beautiful," he said. "A lion and a dragon locked in combat. Potent imagery." He laid the medallion back down on Gabriel's bare chest. "I take it you're the lion?" He smiled. "Good night, my feline friend."

He reached out a hand and brushed back a lock of Gabriel's hair, then stood up and walked out. He closed the door behind him.

Gabriel watched him go, surprised at the intimacy, and even more surprised that it felt all right, even comforting, like being tucked into bed.

And then the mattress reached out to swallow him and he was fast asleep.

He allowed himself a quick shower in the guest bathroom before dressing. He went downstairs and called Friedrich's name. Gunter showed up instead. He greeted Gabriel in German and motioned toward the dining room, where breakfast was waiting. There was a note on the plate.

Gabriel—I have some business to attend to. I'll see you later today at the club. Regards, V.G.

Gunter was pouring a cup of coffee that Gabriel couldn't resist. He pulled out the chair, suddenly starving. Gunter was apparently used to serving hearty eaters, for he kept bringing the food and Gabriel ate and ate and ate.

He was half afraid it would be gone, that Xavier had cleaned up and that the tape recorder had been discovered and confiscated. And how in God's name could he ever explain that?

But it was there, right behind the magazines as he'd left it. It had shut itself off when it ran out of tape. Gabriel pocketed the device and left the club, headed for a certain youthful mystery enthusiast.

"Can I bother you for another favor, Harry?"

"Anything. What is it?"

"I need something translated." Gabriel pulled he tape recorder from a pocket.

Übergrau's eyes shone eagerly. "Yes? Okay! How do you say? Roll 'em."

Gabriel sighed patiently and started the tape.

"Wir müssen miteinander reden," came Klingmann's nervous voice.

" 'We should talk,' " Übergrau said.

"Nein," said von Zell flatly.

" 'Nooooo,' " said Übergrau, with a surprised lifting of one brow.

"Est ist meine Karriere, verdammt nochmal! Vielleicht sogar mehr wenn die Polizei . . ."

"Ich habe Ihnen doch gesagt, nicht darüber zu sprechen!"

Übergrau was listening intently. "The first one says his career is in danger, maybe more if the police . . . and the other says 'I told you not to speak of it!' "

"Aber . . . Ich denke mir daß die Polizei bereits weiß daß unsere Wölfe nichts damit zutunhaben. Die können einen Test machen . . . an den Körpern," Klingmann said in a low tone.

"He says, 'The police must know that our wolves are not responsible—there are tests they can run on the bodies.' " Übergrau looked alarmed.

"Gut. Ihre geflüchteten Wölfe sind keine Killer. Was soll's? Halten Sie nur Ihren Mund. Sie sind damit besser dram," came von Zell's curt reply.

" 'So? Your escaped wolves aren't killers. What's the problem?' "

"Aber . . . Herr Knight. Er kam gestern morgen zu meinen Büro. Er hat viele Fragen gestellt."

"Worüber?"

Übergrau looked at Gabriel, his eyes wide. "He says *you* came to his office asking a lot of questions."

"Uber die Wölfe."

". . . about the *wolves.*"

Gabriel stopped the tape. Übergrau's golden eyebrows knit into a fuzzy line of misgiving. "Herr Knight, who are these men?"

"Just some friends," Gabriel said, his mind elsewhere.

"Why does that sound like such a very bad idea?"

"Wait, there's more." Gabriel fast-forwarded the tape a bit and started it again.

"Was ist los von Aigner? Ich muß mit jemand anderem reden," von Zell said in a tight voice.

" 'What is it, von Aigner? I have someone else to speak with,' " Übergrau translated.

"Ich habe mir gadacht . . . Wissen Sie etwas über Grossbergs Tod?" said von Aigner.

" 'Do you know anything about . . . about Grossberg's death?' "

"Wieso sollte ich?" Von Zell sounded pissed now.

" 'Why should I?' "

"Nun . . . ganz eifach . . . Ich gab Ihnen Seinen Namen."

Übergrau's eyes were wide blue pools. " 'It's just that *I* gave you his name.' "

"Und?"

" 'And?' "

"Herr Knight fragte mich, ob ich Grossberg kenne."

"Was!" von Zell exploded.

There was the sound of a chair scraping, and von Aigner muttered, *"Oh, mist."*

Gabriel stopped the tape.

"He said *you* asked him if he knew Grossberg."

"Yeah, I, um, I kinda got that part." Gabriel smiled rakishly, but his heart wasn't in it.

Übergrau regarded him grimly. "You know, it would be a great tragedy if the Ritter line were to die out. A great tragedy. Not just for our firm, you understand . . ."

"Harry, I know what I'm doin'."

Übergrau looked unconvinced. "These men are involved with the murders in some way, aren't they? Perhaps we should call the police."

Gabriel nodded, his eyes still hazy with remote possibilities. "Sure. I will. In a bit." He blinked and looked at the young lawyer. "By the way, any luck with that missing-persons search?"

Übergrau muttered worriedly under his breath and picked up a folder. "Frau Hogel left the results with me this morning."

"What'd she find out?"

"There are two forests where missing-persons incidents are unusually heavy. The Nationalpark Bayerischer Wald, or the Bavarian National Forest, and the Naturpark Schwabisch-Frankischer Wald—the Swiss Franconia Forest."

"What do you mean, 'unnaturally heavy'?"

"Between 1970 and 1990 there were ten to twelve cases each year in these areas. In 1991 it went up to seventeen, then back down to twelve in '92 and '93. Both sets of figures are very similar."

"That *sounds* high. Is it . . ."

"Before 1970 the figures had been more like one to two cases a year. And Frau Hogel checked these figures against the same years in Munich. In the sixties, it was one to two cases annually. In the seventies three to five, then four to eight in the eighties, four to ten in the nineties. Not the same kind of jump in percentage at all."

"Hmmm . . ."

"Does something ring a bell?" Übergrau asked, his boyish face frightfully dire.

"If it does, I'll be able to hear it loud and clear," Gabriel mused worriedly. "I'm leavin' this afternoon for the Bavarian National Forest."

He had a hard time extricating himself from the office after that.

Von Aigner had given Grossberg's name to von Zell. Why? What possible interest could von Zell have in someone like Grossberg? What interest did von Aigner have in him, for that matter?

There was no point in going back to Grossberg's office. There was nothing more to be learned there. *The police have taken all of Herr Grossberg's papers.*

He sat on a bench in the Marienplatz to watch the tourists snap photographs and to consider his strategy. The golden statue of Mary gazed down benevolently at the square that bore her name and at the pensive American who sat there. Gabriel stared at the statue, really noticing it for the first time. *Marienplatz. Mary.* So that was where the name came from. It was odd the way she seemed to be gazing right at him—surely an illusion.

And while staring at her, trying to decipher it, he realized what he had to do.

Leber looked up with surprise as Gabriel entered his office.

"The American P.I.," he said dryly. "Come in."

"Hey, Kriminalkommisar Leber. Phew! That's a mouthful. Sure I can't call you K.K.L. for short? No, too hard to remember. How 'bout K.K.K. to make it—"

"Sit down!" Leber scowled.

Gabriel sat obediently. "Anythin' new on the case?"

"Nothing for *your* ears. If that's all you came in for—"

"Not quite." Gabriel slouched down in his chair in a most irritating display of relaxation. "I was speakin' with Grossberg's secretary the other day? Nice girl."

Leber's scowl became almost comic.

"She mentioned somethin' about you guys takin' his papers?"

"So?"

"So why'd you take his stuff if Grossberg was a random victim?"

"Standard procedure. As long as this case is open, I'm going by the book." Leber accented this point by jabbing his finger at the desktop.

"Find anything?"

"No one's looked yet. One of the younger men will do it. As you say, Grossberg was a random victim."

"Did I say that?"

Gabriel looked pointedly at the *kommissar* and drummed his fingers on his leg.

Leber's beady eyes grew suspicious. "What do you mean?"

"Maybe he was, maybe he wasn't. You could let me take a look at those papers. I could tell you for sure then."

"*Tchhhh!*" Leber expelled from between clenched teeth. "Never."

"Why not? If he's a random victim like you say, there's no reason why I shouldn't look at his papers. And if he's not a random victim, you might get an important clue."

"This is the personal property of a German citizen, Mr. Knight! As long as his things are in my hands, I am responsible for his privacy!"

Gabriel raised a sardonic brow. "Um, he's *dead*. Remember?"

"He still is protected by the law! Why don't you tell me what you want to know?"

Gabriel pursed his lips and shook his head. "Can't.

I'm not sure what I'm lookin' for, but I'll know when I see it."

Leber grunted derisively. "I don't have time to talk nonsense."

"If I can prove to you that I know somethin'," Gabriel said slyly, "that Grossberg *wasn't* just a random victim, will you let me look at his papers?"

Leber's eyes narrowed into slits. He studied the American, a sneer pulling his fleshy lips. "I'm listening."

"Good. Keep it up."

Gabriel pulled the tape recorder from his pocket and pressed Play.

"But . . . the police must know that our wolves are not responsible. There are tests they can run . . . on the bodies."

"So? Your escaped wolves aren't killers. What's the problem?"

Gabriel stopped the tape. Leber sat up, his mouth quivering around a word like a twelve-year-old pursing for a kiss. "Was . . . was that Doktor Klingmann from the zoo?"

Gabriel shrugged. "Could be."

"Yes? And who was the other one?"

"Just a minute. There's more."

Gabriel fast-forwarded the tape. He'd marked the spot carefully earlier.

"I was wondering . . . Do you know anything about Grossberg's death?"

"Why should I?" came the voice that had earlier spoken to Klingmann.

"It's just . . . I gave you his name . . ."

Gabriel stopped the tape. He slipped the recorder back into his pocket.

Leber's skin was doing its imitation of a plum. "Who . . . who was *that*?"

Gabriel smiled helpfully. "The papers first, please."

He knew that Leber could simply confiscate the tape, even lock him up. And Leber certainly seemed to be considering it. But in the end he did what Gabriel thought he would. He picked up his phone.

"Stätter. Bringen Sie Grossbergs Papiere herein."

While they waited, Leber glared at Gabriel in what was presumably an intimidating manner. A heavyset plainclothesman brought in a box and left it on Leber's desk.

"I'm going out for some coffee. It usually takes me about five minutes. You'd better have something when I get back, Knight, or I'll—"

"Right," Gabriel preempted.

"I'll teach you more about German law enforcement than you ever cared to know!" Leber seemed to feel better for having gotten it out. He left the room, closing the door behind him.

Gabriel was up and digging through the papers before the sound faded.

"Please, please, please, please, please . . ." he muttered.

He *wasn't* sure what he was looking for. Anything on von Aigner, he guessed, particularly anything that explained what it was Grossberg did for the man. It had cost him a great deal, these five minutes, and it was a bad risk. He had to hope that Klingmann took off for the hunting trip before Leber and his men descended at the zoo, or it was all over.

He uncovered a large black spiral ledger. Gabriel flipped through it. Under V, he found von Aigner's name and a list of figures.

2-3-93	1 exotische	4,000
3-1-93	erhalten (4000)	
7-10-94	1 exotische	4,000
8-1-94	erhalten (4000)	
1-6-95	1 exotische	4,000
2-25-95	erhalten (4000)	

The dates, about every six months, marched back to 1985. What did *erhalten* and *exotische* mean? Was *exotische* "exotic"? It surely couldn't be furs. Who would buy furs so regularly? Exotic dancers, maybe?

But there was one clue. Right next to the first entry, back in 1985, was the word, in parentheses, "Dorn." Gabriel, on instinct, turned back to the D section of the ledger. Yes! There was an entry for Dorn. He flipped back and forth—the dates corresponded closely with the dates listed under von Aigner—they were a day at most apart. And the amounts given under Dorn were much lower and in parentheses.

```
2-2-93     1 exotische (2,000)
10-30-94   bezahlt 2000
7-9-94     1 exotische (2,000)
1-5-95     1 exotische (2,000)
```

Gabriel suddenly realized what he was looking at— debits and credits. Dorn had *sold* something to Grossberg—*exotische*—and von Aigner *bought* it for double the cost. And it wasn't cheap—Grossberg had paid 2,000 DM for whatever it was and sold it to von Aigner again for 4,000.

What was Dorn selling?

There was a sound at the door. Leber called loudly, "I'm going back into my office now. In a minute I'm going back in there."

Gabriel ripped the Dorn page from the ledger and stuffed it in a pocket. The door opened.

"Hey," Gabriel said breathlessly. He returned to his chair and sat down.

Leber put the box on the floor. His chair, which was on wheels, groaned as he planted his bulk.

"Tell me," Leber commanded.

"Sure. Herr Doktor Klingmann from the zoo?"

"Yes?"

"He belongs to this club, right? And the guy who was askin' about Grossberg? He's in that club too.

Ditto the third guy, the one with the personality of a pit bull?"

"Go on," Leber said, his face softening with interest.

"And the club itself is only a few blocks from where Grossberg was killed. Coincidence? I don't think so."

"So maybe Grossberg *wasn't* a random victim," Leber said, stroking his chin craftily.

"Uh, right," Gabriel said.

Leber's eyes narrowed as some major parade marched across his cerebral cortex. "I don't understand this. But I intend to. You don't suppose . . ."

"What?"

Leber leaned forward awkwardly over his stomach, studying Gabriel with an anticipatory expression reminiscent of a kid presenting his report card. "See, I have a little theory. Maybe the killer is some kind of pet someone made. *Maybe* someone like Klingmann, I'm thinking, now that you tell me this. He had access to the wolves."

"You mean . . . someone *bred* an animal? From a wolf and a . . . a dog, maybe?"

"It's possible," Leber said, working hard to suppress his delight.

"And if it *is* a pet, that would explain why you haven't caught it yet. Maybe someone's hiding it indoors. Someone like Klingmann."

Leber nodded and beamed proudly.

"Well, it's a theory," Gabriel said in a bored voice. He stood up.

Leber's face clouded. "Ah-*ah*! I want *names*, Mr. Knight. The names of the men. The name of the club. And I want that tape."

Gabriel withdrew a blank mini tape from his pocket and tossed it on the desk. "The guy who knew Grossberg is named, uh, *Franz*."

"Franz what?"

"That's the last name. And the other guy, the pit bull?, is *Überlay*. And the club is called the *Friendly Wanderer*."

Leber wrote the information down with great care. "*Gut.* As of now, I want you to disappear. We'll take care of everything. You understand?"

Gabriel tried to look humble. "Yes, Kriminal-komissar."

Sucker.

He used a pay phone to call the number from the ledger page. A gruff male voice answered. "Hallo?"

"May I speak with Herr Dorn, please?"

"Speaking."

"Hi. My name is Smith. I'm an American associate of Grossberg's? Are you aware that Herr Grossberg has . . . passed on?"

"Dead? *Ja,* someone called yesterday. Bastard. He fucking owed me money. Now who's going to pay me, huh?"

The man had obviously learned his English from a colorful personality.

"As it happens, I'll be taking over Grossberg's business personally."

"Ha! That's funny. Who would want Grossberg's business? Being dead's the best thing that ever happened for him."

"I have my reasons."

Dorn considered this for a bit. "So you gonna pay me, then?" He sounded gruff, like he didn't dare get his hopes up.

"From Grossberg's ledger, I see he owed you 14,000 marks."

"That's right."

"If we decide to do business together, I'd be happy to pay you. Could I come by and see your operation?"

There was a suspicious silence. "You're not the police, are you?"

"No, not the police," Gabriel said with a laugh. He hoped he sounded believable.

"All right, then. But you'd better not be fucking lying."

Dorn gave directions. He operated out of a farm-house with a large barn near Giesing.

Gabriel hung up and checked the map. It was about a thirty-minute drive to the south. If he hurried, he could make it there and back before the trip that afternoon.

The barn was vast. More unusually for this area, it was in need of a paint job; its gray paint was folding back to reveal only slightly less gray wood beneath. The farmhouse was in no better shape—it looked like the residence of what was called poor white trash where Gabriel came from. But the place was *private*. Gabriel had driven down a dirt road for five minutes before he'd reached the buildings. There wasn't a neighbor in sight.

Dorn answered the knock on the barn door. "Come in, Mr. Smith."

Gabriel had worked on his "business guy" routine on his way over, but one look at Dorn told him he needn't have bothered. Whatever kind of businessman Dorn was, he wasn't the sort that did power lunches. He was short and swarthy and pungent with cigarettes and a rank smell that Gabriel initially took for body odor. He wore a dirty suede coat and work boots, and he refused to meet Gabriel's eyes.

Dorn led Gabriel into the barn, latching and barring the door firmly behind them. The interior was a real shocker. The entire place had been gutted and remod-eled into a kennel. White partitions formed aisles, and there were rows of stainless steel cages stacked two and three high. Bright fluorescent lights hung on wires from the old rafters, and the floor had been covered in concrete, each aisle tilting down to a large central drain.

The smell he'd sensed on Dorn became ever more pungent as Gabriel progressed inside. Jungle sounds assaulted his ears. It was a kind of Wild Kingdom Sense-O-Rama. The inhabitants of the cages came into view: monkeys, a cheetah, orangutan, and glimpses of cats and other exotic creatures down farther aisles.

It hit him like a sucker punch from his left brain. The heads in the basement of the hunt club, von Zell saying they didn't hunt abroad, the notations in the ledger . . .

Von Aigner wasn't buying furs, he was buying the whole enchilada. "Exotics," as in exotic animals. A little variety for the true sportsman, yes indeedy do.

"You have to ignore the smell," Dorn said. "It's these stinking animals. No matter how much I spray them down, they smell!"

"Some creatures are like that," Gabriel said, barely holding his disgust for the man and his business in check.

Dorn smiled in what was meant to be an engaging way, but his stained teeth and his evasive eyes ruined the effect. "You know, I wouldn't have agreed to meet you. You can never be too fucking careful. But Grossberg, he mentioned you to me."

"He did?"

"*Ja.* I called him just a couple of weeks ago, about the fucking money. I said to him, 'Where's my fucking money?', and he said that he was getting a new business partner and would soon be able to pay me everything. I guess I should have believed him, huh?"

Gabriel stared at Dorn, unable to comprehend what any of that meant. "Uh, yeah."

"So, I'd be interested in hearing your business plan, Mr. Smith."

Gabriel tried to look financially viable. "Oh, I'll probably be needin' the same kind of services as Grossberg."

Dorn twisted his mouth in a confident smirk. "Furs? I have fucking good prices for the coats. If you want me to clean it, it's two hundred fifty marks extra. Or I have a room in back if you want to do it yourself. If you want the meat, the price depends on the species. Tiger, for example, you pay a lot more for the body. I can get fucking good prices for tiger penis."

"I bet."

"I can get anything you want. Cats, Grossberg mostly got. What kind of goods are you interested in?"

This wasn't going exactly the way Gabriel had expected. Could he be wrong about von Aigner? "Actually, I'm more interested in the *other* services you did for Grossberg," he hedged.

Dorn frowned. "You mean the export? *Ne,* what a fucking hassle. I told Grossberg it was my first and last, and I fucking meant it."

"Export?"

"*Ja.* It took me forever to find someone to take those two. All my channels run the other way, you know? Would maybe be cheaper just to kill them, I thought, but I got a good price in the end."

Gabriel's mouth was suddenly dry. "Those two what?"

"Wolves." Dorn tossed it away like it was nothing. He took a few steps forward and spat into a drain. A greenish slime oozed over the iron grating.

Gabriel looked away for a moment to hide his reaction. When he looked back, his face was blank. "Huh. Um . . . where'd the wolves end up?"

"Taiwan. A zoo, the buyer said, but I don't believe it. A restaurant is more like it. Those people, they eat anything."

Gabriel ignored this show of liberal-mindedness, his mind still stuck on simple comprehension. "There were *two* wolves, right? Gray? A male and female?"

"*Ja*! I already said, I'm not doing any more fucking exports."

"Right," Gabriel said, trying to calm his hammering heart. "I was actually more interested in the possibility of gettin' animals live—whole. You did that for Grossberg too, didn't you?"

Dorn shrugged and prodded a booted toe at the

gunk still hanging on the drain. "It's all the same to me. Live. Dead. Skinned. Meat. You have to bring your own cage. I don't deliver."

Something seemed to cross Dorn's mind, for he looked over at Gabriel slyly. "Is that what you're into, Mr. Smith? Hunting? *Breeding* maybe?" He leered.

"Huntin'. That's it." Gabriel restrained himself from throttling the guy.

"Hunting, huh? I can pick out some mean ones for ya. Or weak ones. Whatever you want. Panthers are good. I got a black panther right now."

"Really? That's sounds promisin'." Gabriel smiled. "Say, where'd you keep those two wolves anyway?"

"Why are you so fucking interested in those wolves?"

Good question. Gabriel's writer's brain searched for the appropriate line of dialogue while he pretended to be fighting a sneeze.

"Ah!"—sniff—"Well, the guy who sold the wolves to Grossberg? He's been claimin' Grossberg damaged 'em when he picked them up. He's threatenin' to sue."

"They looked all right to me."

"Is that so? No wounds or anythin'?"

Dorn looked insulted. "Not a fucking mark on 'em."

"Good! That's good news. Would you mind if I, uh, checked the cage they were in? See if I can spot any bloodstains or . . . anything?"

Dorn's eyes shifted from Gabriel to the wall as he considered it. Then he began to slouch down the aisle.

"You're fucking lucky I didn't clean the cage. Normally I clean 'em right out, but I didn't need it. I have a lot of capacity here, you know. Sometimes I get in a couple hundred monkeys at a time. This time of year is always slow."

"Yeah. It's a great setup you've got here."

Dorn stopped at a cage. He unlocked it and stepped back.

"Thanks," Gabriel said, smiling at him. "This might take a minute."

Dorn grunted. He still looked leery, but after all, there was nothing in the cage but straw and wolf scat. "I'll be over there," he said. He walked down the aisle and disappeared.

The cage was only four foot tall by five foot wide. Gabriel had to stoop to get in it. Fortunately, the droppings in the cage had dried up long ago. The straw and the scat crunched under his boot.

What the hell was he looking for anyway?

He toed around in the straw, his face contorted in a pained expression. This was hardly fun, but if he could find a bit of wolf hair it would be worth it. He could compare it to what he'd gotten at the zoo—confirm what he already knew. He found some strands over by the food dish. They were gray with white tips, just like the ones from Margarite. He felt a flush of excitement. This was turning out to be a far more productive line of inquiry than he'd ever imagined. The zoo wolves had come through here! How or why was another matter.

He picked up the hairs carefully and put them in his pocket.

He was about to climb out when a glint caught his eyes. There was something silvery peeking out from under the straw near the bars. It was probably just a metal drain, but Gabriel's curiosity got the better of him. He pushed the straw back with his foot.

And stared. Lying on the floor under the straw was an ID tag. He glanced in the direction of the aisle, but Dorn was nowhere in sight. He grabbed the tag, held it into the light.

Parsival   Tierpark Hellabrunn

Gabriel let out a low moan of exhilaration. He stuffed the tag into his jean pocket, thinking that he needn't bother with the hair after all. There was no doubt now. He shifted through the straw some more, searching for the other tag. It wasn't there.

"Mr. Smith?" Dorn was standing outside the cage, shifting from foot to foot and staring at the cage door.

Gabriel climbed out.

"Nope. No blood. Great. I can blow this guy off, then."

Dorn didn't look at him. "Did you want to see that panther? It's a nice fucking panther."

"Sure," Gabriel said, figuring the priority at this point was to get out alive. Humoring Dorn seemed wise.

As Gabriel left, he shook the man's hand and promised to send him a check for fourteen thousand marks. He hoped Dorn ran to the mailbox every day for a month.

They took von Glower's Land Rover to the lodge. Hennemann was Gabriel's closest companion in the backseat. The politician—who was as sober as Gabriel had ever seen him—rambled monotonously the entire way. He told Gabriel that the lodge itself had fifty acres, and it abutted national parkland on three sides. The property had belonged to the Royal Bavarian Hunting Lodge for two hundred years. This lodge, and the club's other lodge in Alfdorf.

And where is Alfdorf? Gabriel asked politely.

In the Swäbisch-Frankischer Wald, Hennemann answered.

The Swiss Franconia Forest. Gabriel looked out the window at the passing trees and said nothing.

They drove through forest for ten minutes before reaching the property. The private road was gravel but in pristine condition. They passed the gate and made their way through dense wilderness on either side until finally, topping a rise, the lodge itself came into view.

It was undeniably beautiful in an epic sort of way— enormous and primitive, like a log cabin with a Mt.

Olympus address. Despite its rustic charm it had an ominous air that was almost certainly lent by the darkness. The day was overcast, and the lodge and its outbuildings were completely enshadowed by trees. Its facade was dark anyway; logs still coated with bark formed the walls, the roof was black as pitch, and the porch was pine stained some dark color.

"*Voilà* gentlemen," von Glower announced as he pulled the car to a stop.

"Yee-haw," Preiss said, giving Gabriel a sly look. Von Aigner snorted derisively. Gabriel pretended he didn't get it.

He felt amazingly stupid unloading his beat-up duffel bag. Who'd have guessed he'd be going on a camping trip with guys who shopped Ralph Lauren?

"Come on, I'll show you up to your room," von Glower offered.

"Hope I'm not puttin' anybody out."

"No! There are more rooms than we've used for years. I called ahead and had the maid prepare an extra."

Inside the foyer, Gabriel stared up at an enormous chandelier made entirely of antlers. A fireplace the size of a small bedroom—roasting spit included—dominated the great room. Indian blankets adorned the pine walls. A large staircase split the room in two. Gabriel slowly followed the others as they ascended.

Von Zell had driven his own convertible, and as the group entered the upstairs hallway, Gabriel caught a glimpse of him swinging shut his bedroom door most unwelcomingly. Gabriel made a mental note of what room he was in. It would be a good place to avoid.

Von Glower opened a door just down from von Zell's. "I hope you'll be comfortable. It's not the Ritz, but it's got character."

"It certainly does."

"There're extra blankets in the *shrank* if you need them. And there's plenty of hot water, so take as long a shower as you like."

"It's great. When, uh, when . . ."

Von Glower looked amused. "We go hunting tomorrow morning. This time of year it's mostly deer."

"Yee-haw," Gabriel said dryly.

Von Glower laughed. "I've got some things to catch up on, but feel free to look around. If you take a walk in the woods, it might help you get your bearings for tomorrow."

"I will. Thanks."

Somehow it felt like he should change. But since he had nothing with him but more jeans and T-shirts, there weren't a lot of options. He wandered downstairs instead and saw that Hennemann and the bar had already found each other.

"Herr Hennemann."

"Guten Abend."

"Oh, it's not that time yet."

"Close enough." Hennemann raised his beer glass in a toast.

Gabriel walked over and sat down nonchalantly. He wanted to look around, but he'd yet to have a shot at Hennemann alone (the cramped car hardly qualified), and there were things he still needed to know.

"I've heard that you're quite the man to know," he began with a smile.

"Uh?"

"Politics. You're *the man*."

"Ah! Well, I'm not *the man* I used to be," Hennemann joked. There was a bitter undertone to his quip.

Gabriel flattered him. "That's not what I hear!" Hennemann looked pleased, but he didn't answer. "So! A politician, a lawyer, a banker . . . It's about all the friends a guy could want, am I right?" Gabriel nudged the older man with a knowing elbow. Hennemann shot him a glance that said he was being incredibly naïve.

"Have you ever worked with Preiss, for example?"

Gabriel continued. "I hear he's quite a hot shot in court."

Hennemann grimaced. "If you need a lawyer, Herr Knight, Preiss is the last person I'd recommend." Hennemann had lowered his voice, and he glanced nervously toward the stairs.

"How so?"

"You met the man. Would you want to be alone in a room with him for an hour?"

Gabriel considered it. "Not especially."

Hennemann's red-shot eyes glanced at Gabriel balefully. "He's a *goat.* No respect for normal human decency. I tell you, society has no interest in a man like that. It's a good thing he doesn't need the money because no one will hire him." He looked at Gabriel's empty hands. "Want a beer?"

"Not just now, thanks. But . . . isn't that what the club philosophy is all about—gettin' in touch with one's primal instincts? Bein' natural?"

Hennemann made a face. "Sure. But do you think animals are like this? Rutting every ten seconds? Even apes have mating seasons, Herr Knight."

Yeah? They also don't lap up alcohol by the gallon at the ol' watering hole.

"Well, what about von Aigner? You guys hang, right?"

"*Ja.* Von Aigner's a good man. Klingmann too I like. He comes by the Donisl and drinks with me."

"Really? You two are so different. What do ya find to talk about?"

"Oh, the club philosophy, mostly. Herr Doktor is very taken with it."

"Did, uh, did you sponsor Klingmann, then?" Gabriel asked with forced casualness.

"Me? No! It was von Zell." Hennemann took a chug of beer and smacked his lips noisily.

"*Von Zell* sponsored Klingmann?" Gabriel repeated blankly.

Hennemann nodded and burped quietly.

"See, I never would have thought that. They don't seem to get along too well."

Hennemann tilted his head to consider it. "No, I suppose not too well lately. It was better at first, though never . . . You know, I always found it strange myself. Von Zell is not the *friendliest* person. *Ach!* Who knows? Maybe he only wanted to shake things up."

"Could be," Gabriel said thoughtfully.

Hennemann finished his beer and immediately poured himself another. "Are you ready now, Herr Knight?" He had a painfully hopeful expression.

Gabriel got up. "Actually, I was gonna take a walk."

Hennemann's face betrayed his opinion of such an activity. But he raised his glass and toasted a *bon voyage*.

The woods were chilly. There was still plenty of daylight left, but the shadows of the trees made it feel like twilight and thus gave the illusion that darkness was hanging just above, like a blanket about to descend on a bed. It seeded an anxiety that night would sneak up and catch the happy wanderer far from home. In the dark.

Or perhaps it was just that Gabriel was no Daniel Boone. Nature to him was the sprawling bougainvillea that leapt from Southern balconies in May or the clematis that draped his grandmother's porch with intolerable perfume. It meant going barefoot on the asphalt on Bourbon Street in the sweet reprieve between chill and molten tar. *Pine needles*—that was another story altogether.

But there were paths through the woods, clear, soft paths of dirt so fine it looked like flour dusted from a sieve. Even a city boy could follow a path like that (though they might not be prepared for what they encountered upon it).

The path that began across the lawn from the front

porch went directly south. Fifteen minutes out, it intersected with a path going east-west, and Gabriel turned left, hoping that he would find a circular route back to the lodge.

The walk was quite bizarre. Perhaps it was the increased supply of sharp, thick oxygen working like a drug on his smog-thickened brain, but there was a strange quality to the woods unlike anything he could recall having experienced before. It was the trees, marching away forever as one's eye cut through the woods. It was like some Escher illusion, trunk upon trunk upon trunk until your depth perception admitted defeat.

But it was precisely this quality—this ability to peer straight through into an endless horizon of trees that, he realized, was odd. Not being a forest person, it took time to realize this and more time to realize the cause. The forest floor was amazingly clean—not thick with dead brush and twigs and brambles as one might expect—and the trees, most of them, had no limbs whatsoever until twenty feet or more up, allowing the eye to continue on and on, unhalted by walls of green boughs and bushes. And with the late afternoon sunlight filtering through the trees in visible beams . . . It was like something from a storybook, these woods, like something from *Little Red Riding Hood*.

He walked on, speeding up into a trot, looking out for another north-south path that would take him back to the lodge. How far had he come? Forty minutes at least—surely there was a quicker way back to the lodge than turning around.

He began to get an uneasy sensation of being watched, a sensation that reminded him of the one and only time he'd gone snorkeling. There, in the silent water, with the sense of sound completely removed, he'd felt peculiarly vulnerable, like a deaf person standing on a road. His insubordinate imagination had called up scenes from *Jaws*, and he'd spun around to look, certain that something unbearable and deadly was headed his way, the ocean's equivalent of a Mack truck.

His writer's imagination was like an overbuilt muscle, and as any serious bodybuilder who's ever tried to buy a pair of pants could tell you—it could be a damned nuisance.

It was being one right now.

He was jogging, something his out-of-shape lungs could not keep up for long. He slipped a cold hand inside his shirt and pulled out the talisman, hanging it outside his jacket, where it bounced with each step. The woods were thickening on his right, and the ground was beginning to undulate. He ran down into a ditch and nearly slipped on some orange-colored mud. His thighs ached as his feet pushed him up the rise on the other side.

And then, when he was beginning to think about turning around, he ran into a north-south path. Ten minutes later, he was on the front porch.

"Did you have a nice walk?" Hennemann asked as Gabriel came in the door. His speech was already taking on that overcompensated elucidation.

"Wunderbar," Gabriel choked. He turned his back to Hennemann to remove his coat, tucking his talisman into his shirt as he did so. His breath was coming in embarrassingly ragged gasps.

"Von Aigner was just down. He said if you came in, I was to invite you to join him in his room."

Gabriel tried not to show his surprise. "What room would that be?"

"Across the hall from your room, Herr Knight. You want a beer now?"

"I guess I do."

Gabriel took his stein and climbed the stairs, still trying to slow his breathing and warm the ice water running in his veins. There had been nothing in the woods, only his own febrile juvenility, just as there had been nothing at the Huber farm the other night. He rapped lightly on von Aigner's door.

"Kommen Sie!"

Gabriel was perplexed to see that the bedroom was empty, but then he heard the sounds of splashing. "Von Aigner?"

"In here," came a voice from the bathroom.

"Sorry. I'll come back."

"No need. Make the door more open."

Gabriel pushed on the bathroom door. Von Aigner was sitting in a tub full of hot water. On a chair next to him were a glass of beer, a plate of cold cuts and cheeses, and a basket of rolls. He was chewing busily, one meat-wrapped roll in his hand.

"You want?" he asked Gabriel, motioning to the plate.

"No, thanks." Gabriel raised his stein as though in explanation.

"Sit on the bed." Von Aigner pointed toward said object, which was visible through the doorway. Gabriel complied.

"Von Zell doesn't like you," von Aigner said, chasing this revelation with a loud and liquid belch.

"He doesn't? I'm hurt."

Von Aigner grunted. "You joke. I would be careful if I were you. Tomorrow. On the hunt."

Von Aigner put down his roll and clenched his meaty hands into fists, then made the unmistakable mimicry—one arm stretched—of a rifle being pointed. *Ka-blam.*

"You're not suggestin' . . ."

Von Aigner picked up his roll and took a large bite, as though he'd missed it. He shook his head, crumbs making an escape from his beard to the water below.

"A friendly warning," he said with his mouth full. "Look out for your back."

"You think von Zell is capable of murder?"

"He is capable of anything."

Gabriel took a drink of his beer, annoyed by the

stupid lid that bumped his nose. Von Aigner pieced together a second sandwich.

"Are you? Police?" von Aigner asked carefully.

"No."

The huge man—his stomach mounding out of the bath water like Nessy on Loch Ness—grunted. "That's good."

"But I *was* wonderin' . . ."

"What?"

"I . . . well, this is embarrassin', but I kinda overheard you and von Zell at the club. You mentioned that you'd given von Zell Grossberg's name?"

Von Aigner wiped greasy fingers on his chest and stared at Gabriel, his sandwich held in one hand like an unfinished thought. "What big ears you have."

Gabriel smiled self-deprecatingly. "I don't blame you for not admittin' it to me earlier. That you knew Grossberg, I mean. I've run into him before, usually in connection with certain *exotics*."

Von Aigner's eyes narrowed. "You *are* police, then."

There was an anger behind his voice that was quite eerie. Gabriel had a brief vision of the bulk that was von Aigner launching itself from the tub and laying into him. Hell, just laying *on* him would be fatal.

"Not at all," Gabriel said calmly. "Just a hunter. Like I said."

Von Aigner considered this as he took another bite and chewed. "Grossberg got exotics for you also?"

"Not for me directly, no."

Von Aigner said nothing, his brow knit in thought.

"Why did von Zell want the name of your exotics contact? Do you know?"

Von Aigner licked his fingers and ate the last bite of roll with focused precision. "I thought he would maybe leave to make his own club, or maybe hunt alone. I would cry no tears to see him go." He picked up a loose piece of cheese. "You are more the international hunter than you look like, Herr Knight. If you hunt exotics."

"Oh, I've hunted exotics, all right. Speaking of which, have you ever heard of the Black Wolf?"

Von Aigner belched in a sustained note. "*Ne.* We've never hunted wolves."

"Oh."

"Though we could if we wanted to, and we would not need Grossberg to do it."

Gabriel studied von Aigner leerily. "What do you mean?"

"They're all around here," von Aigner said, waving a hand toward the window.

"What?"

"*Wolves,*" von Aigner said loudly and with much tongue, as though Gabriel were hard of hearing.

Gabriel felt his heart trip in his chest. "You must be mistaken. Wolves are extinct in Germany."

Von Aigner laughed. "Not here. I hear them at night myself all the time. *Arrrooooooo!*" He stuffed a piece of *Liebercase* in his mouth and chewed openly, grayish matter visible on his tongue. "Like to make your blood go cold. Take my advice—don't go out there at night. I never do."

Von Aigner went to wash down his mouthful and found the stein empty. He looked extremely put out.

Gabriel headed straight for the room he'd seen Klingmann occupy. He'd learned a lot in one day and, in a word, he was tired of mucking about. He thought he now held the cards he needed to pin the lying sack of *scheiße* to the wall, and he was more than worked up enough to do it.

Gabriel found the good doctor lying on his bed, reading a scholarly journal. Klingmann did not look pleased to see him. "What is it, Mr. Knight?"

"Oh, just hangin' out. Nice lodge, huh?"

"Very nice. As I would expect."

"Have you been here before?"

"No. I'm sorry, but I would like to read."

"Oh, I don't mind."

Gabriel went over to the window. Outside, shadows were stretching across the lawn as if in a race to see who could reach the woods first. Gabriel stuck a hand in a pocket and brought something out. He juggled it from hand to hand, leaning against the glass.

"Kinda surprised me that you were even in this club. Seems like huntin' is an odd pastime for a zoologist."

"Animal behaviorist," Klingmann said stiffly. He looked a little guilty nonetheless.

"Wouldn't you say?" Gabriel probed, turning brooding eyes toward the bed.

Klingmann put down his journal in exasperation. "There are *reasons*, Mr. Knight. The point is not to provide a carcass for the family table, after all!"

"You're tryin' to get back to your primitive nature, then?"

"Yes," Klingmann said, surprised. His brow furrowed in irritation. "What *is* that you're playing with?"

"What, this?" Gabriel tossed the object to Klingmann, who looked all the more irritated as it went flying through the air. He caught it with an annoyed sigh and looked at it.

In an instant his demeanor metamorphosed. His face lost its arrogance in a horizontal swoop, like someone erasing a blackboard. He seemed to have trouble catching his breath.

"Doc?" Gabriel said.

"Where did you get this?" Klingmann managed. He looked damn scared.

Gabriel strolled over and sat on the edge of the bed. "In the kennel of a black-market animal dealer."

"I don't understand."

"The wolves were shipped out. *Adios, amigos.* Deported."

Klingmann met his eyes reluctantly. "Where to?"

"Taiwan."

"Oh."

For a moment Klingmann said nothing; he just fingered the tag.

"I don't understand," he said again.

"Let me explain it," Gabriel said malignantly. "You wanted to get into the club. Von Zell offered to sponsor you for a small favor. He wanted two wolves. You helped him get them out of the zoo. Have I got all that right?"

Klingmann's face was suffused with humiliation. Gabriel felt a twinge of satisfaction at the sight. "If this information gets out, my career will be finished."

Gabriel leaned in, his eyes relentless. "Then you'd better start talkin'."

"I don't know anything about the killings!" Klingmann burst out. "I swear! I was *shocked* when I read about the first one in the paper! I went to von Zell. He said it was a fluke, a coincidence! The wolves were fine, the wolves were under control, it couldn't be *my* wolves."

Gabriel looked at the worm disdainfully. "It *wasn't* your wolves."

Klingmann studied him searchingly, as though trying to gauge the truth of this. Relief flooded his face. "Are you certain? Thank God! I didn't think so, but . . . Thank God!"

"It wasn't them." Gabriel plucked the tag from Klingmann's fingers. "How'd you get them out of the zoo anyway?"

"Von Zell and some other man came late one night with a truck. I let them in the service entrance. I . . . I had drugged two of the wolves earlier. It was simple enough to pick them up and put them on the truck. The night boy, he was lazy. It took him forever to do the rounds."

"Did von Zell tell you why he wanted the wolves?"

Klingmann lowered his eyes, the burn creeping across his forehead. "He said he wanted to study them, that he had a kennel prepared. He said he admired them, as I do."

He looked up, his eyes desperate. "I would never do such a thing, but von Zell, he came to one of my lectures months ago. He—he *courted* me, telling me about the club, the philosophy, the prestige. So many of the ideas fit my own feelings. I *had* to get in. Don't you see?"

Gabriel rose, not about to assuage Klingmann's guilt. "Thanks for the talk."

"Herr Knight, can I . . . can I please keep the tag?"

Gabriel pretended to consider it. "Nope. Be seein' ya, Doc."

And he left Klingmann sitting there, journal forgotten.

He was shutting Klingmann's door when he heard a soft noise behind him. He turned to see von Zell locking the door to his room. Gabriel quickly stepped into the middle of the hall and pretended he'd been passing through. Being caught coming out of Klingmann's room was probably not a good idea. He didn't feel like taking any of von Zell's abuse at the moment.

Von Zell turned slowly, his head cocked to one side.

"Hey, Baron von Zell."

Incomprehensibly, von Zell began to make oinking noises. He walked slowly toward Gabriel, raking air in through his nostrils like fingernails on a chalkboard: *snort, snort, snort, snort, snort.*

Gabriel backed away.

"This little piggy went to London," von Zell said, a rapt look on his face.

"That's nice. I—"

"*This* little piggy went to Rome. *Snort, snort.*"

Gabriel's back hit the wall. He stared at von Zell and thought, *Okay. I get it. He's absolutely mad. You can end the demonstration now.*

"And *this* little piggy . . ." Von Zell stepped into Gabriel's face and jabbed a finger at his chest, "went *wee! wee! wee!* all the way home to America!"

Von Zell began to laugh uproariously. Gabriel stood there, at a loss as to how to proceed. It occurred to him that escape was a good idea. He tried to push his way along the wall. He took one step, and von Zell stopped laughing abruptly and grabbed his shirt with two hands, yanking him back.

"No, I've changed my mind. You're not like a pig at all, are you, *Herr Knight*?"

"No?"

"No. You're more like a *cat*. That's what you remind me of: a sneaking, slinking, sly little *cat*."

Von Zell's face was only inches away from Gabriel's, and his eyes were so intense, Gabriel swore he could feel the heat of their gaze.

"I'm not really—"

"And I *hate* cats," von Zell interrupted. "I *loathe* them."

"Yeah. I get the point. Excuse me." Gabriel tried to sound both bored and firm.

"No, we're not done here. I have one more thing to share with you, Herr Knight, and that's a note about *curiosity*. You know what they say about the *cat* and *curiosity*, don't you?"

"Um . . . Something about winning the race?"

It was not the smartest move he'd made all day, but his tongue had a way of spitting things out without notifying his brain. Von Zell flushed and shoved Gabriel back against the wall with incredible force. Gabriel wheezed as the breath was forced from his lungs.

"No! Think again!" Von Zell's anger was barely in check, looming behind his eyes like thunderclouds. "I'm sure you'll remember it if you *try*."

He gave Gabriel one more push, then retreated and walked quickly down the stairs.

When Gabriel was certain von Zell was gone, he tried the door to his room. Locked. He looked around the hall to make sure he was alone, then squatted down to take a closer look—the door was thick; the handle and lock looked formidable. Of course, he could try picking it, but this wasn't exactly a place one could settle down for some serious tinkering.

Anyway, he had a better idea. He knew he was behaving irrationally even as he went into his own room, went to the window, moved aside a chair, and propped back the curtain. He recalled this feeling before, when it had been about Voodoo in New Orleans—that feeling of plummeting ahead no matter the cost, irregardless of personal danger, *defiant*. He was a teenage motorcycle rider going 100 M.P.H. down a country road, or a child whose mother says, "Don't climb on those rocks," and the child turns right around and begins to climb. But was it defiance really? Bravery? Or was it more of a single-mindedness so focused that all obstacles are brushed off the consciousness like a fly off a picnic table?

Back in New Orleans, when he'd felt himself plummeting this way (out of control, really—yes, he was out of control), he could tell himself that it was because it was personal; it was about his nightmares, his love, his family, his destiny.

What the hell was his excuse this time?

He leaned out his window and saw what he'd seen from the outside of the lodge—that the walls were made of rough-hewn logs: rounded, grooved, tractable with bark. Why, it was practically a staircase out there, at least compared to his grandmother's siding, which he'd routinely scaled every Saturday night when he snuck from his room.

Von Zell's window was only fifteen feet away. It was open to let in the air.

The side of the lodge was deep in shadow, lending stealth to his endeavor. But the actual job of getting to von Zell's window was much harder in fact than it had been in his head. The bark fell away beneath his feet, and the crevasses between the logs had a cement-like filling, allowing his desperate fingers only so far inside. When he finally reached the window, he was cursing his bright idea and quivering from the strain.

But he was about to have his revenge.

He crawled over the bottom of the sill and took a moment to catch his breath, looking around. For the bedroom of a psychopath, the room was stupefyingly uneventful. Von Zell's large leather carpetbag was placed in a particular manner to one side of the room's *shrank*, or armoire. The bed was tidy. Gabriel opened the *shrank*. Yes, von Zell had unpacked, and his things were neatly stacked or hung, including a killer pair of black leather riding boots.

Gabriel searched the bed, checking under the pillows and dipping a hand between the mattress and box springs. Nothing. He checked the carpetbag. Empty. He checked the drawers in the nightstands next to the bed. On the left-hand side were a watch, a small alarm cock, and von Zell's black appointment book—the one he'd left in the basement at the club.

Gabriel had already looked at the book once, but he picked it up again. He knew a lot more now than he'd known then, including whose book it was and how suspicious the son of a bitch had turned out to be. He checked the calendar for the past months, but didn't see any mention of picking up wolves, no mention of wolves at all. But then von Zell would hardly jot that down next to his luncheon and dental appointments.

He came to that page again, the one with the names and figures listed.

Preiss—100,000
Aigner—~~1 m.~~ 700,000
Hennemann—30,000

Loan amounts, no doubt. And the von Aigner figure—300,000 marks, could it be? Had von Aigner really paid back such a large amount recently? Or had von Zell given him an incentive to reveal Grossberg's name?

He was about to put the book down when he saw

a tip of a white envelope sticking out of the back pages. He pulled it out. It was addressed to von Zell— no return address. Inside was a single sheet of paper. The short text was written in German, but Gabriel recognized the words *newspaper, wolves, zoo,* and *police.* There was also a figure: 500,000 DM. It was signed Grossberg.

"Son of a bitch," Gabriel said out loud. It was a blackmail letter. Grossberg had known about the deliberate kidnapping of the wolves; he had probably driven the truck. And when he'd seen the killings in the papers, and the blame go to the wolves, he'd decided he needed to be paid for his continued silence about their true whereabouts.

So von Zell was the new "business partner" Grossberg had bragged about to Dorn. It looked like von Zell thought otherwise. *Do we have a motive for Grossberg's murder, ladies and germs? Yes, I believe we do.*

Gabriel put the letter and the book back the way he'd found it. He was about to leave when he decided to check the bathroom. The tub and sink were both spotless. There was nothing in the medicine cabinet. A small travel kit was on the back of the toilet—there was nothing but the usual sundries in it.

As an afterthought, Gabriel pulled up the rug that lay in front of the tub. The white tile floor was clean.

He gave the rug a quick scan, and something caught his eye. It was a small Oriental rug, expensive by the look of it. Perhaps von Zell had brought it from home—a little luxury to make the rustic life all the sweeter. The pattern was a mix of colors, mostly reds and blues.

But there was something out of place. A spot of brownish-orange. Gabriel took it closer to the light and held the section up. Yes. It wasn't yarn, it was a stain of . . . He brushed one nail against it, and a few dust motes puffed up. Dried mud. Dried orangey mud.

Gabriel studied it. It was a spot about three inches

by two, and it was darker in ridges. There was a pattern there. He frowned, trying to discern it. It was hard to picture someone as neat as von Zell wearing muddy boots into the bathroom. Besides, that wasn't a boot print was it?

His imagination supplied an answer; he had a mental flash of von Zell, naked and sweating, crawling in his bedroom window and walking with bare, muddy feet into the bathroom, stepping into the bath.

Yes, he recognized the pattern now—it wasn't a boot print, the ridges were toes. It was a footprint—a bare footprint in orange mud.

Von Zell was sitting in a corner of the great room absorbed—or at least pretending to be—in a hunting magazine. Gabriel thought he went unnoticed as he slipped outside. He was relieved to know von Zell was inside and not, therefore, in the woods, particularly since he had to go back out there.

Now it truly was getting dark. The sunset was happening somewhere in the west, as indicated by the golden glow hanging over the trees. The rest of the sky was turning a nice, solid indigo. He grabbed a lantern and some matches from the barn and a pair of thick gardening gloves while he was at it.

He took the short path still visible in the gathering twilight, back to that dip in the woods, the place where he'd seen the orange mud. When he reached the culvert, he lit the lantern, the better to examine the ground. There was a trickle of water in the bottom of the ditch, perhaps from some underground stream. He followed it back into the woods, his legs spread to either side of the stream, his head bent low. About ten yards back he saw what looked like a shadow near a leaf. He brushed the leaf aside and lowered the lantern.

In the mud was a huge paw print—identical to the one he'd found at the Huber farm.

It was exactly what he'd been looking for, but he'd

unconsciously hoped not to find it. Indeed, he found himself quite unprepared. He heard something rattling and actually swung around before realizing that it was his teeth. He was shaking like a can of paint in a mixer. What was it he'd just been thinking about being recklessly brave and defiant?

He had to talk himself into continuing. It was true, he was in the woods without a weapon and it was nearly dark. Yes, the Beast was here. Somewhere. He even had an idea that it didn't like him very much.

But he did have the talisman. That would do something to protect him. Wouldn't it?

He turned and continued down the culvert, his eyes still searching. He found another print—a partial— near a rock farther down. And then a third. This one was on the bank to the left, as though entering the culvert. He looked up the side, raising the lantern. There was a hill on that side, a good-sized hill, and it was covered with brush. This part of the woods was quite wild and had been allowed to stay that way.

He walked up the bank slowly. He put on the gloves to better push aside the stickers and the brambles that clutched at him. He was looking for some kind of a path here, a path not made by human hands, and there did seem to be an opening, lower down, where the bushes were not as thick.

He pushed his way through and came, after a few minutes, to the side of the hill. There, in what was a small clearing in the brambles, he saw an entrance to a cave.

And he knew he'd found the lair.

The cave entrance was only about four feet tall, so he had to stoop low. It continued at this height for a while, perhaps ten feet. It seemed a lot longer. Then the rock began to slope upward, and the narrow passage opened into a small room.

He was still straightening up when the smell assaulted him—a horrible smell, rank, musty, and unmistakable. It was the smell of carrion—the sickly sweet smell of death.

He clasped his free hand to his nostrils, desperate to get away from the tangible net of it. But he had to breathe. He inhaled through his mouth reluctantly, feeling the odor like Teflon coating his tongue, his throat.

"*God*!" he gasped, wanting desperately to retch, to *turn around*.

Instead, he raised the lantern and scanned the room, wanting to finish so that he needn't come back. There was nothing in this room but rocky outcroppings from floor, wall, and ceiling. But there was another low passageway beyond. He would have to go on.

He fished in a pocket for a handkerchief and didn't find one (not surprising since he never carried the things). He pulled out his T-shirt instead and used the bottom hem of it to cover his nose and mouth. He went into the second passageway.

This time the low channel continued on even longer, twenty feet perhaps. And before it ended he began to hear the sound of a watery drip up ahead.

When the ceiling sloped up again, he stepped into a large cavern. It gave the illusion of vastness, anyway. It was absolutely pitch black in there, and the lantern itself seemed intimidated by the smell, for the flame cowered down. He could see little but the wide outward slant of the walls on either side of him, indicating that they were broadening out to encircle a very large space. And there was that sound, that dripping, which sounded loud and echoed in the stillness.

What else was out there in the uncompromising dark? His sense of repulsion over the smell faded as fear began to make such concerns seem trivial. He scanned the darkness for the glow of eyes, but nothing in the beyond separated itself from the dark. He fought to slow his breathing, telling himself that whatever lived here was currently back at the lodge. He took a few cautious steps forward.

The dirt beneath his feet gave way.

He was slipping, falling. He dropped the lantern and grabbed at the ground under his hand. His right foot disappeared into nothingness, but he managed to catch himself and scoot back on the dirt. The lantern, thankfully, had not gone out. He picked it up and held it out in front of him.

The light shone on the dirt, then black swallowed it up. He was on the edge of some large rift. He crawled on hands and knees closer to the edge, the smell coming in nearly visible waves now. He held the lantern out with one unsteady hand, the other desperately masking his nose. He looked down.

Below him was a deep pit, a hole, at least fifteen feet deep, perhaps much deeper, and easily as wide. At first his mind rebelled against identifying what his lantern danced off down inside this hole, and he only saw jutting, broken edges; rotting, darkened lumps; and scraps of stuff incongruously placed, like the red-checked calico that wavered just inside the reach of his flickering light. Then his eyes settled on a pattern of yellow daisies on white just below him. The fabric was stretched over a rounded mound of black straw, and below the straw were dark holes—gaping and sunken in a . . . Like an image snapping into focus, he saw quite suddenly that he was looking at a face. The gay daisy handkerchief was still atop the dun-colored hair, and the face was decayed and shriveled. And then every form below defined itself in the gloom—every lump and jutting limb, a shoe-clad foot, torn, half-eaten haunches.

The pit was filled with rotting corpses.

"AAAAG!"

It wasn't exactly a scream; it was more a cry of denial. The lantern fell from his hand and landed with a dull wet thud on the daisy-clad child below, then the flame went out. Moaning, he scrambled backward on hands and knees in the absolute darkness. He banged into unyielding rock and turned, felt with his hands, found the opening.

He crawled, blind, through the long passageway and then into the first room, where the entrance to the cave was illuminated softy by the dying sunlight outside. He'd almost made it to the opening, still crawling mindlessly, when his stomach caught up with his brain and vomit filled his mouth. He turned to an outcropping near the door and spewed.

In the dull light from the entrance, so seemingly bright after the blackness of the inner cave, part of his mind saw in detail his hand placed on the rock, fingers splayed, dustings of hair disturbed by the movement wavering up for a moment, caressing his skin. It saw this in an odd, surreal kind of clarity, almost like a déjà vu, while the rest of his mind and body were busy elsewhere, expelling everything in his gut in an act of pure terror and revulsion.

It was several minutes before he managed to propel himself, on exhausted legs, through the mouth of the cave and stumble back through the trees.

Lair. Lair. Lair.

His mind repeated the word over and over while he stumbled down the path.

He'd found its lair.

He had flashes as he ran of the Beast—IT—coming down the same path but from the opposite direction—from civilization *to* the lair, its strong forelegs pushing steadily on, despite the fact that it was dragging a human corpse in its jaws.

Why take the bodies there? *Oh, why do you have such big teeth, Grandmama? To eat, eat, eat.*

Perhaps too to hide the evidence. *But it's not hiding anymore.*

He broke into the clearing at the lodge and went quickly inside.

"Are you ready for another beer yet, Herr Knight?" Hennemann called out, his voice thick with drink. Von

Aigner was downstairs too, sitting at the bar, hogging the pretzel dish.

Gabriel wanted to scream or laugh. He swallowed it. "No. I h—have to see Friedrich."

Von Aigner raised a curious eyebrow. "He's in his room. Upstairs."

Later, Gabriel was to wonder at his decision. Even at the time he knew that it wasn't particularly wise. But he'd reached a point—even if it was just for a brief reactionary moment—when the burden was too great to shoulder alone. And there was von Glower, with his shoulders broad enough to take on the world. Shoulders like perhaps Wolfgang's might have been, had he lived, or even his grandad's. Somehow, Gabriel knew that von Glower would loathe what von Zell was doing as much as he did himself.

He was not wrong about that.

One look at Gabriel's face and von Glower jumped up from his desk. "My God, what's happened?"

"In the woods . . ."

"Show me."

Von Glower put on a thick coat and insisted they stop at the barn for lanterns and a rifle. He questioned Gabriel several times about what he had seen, but Gabriel only shook his head. Although the woods were dark now, he raced down the path unerringly. His panic had ingrained its contours on him like a melody on vinyl.

When they reached the culvert, von Glower stopped him by tugging on one arm.

"Gabriel, what *is* it? Did you see an animal? A bear?"

Gabriel shook his head. "There's a cave," he said, trying to catch his breath.

"A cave?" Von Glower sounded doubtful.

"This way."

Gabriel walked back along the culvert and pushed

through the brambles. Soon, they were both at the cave entrance. Von Glower looked baffled.

"Go in," Gabriel said, having no intention of going in himself. "It's in the second room. Be careful—there's a . . . a drop."

Von Glower's dark eyes looked worriedly at Gabriel, and he nodded. He stood for a long moment, staring at the entrance, as though he really did not want to go inside. Gabriel recognized the fear, but was surprised to see it in von Glower. It was a momentary lapse; he soon stooped low to crawl in through the opening, his lantern held in front of him. Gabriel waited, pacing outside.

Von Glower emerged from the cave ten long minutes later. When he came out, he looked paler, more stricken and ill than Gabriel himself had been.

"My God," he said, his chin trembling with shock.

"It's von Zell," Gabriel said bitterly.

Von Glower looked at him sharply. "Von Zell?"

"He's . . . he's a—"

Von Glower grabbed his arm. "He's a *what*, Gabriel?"

Gabriel swallowed. "He's a werewolf."

He waited, expecting von Glower to laugh, but he just stood there, studying Gabriel with those worried, dark eyes, his brow furrowed in thought.

"I think you'd better explain," he said gently.

And so Gabriel did. He explained about looking into the wolf killings for the Hubers, about being suspicious of Klingmann and following him to the club. Von Glower seemed to take this in without much anger or surprise.

"Here's what I think happened," Gabriel said. "Von Zell got caught up in this philosophy of yours. Maybe at first he only *thought* he was a wolf. But he must have had some kind of . . . I don't know . . . genetic code—maybe a werewolf way back in the family tree somewhere—that allowed to him to actually *physically change* once his mind got worked up enough by the philosophy and the hunting to trigger it. Anyway, he changes now, that's certain. The killer isn't a wolf *or* a dog and certainly not human; it's some huge wolf hybrid."

"What about the zoo wolves? The newspapers say—"

"It was a setup by von Zell. He must have been killin' around here for a long time, and at your other lodge in Alfdorf. He'd grab people when they were alone and drag them back to the cave. But for some reason—maybe he's just gettin' more and more insane—he got tired of being subtle. He decided he wanted to kill closer to home, not have to dispose of the bodies, maybe even spread some terror. But he didn't want to be caught, so he cooked up a scheme to let two wolves out of the Munich zoo—wolves the killin's could be blamed on. He seduced Klingmann into wantin' to join the club to get his help in kidnappin' them."

Von Glower said nothing, but his handsome face was etched with concern.

"But then he had to get *rid* of the wolves," Gabriel continued. "So he offered to reduce von Aigner's debt for the name of your black-market animal dealer. It was a guy named Grossberg. He helped von Zell get rid of the wolves. But Grossberg tried to blackmail von Zell. Von Zell killed him just blocks from the club. He must have arranged a meeting and then . . . changed before keeping it."

"This is incredible."

"I know."

Von Glower paced anxiously. "It's difficult to believe there's an actual transformation, but as for the rest of it . . . I've seen his savagery in hunting. With the way he's been acting, I'm not surprised that he's turned that rage on other human beings."

"There's an actual transformation, all right. I have samples of hair and a paw print."

Hair. Wasn't there more hair in the lair? Yes. He'd seen some. He could go back in now and get it to show to von Glower, but the thought of entering the lair was hideous. He decided not to mention it.

"How curious," von Glower said, soft and low.

"We have to . . . to kill him," Gabriel said, suddenly worried that von Glower would want to study the process rather than end it.

Von Glower nodded solemnly. "Yes. I agree."

Gabriel bit his lip. "I don't think the police would believe me."

Von Glower let out a breathy laugh. "*No.* No, they would not." He drew himself taller. He seemed to have reached some kind of decision, and now the von Glower that Gabriel had so admired was back. He had assimilated the situation, and he was more than ready to act.

"It's not their concern anyway," he said. "This thing belongs to you and I."

Gabriel nodded slowly.

"You, you have a stake in this for the Hubers. As for myself, I feel responsible. I obviously chose even my chosen few very badly."

He smiled a sad, ironic smile and placed a hand on Gabriel's shoulder. "We'll hunt him tonight."

They'd agreed to meet at the stables at midnight. The rest of the men would be asleep by then, von Glower explained, and their interference was one thing they didn't need.

How do you know he'll be out? Gabriel had asked.

It's our first night here. If he's what you say, don't you think he'll want to be out?

Yeah. Gabriel thought he would. The question was, did Gabriel himself really want to be out? Answer: no.

Now that it had come down to this, now that the chase was over and the knife was put in his hand, he found himself much less enthusiastic about his role. Had his ancestors enjoyed it? The killing part? He could still remember Malia, hanging over that fiery chasm. Whatever his commitment, whatever was right and wrong, he'd die before putting himself through that again.

But this wasn't Malia. This was grade-A asshole von Zell, and he was eating people. Somebody had to stop it.

The stables were aglow with lantern light when Gabriel arrived. Von Glower was saddling a horse.

"What rough beast slouches toward the hunt, its prey to be undone?" he said darkly as Gabriel walked up.

"What's *that* 'sposed to mean?"

"Just a little hunting joie de vivre to get you in the mood."

"It didn't work," Gabriel said, eyeing the horses with apprehension. "We're not ridin', are we?"

"Yes. We'll be safer on horseback. The horses will let us know when he's close. Plus, we can move much faster if we have to chase him."

"Right. This is, um . . . we don't ride much in New Orleans."

Von Glower looked up at him, surprised. "Oh. I didn't realize . . ." He tightened the saddle's buckle on the horse's underbelly. "Well, just hang on. Let the horse know who's boss. You'll be fine."

Von Glower offered him a hand up. Gabriel reluctantly put one booted toe in the saddle and pulled himself upward. He found himself sitting on the horse. In truth, he'd never been on a horse in his life. It was a lot higher up than he'd imagined, and his legs didn't particularly care for the spread forced by the horse's broad back. His inner thighs began to itch. The horse whinnied uneasily, obviously not any more happy about the pairing than he was.

Von Glower grabbed a rifle from a table nearby and held it out. Gabriel looked at it. He wanted to take it, but there was no fucking way he was going to go on his first ever horseback ride—through the woods, in the dark—while holding a loaded rifle.

"Think I'll pass," he said dryly.

Von Glower frowned, and Gabriel felt his stomach twist in embarrassment. No doubt his obvious lack of skill would be grating on a man like von Glower, a man who could probably gallop bareback while shooting at a target a hundred yards away.

"Then you'd better stay close to me, Gabriel." Von Glower laid a hand on his leg to press home the point. "And close to the *gun*."

They rode out across the lawn and into the woods, their way lit by powerful torch flashlights that von Glower had attached to the saddles. Gabriel was alarmed at the bounce involved in this riding business and how it threatened to unbalance him with every step. He watched Von Glower's back—starkly lit by Gabriel's torch—and tried to mimic his posture. He saw von Glower reach up to mess with his hair on the right side, then on the left, putting it behind his ears, it looked like. He was completely at ease in the saddle.

The plan was simple. Farther down the right-hand path from the lodge, just past the point where Gabriel had turned left earlier that day, there was a ravine. They were to push von Zell toward the ravine, using the horses. There, with his back to the chasm, he would be cornered and could be shot.

Gabriel felt less comfortable with this path than he did with the one he'd taken to and from the cave several times. It was odd how things grew on you so quickly, and how disconcerting it could be when they were unfamiliar. The way his higher position seemed to place him within grasp of the trees didn't help.

Somewhere in the distance he heard a howl.

It was a sound so eerily human yet so utterly Other that it made the hackles on his neck rise. Every instinct bade him to turn around and go back the way he had come, perhaps bar himself into the stable.

He hissed loudly, "Friedrich!" just to hear some human sound, to say "did you hear that?," but von Glower was getting farther ahead, and he didn't turn around.

Gabriel's horse, on the other hand, was more than prepared to acknowledge the howl. It had slowed and now it stopped nervously, taking reluctant steps forward, as if unsure what was less horrifying—to lose sight of its mate or to continue on toward that sound.

"Come on!" Gabriel pushed his knees into the horse's sides. "Go! Giddy-up!"

At this, the horse came to a complete standstill.

"Friedrich!" Gabriel called out, raising his voice full tilt now, but the baron was melding unheedingly into the shadows up ahead, unhearing, and now he was gone.

"Shit!" Gabriel slapped the reins down on the horse's neck. At that moment the howl came again, and the horse came to its own conclusions about the safety of the stable. It reared a bit and then quickly turned around on the path and began to gallop back the way it had come.

Gabriel managed to stay on through the turn, but he was canted to the left, and when the horse lurched forward to run, Gabriel went sprawling to the side and smacked straight into a tree.

He was not knocked out or even stunned. No, he was fully conscious as he heard the sound of the horse's hooves fading into the distance. He stood up painfully. "Shit!"

He was left in utter darkness. The horse was gone, as was the flashlight. Von Glower too was gone, along with the gun. Yes, this was going rather well.

But as his eyes forgot the brightness of the flashlight, they began to acknowledge the lesser glow of a three-quarter moon hanging over the woods. If he looked straight up he could see it, off to the left. He looked in one direction and then the other on the path, trying to decide what to do. He thought it likely that von Glower would soon realize he was gone and come back. The stable, on the other hand, seemed *way* too far away.

He began walking toward the ravine.

He heard the howl again, and this time it sounded close, perhaps two hundred yards away. He had put the talisman on over his shirt, but this no longer seemed enough. He pulled the chain over his head and wrapped it around his hand. He held the medallion out ahead of him like some kind of cross on a Dracula hunt, his teeth chattering.

Now there was silence in the woods. Now there was no howling. And yet something inside him, imagination perhaps, told him the Beast was close, perhaps hidden just behind the trees to one side of the path or the other. He began to feel that strange underwater feeling again, that desire to swing around, certain the thing was sneaking up behind him. Would the talisman have any power at all if the thing jumped him from behind? Would it have power anyway?

And then, when he thought he couldn't get any more afraid, the Beast stepped out onto the path. It stepped out, stood there, and growled at him, growled low in its throat, its fangs bared and dripping saliva.

"Ohmigod," Gabriel said. Pure terror washed over him, like a wave inundating a small boat. It threatened to incapacitate him, this absolute fear, fear of what he saw standing there in the moonlight.

Frau Huber had been right—the Beast wasn't a wolf. It didn't look like the wolves at the zoo at all. They had long, graceful legs, and this thing was shortened—its legs squat and meaty. And its hair was thick and wiry, springing up and out in a disconnected chaos that seemed to glow an earthy red in the moonlight. But the head was the worst—large and oddly square, with a short, brutish snout and teeth that were long and pointed and overstuffed along the gums. These teeth had only one purpose—to rip, to render, to annihilate.

The growl was low, rumbling, black as pitch, demonic. It grew in intensity as the thing crouched.

Gabriel thrust the talisman forward, certain that he was experiencing his last few seconds of life—his last sight, this hideous Beast's crouching spring. The thing's growl softened to a whimper as the medallion was thrust forward. It backed away!

At first Gabriel merely watched this with overwhelming relief. Then he saw the Beast's eyes dart sideways into the woods. It was going to turn off the path.

No.

He stepped forward, thrusting the talisman again. It wasn't because he felt like pursuing the creature; it was because he couldn't stand the thought of that thing gaining cover in the woods, becoming invisible. The move worked. The Best, von Zell, whimpered again and backed up on the path.

And Gabriel walked the creature down the path, step by step—*thrust,* step, with it backing up in front of him. He wondered, *Where the hell is von Glower?* And then, *Where the fuck is that ravine?*

They passed the east-west path on their left. But where was von Glower? Why didn't he come riding in and shoot the damn thing?

When he was certain they must be at the ravine at any moment, the Beast, perhaps, felt it too. Yes, it would know these woods. It seemed to gather itself together, and when Gabriel thrust the talisman, it made a kind of yelping cry, but it didn't back up. Instead, it leapt off the path to the right and ran away.

"Shit!" Gabriel said. "Shit!"

He was covered with perspiration. His legs threatened to give way—the muscles jiggling like a Jell-O mold in an earthquake. He hadn't realized how tense he'd been, how terrified. He'd had the Beast in check for a good five minutes. Where the hell was von Glower with the gun?

At the ravine.

He moved forward down the path, exhausted. Within a few moments the path opened up and ended in a small clearing surrounded by rock. Up ahead in the moonlight he could see the end of the woods there, the cliff edge that fell away. Somewhere down below he could hear a running stream. There was no sign of von Glower.

He lowered the talisman wearily. "*Damn* it!"

It was then that he was struck from above. Something that felt like a wrecking ball swung into him. Its momentum sent him sprawling to the ground. The talisman flew from his hand like a shot put just about the time he realized that what had struck him was the Beast. It had leaped on him from the rocks above, and it had succeeded in its gambit.

He no longer had the talisman.

He screamed in pain and revulsion as the Beast bit, hard, into his left thigh. He thought for a moment that the bone would snap in two, such was the torque on the creature's jaws. The pain burst upon him hot and wild. He screamed again.

Then he heard the sound of a horse at full gallop. Von Glower pounded into the clearing and reared his mount to a stop. The Beast let go of Gabriel's leg and backed up, confused and startled. Gabriel sat on the ground and looked at the creature a few feet away, its muzzle thick with his blood. Then he looked up at the man on the horse.

Von Glower took in Gabriel's wound. He too looked at the wolf, his large, dark eyes meeting the red feral ones below.

"Shoot it!" Gabriel screamed, the words pouring forth of their own accord. "Kill it, goddamn it!"

But von Glower just sat there, reins in one hand, rifle in the other. The Beast crouched low, backed up a step. It swung its head from Gabriel to von Glower, its throat issuing a never ending growl.

Its eyes. Its eyes were human.

"Kill it!" Gabriel screamed again, unable to comprehend von Glower's inaction.

"You must do it!" von Glower said, snapping out of his daze. He tossed the rifle through the air.

Gabriel was so shocked that for a moment he didn't move. Then, powered by some survivor's instinct, he reached up one hand and caught the rifle. It was not a move he could have done with any number of practice rounds. He simply did it now. He looked at von Glower disbelievingly.

"Shoot it!" von Glower cried.

Now the Beast, the wolf-thing, snarled in absolute rage. Gabriel never even had time to stand. The thing tensed its legs and leaped into the air, directly at Gabriel.

He saw its underbelly, white and thick in the moonlight. The gun was already pointed awkwardly upward. He tilted it slightly and pulled the trigger.

The creature fell to the ground, a dull, dead weight. It landed at Gabriel's feet, and he scrambled backward on his hands and butt, expecting the thing to bite him again, but it didn't.

Von Glower dismounted and turned his back to Gabriel, messed with something at the saddle. Gabriel looked back and forth between him and the wolf. He tried to stand up, but his left leg screamed in pain.

"Let me help you," von Glower said. And then he was there, warm and strong. He grasped Gabriel around the chest and pulled him upright onto his good right leg. Gabriel dropped the rifle, feeling weak and nauseated now from the pain, from the aftermath.

They both stood and watched, mesmerized, as the Beast's hair retreated into its body, as the thick legs and torso turned pink, as the head reshaped itself.

Finally, von Zell lay there, naked, a gaping wound in his chest.

"Poor von Zell. You got him right in the heart," von Glower said with a mix of regret and amazement.

"Dumb luck," Gabriel replied, his tongue numb from shock.

"Fate," von Glower said.

Gabriel looked up at him vacantly. "Fate? Fuck that. I should be dead. Why didn't you shoot?"

Von Glower didn't answer. Instead, he bent down to look at Gabriel's leg. He gently pulled the ripped pant material aside. "It's a nasty wound."

"*Ouch*! Yeah. It bit me."

The words came out of his mouth without thought, but the second they hit the air, he *heard* them, really heard them, and realized what they meant.

"God! Oh, my God! It *bit* me! Fuck! *Fuck!*"

He tried to step back, panicked, but von Glower held him steady. "It's all right, Gabriel!"

"No! It bit me! I . . ." And then he realized that it *was* all right. He expelled a huge breath. "Christ! You made *me* shoot him! Thank God you made me shoot him! I killed him and broke the curse. I'm all right."

"You'll be fine."

"But how'd you know? How'd you know that *I* had to shoot him?" Gabriel looked at his rescuer, his face as blank and wondering as a child's.

Von Glower smiled shakily. "I don't know. Instinct, I guess. I saw the wound and . . . It's part of the lore, isn't it? I must have seen it in a film."

"Jesus! Do you think we should . . . should we burn it, or . . . ?"

"I'll take care of it." Von Glower stood and draped Gabriel's arm over his shoulder. "But first, let's get you back to the lodge before you pass out. You've done enough for one night."

Gabriel allowed himself to be put on the horse. Von Glower was gentle, and Gabriel perhaps should have been more grateful or at least aware, but he was too distracted by the body of von Zell. He allowed himself to be fussed over, unconsciously, as though he'd been born to it.

He was busy thinking about how, now that von Zell was dead, naked and dead, he didn't look quite so much like a grade-A asshole. He looked rather pitiful really, wretched and sad and brutalized.

It was only the *Schattenjäger's* second kill, after all. Gabriel continued to stare at the corpse as von Glower led him away. He stared until the white of the flesh had been completely swallowed by the darkness.

Chapter 6

Starnberger See

The morning was cold and overcast with an insistent light drizzle that came and went as frequently and as suddenly as a five-year-old running in and out of the house. Grace had planned to arrive early because she wanted a few moments alone. Even so, she had underestimated the impact of the place.

From the parking lot a path headed north along a fence and through a wooded area. It ended at a chapel, a memorial chapel for Ludwig, that was locked with no signs of life. She walked around the building and found that it overlooked a cross, farther down, and then the lake itself. She walked down the grassy hill slowly, the water already mesmerizing her. The only sounds were that of birds and of the water gently lapping.

There was a sign at the cross, but she didn't read it; she knew what it would say. It was the water itself that drew her on. She did not hesitate, but climbed easily through an iron rail fence that protected the small beach from the tourist rabble. She walked to the water's edge and stared down into the greenish-gray water, watching it lick the rocky sand.

He died right here.

She shivered and drew her coat more tightly around her. She'd seen a postcard from the 1890s in the museum; it showed the king lying among the reeds at the bottom of the lake, an angel hovering overhead, looking at the viewer and placing a silencing finger to her lips. *Don't speak of this,* the label had said. And this was what she pictured now, Ludwig lying just under the water, eyes open, hair waving in the current . . .

"Hello."

She jumped, startled, and turned to see an elegant-looking blond man in a long woollen coat.

"Sorry. Josef Dallmeier here. Are you Grace?"

"Yes. Hello."

She reached out and they shook hands through the fence. "It's this place," he said. "I really feel him here."

"I know what you mean."

"There's a bench over there if you like." Dallmeier inclined his head down the fence. Grace blushed at her trespassing and climbed carefully back under the rail.

"It was very nice of you to meet me."

"No problem. I love talking about Ludwig. My partner gets sick of it."

"Well, you've found a very open ear, Herr Dallmeier."

"Josef, please."

They sat down on the wooden bench. Dallmeier put his hands in his coat pockets and propped out his long legs. He was very thin, with a delicate long nose and a small, freckled mouth.

"I found your Black Wolf," he said pleasantly.

Grace nearly fell off the seat. "Really? Where?"

"He was an associate of Bismarck's. Did you bring that letter, by any chance?"

She gave it to him. He devoured it like a missive from his dearest love. He looked the envelope over carefully. "This looks authentic."

"Oh, it is."

"You found it where?"

"I'm staying at the Ritter family castle in Rittersberg. It was in . . . uh, inside a book in the library."

"It looks like it was never sent."

"That's what I thought."

Dallmeier read the letter again. "I don't understand. Was this Christian Ritter in law enforcement or . . ."

Grace smiled tentatively. "Sort of. What did you learn about the Black Wolf?"

"Of course. Sorry. Actually, I'd read about him before, but I didn't realize that was who you meant. His name was Paul Gowden. I found a reference to his having the nickname 'the Black Wolf' after you telephoned."

Grace's brow knit in disappointment. She'd been expecting . . . what, exactly? "Paul Gowden? Who was he?"

"Gowden lived on the fringes of the Prussian court," Dallmeier said, sitting up attentively. "He wasn't titled, but he liked to put on airs. By all accounts he was handsome, charming, even dangerous. Since you brought him up, I dug a little deeper. I think I've found some things that are *probably* true. It's said he came from abroad in the mid 1800s but claimed high German blood. Supposedly, his family's title and lands were lost in some catastrophe or another."

"Do you know where he came from exactly?"

"No. He was also said to be ruthlessly ambitious. Gowden probably found out who held the power in the Prussian court—Bismarck—and offered his services. Bismarck no doubt used him. He knew talent when he saw it—of that sort, anyway. And if this letter is accurate, and Gowden really was close to Ludwig . . ."

Dallmeier looked at the letter again. He had the distracted anticipation of a scholar smelling a major paper, maybe even a book. As for Grace, she wasn't sure what to make of it.

"What about 'Louis'?" she asked. "Didn't Ludwig have a paramour called Louis?"

Dallmeier looked at her sharply. "Yes. Maybe even several. Anyway, there are a few different references to a Louis, but none have ever been identified for certain. Ludwig's penchant for renaming people confounds most searches. Maybe he even meant for it to."

Grace bit a nail worriedly. "Hmmm. Is there anything else about Gowden?"

But Dallmeier seemed agitated, as though she'd sent his mind down a path he'd not hitherto seen. "Hmmm? Oh. Well, there's this: whatever Gowden did for Bismarck, it must have been something remarkable. Bismarck was *not* a generous man. He liked to string people along with promises but rarely came through. He did for Gowden, though. He gave him a royal title and lands in 1871."

Grace was watching Dallmeier, her thumb still poised at her mouth. "Then what?"

Dallmeier shook his head, irked. "I don't know. That's the last reference I found."

"But he couldn't have just disappeared!"

Dallmeier smiled tightly. "Maybe he did just that. In those days, if you suddenly were granted title or lands, you might move away and change your name. That way you could act like you were born to it, and no one would know better. Gowden was arrogant enough to want that kind of freedom."

Grace thought about it. "If Gowden did change his name or move away, isn't there a way to track that down?"

Dallmeier was nudged from his own brooding interest by the insistence in her voice. He raised a brow at her, bemused. "You're very determined."

Grace glowered menacingly. "*Deadly* determined."

Dallmeier smiled. "Well, let's see . . . A copy of the entitlement deed would tell you his new official name and title. Assuming the document wasn't lost or destroyed in a war, that is."

"How would I go about getting that?" Grace pulled a notepad and pencil out of her purse and waited expectantly.

Dallmeier sighed. "If it is that important to you,

why don't I look? I know the bureaucracy—and the language."

"Are you sure?"

"Yes. You wouldn't believe the red tape in German government. Just remember, the records could be long gone."

"I understand." Grace smiled gratefully, but her stomach was tied in knots. There was something in all this that was extremely troubling. Could Gowden, a.k.a. the Black Wolf, really have been a werewolf? Or had Christian Ritter been mistaken?

"Was there anything else you wanted to know?" Dallmeier asked.

"As a matter of fact . . . Have you ever thought about contacting Chaphill about the diary?"

Dallmeier looked doubtful. "No. His book was written, what, thirty years ago? He's British, I think."

"Sounds like it."

"To tell you the truth, that book made me so angry, I never even finished it."

Grace studied Dallmeier. "Because it said Ludwig was gay?"

"No!" Dallmeier scoffed.

"*Was* he?"

Dallmeier took a long sigh and slouched down on the bench again, planted both feet carefully. "Yes. That's the simple answer. Oh, some of our stodgiest historians still deny it, but it's pretty much common knowledge."

"But there *were* women."

"There were women, especially when he was younger. But as he grew older, he became more true to his stripe, as they say."

Grace was disappointed for some reason, as though she'd lost him herself. It was ridiculous. The man lived in another time.

"So what makes you angry about Chaphill?" she asked.

Dallmeier grunted. "He implies—no, more than implies, he *states*—that it was Ludwig's homosexuality that drove him insane, made him a recluse. He might as well have said he grew hair on his palms!"

Grace looked away toward the lake, blushing. She knew, of course, to what he referred, but it struck an altogether different chord for her.

"The diary entries," she said, "All the oath taking."

"Exactly! Since Chaphill that seems to be pretty much the standard interpretation, and it really . . . it really . . . Bah! I don't like it."

"You don't think the diaries were about Ludwig being gay?"

"No." He paused, then exploded passionately. "Ludwig was no prude! He loved Byron and the French court! He understood his feelings, and I don't think he was ashamed of them."

Grace was watching him silently. It was occurring to her that this was a personal crusade.

"You have to understand the man!" Dallmeier went on. "He didn't care what anybody thought—about anything! If he didn't care that they complained about his spending a fortune on those castles, why should their narrow-mindedness about sexuality make him feel guilty? No, all evidence is that he pursued exactly whom and whatever he wanted to pursue. If he was tormented, that's not what did it."

Grace thought about this for a while as they watched the lake in silence.

"What about the hunting accident?" she asked.

Dallmeier exhaled a calming breath. "It was a major turning point. I know this great old man—Stephan Horning. His grandfather was Richard Horning, Ludwig's equestrian. He told me that Ludwig started to go mad after the accident."

Grace bit her lip anxiously. "Do you know what happened, exactly?"

Dallmeier shrugged. "Ludwig fell off his horse and seriously injured his leg. He never really got over it. Maybe Horning would know more."

"Do you think I could speak with him?"

Dallmeier grunted as though no longer surprised at her tenaciousness. "Perhaps, Grace. He's a friendly old man. I will call him for you if you like."

They sat there for a moment longer. The lake beckoned, encouraged contemplation, but Grace knew she didn't have the luxury.

"Say, do you think I might see Horning today?" she asked brightly.

Dallmeier looked at her, one eyebrow cocked in surprise. "And I suppose you want me to get right to that entitlement deed as well?"

Grace cracked what she hoped was an encouraging smile. "I'm Japanese. We have this thing about perpetual motion."

"What a slave driver!" Dalmeier growled. "All right, Miss Nakimura. Let us say good-bye to the spirit of Ludwig and depart."

While Grace waited at Schloss Ritter for Dallmeier's call, she decided to follow up on another idea. She telephoned the publishers of Chaphill's book. They informed her that Sir Richmond Chaphill was deceased, but they gave her a phone number for his son in England.

Thomas Chaphill was pleased enough to hear from a fan of his father's work. At first.

"I understand your father was allowed to see Ludwig's diary," Grace said after she'd buttered him up a bit.

"Yes. Of course, I was quite young then, but I remember him being very excited. You see, the London Chaphills are related to the Wittelsbach family by marriage."

"I see."

"So my father pulled some familial strings, you might say." Chaphill laughed nasally.

"Did he make a copy of it by any chance?"

"Heavens! I shouldn't think so."

"What about notes? Did he takes notes perhaps?"

Chaphill was silent for a moment. "Ah! Yes, I remember now. I believe he did translate it. Into English, just for himself. I remember he had pages and pages of these notes. I take it Ludwig's handwriting made the German quite impossible to work with."

"He *transcribed* it?" Grace said, astonished. "Do you know what happened to his version?"

"My goodness!" Chaphill said, dismayed by her passion. "No, I don't, really. When he passed on, we put his papers away. They're probably still up in the attic, but whether or not they included *that* . . ."

Grace squeezed her eyes shut. Chaphill sounded not only uninterested, but he was starting to sound a little offended as well.

"I know this must sound *very* odd, but this is so critical, Sir Chaphill."

"Well, I do apologize," Chaphill said coolly. "But even if I did *search* for the document, and even if I could *find* it, I really don't think it would be proper to let it out of my possession. My father was entrusted with that diary under strict guidelines. If he'd been permitted to publish it or pass it around, he would have, Miss Nakimura."

"I have no interest in publishing it, *believe* me. This is a strictly personal matter. I give you my word."

"I'm afraid I can't help you. You'll have to apply to the proper authorities in Germany."

Grace went downstairs, feeling pouty, and complained to Gerde for a while. Gerde was sympathetic, but in the end she only smiled enigmatically and said, "If you really need the diary, you'll find a way."

In other words, she wasn't a lot of help. Fortunately, Dallmeier called with better news. He'd arranged an interview with Horning.

Horning's farm was near Halblech, forty-five minutes north of Neuschwanstein. Grace didn't mind the drive. If she'd had all the time in the world, in fact, she would be enjoying this immensely—driving around the most intimate places of Bavaria, looking into a historical mystery . . . It was as close to an ideal job description as she could imagine.

If only she didn't feel the clock ticking so loudly. She thought at first that she was being driven by her own ambition, by her need to get something meaty and tangible to lay down in front of Gabriel—to show her worth. But when the feeling only grew, she began to suspect that there was more to it than that, that there was something major at stake, as Mrs. Smith had implied—and not just on Gabriel's end of the equation.

The farm was old but immaculately kept, the fields covered with the finest green dusting of some early crop. The house was large and freshly made up with dark pine window shutters and boxes filled with orange and purple crocuses. Horning himself sat out in the yard, puffing on a pipe. He was old, in his seventies at least, but he looked fit with his ruddy face and thick white hair. He sported worn lederhosen, a white shirt, and a thick wool coat and feathered hat. Grace wondered if he'd done the traditional thing for her, then decided that he looked too comfortable in it.

She pulled into the driveway and waved. The old man raised his pipe to her. As she climbed from the car, he called toward the house in German. A beautiful young blond girl came out in jeans and a sweatshirt.

"Mr. Horning? Hi. I'm Grace Nakimura." She walked over and extended a hand.

"Ja. Sehr gut. Stephan Horning hier." The old man had a broad smile. He looked over at the blond girl.

"Hallo, I'm Stephanie. My grandfather asked me to meet with you. He doesn't speak English."

"That's great. Thank you, Stephanie."

The three of them settled into the comfortable wooden chairs Horning had set up on the lawn.

"I was hoping your grandfather could tell me about Ludwig's hunting accident," Grace began.

The girl spoke with her grandfather in a German that sounded heavily dialectic. Stephan Horning's enthusiasm was evident, but the actual words were mostly unintelligible.

"In 1873 he had the accident. Grandfather says he went bad after that."

"Does he know exactly how the accident occurred?"

"It was on a trip to Schachen. The king was riding with a friend when it happened."

"Who was the friend?"

Grace could tell the answer before the girl translated, for it was prefaced by one of those *"Ne's"* that grew longer and more guttural the farther south one went.

"Papo—that's what Grandfather calls my great-great granddad—he never said a name, only that Ludwig was with a friend. Papo didn't like the king's friends much."

Damn.

"And Ludwig fell from his horse? Was there any chance that he was maybe pushed or . . . or something?"

The girl repeated this question for her grandfather. The old man's smile eased away, and he sat for a moment and looked at Grace, considering. It was an odd sort of look, a curious weighing of some matter, and Grace hoped it meant that she was on the right track.

Stephan Horning finally spoke again in that throaty, gulping language.

"He says he did fall from the horse, but that's not what hurt his leg," the girl translated. She looked surprised herself. She spoke to her grandfather on her own accord, trying to get the story straight.

"He says Ludwig insisted that the servants tell no one, but the real cause of the accident was a wolf. Ludwig ran into a wolf in the forest. The horse reared and threw him, then the wolf attacked. Ludwig was bitten in the leg."

Grace felt a strange numbness spread through her. The birds were suddenly loud and the smell of the old man's pipe, suddenly pungent and pervasive. It was a moment she knew she'd remember for the rest of her life.

The old man was speaking again to his granddaughter.

"Grandfather says that he hardly ever tells anyone this. But then, no one ever asks."

"Ludwig was bitten by a wolf," Grace repeated slowly.

"Yes. And then the wolf ran away. The servants searched in the woods for days but never found anything."

"Schachen is in the Alps, right?"

Stephanie nodded. "Near the border. Grandfather took me there once. It's beautiful."

"What about Ludwig's friend, did he see the wolf too?"

"Papo never said, but it was the friend who carried Ludwig to the lodge."

Grace thought about it, her heart beating dully in her chest. "What happened after Ludwig was bitten?"

"He was sick for a long time. They thought the bite had gone . . . um, infected maybe? Very high fever. He was out of his mind. He didn't want any doctors. There was only his friend and a few servants to tend him."

Grace had a clear picture of Ludwig, tall and dark with pale, pale skin, lying in a palatial bed somewhere—maybe Herrenchiemsee or Linderhof or even the Residenz in Munich—delirious, raging, out of his mind with pain, and beside him, tending him . . .

"This friend who nursed him—was it the same one who was on the trip?"

Stephen Horning considered this for a bit, then spoke to his granddaughter.

"Yes. Probably. You see, Ludwig didn't have *many* friends, but he often had someone . . . a very . . . close friend, a man usually. Papo really didn't like these men, so he always just called them 'Ludwig's friend' or 'Ludwig's companion.' "

The girl looked away uncomfortably, and Grace got the point. Richard Horning had known, as no doubt all of the servants had, that these men did more than share the king's leisure time.

"And then Ludwig recovered?" Grace said. "After a few months?"

The girl and the old man discussed this point.

"No. His wound got better, but the fever did something to his brain. He was never the same again, Granddad says. Never."

Frau Horning—a very pretty old woman—came out and served them iced tea. It was sweet and dark, and although Grace normally avoided caffeine (unlike the bean slave Gabriel), she welcomed its kick now. Horning knocked his pipe out against the chair, stubbed a toe at the ash until it had disappeared, then filled his pipe again in a methodical rite.

Grace spoke. "Can your grandfather tell me *how* Ludwig changed after the accident?"

Horning described the king's growing reclusiveness, obsessiveness, and fits of rage. These were things the museum too had touched upon, but Horning's insistence on the accident as the origin point was quite determined.

"The servants must have been terrified," Grace said sympathetically.

"Oh, yes!" Stephanie said on her own. She discussed it with her grandfather.

"They were terrified, but not just because of the king's temper. After he got angry, he felt very badly and gave them gifts. But they were afraid more like . . . more for the king and for themselves."

"What does he mean?" Grace asked, leaning forward.

"There were all kinds of rumors. Papo made fun of

them, of the servants for being so superstitious, but he was scared too. Like the sleigh rides. Ludwig had many bad nights, and when it was very bad he would call for the sleigh. He made the servants go faster and faster—really dangerous. And sometimes they couldn't go fast enough and he would make them stop and he would go running by himself. They were terrified he would hurt himself or get lost out there, but he always came back.''

Grace looked down at the grass for a moment, trying to keep her composure. The green was iridescent, too rich to be real. "Was there anything else—any other incidents that made the servants superstitious?"

Horning considered this. Finally he spoke again.

"Yes," Stephanie translated. "Near the end Wagner came to Neuschwanstein, and he and Ludwig would lock themselves upstairs in the hall. Then there would be music and very strange noises. One time one of the servants called Papo in to hear them because the other servants were so afraid. Papo said it sounded like the devil himself was screaming."

They were quiet for a moment. The images the girl's words conjured were so clear and detailed after having visited the castle, and having seen the paintings and the portraits of Ludwig, after knowing his eyes in the dream. . . . Horning was speaking again.

"Papo said once that Ludwig knew he was going mad. When Wagner played, it was the king screaming, screaming for his own lost soul."

The old man had tears in his eyes now. Big, swelling pools on the edges of his lashes. His chin trembled. He fought it, as men do. He cleared his throat and wiped his nose roughly. He looked away.

Stephanie reached out and slipped her delicate hand into her grandfather's rough, tan paw.

"My grandfather loves Ludwig very much. All of the common people did. Ludwig went home with Papo many times. He liked to play with the children and eat meals there. He was really happy in Papo's house, where he could just be a person."

Horning had reclaimed himself. Now he wrestled with the one old, gnarled finger where a large ring sat. After a moment he worked it free and held it out to Grace.

She looked at it closely. It was an ornate gold ring, heavy as a rock. Its widening bands held engraved images of Ludwig—young on one side and older on another, both surrounded by the Bavarian crest and flag. In the center was a large oval ruby. Grace could see something dark underneath the red.

"Ludwig gave Papo that ring. It has a lock of his hair in it." Stephanie had a touch of pride in her soft voice. "Granddad was given it on his eighteenth birthday, and when he dies, it will go to my father."

"It's beautiful," Grace said to the girl. "*Sehr shön,*" she said to Horning with a warm smile.

"*Ja,*" Horning said, smiling back. "*Mein Ring von Ludwig. Sehr shön. Sehr geliebten.*" Beloved.

Grace didn't even bother going back to the castle when she drove into Rittersberg. Instead, she parked outside the *gasthof* and went inside. Yes, the Smiths were upstairs, Werner informed her, and he went to fetch them.

Mrs. Smith looked considerably better than she had the last time Grace had seen her. In fact, she hurried over to the table with thigh-rubbing eagerness and large liquid eyes.

"Oh, Grace dear, I'm so glad you came! We walked up to the castle this morning, but you were out. I've been so worried!"

"Would you like something to drink, Miss Nakimura?" Mr. Smith offered.

"Yes, please. In fact—have you eaten lunch? I know it's late, but—"

"Sweetie, my stomach doesn't wait past noon, but you go right on ahead."

So Grace ordered the quickest thing she could see on the menu—a large mixed salad. She filled in Mrs. Smith while she ate.

She'd made a decision on the way over to tell the Smiths everything, and she did. She didn't know why she trusted them exactly, except that she couldn't imagine them being anything more than they appeared. *And* they were the only ones who might actually believe her. If she called Dallmeier and told him what she was thinking . . .

Even she couldn't believe what she was now thinking.

"You think Bismarck sent this man—this Paul Gowden—to befriend Ludwig . . ." Mrs. Smith said, trying to make sense of Grace's rattled story.

"Seduce him."

"Seduce him, and that Gowden was a—a werewolf."

Grace nodded. "Christian Ritter thought so."

"Oh, my!" Mrs. Smith's lower lip cowered as her teeth pulled it nervously. "Yes, that explains it. I've been dreaming of wolves. Horrible, hideous dreams!"

"Me too!" Grace told Mrs. Smith about her dream of the sleigh and the painting in the museum.

"My dear," Mrs. Smith said with serious, wide eyes. "Ludwig was trying to contact you!"

"Do you think?"

"Yes, I do. Was there a black wolf in your dream?"

"No," Grace said slowly, trying hard to recall. Oddly, she *could* recall. Most of her dreams evaporated like ether once she was awake, but she did remember quite clearly the wolves that were chasing her. They weren't black. In fact, she couldn't remember feeling that they were all that important—not as personalities, not like the silver wolf in the . . .

A slight gasp of realization escaped her. "It's true. Ludwig was a werewolf; *that's* what he was trying to tell me in the dream."

Mrs. Smith looked at Grace, her head cocked to one side. "Yes, I see," she said, not at all surprised.

"Gowden changed him—at Schachen. He bit him."

"Do you know why, dear?"

Grace twisted her fork between anxious fingers. "I don't know. If he was working for Bismarck, maybe he wanted Ludwig insane. Or . . ."

Something else had occurred to Grace, and she wasn't at all sure where it had come from.

"Or *what*, dear?"

"Or . . . Maybe Gowden was supposed to *kill* Ludwig, but he changed his mind. If he was the one Ludwig called Louis, they'd been together for . . . '64 . . . '73 . . . nine years! Maybe he *did* care for Ludwig, at least enough not to be able to go through with it."

"Yes!" Mrs. Smith nodded. "That's exactly what crossed my mind as you were talking!"

"So he just bit him. Made him into a werewolf. Maybe he even *wanted* to make him into one. This book I found on werewolves talked about their desire for a pack."

Mrs. Smith rushed in excitedly. "Perhaps Gowden really *was* in love with Ludwig. By changing him into a werewolf, he could satisfy Bismarck and himself at the same time. Ludwig would hardly be fit to rule after that."

"And he wasn't," Grace said unhappily. "He wasn't fit to rule. It explains everything. Can you imagine? He must have been terrified that it would show, that he couldn't control it. He must have thought others could see his terrible secret just by looking at his face! And that's what the diary entries were about—he was promising not to give in to it—not to change. But he couldn't help himself."

Mrs. Smith was tapping the table pensively. "We went to visit one of his castles on our way over here. I'd never felt such a *sad* place. Now I know why."

"And it explains the paintings in the Singer's Hall. At least, I think it does." Grace looked up at Mrs. Smith. "Is Ludwig the spirit guide you saw in the tarot?"

Mrs. Smith shook her head slowly. "No. The spirit

is definitely female and much stronger than a human spirit. Someone or something is acting on Ludwig's behalf, trying to get the message through. Perhaps there's something we're supposed to do for poor Ludwig, or perhaps Gabriel—"

Mrs. Smith stopped abruptly. Her lips tightened to a determined line.

"Perhaps Gabriel what?" Grace demanded.

"Nothing, dear," Mrs. Smith said firmly. She reached over and patted Grace's hand. "Only that we must warn your *Schattenjäger* at once. Have you already told him about the Black Wolf?"

"Yes," Grace said, nearly sick with worry, "but not enough. Not nearly enough."

"Then we'll call him right away."

"Can't *you* contact Ludwig yourself? You're a medium, aren't you?" Grace blushed at her own question, not sure what was more embarrassing—that she'd been so reticent about Mrs. Smith's "skills" earlier or that she was so gullible now.

Mrs. Smith shook her head. "I've been trying to contact whatever is out there all yesterday and all today. I *feel* it, but I'm not getting a clear signal. To tell you the truth, communicating with the dead is not really my specialty."

Grace frowned.

"But I was thinking . . . With Gabriel's gifts—even if they're latent, mind you . . . I could probably help to focus and strengthen his powers. You know, boost his radar. Gabriel and I *together* might establish a channel."

Mrs. Smith smiled at Grace hopefully. "Why don't you give him a ring, dear?"

Grace's face burned. She looked down at her hands. "I don't have a phone number," she mumbled. "No one will tell me exactly where he is."

Mrs. Smith exchanged a knowing glance with Mr. Smith. Then she picked up her spoon and carefully stirred her coffee.

When Grace got back to the castle, Gerde was waiting for her anxiously. "Grace! You had a call while you were out."

"Josef Dallmeier?" Grace asked, hoping it was that entitlement deed.

"No, a British man named Chaphill. He said something about having a change of heart."

Grace stared at Gerde, unable to believe her ears. "You're *kidding* me. Oh, my God, I have to call him right away!"

"Wait! You may not need to do that. He asked me for a fax number, and I gave him the one at the post office in town. Then Frau Hogel rang and said she'd gotten the fax. It's a long one. Fifty pages."

"Oh, my god!" Grace turned herself around several times before successfully aiming for the front door.

"What is it, Grace? Is it important?"

"You wouldn't believe. I'll be right back with it, okay?"

Miss Nakimura:
I can hardly believe this myself, but the strangest thing happened after you called. I kept hearing noises up in the attic. This is a huge old place, you see, and it's difficult to hear anything, so these noises were quite loud. When I went up to investigate, I saw that a stack of boxes had fallen. One had opened and papers were strewn across the floor. I picked them up and saw that they were my father's translation of the diary. I packed those boxes myself, Miss Nakimura, and I don't recall ever seeing those pages. In any case, I had the strongest feeling about what I must do. Perhaps I'm a fool, but I've decided to trust you. Please do not share these with anyone and destroy them when you are through.
Good luck. Sir Edmond Chaphill.

Grace felt chilled as she read this, and for the first time she really *knew* that something much larger than herself was calling the shots. She felt tears sting her eyes. She was not a religious person by any means, but she closed her eyes and offered up a silent prayer of thanks.

Then she walked back to the castle to read Ludwig's diary.

11th June, 1873. Louis has convinced me to think matters through more thoroughly before I act. A trip it shall be, then. To Schachen. It shall not alter my purpose, I feel, nor shall his compelling. The treaty is the ruin of my beloved Bavaria and must be disposed of, whatever the cost! I regret now ever having made the decision. Of course, Louis makes the same arguments now as he and so many others did then, but I have grown deaf to that point of view. War or not, Bavaria must wear her own crown.

3rd July, 1873. Pain, pain, pain. The pain is so bad, I cannot hold a pen to write. Oh, what has happened! But the pain is not the worst of it. The *horror* is far more unbearable. He says that we can be truly one now, that it is a great adventure. When he is next to me and I can look into his eyes, I believe him. But the moment he turns away, I feel the horror of it! I can feel the flames of hell upon my heels! Oh, most unnatural state! Surely God cannot look upon such a creature. I pray to the blessed Virgin every day for intercession for my soul!

5th January, 1874. By the power of Mary, Mother of God, I swear to refrain from the ultimate sin and to remain steadfast in my flesh. Sworn by the power of the lily. L & R.

16th May, 1875. I will not falter, but will remain true!!! No matter the torment or longing, I will not yield. I will control the process, God grant me strength and will. By the grace and power of the monarchy and its allegiance. De Par Le Roy. L & R.

10th September, 1880. It is all finished. My life, my world, everything. Elizabeth warned me and I discovered the truth at last. *He was set upon me by that Prussian jackal! It was all a lie, the Great Lie!*

Oh, most venomous viper at my very bosom!! Oh, lowest of the least worthy who ever breathed! My Judas! My devil! He dares still swear he loves me. I spit on his words! If I could tear my heart out and fling it after him in the dirt, I would, I would!!

21st December, 1880. He continues to come and beg at my door, the devil. I will never look upon his hideous face again. He is afraid I will tell, and I might, I might! To destroy him, I might! When I think on the Change, now that things are clear, I wonder—what was his true intent? Was it an accident, as he swore to me then, or had he plotted with that jackal to destroy me? If so, why did he not simply kill me then instead of putting me in this torment? Could he have hated me *that much*?

No. I know that part of him at least. He truly revels in this life. He could not have guessed how much I would hate it. I wish to God he had simply ended it there in blood and death!

10th June, 1881. Terror! Rapture! During W.'s performance tonight I felt a strong pulling, and the horror nearly came upon me right there! Then the music turned and the feeling was gone. What can it mean?!!! Can music truly have such power? I must confide in the Great Friend. If anyone on this earth understands the passion and potency of opera, it is he!

2nd August, 1882. The experiments go better and better. It has given me something to hold on to, and the terror of the nights has somewhat eased. Now that I have hope, I am better able to fight the sickness. The devil still comes and waits outside in the night and calls for me, but I have learned to stop up my ears and resist him. He comes less and less frequently as a result, thank the blessed Mother of God. I still must fight my own internal urges but She and W. give me courage to do so—most of the time.

W. has proved as loyal and determined as ever I believed he would be in a matter of my salvation. He says he has the formula now; it remains only to put the finishing touches on the completed opera and to draw up the diagram for the crystals. Can this living death truly end? I scarce dare to hope!

April, 1883. The Great Friend is dead! How unjust that he should be taken from me now! Where is my chance at salvation? *Why has God condemned me twice?*

10th October, 1885. There MUST be made clear funds for the crystals. Lies, everyone lies! My own servants! What must I do? Must I sell one of my beloved castles? The crystals MUST BE MADE! I grow daily less able to control my own will (how long will I be able to resist the ultimate sin?), and the music is worthless without the device. Time is running out for me. There are rumors and plots and conspiracies. Please, God, the crystals MUST BE MADE!

Bayreuth, Germany

It was sunny and clear when Grace reached Bayreuth. Wahnfried, the residence where Wagner spent the last years of his life, had been made into a museum. Grace found a side street on which to park and hurried back to the villa. She felt her search was narrowing; the picture was coming into focus as if a lens was turning somewhere. The diary had given her the last piece of the puzzle—Ludwig's hope. And his hope had lain with Wagner.

As if an omen of good faith, she was greeted at the door of the villa by a large bronze head of Ludwig— the young Ludwig, face tender and vulnerable. She smiled at him reassuringly and pulled open the heavy door.

"*Guten Tag,*" the attendant said.

"*Grüss Gott,*" Grace answered.

The entryway was small, with a built-in display case that served as a desk for the museum attendant. He was a young man, mid-twenties, blond and studious-looking with wire-rimmed glasses. He had a sheaf of papers in front of him, and as Grace paid for her ticket, she noticed that it was musical staff paper with hand-marked notes.

"*Danke*," she said as he gave her change.

"You're American?"

"Yes," Grace answered with a sigh. It was amazing how few people here would give a foreigner a chance to speak the language.

"You'll have the place all to yourself today. We had a tour group this morning, but it's been quiet since then. If you have any questions, please ask me. I love to be interrupted."

He smiled at her, and his soft pink skin flushed a little at the throat.

"My work is not going so well," he explained hurriedly, as though she'd think he was being facetious.

Grace promised to interrupt frequently and lengthily, and went into the museum.

She passed through the displays like a crow circling a wheat field—eyes darting to see through the hubris and history for something that was actually relevant. Had anyone seen her, they would have thought her quite odd with her peering, dissecting, and dismissing rush through the displays.

Ludwig hadn't entered Wagner's life until 1864, so the early years were bypassed quickly. Then Wagner's fortunes had changed. Fleeing from city to city, deeply in debt, he'd been quite in trouble until his own personal savior appeared, a rich patron, a royal patron, a devoted, adoring, smitten fan—the teenage King Ludwig. Here a locket portrait of the king given by Ludwig to the "musical genius." And money, of course. What did Ludwig care for money? Sacks of it to save Wagner's neck, promises made by Wagner, promises later broken. But the performances! Ludwig's generosity saved the music. He insisted upon Wagner in Munich, a city that despised the composer. He opened doors.

Page after page of original sheet music in the maestro's own hand—*Lohengrin, Parsifal, Der Ring des Nibelungen*. Grace passed them without pause.

And finally, in a small room, a tribute to Wagner's patron saint. The sunlight filtered in through a stained-glass image of Ludwig, all royal blues and deep reds, hair black-painted glass, features etched from a portrait. In a cabinet was correspondence between Ludwig and Wagner. Grace scanned them. From the king were mostly flowery praises, almost embarrassing in the rational world of the 1990s, so vociferously emotional and extravagantly phrased. But then, the king was no doubt inspired by Wagner's operas, which were nothing if not overdramatic and ponderously self-aggrandizing.

The last letter in the case was from Wagner to Ludwig. Grace almost dismissed this one too when the date caught her eye. She read the English translation on the sign next to it.

> July 1882.
> Great and beloved King. Monsieur Beaujolais and I have finished the diagram. We checked the figures many times, and M. is confident that it will work. Eight identical fixtures are to be made from the diagram and placed in the theater *exactly* as specified. I'm sending the diagram with your courier.
> Be full of hope and have courage. Your soul is more precious to me than mine own—we shall win it peace or die trying. Your own Wagner.

Grace gripped the display case with cold fingers. It confirmed what she'd read in the diary. Ludwig and Wagner had conspired on something, but what? Where was the diagram the letter mentioned? Grace looked through all the displays in the room but found nothing. She hurried into the next room. There was more here on the building of Wagner's theater in Bayreuth. Grace hurried past it.

In the last room was an account of Wagner's death in 1883. He'd been visiting Venice and had suffered a heart attack in a gondola. A few days later he had died quietly at his desk. Cosima had been inconsolable. Ludwig had been inconsolable. The world had been inconsolable. Especially, no doubt, Wagner's debtors.

Then she saw it—a desk against the wall roped off with red velvet theater ropes. A sign said *Wagner's desk exactly as it was the day he died.*

Grace leaned forward over the ropes. There were papers on the desk. Had they really been untouched? Wouldn't Wagner have been working on "that project" just before his death? Grace glanced around, but there was no one in the room. She'd seen no once since she'd entered except for the young man at the entrance. She ducked under the rope.

In the middle of the desk, on a faded green blotter pad, was a large piece of paper. It was a diagram of a theater. The name at the top said *Residenztheater, München.* The diagram was a cutaway of the theater, showing each individual seat, the stage, the doors, everything. This layout was formally printed, but on top had been added measurements and lines in pencil—from the stage to the back of the theater, from box to box, measurements from floors to ceilings and wall to wall. And large X's were marked along the ceiling at precise intervals, each also measured with lines and numbers, distances from each X to the stage, walls, floor, back center box seats, all enumerated.

It was definitely a diagram, but was it the diagram Wagner had mentioned in his letter? Grace thought not, for that letter had referred to it as a diagram for some kind of "fixture" or "device" of which eight copies were to be made. But this theater diagram had to be related to the bit about "placing the devices in the theater exactly as specified." There were eight X's, four on each side of the theater. But what were the devices? And why did their placement require such mathematical precision?

A stack of correspondence lay to the left of the blotter. Grace glanced behind her again and then carefully riffled through them with the historian's awareness of the fragility of paper. The one on the bottom had a large drawing of a diamond shape on it. Grace pulled it out and studied it quickly.

It was from a Monsieur Beaujolais—the man mentioned in Wagner's letter to Ludwig. It was in French, and Grace understood none of it. But what was clear was that the letter, several pages long, was a discussion of mathematical formulae. Equations and drawings of what looked like sound waves were abundant. And then there was the drawing of what had to be, not a diamond, but a crystal. The drawing was meticulously rendered, with every facet to be cut scribbled with measurements and angles. This, then, was one of the crystals of which Ludwig's diary spoke. *The crystals must be made!* Grace leaned forward again to study the schematic of the theater, the positions of the X's.

Chandeliers? Could it be crystal chandeliers? *All this effort for chandeliers?*

She put the letter back and ducked under the rope, her mind cogitating. A diagram of the Residenztheater. And crystals, possibly crystal chandeliers. Sound waves . . . Acoustics? Did it have something to do with acoustics?

Then she remembered she had brought the diary with her. She pulled it out of her purse and flipped through it.

10th June, 1881. Terror! Rapture! During W.'s performance tonight I felt a strong pulling, and the horror nearly came upon me right there! Then the music turned and the feeling was gone. What can it mean?!!!

Can music truly have such power? I must confide in
the Great Friend. If anyone on this earth understands
the passion and potency of opera, it is he!

Grace stared at it for a moment, her brain rebelling
at comprehension. The diary, the strange sessions in
the Singer's Hall . . . *Ludwig screaming*. Acoustics.
The X's on the theater diagram, the measurements
and calculations, reminding her somehow of a blueprint for a bank heist. A plot, a plan, a new performance, not here in Bayreuth, where all of Wagner's
new work was done at the time, but in Munich once
again.

They had been laying a trap.

The words came into her resistant mind like a
floodgate opening. She saw the werewolf lore book
in front of her as clearly as if she'd been holding
it there.

*The true werewolf may shyft forme at wil, but the
Chaunge may be forced upon them by certeyn sounds
swich as the howling of a wolf or the presence of a
ful moon.*

*I felt a strong pulling, a pulling, pulling, pulling and
the horror, the nightmare, the living death nearly came
upon me right there . . .*

Wagner and Ludwig had been working on a way to
force the Change with music.

A trap to catch a werewolf.

"Excuse me," Grace said. She startled the young
man.

He jumped a bit in his seat and giggled nervously.
"Sorry, I was trying to hear a phrase. Sometimes my
ears forget to hear the outside world when I'm doing
that."

"I am interrupting, then."

"No, please!"

"Grace Nakimura," she said, holding out her hand. The young man accepted it with a tinge of surprise.

"Georg. Georg Immerding."

"Georg, I was wondering if I could ask you something."

"Of course." He closed his noteboook and pushed it to one side.

Grace hesitated and took a deep breath. "Georg, have you ever heard about a lost Wagner opera?"

Georg recoiled backward and nearly lost control of the stool. He caught himself from falling by gripping the top of the display case with one hand and waving the other erratically in the air.

"Georg?" Grace asked, alarmed.

"No. Sorry. I'm okay." He squeaked. He settled his stool firmly back on the ground. "Did my brother send you here?"

Grace raised an eyebrow. "Uh, no."

"No. Of course not. It's just that my brother laughs at my ideas. He thinks lost operas are for fools."

"So you do think there *is* one?"

"Only in the dreams of unemployed composers." Georg smiled wistfully. "Of which my brother is not one. He's the conductor for the Munich opera."

"Really?" Grace was impressed.

"Oh, yes," Georg said with a trace of rancor. "So you see, he doesn't need to imagine such things."

"But what if there really *was* one? Have you ever seen the panels in the Singer's Hall at Neuschwanstein?"

"Many times," Georg said, his eyes shining. "It very much looks like a Wagner."

"And Ludwig wrote to the Munich conductor about a new opera too, am I right?"

Georg looked at Grace appraisingly. "Are you a musician?"

"No. I'm more interested in Ludwig, actually. I think he was planning something with Wagner. In fact, I know he was."

"I wish I could help you. The thing is . . ." Georg stroked his chin dejectedly. "My brother says Wagner would not have worked on a secret project for Ludwig. It was not in his nature. If he had a new opera, he would have told everyone—*on* and *on* he would have told. It was in Ludwig's nature to *want* a private opera, but not in Wagner's to give him one."

"But he *wasn't* writing it for Ludwig alone. The letter showed that it was to be performed in Munich."

Georg shrugged, but his face betrayed a desire to be convinced. "Even so . . . If he ever started such a thing Cosima, his family . . . they would know."

Grace thought about it, biting her lower lip stressfully. "Unless he had a good *reason* for secrecy."

"Like what?"

Grace couldn't bring herself to say it, even if she'd had time to explain, which she didn't. She sighed. "I'm not sure. Have you ever seen anything else that pointed to a lost opera? Anything here maybe?"

Georg looked down at his nails. "Well . . . There is something in the archives. I was not supposed to look at it, actually."

"What?" Grace leaned on the display case and bent forward to get a look at his face. His long blond bangs hid his eyes. "Georg?"

"Cosima Wagner's journal. It is in a case. One day I opened it when no one was here."

"What'd it say? Can I see it?"

He glanced up guiltily. "No, please. I should not have looked myself. It is nothing anyway."

Grace made up her mind quickly. She stood up straight and put her hands on her hips. "All right, Georg. I'll show you mine if you show me yours."

"What?" he said with an embarrassed giggle.

"Diaries. Have you heard of Ludwig's?"

"Of course! But no one's allowed to see it."

"I have a copy. With me."

Georg shook his head in disbelief. "No."

Grace pulled it from her purse and slapped it on the counter. "This is a handwritten English translation made by Sir Richmond Chaphill when he was writing Ludwig's biography."

Georg looked at the sheaf of papers with wide eyes. "Not possible," he repeated in a much smaller voice.

"Go get Cosima's journal, Georg," Grace growled.

Georg went.

They locked the front door to the museum and spread both documents out on the counter, then huddled together like children studying ants. In the silence of the hall, Grace's clear voice range out.

" 'August, 1882. The experiments go better and better. W. has proved as loyal and determined as ever . . . it remains only to put the finishing touches on the completed opera and to make up the diagram for the crystals.' "

"My God!" Georg whispered. "*Completed*! An opera completed in 1882. Is it possible?"

Grace's dark eyes were laden with intent. "What do *you* think?"

Georg flushed under her gaze. "Okay, listen to this." He translated haltingly. "July, 1881. Richard returned from his meeting with the king. Never have I seen him so pale. I was worried for his heart! He would not speak with me, but immediately shut up himself in his study and started working on a new project. He will not tell me the first thing about it. He will only say that it was time he repaid his king.' "

Grace was leaning over the counter, her face inches away from Georg's own. "My God! That must have been the start of it—of the new opera!"

"Yes, but *what* happened? Why was he so pale? Why so secretive?" Georg asked, his eyes searching hers.

"I—I'm sure there was a reason." Grace faltered. She couldn't hide much at this distance, so she hastily changed the subject. "The real question is, if the opera was completed, what happened to it? Where did it *go*?"

Georg's eyes went wide. He began flipping through the journal. "When I saw this before, I thought I was imagining things, but . . . Listen."

" 'May, 1883. I sent Richard's sealed package to the king as he instructed me the day before he closed his eyes forever. I could not even bring myself to care what was in it, though heaven knows there were times when I wanted more than anything to know what was going on between those two. That seems so stupid now, now that life itself had ended. Whatever it is, I hope it brings the king good memories of Richard. He did so much for my beloved.' "

Somewhere down the hall, a grandfather clock was ticking. In the silence of the moment it seemed as loud and measured as approaching footsteps. Grace, oddly, was suddenly aware of the ticks, *one, two, three;* then she looked up at Georg and he at her, and they both spoke in breathy unison two simple words.

"The package!"

On the way back to Rittersberg, Grace's elation made the miles blur together as though even the clock bent to her will. But by the time she reached Augsburg, time had reasserted itself and pressed her spirits back down. She felt she'd solved the mystery of Ludwig, at least the heart of it. Exactly how he had died and why his plan went wrong, that was another matter.

But more important, she realized that she still had no clue as to how this fit into Gabriel's case. For that matter, perhaps it didn't. Perhaps it was only her openness to the idea of werewolves and Christian Ritter's letter that had brought Ludwig's plight to her. Perhaps it had nothing to do with Gabriel at all.

That's not what Mrs. Smith says.

Then Grace realized that she knew almost nothing about Gabriel's case. Something about killings in Munich that might be the work of a werewolf. Something about a hunt club and suspects. Somewhere, Gabriel was off doing what *she* was doing, what he'd done in New Orleans (so recklessly, so dangerously), and she didn't have the first clue where or what or whom or how. She'd gotten so caught up in her own research, so eager to make her own mark, that she'd forgotten that he was off somewhere making his as well, perhaps even mucking about with a *real* werewolf, mucking about in that brash, bungie-jumping way of his.

And she was suddenly very afraid.

Gerde was sitting on the sofa, trying to solve a crossword puzzle. She had the phone perched next to her, and the blankness of the page confirmed her distracted state. She got up as soon as the front door opened.

"Grace, I've been so worried! Is everything all right?"

"Yes," Grace said, though she suddenly was sure it wasn't. "Did Gabriel call?"

Gerde shook her head, her face pensive.

"When was the last time you heard from him?"

Gerde rubbed her hands together anxiously. "Not since he left. There was that letter to you, and that is all. I decided to call Herr Übergrau a few hours ago, and he sounded worried himself. The last he knew, Gabriel was leaving for a hunting trip."

"Hunting trip?" No two words could have sounded more ominous. Grace felt a sickening rush of dread.

"Yes. I don't understand it. Is he still working on the case, do you think?"

Grace bit her lip. "His letter said something about suspects in a hunt club. He must have gone off with them."

Grace realized she'd never shared the letter with Gerde and felt terrible.

"Oh, and there was a call from Herr Dallmeier," Gerde continued. "He said he has the information you requested if you want to call him back."

Grace fished in her purse and found Gabriel's letter. "Here. Read it. I'll go call Josef, and when I'm done we should talk to Werner. He knows where Gabriel went, doesn't he?"

"Yes, it . . . it was the Hubers' farm near Munich," Gerde said, looking down as if feeling guilty about having withheld the information for so long.

"Well, it will be someplace to start. As soon as I'm done with my phone call, okay?"

"All right." Gerde nodded. She watched anxiously as Grace ran up to the library.

"Josef? It's Grace."

"Grace! You're in luck. I found a copy of the entitlement deed. It had been filed in Berlin. Fortunately, it was among a shipment of city papers that were taken out and hidden during the war. They were recovered only ten years ago."

"That's great. What does it say?" Grace asked impatiently.

"Gowden did change his name. The new one is on the deed."

"*Read* it."

Grace's stomach was suddenly in knots, and the phone receiver grew slick in her hand. She had the terrible feeling that she would recognize the name, that what was about to be said would change everything.

Dallmeier read it. Her instincts had not been wrong. As soon as the words were out of his mouth,

Grace screamed and dropped the phone. It was still
rocking on the floor, Dallmeier's worried voice calling hollowly through it, as her feet pounded down
the stairs.

Chapter 7

He was dreaming of Gracie. She stood alone in a ball-room, an immense ballroom, and she was wearing a dress from another era: low-cut, tight bodice, full, arching skirt in some kind of creamy silk, all lace and glimmer. Her hair was piled up in ringlets, and white pearls wove their way through the black luster that outshone them. Her face was softened without the bangs and the blunt A-line cut that usually touched both cheeks. It was a beautiful face and so familiar.

God, he hadn't realized how much he'd missed her! He tried to approach her, but he didn't seem to have a body. He could only watch as she glided silently across the polished marble floor and stopped in front of a large painting.

It was a life-size portrait of a young man dressed in regal blue with epaulets and medals and a bright red sash. The young man's pale, narrow face was sur-rounded by a mist of black curls, and his blue eyes were as deep an indigo as his uniform.

Grace reached out her hand to touch the painting. She trailed her fingers longingly down one long arm, and when their slender tips reached the painted ones, they curled around each other. She pulled, gently, and the man stepped from the painting into the room.

And now they were dancing and the man held her in his arms. So tall was he, and handsome. Her pale skin against his starched royal blue was a song filled with longing as they moved. It was a picture too perfect, too compelling to be denied. He leaned down his head and

kissed her.

Then they were spinning, spinning, two dark heads locked in an embrace, locked in a kiss that would waken the dead, a kiss that could exchange souls, and Gabriel's dream eye watched the sweep of Grace go by, the creamy skin of her back above the tight silk, as they spun around again. He felt a swelling tide of jealousy and desire, wanted to tear the young man away and take his place, and then realized that

he had.

In an instant the bodiless spectator he had been vanished and she was in his arms, as real as anything. He could feel the cool stiffness of the silk against his arms where he held her, against his shirt, against his pants. He drew her in more tightly, pressing her against him, while his mouth experienced her greedily, sweetly, like a long drink of cool water to one parched of thirst. He drew her in with his lips, his tongue, wanting only to fall into this moment and never return.

He thought, *So this is what it's like.*

She pulled back, one hand pushing against his chest. Her lips left his, and he opened his eyes and saw, over her shoulder, the young man in blue. He was standing across the room, watching them, and as Gabriel's eyes met his, he raised his arm and pointed, like a mute beacon, toward Gabriel, beyond him.

Gabriel turned his head to look. Where the painting had been there was now a mirror. Reflected in the glass was Grace, reversed, and standing next to her, where he should have been, stood

a wolf.

He turned to look at Grace, his eyes searching for the contradiction. Her expression was loving and woeful. She caressed his puzzled face with her hand and opened her mouth to speak.

Beware the Black Wolf.

* * *

He was rushing through the darkness. He could hear Leber's voice saying,

Two wolves missing from the zoo.

Then he was back in the cave, in the lair, and he could hear the sound of his own retching, and he could see his hand splayed flat on a rock for balance and by that hand

von Zell in the moonlight, coarse fur thick and bristly, *red* fur, red like the hair from the farm.

Von Glower emerging from the cave. He opened his mouth, but what came out was not what he said that day, at that moment. What came out was

An Alpha werewolf will not harm a beta of its own making with its own hand

KA-BOOM

They are at the ravine, and von Glower rides up on his horse and the wolf. The red wolf is standing there growling, snarling, and Gabriel screams

Kill it! Shoot it!

and von Glower throws him the gun

You must do it.

Von Glower in the dark woods, ahead of him, messing with his hair—no, his *ears*. And the wolf's howl cutting through the night and Gabriel calling out

Friedrich

and von Glower not turning, *not hearing*.

Two wolves missing

Leber said.

WHY TWO? WHY DID VON ZELL WANT TWO WOLVES?

And there he was, von Zell, sitting there, looking smug in the chair at the club.

We used to hunt together quite a bit. I suppose I've simply outgrown him

And then Gabriel was in the lair, the choking, cloying lair, and he was looking down at the bodies in the pit, illuminated by the lantern: the corpses, some of them just bones, the tattered remains of faded clothes, some of them fresh but some of them so old.

Started acting strange about a year ago

So old.

Von Glower was telling von Zell he'd acted stupidly about something

SO OLD.

When a healthy beast kills, it takes only what it needs to survive and it does so respectfully

"But the killer is *not* a man," Gabriel mumbled out loud.

A healthy *beast*

SO OLD!!!!!

The creature he'd imagined, the beast running down the wooded path at night, dragging a body back to the lair silently, carefully, hiding the evidence

In broad daylight

Leber was leaning forward at his desk

Body parts left lying like a trail of bread crumbs

Not this pointless slaughter

And the hand was on the rock; he was retching, retching, retching, and the hand was on the rock and next to the hand was hair, animal hair, long and thick like that at the farm but even in the dim light from the cave opening he can see it isn't red, it has no luster, no tinge of auburn, no inner light.

Two wolves

It was black.

Acted stupidly

It was *black.*

Then it is on your head

IT WAS BLACK.

"No!"

He woke up and found himself on the floor of the Huber farm. He'd fallen off the couch at some point, and the afghan was tangled around his legs.

And he was in the grip of a terrible, wrenching, debilitating pain. It was coming from everywhere and nowhere, from the marrow of the bones in his limbs, from his head, which was bursting asunder, from his stomach, which was surfing on waves of nausea, from his lungs, which felt like they were breathing liquid fire, from the stinging, burning, crawling wound on his leg.

"No!" he cried again. The plea was born in his mind as a scream, but it came out as a guttural whisper. Even his throat was on fire.

And he knew what was happening but couldn't, wouldn't, *wouldn't* believe it until he looked down and saw his forearm, bare in the moonlight, *ripple,* the muscles beneath the skin dancing and cording and slipping across the bone.

"*No!* Oh, God, no! *Jesus,* no! Please, God! *Please!*"

He'd killed von Zell, but he'd missed something: *von Zell's* changer—the alpha wolf, the black alpha wolf. *Von Glower was the alpha.* He hadn't thrown the gun to remove Gabriel's curse. He'd thrown it because *he couldn't kill von Zell himself.*

And then the pain in his gut bent him on the floor like a bowing marionette. He screamed as he felt his spine shift, tear, *bend.*

Oh, God, let it end, let me wake up. Make it stop. Let it end.

And then he heard the sounds of the door opening and footsteps.

"Gabriel!" It was Grace's sweet, frantic New York voice.

"Go. Away." He managed to choke out. "Get out. Now!"

"It's all right, dear," came an incongruously relaxed and soothing voice. "We know all about it, and we know just what to do."

Rittersberg

The cold forced him to rise from unconsciousness. When he opened his eyes, shivering and naked, he saw that he was lying on a chilly earthen floor. The smell in his nostrils was dank and musty, like a basement or . . . or a cave. And when he managed to raise his head (which weighed about a hundred pounds) on his neck (which felt like it had the worst case of whiplash ever), he saw that he was in a stone room. *A cell.*

He immediately panicked. In a pitiless wave of remembrance he knew everything. And although he couldn't recall exactly what had happened last night—it was as hazy as a bad dream—he knew, from the broken feel of his body and from his nakedness, that he must have . . . must have *changed*.

And now he was in prison.

He scrambled to his feet, his fear overriding his bruised muscles. He looked around, but there was nothing in the room but a cot—not a scrap of clothing, not even a blanket with which to cover himself. He was to be treated like an animal, then.

And just about the time he was going to open his mouth and scream, he heard a loud sound. It grated on his ears like the whetting of a blade on stone, and he realized it was the lock on the door outside, only amplified ten times. And then the door creaked open.

A slightly built older man entered. He had a long, sober face and little hair, and his outfit was pure Americana circa 1976. He held out a neat stack of blue jeans and T-shirt and averted his eyes.

"Put these on now," he said, trying hard to sound ordinary. "Then come on upstairs. We have a hot bath waiting for you at the castle. Those scratches'll need tending."

It was the worst fifteen minutes of his life. He would remember it a long time afterward, with unwelcomed clarity, and with the memory would come a humiliation so overburdening it made him wish for a loaded gun and the courage to place it to his temples. For a long time afterward.

And this was how it began. He watched the man

leave, and then he put on his clothes. Now that he knew where he was, the worst of the fear had gone and his aches and pains reasserted themselves petulantly. He felt as though he'd gone ten rounds with a five-hundred-pound gorilla. Bending his knees to get into his pants, he had to bite his lips to keep from screaming out loud. And the nausea, wave after wave, like the worst flu he'd ever experienced, and the shivering, wretched shivering. He had a fever. He was burning up.

And when he'd finally accomplished it, when the clothes were more or less on his body, he walked weakly to the door and tried to straighten himself up, tried to firm up his throbbing spine.

Then there came a walk up a flight of stone stairs, supported, reluctantly, by the tall man who said something about being Mr. Smith from blah blah blah. A walk up the flight of stairs into the light, like emerging from the tomb. And at the top came the worst of it. The faces.

Werner's face and the postmistress's face and the priest's face and the baker's face and the faces of all the other villagers waited in the Rittersberg town square. Waiting there, like a crowd gathered at the scene of an accident. Waiting there, as if hoping to catch sight of some blood. And right up in front was Gerde's face. And Grace. Worst of all, Grace's perky, familiar little face.

All looking at him. Trying to smile. All drenched in pity. Pity. Pity. *Pity.*

Welcome home, they said, in English, in German. And Werner's hand on his shoulder—*You got one of them. You got the one that killed Toni Huber. You did well.*

(a lie)

And Grace chattering nervously. *We have a hot bath and Doktor Strutz here to look at you, and Gerde made breakfast—aren't you starved? I bet you're starved.*

And on and on and he tried to push through them,

and his face must have shown something, for Gerde was saying, *Let's just get him to the castle. He must be tired. He looks tired. Let's just . . .*

And the car and he was getting into it and he could still see the faces outside. The specious sympathy on the faces. And then the drive up the hill to the castle and still Grace was chattering, her hand coming lightly to rest on his arm now and then (as if to show that he was not repulsive, which, of course, he was), and he couldn't bear to look at her, couldn't stand it that she could see *him*, not this way, and more chattering as the car doors opened and the sunlight pierced his brain and then they were in the cool dimness of the castle and how strange that it was still the same, that everything was still the same—everything, everything, everything except for him.

And finally he was in the bathroom, finally he could disappear, finally he could close the door and shut them out, all those faces, all those words. He locked the door and took off his clothes, and now the pain in his body was nothing, was welcome, was his due, and he stepped into the tub and sank into the water and covered his face with a hot, wet washcloth.

And sobbed. Silently.

"No, we *can* pull it off," Grace insisted.

"Only if we can find it," Gerde said doubtfully.

"Why don't we just wait and see how the session goes?" said Mrs. Smith.

"That might be best," Mr. Smith agreed.

They were all at the table in the castle's dining room. The table was set and the dishes were still clean. The smell of coffee filled the room.

"*Ahem.*" Mr. Smith cleared his throat, and the others realized Gabriel was standing in the doorway, leaning against the doorjamb, arms folded.

"God, I could smell that from upstairs," he said. He walked stiffly over to the table and picked up the coffeepot. Hot, dark liquid streamed into a cup.

"Are you feeling better?" Grace asked. "Doktor Strutz is waiting at the *gasthof*. I can call him."

"Not just now, Gracie." Gabriel pulled back the empty chair—its feet scraping loudly in the awkward silence—and sat down gingerly.

"So where's the chow?" he asked, looking around at them brightly. His fair complexion was mottled with pink—from the hot bath, Grace wondered, or the fever?

Gerde got up and went into the kitchen. Mrs. Smith went in to help. Grace got up too, but she headed for Gabriel instead. She placed a cool hand on his forehead.

"You're burning up."

"I'm fine," he growled. He pulled her hand away and shook it. "Nice to meet ya."

A crease of irritation appeared just between her brows. He seemed to recognize it, for he smiled fondly.

"Fine! You're fine. A hundred and three, no big deal. Sorry I mentioned it." Grace went back to her chair.

He drank the coffee greedily, as he always had. He winced at first, then drank some more.

"How'd you get back to the Hubers', anyway?" Grace asked, still a little put out. "I thought you were on a hunting trip."

"Didn't feel much like hangin' out after . . . once I was hurt. Frie—" He paused awkwardly. "They dropped me off. I was gonna drive back here, but I was so . . . so tired."

He said it lightly. He cleared his throat.

"Good thing. I really didn't think we'd find you."

He said nothing. He glanced at the kitchen door.

"There's so much to tell you," Grace said breathlessly. She leaned forward, studying his face. "God, a million things! You're not going to believe this, but remember that letter to Ludwig? Guess who the Black Wolf was that Christian Ritter was tracking?"

Gabriel looked down at his knife. His pinkness deepened. "Von Glower," he said stiffly.

"Right! Here I was tracking down this whole Black Wolf thing with Ludwig—by the way, he changed *Ludwig* into a werewolf too. Can you believe it?"

Gabriel looked up at her sharply.

"And the whole time, I couldn't quite figure out how it might be related to what *you* were doing. 'Course, it would've helped if you'd *told* me what you were doing."

She paused in her spiel to let that sink in. He looked away.

"Then Dallmeier found the entitlement deed. You see, the Black Wolf was Ludwig's lover. His real name back then was Paul Gowden, but Bismarck gave him a title—probably for his help in closing the Prussian treaty—and he changed it. Changed it to Baron Rudolf von Glower. He even appears in Ludwig's diary as the R in 'L & R'.

"In fact, Dallmeier helped me track von Glower while you were, um, out of it yesterday. Rudolf von Glower left Germany in 1890. In 1927 his alleged son returned to claim the family lands and title—an Endro von Glower. He was around until 1942, then went abroad again. In 1970 a Friedrich von Glower showed up. You know what I think? I think it's all the same guy. The inquisitor's manual said werewolves are essentially immortal. I don't think it's been new generations at all. He has to go away once in a while so people don't catch on about his age."

The kitchen door swung open, and Gerde emerged with a platter of meats and cheese. Gabriel looked relieved.

"That's good, Grace," he said flatly. He looked at the platter and patted his stomach. "Man, I'm ravenous!"

Gerde stopped in mid-stride and stared at him. The spoon on the platter rattled lightly as her hands shook.

Gabriel turned scarlet and went back to messing with the cream pitcher.

Grace stood up. "Let me help." She moved to Gerde's side and took the platter. Gerde's eyes welled up with sudden tears, and she ran back into the kitchen.

"Uh . . . Looks good, huh?" Grace said cheerfully, putting the platter on the table. The cold array of sliced pressed meats and thick local cheeses stared up at her. "Uh, doesn't it?" she asked doubtfully.

His chin trembled and he exploded. He pushed the table away roughly, sending it skidding several inches. His chair clattered to the stone floor as he strode from the room in a rage.

She found him outside on the doorstep. He was pacing angrily, one hand pressed against his mouth. When she came out, he turned his back to her. His shoulders were tensed so hard she could see the corded muscles beneath his shirt.

"I'm sorry," she said. "I didn't mean what you *thought* I meant. It's just that I know you're probably sick, and those cold cuts . . ."

She trailed off. He said nothing.

She took a deep breath. "I know this must be hard, but we're going to fix it."

"No, Grace! You have *no* idea how it is, okay? You have no *fucking* idea."

He turned to face her, and she saw the violence of his rage, and the shame.

She looked away, embarrassed. "No, I guess I don't."

"No *fucking* idea," he mumbled again, as if to himself.

She glanced at him sideways, wanting desperately to comfort him. "I know you're upset, but I really think we can fix it. You see, Ludwig had a plan. . . ."

"You can't *fix* it, Grace," Gabriel interrupted darkly. "I fucked up, okay? You won. You were right, you figured it out, you're the smart one. Me, I was wrong. I blew it. I screwed up. I flunked out. I bit it. Okay? Does that make you happy? It's over. You go on and take over now. I'm sure everyone will love you."

Grace shook her head impatiently. "Cut the crap and listen, will you? There's this opera that Wagner wrote, and it—"

Gabriel snorted bitterly, then he laughed out loud, a loathing laugh. "Grace! Come on! You should have just left me there."

Grace's face darkened. "What are you *talking* about? Left you *where*? At the Huber farm? And what good would *that* do? You'd just be roaming the countryside like . . . like von Zell! At least *here* we can put you behind bars when it happens, so you don't—"

But he moved to her side in one quick stride. He gripped her arm painfully, his face so terrible, the words died in her throat. She immediately regretted what she'd said. She finally saw, really *saw* how it was. She too had been in a kind of denial.

"Just kill me," he said quietly, his fingers digging into her arm. His eyes were so filled with darkness, they were unbearable.

"I can't," she said, her voice thickening. "Gabriel, I can't. I won't."

Other words, words that had come to her mouth from out of nowhere died unsaid. But perhaps he felt them anyway, for when she reached out her arms and gathered him to her, he didn't resist. He buried his face on her shoulder and allowed her to hold him like that for a long, bittersweet time.

"Now, hon, here's the plan," Mrs. Smith said. She leaned over the couch where he lay. He could see the light overhead shining right through her beehive in a kind of dyed filament glow.

"You just hold this ring here that Grace got and

close your eyes. We're gonna try to make contact. You and me together, all right?"

She sounded exactly like something from a UFO documentary. He turned his head to one side so he could shoot Grace a look.

Go on, Grace mouthed. Gabriel sighed.

"Don't forget the opera," Grace added for the tenth time.

Gabriel grumbled low in his throat.

"Now don't block, dear. You have the gift and you've already been in contact with him, so there's no need to play skeptic. You don't need to worry about saying anything, I'll do the communicating. You just do your best to get into his mind—that lock of Ludwig's hair in that ring should help you do that. If this works the way I hope it will, you'll help me bridge the gap to the other side. Now come on. Close your eyes."

Gabriel sighed again and closed them. He'd insisted on having everyone out of the room, but Grace had insisted on staying.

At first he fought Mrs. Smith's low, soothing voice as she talked him down, fought it rebelliously, derisively, silently. But at last fatigue overcame him, and he fell into the hypnotic tones, as silly as they were. He stopped thinking about how silly they were and fell.

Neuschwanstein, 1886

Ludwig opened his eyes to the sound of scratching on the door. He hadn't been sleeping, only trying to shut down the panic that threatened to consume him. At the interruption any progress he'd made evaporated like the illusion that it was.

"What is it?" he called impatiently.

Weber entered, shuffling forward on his knees, his face studying the carpeting.

"Your Majesty wished to be informed . . . they are on the move at Hohenschwangau."

Ludwig sat up immediately, ignoring the pain in his head. "Are they coming this way?"

"They have not yet left, Highness, but the carriages are in the courtyard."

"What about the guard?"

Weber shifted his weight awkwardly from one hand to another. "They . . . most of the farmers returned home last night."

Profanities began pouring from the king's mouth unbidden. His rage sparked to life like a match being struck. The worst thing was that he never seemed to be the one lighting it; nor could he predict its blaze.

"Go get more men!" he screamed when he'd regained control of his words.

"Yes, Highness." Weber scuttled backward from the room and shut the door softly.

Ludwig ran down to the hall to his study, which had the best view of the east. He tore it open and peered out, trying to get a look. But it was night—he hadn't even realized it was night. Hohenschwangau was small from here, even in broad daylight. Even so, he could see movement in the courtyard—torches. And horses, many horses. Although he could not see them, he felt their life force, ever so faintly, even across the distance.

He uttered a curse and stumbled backward. And there, in that moment in the study, it entered his heart like Cupid's arrow—an acceptance of the inevitable. He relinquished, finally, the last thread of hope, of determination to complete his plan, to somehow save himself, to have a life beyond this horror.

It would never be.

The rage sloughed away like a discarded skin, and what was underneath was cold, stark fear.

"Mother of God," he pleaded. His knees wanted to buckle right there, but he dragged himself back to his bedroom, pulling open and then shoving shut each door along the way. It was a habit he'd gotten so used to he didn't even notice it anymore. Block the doors, block the line of sight, never let anyone see you.

And in the bedroom he stumbled to the chapel and closed that door too, then locked himself in.

It was a tiny room, and he loved it that way, for he wanted the arms of God around him, to feel, with the Virgin on the altar, that he was in a womb, the blessed womb. But how he'd felt the loathing of these walls— those arms—at times. Loathing for his putrid soul!

He collapsed in front of the altar, *hugged* it.

"Mary, Mother of God, be with us poor sinners now and in the hour of our death. . . ."

And he reached out a hand and clasped the Madonna and child—both with faces pitch black after the Virgin of AltÖtting—and poured himself into her. He poured out his rage and frustration and terror, and it oozed forth in thick globs as though he'd slashed his psychic veins. He emptied himself, and for that moment, emptying himself was all that he desired.

And when the torrent became a trickle, then stopped altogether, the fear was gone and he was in a place of unnatural peace, like the eye of a hurricane. Yes, they would come for him. But he didn't have to remain in custody. He didn't have to allow them to lock him up, to study him. His secret, his shame, did not have to go down in the history books.

These were the things that terrified him. And like a child told that although night would come, the light did not have to be turned out, he felt enormously comforted. They could take his body, but they could not force him to remain in it.

As for the other matter, the reason why he'd believed he *had* to live, he suddenly, in a clear, calm voice, received the answer for that as well. And he realized that he was free. He'd carried the burden for a long time, and now he had no choice but to hand it to another. It was not a matter of opting out; there was simply no choice. He felt unimaginably lightened and wept tears of gratitude as he thanked the Virgin profusely, tenderly, for her guidance.

Then he kissed her black face and went out to do what had to be done.

On the dresser in the bedroom was a gold and lapis box with a swan on the lid. With steady hands and clear eyes Ludwig opened a secret compartment at its base and removed a gold key.

This he took into the study to a large cabinet of carved wood with turrets and fake windows—a model of Neuschwanstein itself. He fitted the key into the lock on the door, opened the cabinet, and gently removed three rolls of paper. Each roll was tied with a scarlet ribbon. He carried them carefully to his desk.

From the bottom drawer he removed a piece of vellum so thin it was transparent. A Wittelsbach crest and a Bavarian flag were placed to either side at the top of the page. Four small swans etched in blue and placed at odd intervals were the only other markings. He carried the vellum over to the sitting area, where a blueprint of the castle hung. He placed the vellum carefully on the glass, lining up the flag and the crest with matching icons on the plan. And then his blue eyes, still lashed as thickly as a babe's but red-rimmed and exhausted, sought out the positions of the swans carefully. One fell in the bedroom, just to the right of the living room door. One was in the Grotto, at the bottom of the left-hand wall. One was in the Singer's Hall under the third painting on the left, and one was in the room at the top of the tower.

He glanced around suspiciously, but there was no one there. There never was.

He withdrew the vellum and took it back to his desk. Then he drew out a piece of his finest writing paper and a new pen with his own crest on the hilt. He opened his ink well and began to write.

June 17, 1886

My Sweetest Dove,

By the time you receive this letter, it will have
ended for me. My Uncle Luitpold and the traitors
mean to finish me, to wrap me in their lies and put
me away somewhere. I cannot let that happen.

Oh, my beloved, you and your friendship make up
the happiest memories of my life! You have always
been true to me, and I shall love you forever. Please
remember that, and know that I wish to bequeath you
the world. I must instead ask a terrible favor.

You have known something of my torment these
past years. I have written to you of the plan that I
had for setting myself free of it. Well, dearest one, it
has become too late for me to complete this work.
They will not let me, though it means my soul! I can
only beg you to believe in me, to believe in the impor-
tance of the work, and to do your utmost to carry
it through. Will you, my only friend? Will you save
your Ludwig?

Here is what must be done. I intend to hide, this
very day, four documents in secret compartments in
Neuschwanstein. Enclosed you will find a vellum that
will reveal the locations of these compartments. Use
it on the map in my study. Remove the four documents you find in the compartments and take them to
the conductor in Munich.

Three of these documents are the three acts of a
new opera. The fourth is a diagram for a chandelier.
Eight of these chandeliers must be built exactly and
placed in the Residenztheater as shown on the diagram. When you have done this and the opera is prepared, you must invite the following person to the
opening performance. His name is Baron Rudolf von
Glower, and he lives in Prussia. Place him in the *mittelloge* and make certain that the sharpest and quickest
armed guards are stationed near the door and are prepared to protect the crowd with their life. This is all.
The rest, I believe, will happen naturally.

I know I sound insane, as insane as they say that I
am, but if you do this you will finally learn what has
been my torment and you will see for yourself my
tormentor! More, if all goes as I believe it must, you

will have saved my immortal soul and admitted me to heaven.

May God grant you peace and love and an eternal crown for your never ending loyalty and affection for me. I shall miss you. Your own and forever Eagle

When he lowered his pen, tears were streaming down his cheeks. He picked up the letter and blew on it through quivering cheeks. He folded both it and the vellum carefully and found an envelope in the drawer to enshroud his missive. On the front he wrote *Empress Elizabeth of Austria.* Then he stuck the envelope in a pocket and stood up, gathering the three parchment rolls to his chest like children.

To the Singer's Hall, up the stairs. And now he swore he could hear the clatter of hooves on the road below the mountain, the anxious grinding of carriage wheels.

The stairs were dark, and he cursed the servants. Every room, every crevice, was to be lit by candles at all times! He called out, but no one came. He placed one large hand against the wall and mounted the stairs in darkness, his night vision providing sight enough, though he hated to be dependent upon it, to feel the unnaturalness of his own physiology.

The Singer's Hall itself was still lit, albeit with candles burned nearly to the quick. He located the painting and knelt down stiffly. How did these things work? He could remember vaguely, being shown the compartments just after they were installed, but . . .

He banged his hand against the wall over and over, left and right and up and down. Just as his frustration threatened to rush in, he heard a click and a piece of the wall popped up.

Yes. Yes, excellent, he thought. He'd never have seen it. It was impossible to spot, even with *his* eyes. He tucked one of the rolls carefully into the small compartment, then swung the panel shut. All signs of it vanished at once.

He gave a sigh of satisfaction, then grunted as he pushed his heavy frame upright. Down, down, down to the grotto.

The compartment in the grotto he remembered better, for it was on the under-slant of a rocky protuberance just at the turn. He banged his hand more softly this time, afraid that the fake materials that made up the rock face would not withstand a pounding. The compartment popped open after just a few tries. He planted the second act of the opera.

Then the bedroom.

As he entered, he realized that the tower—his next stop—was locked. They kept it locked, *he* ordered it locked, because its entrance was between his rooms and the servants' and he always had a nasty feeling about them sneaking up there (for what purpose he couldn't fathom, but they hardly needed a reason to be vile). Now he picked up a silver bell from his nightstand and rang it, hiding the third roll of the opera behind his back.

Mayr, his valet, entered. He knew it was Mayr because of the black mask that covered his face. An ugly face had Mayr. Ludwig could not abide ugliness. In brutishness he saw an unmerciful reminder of himself.

"Send this letter off with a messenger at once! And bring me the key to the tower!" He held out his letter to Elizabeth.

Mayr reached up without looking, and the king placed it in his hand. Mayr tucked it in his waistband carefully so that it would not wrinkle, as he'd been taught to do. Then he hesitated, kneeling there on all fours.

"What are you, *deaf*?" the king shouted angrily. "Go get the key!"

"I believe it is lost. I shall go look for it," Mayr said.

"*Find* it," Ludwig thundered. "Don't look, *find* it. At once! And get someone off with that letter!"

"Yes, Your Highness." Mayr crawled backward from the room.

Lost! Indeed!

He rushed to his bedroom window and pushed aside the heavy drapes. Outside, the night was black, and the scent of it was tantalizing. It was so seductive, night, like a black pool you had only to lean toward to fall into.

"No," he said out loud. He shook his head and tried to concentrate, to hear, to see anything that might be moving on the road below. He heard horses faintly, but whether from the road just out of sight or his own stock in the courtyard, he couldn't tell. He let the curtain fall, feeling his anxiety outstrip his nerve once again. He hurried over to the bedroom wall.

He glanced around—both doors were shut. He struck the wall again and again. The panel popped open, and he hid the third and final act of the opera.

Now the diagram.

He hurried into the chapel, trembling. Where was his calm, his resolve? To decide to act had been a relief, but now the horror of the next few hours began to impose upon him, like Jesus in Gethsemane. He wanted it to be over, but he did not relish the process. The thought that they might lay hands on him . . .

He muttered a quick prayer to the Virgin, but there was no time to stay and seek solace. He picked up the diagram from the altar. It was rolled tightly, as the opera had been, but this paper was as thin as tissue. It had lain here since Wagner's death, a promise to the Virgin, an oath that Sin would be conquered. He promised her this once more in a muttered prayer and tucked the roll inside the breast of his coat.

And then he did hear it, something on the path, a clatter. He rushed to the bedroom and rang the bell again, loudly.

No one came. He paced. He rang again and screamed out Mayr's name, Weber's. At last he heard scratching.

"Open it!"

Mayr crawled in.

"The key, the key, *the key*!" Ludwig ranted, unable to bear it.

"I'm still looking," Mayr said, and he began to back out even before he'd been dismissed. But Ludwig was too beside himself to correct the swine. Let him go, then, let him go find that damn key! Why were they all *always* so incompetent? And now his life, his very *soul* hung on the idiocy of his servants, as he'd always known it would. And they wondered why he raged so!

For ten minutes he waited, nearly unable to contain himself. He considered hiding the diagram under the bed or anywhere else, but no. Elizabeth would never find it there. He'd told her where to find it already. It must go in the tower.

Surely he was panicking for no good reason. Surely his men could hold them at the gate for at least a few hours. Surely what had arrived so far was just a vanguard, and they would have to wait down there and then discuss it the way that politicians do. Why, it could be days!

There came a scratching at the door.

"Enter, Mayr, damn you to hell!"

Mayr slipped inside. "I have the key to the tower, sire."

He held it up in one pathetic paw. Ludwig strode across the room on his long legs, his polished black shoes shining against the rugs. He snatched the key and a candle from the bedside and, unable to help himself, shoved Mayr down with one heavy thigh as he headed for the entry hall door.

Mayr had shut the door, as always. And as Ludwig jerked it open, he saw that the hall was dark. The candles were out, and that was particularly odd for this room, the first room the servants had to pass through to get to his quarters. Why had Mayr not lit them? Why were things falling apart?

He paused there, silhouetted in the doorway. Beyond, shadows danced away from the light, black and confusing. If he put out his own candle, his eyes would adjust quickly to the dark, see through the shadows, but he didn't want to put it out.

He hesitated. His heart beat loudly in his chest, sounding an instinctual alarm. He told himself he was being paranoid. All he had to do was cross the room and there, there was the door to the tower. He couldn't weaken now, not now.

He began to cross quickly. And just as he'd reached the tower door, just as his hand moved to put the key in the lock, he was grabbed from behind.

He cried out in rage and fear and spun around. The vicious movement of his body dislodged the determined hands, but as soon as he'd turned they grabbed him again. A match was lit and a candle. A man, a small white-bearded man, came walking slowly toward him, holding the flame like a ghost.

"Your Majesty, it is the saddest action of my life that I now perform. Four alienists have provided a report on Your Majesty, and in the light of their findings Prince Luitpold has taken over the government. I have orders to accompany Your Majesty to Schloss Berg this very night."

He could have fought them. Might have wounded several. They had no idea how strong he was. *They had no idea.* But the fight slipped from him in the shock of the moment, the unreality of that little man's face speaking those words. It was inconceivable that this could really be done, that it could dare to be done *to him.* And *Berg, Schloss Berg,* where crazy Otto lay: *Berg of the insane.*

Guilt and shame came upon him as thickly as it had ever done. *I deserve this,* he thought. *This is what happens to the damned.*

"How can you declare me so? You have not yet examined me."

The small man smiled sadly. "Your Majesty, the overwhelming documentary evidence is proof enough."

As Ludwig, once king, was led from the room, Mayr watched. He slowly pulled his loathsome mask from his face, a triumphant, mocking smile revealed. He took an envelope from his pocket on which was written *Empress Elizabeth of Austria* and dropped it, scornfully and with great intent, on the fire.

In Rittersberg, Gabriel moaned on the couch and twisted his body as if seeking to flee the experience. Mrs. Smith, sitting upright on the floor next to him, had fallen into a kind of panting silence; a stillness that echoed after the long, steady drone of her voice. She was sweating, her mouth and eyes pinched tight. She'd removed her polyester suit jacket before they commenced, and her dimpled upper arms were pale and clammy. Perspiration on her lip and cheeks turned her heavy pancake makeup into a moist, clay-like texture. Grace's face too was wet, though not for the same reasons.

Mr. Smith had entered after the pair had gone into their trance. He got up now from his chair.

"I think that's enough," he said, moving toward his wife.

Grace was lost in the images knit by the words, but this unexpected decision snapped her to at once. "Wait! The diagram! We still don't know what happened to the diagram. Ludwig had it on him when he was arrested."

Mr. Smith glanced at his wife, apprehension and reluctance reeking from every pore.

"*Please*. We might not make contact again!"

Mr. Smith looked up at Grace sharply.

"A few more minutes," he agreed, and Grace knew that it was only because he'd decided that this would not be repeated, whatever the cost. He leaned close to his wife and whispered in her ear, "*The diagram, Mother.*"

And Mrs. Smith, beginning haltingly in a flat, husky voice, took back up her narrative.

*   *   *

Horse hooves. Swaying. His eyes were closed, but he didn't need to see the view to know where they were. Over the past dozen years his sense of direction had developed until even conveyances that were as unnatural as carriages could not throw him off. They were a hard day's run from home now, and they were approaching water. They were nearing Starnberger See.

He squeezed his eyes shut more tightly, unable and unwilling to connect with what was happening around him. The carriage slowed. The surface under the wheels changed to cobblestone. It was what he had been waiting for.

He opened his eyes and saw that they were in a small town. Seeshaupt. It was at the southernmost tip of Starnberger See, and Berg castle was at the northernmost. They were stopping to change the horses. The beasts were exhausted and quivering from the long and steady pace they'd set. Ludwig could feel their racing heartbeats.

He offered up a prayer of thanks to Our Lady. This was exactly as he'd hoped—that they would stop and that it would be someplace he knew. The odds were in his favor, for he'd traveled most of the routes between royal residences since childhood, and the route from Hohoenschwangau to Berg was no exception. And this same area, these same towns, had witnessed his nocturnal odysseys for many a year. Yes, Seeshaupt was exactly what he needed.

But even as the carriage pulled to a stop, there were men in uniform running alongside, men from the other carriages guarding the doors.

He leaned down and forward to bring his eyes to the height of the window and peered out over the heads of the men outside. It was a dark night, and a light rain had begun to fall. Torches were lit. The slick cobblestones glimmered in the flickering light.

In front of the carriage the men parted abruptly, and Ludwig felt the approach of a diminutive doctor before he saw the white hair emerge from between the guard's woollen coats. The doctor nodded curtly at his charge and tapped lightly on the window. Ludwig pushed it open on its hinges.

"Does His Majesty require any services while we are here?"

Ludwig's heart lurched, and he fought to keep his face from betraying him, to coax his voice into a casual and reasonable tone.

"Across the way is the post office. The postmistress lives directly above it. Would you be so kind as to knock on the door and ask her to fetch me a glass of water?"

Gudden bobbed obsequiously. "Of course, Your Majesty."

He had a desire for goodwill, this little man. He coveted a veil of affability over this brutal proceeding. Ludwig knew his type well and despised it. Gudden was a politician, or he'd never have been appointed to such a task, never have had his Uncle Luitpold's ear. And politicians always kept their options open. After all, if Ludwig was to somehow regain control, it would be wise to have displayed mercy.

But Ludwig would never regain control and he knew it. Black thoughts about Gudden, Luitpold, even about the men who drove this carriage, threatened to swamp him. Bloodlust and revenge as black as sewage drifted through his mind. He pushed them aside with great effort. His eyes followed the doctor across the courtyard and to the post office.

In truth, he was amazed that he was able to control himself now, his rage, his fury, *now* when he'd had so little success at it for so long. But this was the last round of play, the final yards of his mad dash. He had little choice.

Gudden was knocking on the post office door himself, as Ludwig hoped he would, to show the king that he was the humble servant, whatever the current circumstances. And now the door was opening and a pale, worried face looked out, then slipped back inside at once to do what was bidden.

Ludwig leaned back to wait, his entire body heavy and tingling with the rushes of dread and adrenaline, with the struggle to suppress the need to hurt, the urge to *flee* that washed through his veins.

It will work. If I'd asked to use the bathroom or stretch my legs, they would have followed me, guarded me, but this is one single old woman performing a servile task. They will let her pass, and they will turn their backs to us, unthreatened, uninterested. It must be so. It must work!

And when he opened his eyes, he could see Frau Vogl in a dark shawl and skirt, hurrying across the square, a glass held up and out in front of her like a lantern, her skirt skimming the wet stones.

He sat up, his mouth dry. He reached a hand inside his coat and felt the parchment of the diagram there. He pushed the window all the way open.

And she was standing there. The men, as he'd hoped, parted and stood about, their backs to the carriage, their eyes looking out as if watching for a mob perhaps, or even a lone loyal farmer with a pitchfork.

Frau Vogl held the glass toward him and turned her head. Her face fell into the light from the lantern hooked in the driver's seat. It was drawn and anxious. He'd sat in her rooms and had tea with this woman.

"Are you all right, Your Majesty? Is there anything I can do?" she whispered.

He took the glass of water from her slowly. "Yes, there is something you can do, most urgently!"

"Anything!"

His eyes shifted, intently taking in the creatures that surrounded them—none were looking. He slipped the rolled parchment from his coat. "Hide this."

Frau Vogl hastily took the parchment and tucked it into her shawl.

"It must be sent to Elizabeth," Ludwig whispered. "Empress Elizabeth of Austria. And tell her . . ."

He stopped, swallowing painfully. In his anxiousness to accomplish this new plan he'd been carried on a wave of intent. And now that he was about to complete his goal—to smuggle the parts to Elizabeth, to lay the burden of the task at her delicate feet—as his last chance at instructions were parting his lips, he suddenly realized that *she might fail.*

After all, hadn't he?

"And tell her that if for any reason she is unable to complete the plan that I outlined for her in my letter, if the man I spoke of manages to . . . to *retain* his freedom, then she must . . ."

He paused, his heart burdened with fear and self-pity. He could see the little chapel in Neuschwanstein where he'd so often poured out his soul.

". . . must take this diagram and place it with my heart in the urn at AltÖtting. It is to be a token to the blessed Virgin of my faithfulness."

Frau Vogl's eyes were wide and dismayed. It seemed to strike her at once the exact circumstances of this odd party in the night. Her face contorted, aghast, but to her credit she did not protest or argue. "I will tell her just what you have said, Your Highness."

"Thank you, Frau Vogl."

"Your people love you, Your Highness."

"I know."

Then Gudden was there and his slick smile bade Frau Vogl good night. Ludwig settled back into his seat, not wanting to see the polite nod aimed his way, the false sheen of congeniality, or anything else the night had to offer.

It was finished. He had done all he could do. Now there was left only to prepare himself for what came next and to find the means and the moment to accomplish it.

Gerde brought in cold compresses. Mr. Smith was trying to guide Mrs. Smith's padded frame onto the floor, for she looked ready to fall over, her limbs trembling with fatigue. She had gone silent, her voice winding down and down and finally stopping completely. And still her eyes were pressed shut, her face ghastly. He was calling to her now, over and over.

Mother. Mother. Mother.

And even in the silence it was clear that they were, both of them, still *back there.*

Mr. Smith gently lowered his wife to the floor. He rolled her onto her back and took a cold cloth, bathed her face with it, repeated her name loudly.

Mother. Mother. Mother.

Grace crawled on her knees over to the couch. Gabriel wasn't moving at all. He was utterly still, as if lost in a deep sleep, and behind his lids his eyeballs jittered as if riding the dreamland express. His skin, which was pale anyway, had gone fish-belly white. The brown dots of his freckles stood out in mute contrast, exaggerated and startling.

"Gabriel?" She leaned forward and spoke in his ear, but there was no response. She reached back and grabbed the second cold towel from the bowl and began wiping his brow with it. She recalled how intent his emotions had been earlier and the physical agony he'd been through in the night. He always seemed so vital, so rebelliously alive, but now a worry filled her. If this process could wipe out Mrs. Smith, what might it be doing to his already taxed heart? Particularly since he'd just expressed to her his desire to give up, to admit defeat.

Just kill me.

"Gabriel?" she said again, sharply, and she shook his shoulder.

Late afternoon. The daylight was still bright enough to aggravate his headache and sting his sleepless eyes, but Ludwig forced himself to pull back the curtain of his room and look out. He'd requested another walk, and he saw the guards gathering in their long coats.

Beyond, the lake shone as the sun, already beginning its early winter descent, broke from the dark clouds. It turned the choppy green surface of the water to a bruised white that merged with the clouds above.

He dropped the curtain and turned to pace, wringing his hands in agitation. The room they'd locked him into was one of the guest suites, and the small dimensions of it were hopelessly unamenable to his long stride.

If he could just get alone on his walk, or even with Gudden and, say, one guard, he thought he could accomplish it. But not with more than that. With two or more guards the risk of failure was too great, and once he tipped his hand they'd never let him alone again; he'd be watched day and night. He had one advantage and one advantage only—the conviviality of the good Doktor Gudden, the sense he'd managed to instill that he was cooperative, beaten, sane. He'd courted that feeling this morning on their walk, feigning an interest in the doctor's career. The guards had gone with them then, but he'd hoped . . .

It must be soon. He could not hold out much longer under the mental strain, could not dam up the rage and hopelessness much longer, and the thought of it happening here, the Change, in front of that horrible little man . . . It was so utterly profane.

A light tapping on the door.

"Come in," Ludwig called politely.

Gudden's cheerful face appeared. "Are you ready? The temperature is quite pleasant outside, Your Highness."

"How kind you are," Ludwig said. It was so out of character that he felt the awkwardness of it hang visibly in the air, but Gudden, who knew him not at all, only smiled in a self-congratulatory way.

"Your well-being is my duty and my pleasure, Your Majesty." The man even bowed before gesturing toward the open door.

They were walking down the hall when Ludwig said, "I wanted to speak to you of my uncle."

Gudden tilted his head to one side curiously. "If you wish."

"There are certain things that must be imparted to him if he's to rule in my stead."

Gudden turned to look at him with amazement. "I must say, Your Majesty's good nature makes quite an impression."

"My people come first," Ludwig said humbly.

They emerged into the late afternoon air, and Ludwig gulped it down desperately, his veins singing with the terrible strain of his claustrophobic confinement. How insufferable after only one night and one day. How not to be borne!

Four men stood to attention, their rifles on their shoulders.

"We'll go alone," Gudden said casually, with a dismissive wave of his hand. He did not even pause as he said it, but continued to walk down the path. Ludwig followed, his face composed but his heart pounding frantically.

"I am anxious to hear your advice," Gudden said magnanimously.

"No more anxious than I am to give it," Ludwig said, forcing a smile, "when we have achieved a bit of privacy."

Mrs. Smith had wakened and she was propped up against Mr. Smith's chest, too weak to rise from the floor. She was crying softly, sheets of tears running down her face, but whether it was from what she had seen or sheer emotional and physical exhaustion was unclear. She could not even gather reserves enough to speak. Her brown eyes merely watched as Grace tried to wake Gabriel. And now Gerde too was calling his name, tapping his cheeks, shaking first one arm, then another. The two women glanced at each other, their eyes frightened.

"Help me," Grace said, moving to push an arm under his back. They attempted to raise his immobile form into a sitting position.

Gabriel, wake up. Gabriel. Gabriel.

Gudden was talking, talking, on and on, and Ludwig was not listening to any of it. He was watching the banks of the lake, watching for a good place, for the right spot. The path curved, following the water, and on either side were trees and grass. And now the path was dipping out toward the water, out to meet a natural beach, the trees falling away on their right.

Ludwig checked his watch. They had walked twenty-five minutes. Soon, Gudden would suggest they turn back, but there'd be no turning back today. Twenty-five minutes was far enough, far enough that they might not hear Gudden when he called and if they did it would be over by the time they arrived.

He'd read everything about his condition that he could get his hands on, and he'd questioned Louis repeatedly. Although he'd not often received a straight answer, he knew enough. He knew what had to be done. He'd found sources.

Anything that completely destroys heart or brain so that regeneration can not be facilitated. Or death by the elements: burning, drowning, being suffocated by earth—buried alive.

He had not the courage to inflict such a devastating wound to his head or chest, or the means in his confinement. And even had he the courage and the means, the chance of fouling such a blow was too great. As for fire, he could not begin to contemplate the horror of burning alive. But the lake, surely it would not be too horrible to swim out, to open one's mouth. And if one could induce one's mind to still its instinct long enough to take in that first unnatural breath, would the rest not follow swiftly? He prayed it would follow swiftly.

The doctor was still rambling as Ludwig turned and

began walking with long strides directly toward the
lake. As he crossed the beach he unbuttoned his coat
and shrugged it off, as if shrugging off life itself. Gudden was saying Ludwig's name or some such nonsense
as Ludwig's boots hit the water and the mud began
sucking at his great weight, pulling at his legs as he
strode purposefully out, deeper and deeper.

And now Gudden's calls became cries of alarm.
Help! Help! And the water was up to the king's thighs.
Its coldness shocked him, and his heavy wool pants
made his steps sluggish. He continued wading out,
slowed a little, and the icy water reached up for his
most intimate parts.

He never even heard the splashing behind him, so
intent was his purpose. Gudden's hand reached out
and grabbed him as the water chilled his belly—
grabbed him insistently, urgently.

"Your Majesty, *in God's name!*"

Ludwig shook him off, but the doctor was back at
once, more strong and determined than Ludwig had
anticipated. This time Gudden attempted to wrap his
arms around the larger man's body, to pull him back
toward the shore.

And rage, like a black fruit so ripe it burst, filled
Ludwig with its bitter juice, its tang biting cleanly
through his despair. Before he was even conscious of
a decision, he had turned and had Gudden's throat in
his large hands and was pushing him, pushing him
down.

And felt the pleasure-pain sweep through him like
an orgasm, heard the horrible, guttural sound that he
knew was coming from his own throat, felt the dark,
urgent craving.

No. Not now. Not now!

He furiously pushed Gudden, sending the man careening back into the water, anywhere, just *away*.
Gudden came up once, briefly, his mouth gasping, his
face white and lost, before sinking back into the water.

But Ludwig had already swung around and was

striding forward, his breath heaving, his face set with a dreadful determination.

The water pulled at him languorously, resisting his attempts to march, insulted at his insolence in treating it like dry land. The currents tugged gently, playfully at his legs. The water lapped at his shirt, its icy fingers teasing his chest, turning his heaving breaths into gasps at the coldness. He felt the rage seep from him into the water, the beast pull itself back inside like a tortoise drawing in its head, not liking what it saw.

And still he walked forward, holding his arms straight up in the air for balance. He could see the surface just below his head, so darkly green here, so opaquely bottomless, a foreign kingdom, a new world.

By the time the water reached his chin, he was thinking of Louis. And for the first time in many years it was not all bitterness. He remembered how it was before all that. *Louis,* his black curls falling on his broad, muscled shoulders. *Louis,* his firm jaw and tender mouth, his eyes that burned with passion and danced with intelligence and wit. *Louis,* who loved luxury, silk frills, and velvet jackets, so complementary to his romantic beauty. And yet underneath the gilt there was a body and a will that were hard and unchallengingly male, like something from a fairy tale, like Lohengrin himself perhaps, or Siegfried.

How addicted he'd been! How helpless in the face of that perfection! How trapped by that beauty, enamored with every gesture and nuance! What a garden of earthly delights he'd found in the man's arms.

And how he'd paid for it.

"Curse you to hell," he said softly, tears welling up in his eyes. "May God damn you, my love."

And then the water covered his mouth, stilling his words and washing away his tears. And his heart was so numbed by sorrow, what followed next came without too great an effort of will. He simply opened his mouth and took the water in like a lover.

*   *   *

Gabriel sat straight up, gasping and choking. He pushed away the hands and the voices of concern, instinctively knowing that he needed to focus only on clearing his lungs of the conviction that water filled them, to get oxygen to a brain that was convinced that it had none, to get his mind untethered from the journey it had been about to make and back into this reality, here, while he still could.

When it was clear that he would not choke to death, he heard Grace quietly ask the others to leave and was grateful. Only part of his mind was yet in the present, and that part was still filled with emotions that were not his own. The room quieted and fell silent as Gabriel lay back and closed his eyes—the modern, jagged-edged man fighting to reassert itself over the softer, more tormented one.

Grace sat down in a nearby chair and began to rock, waiting patiently for him to tell her the end of the story.

Mrs. Smith had quite recovered herself by the following morning when Grace found her in the *gasthof*. But there was a sadness around her eyes that lingered, like the red light of a reluctant sunset. Grace slipped into the booth opposite her.

"Where's Emil?"

"Oh, he already went up to call Sissy and tell her we're staying on a few more days. I'm running slow this mornin' myself."

Werner brought hot tea, knowing Grace's likes by now, or at least using that as an excuse to come over. She declined breakfast, but he lingered, as obvious and distracting at the edge of their table as only a very tall old man can be. Grace invited him to sit.

"I wanted to talk to you about Ludwig's plan," Grace told Mrs. Smith. "I've been wondering if it would have worked. I stayed up last night going over the werewolf lore book again."

"Then you probably know better than I."

"You have to burn them," Werner suggested balefully.

Grace glared at him. "*No,* you have to destroy their heart or their brain. A bullet in either location would do it, if the lore book is accurate. I suppose we'll have to hope that it is."

Werner shrugged. "Better to be safe and burn them."

Mrs. Smith changed the conversation with smooth diplomacy. "What have you come up with, dear?"

Grace sighed. "I've been thinking about the opera. Ludwig's letter to Elizabeth implied that he didn't have to be present to have it lift the curse. He obviously thought the armed guards would kill the black wolf when he was forced to change in the middle of the opera house."

"Yes, that's the way I took the letter too."

"But wouldn't Ludwig have had to pull the trigger himself?"

"*Ja,* wouldn't he have to pull the trigger himself?" Werner echoed, leaning forward on one long forearm and stroking his white beard.

"No." Mrs. Smith shook her head. "Culpability is a heavy thing. In the spiritual realm—and in magick— a man who hires an assassin is just as guilty as the man who pulls the trigger. Ludwig and Wagner planned the opera, bought the chandeliers, laid the trap. If the trap had led to the demise of the black wolf, Ludwig's soul would have been freed."

Grace bit her lip, pondered. "So if we can get the opera produced *now* it might still free Ludwig."

Mrs. Smith nodded. "And Gabriel." She laid a warm, dry hand on Grace's and squeezed encouragingly. "I do believe so, dear. Otherwise, why all these dreams? Why have you learned about the opera after so many years of its being lost? Ludwig has *helped* you."

Grace assented with a tilt of her head; she'd accepted this days ago. "But what about Gabriel? Are you sure he can have enough . . . culpability in this thing for it to free him as well?"

"*Ja*," echoed Werner, "can he?"

"He's the one who found the Black Wolf again, isn't he?" Mrs. Smith replied. She lifted her coffee cup to her lips and finished off its contents. "*Would* you mind, Herr Huber?" she asked, showing him its empty proportions.

Reluctantly, Werner got up to fetch the coffeepot. As soon as he'd left, Mrs. Smith leaned forward.

"But we should make sure he's involved in *all* the plans, just to be safe. Financially too, if possible."

"That's not a problem. There's still money left over from our last case."

"And he must be willing, Grace. He must *will* it." This last was said with a low and insistent hush.

Grace's brow furrowed. "Of course. How can he not want it?"

Mrs. Smith looked somber as she picked up an envelope from the seat beside her and handed it to Grace. "This came for him this morning. The postmistress showed it to Werner, and he snagged onto it and showed it to me. Goodness knows, he shouldn't have taken the thing, but he meant well. Everyone's a bit at a loss as to what's right in a situation like this."

But Grace wasn't listening. She was staring at the return address.

Von Glower.

The envelope stayed with Grace for a number of days. She didn't want to show it to Gabriel, despite Mrs. Smith's disapproval of the delay. She was afraid to.

Inside the envelope were a letter and the talisman, which von Glower must have found at the ravine. Grace supposed it was awfully big of him to return it, then realized, with some trepidation, that it was more likely a matter of self-confidence than self-sacrifice.

It was the talisman more than anything that forced

her to finally show the letter to its rightful recipient. She knew how badly Gabriel felt about its loss, and there was no easy way to explain its return. She gave it to him one morning just before leaving town. She and Georg had already retrieved the opera acts at Neuschwanstein—it had been a simple matter of distracting the guards. The niches at Neuschwanstein had never been found; the map of their location had been burned by Mayr along with the letter to Elizabeth. The three acts were unmarred.

On this day Grace was headed to AltÖtting to get the diagram. She was taking Mrs. Smith because there were only so many half-truths she could make up for Georg. Besides, Georg was busy in Munich, astounding and blackmailing his brother Claus, and working on getting the new opera onto the summer festival schedule.

She handed the letter to Gabriel as he sat in the dining room after breakfast. She said nothing in explanation, only gave him an unreadable look and left.

At AltÖtting, she and Mrs. Smith sat through service after service in the tiny chapel, waiting for the room to clear so they could get Ludwig's urn down from its place along the top of the wall. Grace could not stop thinking about the letter. She feared that when they returned to Rittersberg, Gabriel would be gone.

Even when Mrs. Smith, in a kind of rapture after seeing the statue of the Black Madonna and child in the inner sanctum, whispered to her that she believed they'd found the spirit guide at last—she that was in the cards as the High Priestess—Grace felt little more than momentary interest.

It was not the High Priestess that concerned her, but that bit about The Lovers and duality.

Gabriel:
I know you are very ill right now. The change is always painful. I went through it myself when I was only

twelve, and I did not even know what was happening to me. I'm sorry I am not there to help you, but I have a pretty clear sense that you would not welcome my presence. You are safe in Rittersberg. For now that is enough. Let me speak, then, of the future.

You hate me now. I know this. But I have some hope that by the pass of the second moon, when the sickness wanes and the blood has inflamed the greater part of you, you will see things differently. You will need me then and, I think, you will *want* me then.

It is for hope of this that I did not have you destroyed the night you were bitten by von Zell. I could have done so. You were passed out for hours at the lodge. It would have been a simple thing to wake the men, show them von Zell's corpse, and make up a story that would enrage them enough to kill you. I did not. Let that be proof of my true desire for friendship with you.

I have desired companionship for more years than you have lived. I have even, very rarely, taken the risk and Changed others. But the Blood was always too much for the brain, and my Chosen One ended up dead. Or mad.

This is why I started the hunt club. It was my idea that if I could first indoctrinate men's minds to the religion of tooth and claw, they then might be prepared for the Change. As you have seen, it did not work. Von Zell was the best of the lot. If he had turned out well, I would have taken the others. But there's no point in even trying with them now.

You are different. You're a Ritter. Your blood is *already* supernatural. Yes, I know of your family. It was a Ritter that captured my own father, Claus von Ralick. I never blamed you, even though I myself would have been killed had not my mother had the foresight to flee. No, it was not your ancestor but my father that I hated for years, until I learned to appreciate his legacy.

You see, I have studied much over these centuries. When you and I met, I felt instinctively that you would not be destroyed by the Change. You have an enormous streak of the beast in you, and you are innately strong in the Occult. You will be powerful and beautiful in the Change, I am sure of it. I did not intend for it to happen so soon and in such a way, but perhaps fate has its own reason.

But how confused *you* must be. You may feel I used you to dispose of von Zell. I did. He had to be taken care of, and you obligingly showed up. What was I to do? I am too old not to have learned at least this much about the light—you cannot shut it out. Better to let it in and let it simply dim to adjust to the relative brightness *inside*. But the warmth between us, this was genuine, I assure you.

Think well on these things as your body adjusts. Think about meeting me in Munich in two months' time. We can leave Germany if you wish and go anywhere you like. I will teach you how to hunt, how to live safe and well. You can feel the night wind on your face, exalt in running free, taste the heartbeat of the kill beneath your jaws. It is glorious—much more so than the priestly life the Schattenjäger offers.

Don't confuse yourself with ideas of good and evil. Nature shows us that there are no such distinctions. You and I both inherited something from our fathers. Is your legacy any less of a curse or blessing than mine? Join me.

With deepest affection, Friedrich

Gabriel was thinking about duality too as he put down the letter. There was something else in the envelope—he'd known as soon as he'd picked it up. Gabriel stretched out a finger and sent it tentatively inside. His finger touched the cool gold of the talisman, and a harsh jolt of pain raced up his arm. It felt as though the meat were being torn off the bone. He withdrew quickly and uttered a muffled sob.

He'd expected as much, but to have it actually happen was more of a rejection than he could bear. He wondered how Friedrich had managed to touch it that night when he'd picked it up from his chest. But then, he'd wondered how Friedrich could manage many things. It seemed that in two hundred-odd years he'd quite mastered his condition. Or perhaps being a birth heir, an alpha, made it easier on him somehow. Perhaps he'd gone through all this as a child or even in the womb.

More than anything, Gabriel thought about that day at the lair—Friedrich emerging, face shocked. Gabriel was beginning to realize that he had not been acting. After the Change, Gabriel himself remembered little. Was von Glower's exploration of the lair his first opportunity to come face to face with the Black Wolf's victims? With the true smell and sight and texture of his alter ego, his grand philosophy? No wonder he had been so moved.

But not—or so the letter showed—enough to give it up.

The lair. That was what he kept coming back to. He sat in his bedroom at the castle, staring at the wall. He wondered at his attraction to the club, to the philosophy, to Friedrich himself. He remembered this attraction well; there was no denying it. And he knew himself well enough to admit that he'd been custom-made for such a siren's call. Hadn't he always believed in living for the moment, doing whatever felt right and to hell with conventional, straitjacket morality? He considered anyone who did otherwise robots of society, didn't he? Not free men, not open-minded men, not *livers* of life.

Yes, he admired the philosophy still.

But there was Preiss's rutting, von Aigner's gluttony, Hennemann's drunkenness. And then there was the lair. Was this the harsh face of moral freedom?

He wondered what his own hidden lair was. It was the first time he'd realized that he was sure to have one.

When Grace returned at six o'clock, he was already in the dungeon, lying under a thin blanket on the cot. He heard the tentative knock and Grace's voice. "Can I come in for a minute?"

Reluctantly, he said yes.

"We got the diagram," Grace said after Mr. Smith left them alone. But on her face was something else, something more pointed than this piece of news.

"Good."

Her hands twisted nervously. "You read the letter?"

His jaw clenched and his face closed guardedly. "Yes."

She stood there, looking at the floor. "Oh. Well, I was just wondering. I mean, do you want us to go ahead with this? Or . . . ?"

For a long moment Gabriel said nothing. Grace glanced up at him once and, seeing his face, blushed deeply and looked back at the floor. She started to say something, then stopped uncertainly.

"Of course we're going ahead with it," Gabriel said in a tightly controlled voice. "And please, don't ever, *ever* ask me that again."

Grace had the intelligence to look guilty. "I'm sorry. It's just . . . I thought you should be allowed a choice."

"I made my choice long ago, Grace. Long ago." He said this coldly and turned to face the wall.

And Grace, realizing the depth of her error, slipped out silently.

THREE
MONTHS
LATER

Der Fluch des Englehart
(The Curse of Engelhart)
by Richard Wagner

Act I

Many years ago in a small German village, there lived
a young man named Engelhart. Engelhart was a lowly
blacksmith's apprentice. Being orphaned, and having
lived with the blacksmith in virtual slavery since his
parents' death, Engelhart had nothing in the world to
claim as his own. Nothing, that is, but an amazing
talent. For ten years the beautiful wares that had
passed for the blacksmith's own had actually been
wrought by Engelhart. The blacksmith, a greedy and
vain man, forbade Engelhart to ever work the metal
in front of another living soul. But the blacksmith's
ingratitude went further still. He was so plagued with
envy that he treated Engelhart like a lazy and worthless dog. The other villagers followed suit.

Now in the same town there lived a rich baron and a
young maiden, Hildegunde, who was lovely and good-
hearted. Hildegunde was the only one who took pity
on Engelhart and was kind to him. Engelhart loved
Hildegunde madly, but was too shy and too penniless
to speak of it. In the first act, we learn that Hildegunde's parents, blinded by prospective fortune, have
betrothed her to the baron. Hildegunde is terrified and
protests that the baron is reputed to be evil, but her
parents demand her obedience. Poor Hildegunde reluctantly agrees.

The baron, with great public ceremony, sends Hildegunde a betrothal gift of a silver bracelet. But the
bracelet is accidentally ruined when Hildegunde, over-

come by anger, casts it into the fire. She is immediately remorseful and pulls it out, but it is too late; the delicate silver has been badly marred. Hildegunde approaches Engelhart and begs him to help her. Engelhart thinks of his master's warning, but decides to disregard it for Hildegunde's sake. He melts down the silver and constructs another bracelet, identical to the first. When Hildegunde sees Engelhart's great artistry, she falls in love with him. But the couple's mutual bliss is momentary—what about the engagement? The young couple, knowing the baron will never relinquish his claim, decide to run away.

Act 2

The baron hires hunters to track the lovers down. In a public trial, Hildegunde pleads their case in a stirring aria. She tells the townspeople of Engelhart's great skill and his mistreatment by the blacksmith. The blacksmith should be turned out for his cruelty and Engelhart given the shop. Then she and Engelhart can marry and live in peace with their neighbors. Her parents chose a groom for her, but she begs to be allowed her own choice.

It is then the baron's turn to speak. He declares that he has been terribly injured—a victim of a wayward girl. His marriage claim was first—there can be no other! He implies that if the villagers do not help him, he will remove his aid from the village coffers. Then the baron turns to Engelhart. By the rights of the injured, the baron announces, he is empowered to set a curse. The baron curses Engelhart with a terrible and ancient malady—that whenever the moon shines in the night, Engelhart will become a marauding wolf. The village is terrified of wolves, and has been plagued for years by a renegade black wolf that has taken the lives of many children.

The baron further declares that he will still marry Hildegunde, but not until she renounces Engelhart with her own words. Until she does, he will keep her safe from further shame by locking her up in a small room at the top of his house.

The villagers side with the baron. Hildegunde goes to her prison, and Engelhart does indeed become a wolf at night. At first Engelhart is hated and feared by the villagers, but soon rumors circulate about Engelhart the wolf. He is always careful not to harm any human being or any domestic stock. In fact, he scares away robbers and keeps the renegade wolf at bay. No more children are lost to the fangs of the night. The villagers begin to respect Engelhart. And Hildegunde, when she hears of his successful mastery of the curse, commits herself to him forever.

The baron's plan having collapsed before him, having given Engelhart dignity rather than removed it, he flies into a rage. He tells Hildegunde that he will marry her anyway, and on the morrow at that. She will become his wife, or he will see to it that her parents' lives are forfeit!

Act 3

The final act begins with the wedding feast for Hildegunde and the baron. Hildegunde has cooperated, but now she is horrified to find herself the baron's wife. After her poignant opening aria, the baron tries to draw her back to the party. He orders more food and calls for the entertainment.

In strides a traveling show of minstrels. They play and juggle and do acrobatics. One of them, a mime with a tragic frown painted on his face, seems to want to hover near and amuse the bride. She ignores him, depressed and tearful, and he does his best to make her laugh.

After the amusing antics of the minstrel's first song, the music grows dark and menacing. The minstrels mimic serious stage players and run and tremble and hover around the room. They gather in a circle around the frowning minstrel. As they whirl around him, he slowly sinks from sight. Suddenly, the minstrels burst apart like petals, and standing in the center of the room is . . . a wolf. The villagers scream and the baron lurches to his feet. But Hildegunde cries out that it is Engelhart! The wolf does not attack the crowd; it lifts its head and howls.

The baron screams at the wolf to stop, and he screams at the villagers to kill the wolf, but they only stand and stare. The baron begins to pull his hair and gnash his teeth. He gets up and makes it to the center of the banquet hall, where he falls down in a heap of wedding silk and lies still on the floor. What emerges from the pile of silk is . . . another wolf—the renegade black wolf! The baron-wolf runs through the door and into the night. Engelhart leaps after him.

The final scene takes place in the woods outside the village. The villagers follow wolf tracks. They sing of the ferocity of the battle between the two wolves. Hildegunde answers the villagers' excitement with her fears for Engelhart's life. The crowd emerges into a clearing. There the two wolves are engaged in a final deadly embrace. As they watch, Engelhart triumphs and the baron-wolf sinks to the ground.

The baron dies, but Engelhart is mortally wounded. His curse has been broken by the baron's death, but it is too late. Hildegunde sings her love to him while the villagers pronounce him a great hero. Engelhart dies, and all mourn in a sorrowful final aria.

Chapter 8

Residence Theater, Munich

Grace paused to straighten the large placard in the lobby. It had been knocked aslant by some scurrying worker or another, and it tottered on the edge of the stand's metal prongs as if threatening to jump.

The Curse of Engelhart by Richard Wagner in its triumphant debut performance, the placard announced in German. And at the bottom, *Conductors Claus and Georg Immerding. Munich opera festival.*

She frowned at it worriedly. She'd convinced them to keep the name and composer secret until tonight. It had not been easy, but then, nothing in the past three months had been. Georg had convinced his brother Claus to put the new opera at the top of the summer festival, replacing a production of *Lohengrin*. And although the *Lohengrin* funds had paid for much of the event, there had been overruns. Gabriel's funds were tapped to pay these and, naturally, to buy the chandeliers, which had been outrageously expensive.

But they had pulled it off, thanks to Claus's ambitious desire to be the first to bring the new Wagner to the world. Grace had no idea how much von Glower knew of Ludwig's plans. Hopefully, he knew nothing of them, or at least not enough to become suspicious the moment he walked in the door this evening and picked up a program.

She sighed and headed for the auditorium.

*   *   *

As feared, things were not going to plan. Where she'd hoped to see a finished product, she saw instead that the last bit of scaffolding was still in place, and that two of the workmen were still attempting to affix the eighth and final chandelier.

On stage, the soprano solo from the beginning of Act III was being given one last run-through. The aria still sent chills down her spine, despite the fact that she'd heard this thing a hundred times or more in the past few months. The chills had a more ominous cast today.

"Herr Silbermeier?"

The chandelier foreman glanced at her warily. "Very close now."

"I know you're working as fast as you can, but we're opening in one hour."

"In one hour it will be done."

"No! But I . . ." Grace took a breath and tried to sound calm. "I told you, I need to run through some music once you're done."

Silbermeier grimaced. "You're lucky we even could make these in so little time, then drive them down special this morning."

"I know," Grace said, forcing a smile. "And I appreciate it."

Herr Silbermeier's sullen eyes challenged hers. It was clear that there wasn't anything she could do to rush him.

"All right," Grace sighed. "But you installed them exactly according to the theater diagram, right?"

"As good as we could."

Grace gripped a nearby seat as the floor swayed beneath her. "What do you mean 'as good as you could'? I gave specific instructions that the diagram was to be followed *exactly*."

She sounded shrill even to her own ears. Silbermeier frowned and pulled out a copy of the theater diagram from Wahnfried. He tapped the name at the top. Residenztheater, München.

"This is the Residenztheater, yes? But not the same Residenztheater. They rebuilt it. After the war."

Grace looked around, aghast. The theater looked antique—with cherubs and angels and gods and various other baroque adornments, now all faded and chipping. Even the red seats were threadbare.

"But everything looks so old!" she protested.

"Yes, they take everything out and save it. Then, when war is over, they make a new building. Put back in the pieces from the first one. They did this in many buildings in Munich."

It dawned on Grace that he was telling the truth, the way a perfectly obvious and perfectly critical answer one had missed on a final exam occurred to one later, in the hall.

Somewhere out there, Silbermeier was still rattling on: ". . . this one is a bit smaller. So we put the chandeliers same distance to each other, but there's less space to walls. Here and here."

He pointed out the areas, but Grace was too overwhelmed to do more than glance at the diagram. "I see. Thank you, Herr Silbermeier."

Yes. Thank you. Thank you for pointing out what an idiot I am! I'm a goddamn history major, for Christ's sake! I should have known.

But somehow, in the midst of everything else, it had simply never occurred to her. Grace moved away, feeling quite ill. She told herself it would work anyway—that it *had* to work. Surely the acoustics couldn't be *that* sensitive. And, really, it did not bear thinking what would happen if they were.

Grace drifted down toward the stage, barely conscious of her actions. Claus spied her first. "Grace, there you are! We really need to let people go. We've only got . . . God! Less than an hour."

She nodded dumbly. "The chandeliers won't be ready in time for the test run. They can go."

Claus looked relieved. He clapped his hands and

dismissed the nervous singers, following them backstage. Georg remained at the conductor's stand, pag-
ing through the music intently.

"Georg?"

She could have used a kind word, but Georg had
his own troubles.

"God!" he groaned. "I'm not ready."

He stared at some dreaded stanza or other. Grace
took a deep breath and put a hand on his arm. "*Relax.
You've done well. You've done all you can do.*" It
wasn't clear if she was telling him or herself.

"Have I?"

"Of course. It's too late to worry about it now anyway. So enjoy it—this is your big debut."

But Georg's stricken face and shaking hands revealed a massive case of stage fright. "I know. I'll
probably be fine once the music starts. It's a *great*
opera, Grace. Wagner's best. You don't know what it
means to me that you—"

"*Shhhh!*" Grace hissed with a dire expression.

Georg laughed. "All right! I won't reveal your secrets. Assuming I even knew them, that is." He looked
at his watch and his anxiety returned. "God, I can't
believe the time! I'd better go get dressed myself."

"Wait! Before you go . . ."

"What is it?"

Grace tried to look innocuous. "Um, I just wanted
to say that . . . Well, given that this is the first performance of a new Wagner, the crowd might be kind
of *volatile.*"

"An *opera* crowd?"

"Well, yes. I mean, it's an emotional thing. So I
wanted to suggest that you ignore any distractions that
might occur. No matter what happens, *just keep playing.* Particularly in Act III. Okay?"

Georg looked at her as though she'd asked him to
conduct in the nude. "Grace, what are you *talking*
about? This is the debut of a *brand-new Wagner.* I'm

not going to . . . to *stop* if the Maestro himself comes floating out on stage!"

"Great. That's all, then. That's all I wanted to say." Grace forced herself to smile at him.

Georg shook his head as if to rid it of the confusion and reached for her hands. "A kiss for luck." He leaned down and kissed her cheek awkwardly; then he jogged up the stage steps and was gone.

"Good luck, Georg," Grace called after him.

It was answered only by the increasingly sour weight of trepidation in her stomach.

She knew she ought to go back to the office and check on Gabriel. But after what Silbermeier had told her, she wasn't quite ready to face him. She ran up-stairs instead, to the old spotlight room she'd found earlier. As promised, a crew member had delivered one of the powerful new spots they'd borrowed from the theater next door. She opened the little door in the wall and wheeled the spotlight over to it. She turned it on and saw a bright circle of light hit the second tier seats opposite. She moved the handle in back until the beam was focused on the *Mittelloge,* the large box at the rear of the theater, just over the entrance doors and main aisle on the first floor. The spotlight lit up the box—it was certainly bright enough. She turned it off, careful not to shift the position, and left the room to go check the box itself.

Everything had been cleaned yesterday, and the *Mittelloge* was in perfect order. Three rows of four, four, and three chairs respectively filled the box, but not all of them would be occupied tonight. Von Glower had been sent tickets for two with seats in the front aisle of the box—a gift, the card said, from an admirer. Kommissar Leber and one of his men were to be the only other occupants. The empty seats here were the only ones in the house.

Back in the hall, Grace pulled the door tight and latched it. She tested its strength one last time. Once secured, she thought it would hold. The doors hadn't had a lock, so she'd had a locksmith come by and outfit one last week. The key was down in her purse in the theater office.

And now that there was no other excuse she could think of for avoiding it, she headed down there herself.

Gabriel was lying on the couch, a blanket covering him. His fever and sickness had lessened steadily over the past month, until he'd seemed almost normal except for a persistent aching in his joints and a tendency to want to sleep in the daytime and be up at night. But with the stress of the performance, and all that was riding on it, he'd had a bit of a relapse the past few days. She could see him shivering under the blanket's meager warmth.

She knelt down by the couch and brushed back his hair. Yes, he was quite warm.

"Not the hair, Grace," he muttered.

Grace smiled. "You've looked better."

"Looking better is my specialty," he answered without opening his eyes. "Are we ready for the test yet?"

Grace tried to sound nonchalant. "I'm sorry, but there's not going to be time for the test. The last chandelier's still going up. It'll be done in time for the performance, but we won't get a run-through."

He opened his eyes. They had deepened in color to a dark, slatey green. The dark circles beneath them underscored the brooding impression. "Grace, that is not acceptable."

His temper, she could feel, was close to the surface. She smiled sympathetically at him, her heartbeat going up a notch.

"I know it's not," she said. And waited.

No explosion came. Instead, he shivered again, his teeth chattering. "I'm so cold."

"I'll try to find another blanket."

"What about some heat? Can't we get any goddamn heat in here?"

"I'll go check."

"What time is it anyway?"

Grace looked at her watch, her eyes unwilling to believe what it said. "Um, six-thirty. In a half hour we're opening the doors."

"Should I go downstairs?" he asked, starting to get up.

Grace thought about the old prop room in the basement. It too had been outfitted with a new lock. She'd wanted Gabriel to wait in Rittersberg, but he'd utterly refused, so they'd compromised on the basement. The lock was in case the earplugs didn't work.

"I still have to get a few things ready downstairs. Why don't you rest here? I'll come get you when it's time."

He laid back reluctantly. "We shoulda tested it, Gracie. We won't get another chance."

"It'll work out," she replied firmly.

From the lobby there was a flight of steps to the basement just behind the grand staircase. *Privat,* the sign over the exit said, meaning not for public consumption, and the basement certainly wasn't. But Grace had been down there several times. She hurried through the archway and descended the stairs.

The basement of the theater was a bizarre, rambling structure of hallways and unlikely rooms, low ceilings and strange, banging pipes. It was like a maze, only with old cement walls where green hedgerows might stand. And if there was a geometric pattern that made some kind of sense, it was outside the grasp of the average human mind to comprehend. There were hallways that formed a rough rectangle along the perimeter, but the inner halls seemed to have been planned by a child with a crayon.

Grace had come down once during rehearsals, and the reverberating sounds of the orchestra and the voices above had a surreal majesty here—an echoing otherworldliness. The effect was enhanced by the music's contrast to the setting, this dank, musty, bowels-of-the-earth space, as if one were Alberich, the earth-bound *Nibelung,* hearing the clear, clean sounds of the Rhine Maidens.

She went into the old prop room and tried, hastily, to provide a spot of comfort in it. She found a chair and wrestled to get it clear of the fray. She brushed it off and placed it in the small clear space she'd made. She shivered, for the basement was quite cold, despite the fact that it was June. She'd have to find some way to remedy that.

She wished Gerde or Mrs. Smith were here—either one would be better suited to this nest making task than she. But Gerde swore she couldn't take the suspense of tonight's grand finale. She'd stayed home, where she would wait for a simple word by phone. And the Smiths had returned to the States weeks ago. With the plans for the opera in place and Gabriel achieving some measure of self-control, Mrs. Smith said she felt they'd played their role. She hadn't given Grace any "impressions" about how things would turn out. Grace wasn't sure she wanted to know.

She left the prop room and hurried through the hallways. She was heading for another room she'd stumbled upon down here, the furnace room. She rediscovered it off the main southeast corridor. Inside was an enormous old coal-burning stove. It wasn't running at the moment, but a large bin of coal stood next to it, a shovel set in it askew.

She opened the bottom drawer of the stove and filled it with coal, getting her hands smudged in the process. She located the pilot button and pushed. The stove made a swooshing sound, then clicked steadily. The flicker of blue and orange flames tinted the glass in the window in the furnace door.

She messed with the control panel for a moment, turning the heat to the auditorium down and that to the basement up. Satisfied she'd done what she could to make Gabriel's interment bearable, she headed back upstairs.

When she emerged back in the lobby, she saw an usher heading for the doors.

"Paul!" she said to him, alarmed.

"There you are!" he answered, turning anxiously. "It's time to open the doors."

Grace looked at her watch, stunned. He was right. It was seven o'clock.

"Oh, God!" Grace muttered. Her stomach did a slow and painful twist.

"There's a big crowd in the street. We must let them get seated or we'll have to start late."

"Can you give me just five minutes? *Please,* Paul. Oh, and you're going to see two special invitations tonight, both for the *Mittelloge*. One is for a Kommissar Leber. Would you show him to the office, please?"

"Okay." Paul looked at his watch. "I open the doors in five minutes."

Grace hurried down the hall to the office. She found Gabriel pacing.

"It's time to go," she said, trying to evince a confidence she didn't feel.

He nodded curtly and brushed past her. When she caught up with him, he was almost to the lobby.

"It's a bit cold down there, but I started the furnace," she chattered. "It should warm up quickly."

"Thanks."

As they entered the lobby they could see the tuxedo-clad ushers standing by the front doors. Paul was looking at his watch, counting down. Grace could hear the murmur of voices from outside, and by the glance Gabriel shot in that direction, she knew he could hear them too. After all the planning, it was impossible to believe this was really the night, that it was about to begin.

But they said nothing to each other, just crossed the lobby and descended the basement stairs. Gabriel went unerringly to the old prop room, though she'd shown it to him only once. He must, she realized, have thought about it often.

Considering the way the diagram of the theater so focused the chandelier X's and the lines of measurement on the *Mittelloge*, Grace thought it unlikely that the music would force a change to Gabriel down here. They had no way of knowing that for certain, though, particularly since Gabriel was still trying to master the urge.

He had told her once, in a moment that was exceedingly rare because he rarely discussed it at all after that first day, that the only thing close to the urge to Change was the flu. When the flu strikes and the nausea hits bad enough to wake you up in the middle of the night, you lie there, trying to tell yourself that you can go back to sleep, that the nausea isn't that bad. But with each minute that passes it worsens, slowly, so that you wonder at first if it's all in your mind, if perhaps your desire for it to go away is actually emphasizing the sensations that are really there. It grows like that until you begin to toss and turn, certain there's a better position to lie in, some way that your stomach will find soothing. And you find those positions momentarily, but then the sickness grows in those positions too, like water seeping in through cracks. And eventually the pain of it, the nausea, becomes unbearable, intolerable, and you get up and you go in the bathroom and you hang out there for a while, feeling the waves grow, until you cannot stand it any longer and the purging comes. And after that purging there's a brief respite before the build-up begins all over again.

That same progression happened with the urge to Change, Gabriel said. Only it wasn't just the stomach that was affected; it was the entire body. Every muscle and nerve began to grow uneasy and twitchy and eventually screamed for transformation, for that brutal, wrenching scratch of a hideous itch.

When he'd told her this, it had still been in the early weeks, and she'd since thought that the urge must have lessened over time, for there are fewer nights now when the cries came in the town square. But he'd never said as much.

"I was planning to get a cot down here and some food and things," Grace said as she swung open the door and flicked on the light. "But I just plain ran out of time."

"It's fine, Gracie." He walked past her and took in the room with a sweeping glance. Then he put his hands on his hips and tapped his foot, still looking around.

"It's going to go like clockwork," she said, feeling a rush of pity for his trepidation.

"It better."

There was more that she wanted to say, but now was not the time. So she gave him a smile and closed the door. She took the shiny new key from her pocket and turned it in the lock. From within she heard nothing.

She had walked down the hall a few steps when a sense of guilt overcame her. She hadn't wanted to tell Gabriel about the rebuilt theater. She'd been afraid of what he would do. His rage was so easily provoked, and it was savage. She hadn't been going to tell him at all, but now that he was safely in the prop room and she was leaving him for the last time until it was over, she was invaded by a sense that her silence wasn't fair. He was the one with his life on the line tonight. He had a right to know.

She went back to the door and stood there hesitantly. "Um, Gabriel?"

"Yeah?" His voice was muffled through the door.

"There's something I think you should know. You know how they just finished installing the chandeliers? Well, the foreman made me aware of a, uh, a small problem."

She paused, but from behind the door there was

only silence. Then he said, very softly, "What problem?"

Grace leaned against the door, hating every second of this. "Well, it turns out that the original Residenztheater was bombed in the war and they rebuilt it. This one is similar, though. *Real* similar. I mean, very, *very* close. They reused the seats and the woodwork and everything. But . . ."

She paused again, and this time there was no sound at all from behind the door.

"But this one is *slightly* smaller. The distance between chandeliers is the same as on the diagram, but there's just a *bit* less distance from the chandeliers to the walls."

She bit her lip and waited for a response. The response was not what she had been expecting. Without warning, something struck the door with incredible force. The wood shook beneath her hand, and there was a loud *boom* that snapped like a gunshot. She recoiled, gasping, and in the next instant understood that he'd struck the door with his fist.

"Gracie, goddamn you!" he screamed, his voice engorged with rage. *"You goddamn bitch! I can't believe you did this! You did it on purpose, didn't you?"*

"Gabriel!"

"You open this goddamn door this minute, do you hear me? THIS MINUTE!"

"No," Grace said, backing away.

"THIS GODDAMN MINUTE! If you can't manage a simple fucking diagram, I'll take care of things myself, do you hear me? MYSELF!"

The door shook again under the cracking blow of his fist. The knob shook violently.

"I'm—I'm doing the best I can!" Grace said, tears making her voice crack. Then she turned and ran down the hall.

She stumbled up the stairs into the lobby, still sobbing, and came face to face with sequins and furs and

tuxedos. The shock was so great that the tears died
instantly in her throat. The buzz in the lobby was elec-
tric; the audience hummed with astonished excitement
over the revelation of the mysterious festival opener.
Grace stared, her dark eyes wide and still moist.

At last she realized that she was drawing attention.
She looked down and blushed—she was not only still
in jeans but she was filthy from coal dust as well. She
pushed her way across the lobby, heading for the
office.

She was slipping her green satin sheath over her
head when a knock came on the office door. For a
moment she was afraid that it was Gabriel, that he'd
gotten out somehow, but she realized it could be anyone—Paul the usher, or Georg.

She zipped her dress hurriedly. "Come in!"

The door opened to reveal a portly, bald-headed
man with a florid face and a tight tuxedo. He nodded
curtly. "Are you Miss Nakimura?"

"Yes. Kommissar Leber?"

"*Ja*. They said you wanted to talk to me?"

"I do! Come in, please."

Leber shut the door and fingered his collar. "What
is this about, Miss Nakimura? I got in the mail two
invitations with a note to come armed. Did you send
them?"

"Yes, I did. You see, we thought it might be a good
idea to seed the audience with a few officers this evening. This *is* the debut of a new Wagner, and we worried that there might be some . . . excitement."

Leber frowned. "Why did you not hire security?"

"Uniforms make people uncomfortable," Grace
lied. "I thought a few plainclothesmen among the audience wouldn't hurt, and we'd be providing a few fine
public servants with a night at the opera as well." She
smiled graciously.

"You are lucky I like music," Leber scowled. He
parted his coat to reveal a holstered gun. "I brought
with me also my associate, Stätter."

"Great. Thank you so much for putting up with all this." Grace stepped forward, hoping to move Leber to the door.

"Is it *really* a new Wagner?" he asked hopefully.

"It really is, Kommissar. I hope you enjoy your evening."

He was beaming as he walked out the door.

Grace found her shoes and checked the contents of her evening purse again to make sure she had everything. By the time she reached the grand staircase, the crowd in the lobby was thinning. The lights overhead flickered once, twice, in warning.

She went up the stairs and passed the *Mittelloge* doors, her pulse quickening as though she were passing a rattlesnake. She went straight to the spotlight room. From the little window she could see the audience settling in down below. The faces were excited, and the rumbling of voices was eager.

She dug her new opera glasses out of her purse. She had to work her way around the spotlight since she dared not move it. After a moment she locked her glasses on the *Mittelloge*.

And as the lights were dimming down, she saw him in the box. There, in the center of the front row, sat von Glower. He had with him a beautiful blond woman, elegantly coiffed, and behind him sat Leber and Stätter, bruisers in tuxes, plump and out of place.

But it was von Glower that mesmerized. It was him, really him, *the Black Wolf*. And she could see instantly why he'd always attracted conquests and not jailers. He was truly beautiful. There was even a kind of odd innocence, a boyish charm in his face that Grace had not expected. Even an air of . . . tragedy? Her heart skipped a beat, and she could imagine what Ludwig had felt that first night, spying on him, as she was, from across the theater.

How brilliant Bismark had been.

She almost felt sorry for him. She shook off the feeling. The important thing was that he was there, in the box, and by the eager smile on his face and his hushed whispers to his date, he suspected nothing.

She lowered the glasses, her mouth dry, her palms moist inside her gloves. Down below, the orchestra began.

He hoped they heard him upstairs—the crashing and the banging. He picked up another missile—this time a side table that weighed half of what it looked like it ought—and sent it careening into the opposite wall. It burst apart into fireplace-sized pieces.

Somewhere inside, he knew this sheer destruction was puerile. He'd regret it later, probably. But that reasoning was not getting much head room at the moment. At the moment his rage was a locomotive, a steam engine stoked to full speed. It took a long time to stop something like that. It would be a while before he'd even want to.

His blitzkrieg maneuvers had nearly cleared one wall. A single item remained, a large painted panel that showed a tree-lined river. The thing was against the wall for a reason—it was six feet wide, about as tall, and very thin. Without pausing in his outburst, Gabriel plowed into it. He couldn't get his arms around it, so he lifted it from the bottom and tilted it up and then over. It slid across Gabriel's bent head and shoulders and crashed to the floor behind him.

It made a satisfyingly loud bang.

He was about to turn around and go after the hapless thing again when his eye was drawn to the wall where the panel had been. There was a vent on the wall with a metal grate. *There was a grated vent on the wall.*

He blinked at it for a moment, Then he picked up one of the legs from that damned table and went after the grating.

The basement hallway was lit by bare, hanging bulbs, but had the feeling of darkness. Perhaps it was the musk

of the underground or the way corridors branched away
so helter-skelter, as if leading off into dead space.

Had there been anyone in this particular section of
the basement, they would have been quite alarmed at
the violent banging that came from the outward-facing
wall. It would have taken a moment to locate that
sound at the air vent, and by then the thin metal grate
was already bending out, crinkling in the middle like
tissue paper—the old, painted-over screws around the
perimeter buckling under the pressure.

And then the grating flew across the hall and
banged against the far wall, crashing to the floor. Feet
appeared—boots, and a body followed. Gabriel swung
himself to the ground, still breathing hard.

From the gaping vent the breeze of the June evening blew over him. The air duct he'd found in the
prop room emptied out into the street behind the theater. When he'd reached the street, he'd been gripped
with an almost unbearable urge to slip into the night,
to let the blood run its course, to stalk. He couldn't
resist popping off the thin screen covering and sticking
out his head to breathe deeply. And while taking this
breath, he'd heard the click of high heels approaching
on the cobblestones, and the stab of carnal desire,
desire to not only *plunder* but to *rend* so suffused him
that he cried out loud. The heels hesitated, as if hearing the cry, and he used the moment to pull himself
back inside, to take an adjoining air duct back, back
into the safety of the basement.

He stood there now, shivering in the hall, the cooler
air reaching in past his hot rage. Or perhaps the shivering came from some other place altogether, from
that place where his mind twitched at the reins of
control. He kicked the fallen grating, sending it spinning down the hall. Then he headed for the rear
stairs—the ones that led backstage.

The stairs that connected the basement and the
backstage were located against the far wall in relative

shadow. So that Gabriel, standing there, his hands on the iron railing that guarded the well of the stairs from becoming an accident hazard, could observe the scene unnoticed.

The music was louder here and clearer, less dream-like. He felt himself becoming more lucid, as if the sounds in the basement had been some drug that confused him. He listened carefully and heard that they were doing the trial scenes—they were well into Act II. He felt a surge of panic, and his heart—so large and foreign in his chest these days—added a heavy bass drum beat to the instrumentals.

Is he out there? Is he watching? Listening? Has he fallen for it, or was he too smart? He's so goddamn smart. Is he here?

He closed his eyes, shame and fear swamping him, threatening to take him somewhere he did not want to go.

He's here. Believe it.

After a while he was able to open his eyes and creep stealthily from the stairwell.

The backstage area was congested with enormous backdrops, with large props on wheeled dollies and ropes and pulleys and mechanical rigging. The crew was identifiable by their heavy jeans, T-shirts, and si-lent-soled tennis shoes. The singers themselves usually congregated on the edges, but there were no costumed players in evidence, for the trial scene involved everyone.

On stage, the baron was laying the curse, the music dark and menacing. His role was bass, and the singer's deep, bell-clear tones could fire the soul of the most obdurate cynic. They vibrated through the backdrop, and even the crew slowed a little, mesmerized.

Gabriel crept toward the dressing room. A youth spotted him, a grip, and his expression of alarm made it clear that the look on Gabriel's face—no doubt accompanied by the usual deathly paleness and bruised circles—was not quite up to passing as normal. Gabriel struggled to smile pleasantly.

The grip must have recognized him from rehearsals, for he didn't raise the alarm. He only smiled back, as nervously as a rabbit smiling at a coyote, and went over to check some bit of rope that didn't need checking.

Gabriel stepped into the back hall. At the doorway he saw a large roll of silver duct tape on a table and confiscated it. It was clutched in his shaking palm as he worked his way past wardrobe rollers and shoes. He'd heard the singers griping about the dressing rooms, and now he could see why. Even the public parts of the theater were faded and in need of restoration—backstage was worse.

The door he wanted wasn't difficult to spot. Someone—no doubt the lead tenor himself—had tacked up a handwritten and star-bedecked sign that said EN-GELHART on a thin, white-streaked door. Gabriel opened the door and stuck his head inside. The room that greeted him was tiny and empty, and it looked as though the tenor had managed to claim it all for himself. Gabriel smiled—a dark, hungry-looking smile—and slipped inside.

The time raced by. The music was magnificent, pounding. But Grace's consciousness kept drifting to a million things, a thousand ending scenarios, and when she tuned back in she was always amazed at how quickly the opera was passing. The bracelet love scene, the flight through the woods, the trial. And then, amazingly, it was intermission.

The spotlight beside her had remained silent and dark, a weapon lying in wait. It felt like an old friend now, so closely pressed to it had she remained since the music began. She couldn't resist staring at the *Mittelloge* through her glasses, though she could make out little and the strain hurt her eyes. Von Glower had not stirred.

She wished there was enough light to see the details of his face. What did he think of the werewolf plot line? Did he imagine that Wagner knew? Or did he assume that Ludwig's part in the libretto had shaped it in his own image without Wagner really understanding the truth beneath the fiction? Was he amused at Engelhart's supposed mastery of the curse? Of the representation of the evil renegade wolf? Did he feel that Ludwig had been a fool? Or was he capable of shame, embarrassment, resentment?

Did he have any idea what happened next?

When the lights came up, Grace was ready, her glass trained on the *Mittelloge* with painful intensity. Von Glower was smiling, his face dreamy, his eyes warm and amused and sparkling with energy.

He loved it.

Grace let out a low moan of relief, and became aware of how stiffly she'd been holding herself. Her fingers and her toes had gone cold and numb. She stretched a little, her glasses still trained on the box.

Von Glower rose to an intimidating height, limbs unfolding like a dragon's wings. She could not believe the breadth of his shoulders. His black tuxedo was expensive and immaculate; his white shirt and tie were blinding. He offered a hand to the woman beside him, smiled at her and said something, something excited, probably something about the opera or the music.

Leber and Stätter were already out the door.

Grace sighed again as the tension left her body. It was one of the last danger points. By his expression, she didn't imagine von Glower was about to leave. No, he'd be back in his seat for Act III.

She couldn't resist slipping out of the spotlight room and following him with her eyes as he went down the stairs with the crowd. She stood at the upstairs balcony and watched him purchase wine, sip it, and chatter excitedly—first to the woman, then to several people near them as heads and eyes turned, caught by his fire. She watched him and listed to the breathless buzz and words of praise and high, bright squeals of excitement all around them. The energy of the audience was infectious.

Then the lights blinked their warning, and Grace followed him with her eyes back up the stairs, fingering the key in her purse as if afraid it might disappear.

The music had begun by the time she took her place at the spotlight. The first piece, performed with the curtain closed, with an instrumental prelude to the wedding feast.

The key had turned softly in the lock, as she'd known it would.

Hildegunde's aria—"Song to the Moon"—swept the theater into a sorrowful melancholy. Grace spared a rare glance for the stage and saw everything in place there—the villagers gathered for the feast, the wedding table laden with food, the baron in his finery and Hildegunde's parents waiting patiently for the bride at the table so they could begin. And Hildegunde herself, framed by a spotlight and off on her own, spilling out her anguish at the nuptials to the silent moon above.

In the *Mittelloge* everyone was seated.

Ba-BUM! The drum beat entry on the minstrel's first song was unmistakable. The clarinets piped in with a high, playful stutter. Grace's ears followed this progression closely, but her eyes were glued to the opera glasses, and the glasses were trained on the *Mitteloge*.

She was therefore not looking at the stage when the minstrels appeared and began their upbeat introduction, a scene that involved juggling.

Wagner, impractical as he could often be, had wisely scripted the minstrels as silent. This not only worked for the story, but it also made it feasible to cast actual jugglers and acrobats in the roles, vocal talent not being a consideration. The exception among the group of five was Engelhart, of course, and the tenor who played him had been the bane of the jugglers' existence for lo these many weeks. Fortunately, the libretto called for Engelhart to repeatedly screw up as part of the comedy. Unfortunately, "screwing up" on cue could be as difficult as juggling correctly. Much time had been spent on getting the choreography right.

And now, focused as Grace was on watching the dark and unmoving figures in the box across the way, she gradually became aware of the laughter of the audience. For such a staid crowd, they were doing a great deal of *tee-heeing*. Grace didn't recall the scene being quite *that* funny. Her ears tuned into the villagers' chorus. Was it her imagination or did she detect a bit of faltering unease in those voices?

Frowning, Grace shifted her glasses to look at the stage.

The minstrel's costumes were bright and jester-like, their faces painted in white and red so as to hide Engelhart's identity. The four professional jugglers were scrambling, not quite in the right places. One was chasing after a ball, and Grace realized, with a sense of dread, that they'd screwed up for some reason—*really* screwed up. The juggler found the ball and came bounding back. The group tried gamely to reassemble before realizing that they were already supposed to be in their next position. They reformed into a line, and one of them roughly pushed Englehart into place and . . .

Grace stared, her breath stopping in her throat. She leaned forward as if that would help, unable to believe what she was seeing.

Engelhart was not Engelhart. Beneath the makeup the face was not right.

Gabriel. *Gabriel* was on stage.

"Oh, my God," she said out loud. "Oh, my *God*."

She nearly dropped the glasses down on some hapless viewer's head. She pulled herself back into the room, gasping, panic ripping through her.

"Oh, my God!"

For an instant none of it made any sense, and the conviction that it was all over, that the entire thing was ruined, loomed over her. It was beyond her what on earth, what the point, what he could possibly be thinking . . .

And then she knew. She knew exactly what he was thinking.

She moaned, low and anguished. She was so agitated that she became dizzy, her body starting to shut down. She put her head between her satin-covered knees and took deep breaths.

Outside, out there on stage where no doubt everyone except the audience was very confused, the final beats of the drum closed the juggling song and the audience applauded and called their approval with great relish. "Englehart" had apparently done an apt job of looking clueless.

And then the swirling dark strings began, the swirling dark pull of the strings, tentative now but they would build soon, build and build. Warner's masterpiece: *the transformation aria*.

She collected herself because she had to. There was no time to go downstairs, to get backstage, to try anything at all. The music was moving on, and soon, imminently, the time would come; either she would be at the spotlight to man it or she would not. There was no time to stop Gabriel now, whatever the consequences.

She sat up carefully and placed a trembling finger on the spotlight's on switch.

The villagers drew back in mock horror as the jesters stalked about, their arms raised menacingly, their painted faces pulled into snarls.

The baron rose, indignant. . . .

What is this dark business? It's my wedding day!

But the guests were entranced. The blacksmith pointed out the new pantomime: *the hunter, the hunter, tracking his prey*.

And indeed, the minstrels had drawn imaginary

bows. They stalked the edge of the stage, looking into the audience for some imaginary foe as the strings throbbed.

Let them continue, it suits my mood, urged Hildegunde.

Englehart looked a little ill behind his jester's paint. He tried to follow the moves of the other minstrels, but soon he was hunched over, trembling. The other minstrels "discovered" their quarry, one by one. They closed in on Engelhart as the tempo escalated. They circled his shivering form, widely, air bows held taut and aimed, faces diabolical. The violins shrieked a warning.

In the *Mitteloge,* the smile of the dark man faded. A light sweat broke out on his brow. He shifted uneasily in his seat, his eyes trained on the stage.

The tempo gathered speed and so did the minstrels. They circled Engelhart, not with measured, stalking steps, but at a gallop now, spinning around and around as their prey clutched his stomach and sank slowly to the floor. The strings began to scream as the minstrel circle tightened, still spinning, until Englehart was hidden entirely from view.

Below the stage, a crewman walked into the pit. He carefully placed his stool in a predesignated spot and opened a trapdoor. He shoved a furry mask and gloves up through the opening. They were flung back in his face, the trap pulled shut. He stood there on the stool, eyes wide, too terrified by the momentary glimpse he had caught to make his hand reach back up and open the trap again.

In a small dark room in the upper right-hand side of the theater, a woman in green satin leaned out a window, opera glasses trained fiercely on the stage.

While the conductor waved madly, trying to chase the tempo to enormous speeds, and the strings screeched in protest and fury, light tinkling could be heard—if anyone was *close* enough to hear it, that is—

coming from large crystal drops on the brand-new chandeliers.

The blond woman in the *Mitteloge* whispered to her companion, *Are you all right?,* for his face was a deathly gray and his eyes had reddened. The arm she was holding quivered as though subjected to a mild electrical current. He nodded unconvincingly and rose from his seat. He stumbled toward the door, one hand pressed to his stomach.

The two large men seated behind the couple turned to watch the man pass. The bald one frowned suspiciously.

The dark man reached the door and tried to open it. The handle would not yield. The door was locked. He turned and flattened his back against the door.

The crystals were shaking in the chandeliers above, vibrating, but lightly and intermittently, like a wind chime on a mildly breezy day. If they were built to withstand storms, they weren't getting much of a trial run today.

And the strings, as the minstrels whirled, could not go any faster or squeal any higher.

The heavyset bald man stood and asked the dark gentleman if there was a problem with the door.

But the gentleman had recovered himself a bit. His breathing, though still heavy, sounded more relieved than embattled, as though he'd just finished a long run. He removed a black handkerchief from his black pocket and wiped his face carefully. He offered a polite reassurance to the bald man; then he straightened, still a bit wobbly, and headed back to his seat. He seated himself and took a steadying breath, smoothed back his hair, and smiled. His smile held a kind of wild and ugly relief, like a killer walking away with a last-minute pardon from the gallows.

The vibration of the chandeliers was not enough; the trap had misfired.

The woman in green did not see any of this. Her eyes were locked on the stage. She was waiting for the next part, the part where the minstrels burst apart, so that she could see Englehart once more. She had forgotten the spotlight entirely.

She remembered it belatedly, cued by something familiar in the score. But by then the moment was upon her. Without even turning to check the *Mittelloge* with her glasses, she reached over and flipped the switch.

The four people in the center box, resettled only seconds ago, were suddenly blinded by light. The bald man, who was enjoying the performance very much, lost his temper at this latest interruption. He cursed loudly and placed a pudgy hand over his brow, trying to see what the hell . . .

On stage, the minstrels burst apart. Only it was not choreographed as it was in rehearsal—with a kind of triumphant presentation. They *disintegrated,* uttering sharp cries that were barely heard over the cacophony of minor chords being pounded out by the orchestra.

And standing in the middle of the stage, the place the minstrels had so hastily vacated, was a large animal—something like a wolf, only squatter and more brutish, less natural, more hideous. The singers on the stage reared back, some bumping into the banquet hall walls, which swayed. A few even fled the stage altogether though, with the music still going, most were professional enough—or confused enough—to remain.

The audience looked at the creature. At first there was silence and then, after a beat, enormous applause washed through the room.

The woman in green, astonished, thought: *They believe it's a stunt.* Perhaps it was because they couldn't quite see the teeth (you wouldn't be able to get past the teeth), for the creature's head was thrown back, and now something joined the strings, something high and eerie and unreal.

In the *Mittelloge,* where the light had prevented anyone in the box from seeing anything on stage, the bald man got up and went to the door, irritated at this intolerable distraction and damned well . . .

He heard a scream and turned.

The dark man. He was rising to his feet slowly, and his body was being racked violently with convulsions. He screamed again. It was a scream of outrage, of protest. His face was swarthy now, a horrible gray, and he no longer looked elegant or boyish. He was frightening. Something about him was wrong, was not right at all.

The woman beside him edged out of her seat. Her words were sympathetic, but her eyes were terrified and her movements spoke of instinctual escape. And the bald man too had instincts and they were thrumming. He unbuttoned his coat and placed a hand on his gun.

Meanwhile, the sound, that one unearthly sound that did not resemble any instrument anyone in the audience had ever heard save two—the dark man and the woman in green—went on, not as loud as the orchestra, surely, but cutting through the music anyway, cutting right into a person's soul.

That perhaps was why most eyes in the audience were still riveted on the stage, despite the fact that some lighting screw-up had caused a portion of the upper seats to be lit. But the woman in green was watching the *Mittelloge*. She was watching intently.

The dark man hunched down, eyes darting around madly. Beneath his black coat things . . . *shifted*. The bald man drew his gun and shouted a warning to the dark man, a command.

And the dark man, before anyone could anticipate it, placed a hand on the balustrade and leapt over it. In one graceful gesture he gathered himself and leapt right *over* it, and then he was sailing through the air before landing, with a grunt, on the red-carpeted aisle a story below. For a moment he crouched there, panting and uttering a low, growling sound, his brow, his face starting to blur, and then he spun around, ignoring the startled faces in the seats around him, and bounded from the auditorium through the double doors.

The woman in green muttered a curse and stood, causing the spotlight to fall with a crash. On the stage, the creature that had been Engelhart lowered its head, its eyes searching the crowd. It tensed its haunches and sprang toward the audience.

A few souls mingled out in the lobby, ushers mainly, and they screamed as the human-like crouching thing in a tuxedo careened from the auditorium into their midst. It headed for the front doors first, but they were closed tightly for the performance. It continued around the perimeter, people diving to get out of its way, then it disappeared down the open archway with the descending stairs, the one marked *PRIVAT*.

In the *Mittelloge,* which was suddenly dark once more, the bald man held his gun in the air with one hand and pounded on the door with another, shouting to be let out.

In the pit, the young conductor, eyes wide, face devastated, was still conducting wildly. The orchestra followed, watching him leerily. They could not see the stage, but they could see that he was losing it.

And the singers, after missing several bars, collected themselves in time for the final line. The blacksmith was against the prop wall, which was fortunately still standing. He reached over and grabbed a torch from a sconce. Holding it up in a trembling hand, he managed the closing line of the scene.

Let's go follow the wolves.

This all happened in the same instant, and in the next, a creature, truly a *creature* this time, bounded out of the auditorium into the lobby, stopped momentarily as if sniffing the air, and then dove down the basement stairs.

This seemed to be the moment for which the basement was built. Or perhaps when built, it was not nearly so dark and dank and eerie. Perhaps it had become that way progressively, like a backdrop molding itself to an anticipated play.

Whether any or none of this was true, what *was* true was that something was going on in the basement. Not something, Something rather, the kind of Something that most human beings would never believe and would, in their heart of hearts (where they knew exactly how vulnerable the tethers that hold the rational mind to its mooring really are), choose *not* to know.

Even Gabriel's rational mind chose not to know. Even, to some extent, von Glower's. The creature that shared Gabriel's altered DNA did not know many of the things that Gabriel knew. There was a gap there— a kind of segmentation that was necessary, not only for the mind of the beast, but more important, for the mind of the human, that kept either experience from becoming too conscious of the other.

Yet the Gabriel-thing knew this: it knew that it was stalking the von Glower-thing. And it knew precisely what it had to do once it found its target. Whether or not it *could* do it did not enter its mind.

It paused at the bottom of the stairs and sensed the air. One of the things it *could* access from its human memory was spatials, location memory. It *knew* the basement in an odd, schematic way. It could remember, for example, the prop room, and even had a vague fear of being confined there.

And now, aided by its sense of smell, it knew other things as well. It could easily smell the tantalizing drift of fresh night air, and it knew the direction from whence it came. It could smell its target, too. . . .

And it knew the target was heading for the fresh air.

It ran quickly down the corridor to the left. As it rounded the turn and saw the open vent, it saw too that the black wolf was heading toward it down a side corridor.

But the brown wolf had gotten there first.

It snarled at the black beast, lowering itself down

on thick muscles and baring its teeth in a clear challenge. The black stopped. Its eyes darted toward the vent, then back to the brown. It retreated a step. It gave a low warning growl but nothing more.

The brown, encouraged by this, began to stalk forward. The black stepped backward for each step the brown took.

Through the winding, jutting, low-roofed corridors, long and short, narrow and wide, they continued this way. It became clear that the black did not want a fight. It was not afraid exactly, the brown beast sensed, for it didn't have the smell of fear and its movements were not submissive. It simply wanted to walk away, the way a father would leave a cub who was getting too aggressive.

This made the brown very angry.

It tried several times to dodge around to the left or right, to get the black against a wall, but the black was sure-footed, confident, and easily evaded such maneuvers.

The brown tried to use its spatial memory, its vague ideas of shape and layout. It was not stupid—indeed, it was exceedingly bright, if limited. It realized that it needed a place where the black could no longer back away, but it couldn't exactly recall . . .

It stopped growling long enough to sniff the air again. And that's when it smelled the fire and its memory pulled up a vague outline of that room, the room with the fire-thing: a box-shaped cave with only one exit.

It began corralling the black toward the southeast corner of the basement. The black continued to retreat, but now that pleased the brown. If it could have, it would have grinned.

They reached the southeast corner along the main east-west hallway. To the right was the opening to the furnace room. The heat came through the doorway in rippling waves. Instinctually, whether from the heat or a sense of the dead end in that direction, the black wolf turned the corner without pause and began backing down the north-south corridor, away from the furnace room.

The brown wolf tried to dodge around the black, to head it off—make it turn back, but the black only mirrored the moves, which made it back away faster. The brown slowed immediately, panicking. It wasn't working! Now they were headed the wrong way!

The brown knew that time was against it. If they continued to back around like this, soon the black would be close once more to the night air opening. In the brown's current position, the black could not be prevented from turning and making an escape.

And then, as they'd almost reached the stairwell leading up, sounds clattered down on them—not just the sounds of the people above, but other sounds— *sounds of human feet on the stairs,* low and stealthy, unmistakable.

The black's calm was broken. It turned its head away from the brown, trying to gauge if it could make it past the doorway before the human arrived. The brown thought it could not, but if the black ran fast, it might be able to startle the human enough to get past it anyway. It decided to give the black another option.

The brown whined in mock fear. It sensed the black's head swing in its direction even though its own eyes were trained on the stairs. It whimpered again and began backing away itself, back, back. It turned the corner back into the east-west hallway.

The brown waited there silently, every nerve humming in anticipation.

The black came around the corner.

The brown stood its ground, its mock fear gone. Now it bristled and snapped its teeth, its eyes full of hatred. The black turned, confused, and began to go back down the north-south hallway, but it stopped immediately and tensed, seeing something.

The brown heard a harsh human cry through the

buzzing adrenaline in its ears. It was instantly followed by a loud *bang* and a metal smell. It knew what made the noise and the smell—a death maker, human teeth.

The black spun around again and ran into the furnace room. The brown, not even pausing to see what was down the hallway, followed at once.

Grace had let Leber out. She was moving the moment von Glower disappeared through the auditorium door. As she unlocked the *Mittelloge,* she mumbled to the detective something about that man—that man *changing,* but he only looked at her like she was insane and pushed past her, gun raised.

She followed Leber and Stätter as they raced down the stairs. In the auditorium the music went on, but those in the lobby were certainly not of the mind that everything was all right.

"There was a dark-haired man," Leber shouted in German as he came down the stairs.

An usher pointed shakily toward the basement stairs.

"And then this huge brown animal went after him!" This was spoken by a woman in a black gown, her face so pasty it was like a white sail over a black ship.

Leber looked at the woman, his face knit in confusion, then glanced at Grace suspiciously. She realized that with the spotlight and the confusion, he hadn't seen the creature on stage at all. Would he have known immediately that it matched the description of his killer?

"Is there another way down?" Leber asked.

Before Grace could decide how to answer, one of the ushers said yes, and Stätter was sent off with the fellow backstage. They were going to use both stairs—try to corner whatever was down there.

"Wait a minute," Grace said. It was as if her words were swallowed up by a vacuum. No one even blinked in her direction. They were all watching Leber as he headed down the stairs.

And Grace realized that letting Leber out was maybe not such a great idea. She hesitated a moment, frozen with confusion and fear. Things seemed to be going progressively wrong, like a bad idea rolling down a hill. Gabriel was down there too, and Leber had a gun.

She went after him.

When Grace was halfway down the stairs, she heard a shout and gunfire. She called Leber's name, but there was no response. She flew to the bottom, her high-heeled feet keeping to the steps only by sheer chance. She looked out into the hall, her dark eyes wide.

There was nothing to the north. To the south she saw Leber disappear into the furnace room.

Leber's large, black-jacketed back blocked the door. By the stance of his legs and the angle of his shoulders, Grace knew he was holding the gun straight out. She prayed that what was in the room was only *one* and that it was not . . .

She pushed past him. He glanced at her sideways and shouted. "Get back! Get out of here!" But she was looking with shock at what was in the room.

They stood at the only exit. To her left was the coal furnace, like a huge squatting fertility figure, its glass door showing fire red dancing deep inside. Straight ahead, backed against the cracked cement wall, was an enormous black beast, almost four foot tall at the head, with long legs and a wide, muscled torso.

The black was snarling at Leber and now at her. It knew it was trapped, and it was furious. It ignored the brown beast. It wanted only the doorway behind the humans.

Grace tore her eyes away from the black and faced what she didn't want to face. On the right-hand wall was a creature very much like the first, though shorter and squatter with a mottled brown coat. She looked at it, her eyes gazing right into its eyes.

Partially out of respect for his privacy, and particularly out of respect for her own sanity, Grace had never seen Gabriel in the Change—*no one* had seen him. He'd been left in the dungeon alone. What she laid eyes on now was both more beautiful and more horrible than she'd ever imagined. The beast was beautiful, the way a wolf is beautiful, and more, because of the intelligence that shone in it. And yet it was profoundly hideous too. Some sense of the unnatural pervaded its being the way death casts an almost visible veil of decay across the face of a man in his deathbed. And there was something heinous deep in the eyes, something heartless and inhuman and predatory. And that image was answered by the teeth, which jutted and snapped and spoke of mortal, fleshy things the way a surgeon's tools spoke of them.

Her emotions were like a grab bag of unassociated scraps. Part of her was embarrassed that she had to see him like this; part of her was concerned that he was here at all and of what might happen next; part of her was overwhelmed with pity; and part of her looked at that face and was *terrified,* terrified in a way that not even the black could provoke, because she had no idea what he would or wouldn't do, would or would not remember from his human side, and the thought of being killed, of being *slaughtered* and *eaten* by *this,* by *him,* was somehow so much worse than the mere idea of being slaughtered and eaten at all.

The brown had been growling and snarling too. But when Grace looked into its eyes, its snarl faltered briefly. Then it turned its head away, its eyes wild and unknowing, and hunched down, increasing its furious challenge toward the black.

Leber was swinging his gun from the black to the brown and back again. By the expression on his face, Grace knew that he was not only afraid, he was in a zone of denial and confusion where he might do just about anything. He now focused the gun on the brown, responding to its increased aggression even if it wasn't aimed his direction.

"Don't shoot!" Grace shouted.

"Get out!" Leber screamed back.

There were only seconds, Grace knew. Should she shove Leber? Let Gabriel escape? But that would only let the black escape too. Her eyes raced around the room, trying to see anything at all that would provide another option. And then, of course, she did. She began to creep around Leber, staying close to the wall. *"Stay back!"* he screamed at her again. Grace ignored him. It was only a few feet to the furnace. The black glanced at her once, but it remained focused on the man and the blocked exit. The brown looked at her and it looked at the furnace too. It stopped growling abruptly, licked its maw, and watched her with those red, horrible, hungry eyes.

Grace reached the furnace, her heart pounding. She stretched her hand around and tugged the glass door's latch. It unhooked smoothly and swung out. She pushed it, hoping it would swing all the way to the other side and stay there. It was a heavy door. It did.

She looked back at the brown, and the brown looked at her.

Then the black leapt. She sensed the movement and turned her head in time to see the muscled haunches unfolding, the body elongating into the air. It was aimed directly at Leber, and its arc would land it somewhere on his upper chest, knocking him to the ground. Leber fired once into the air, wildly. Grace was never to know what happened to that bullet. If it hit the black at all, anywhere, she was never to know. For the brown was also leaping. It had left the ground the moment it saw the black make its move.

It happened so quickly, so very quickly. An instant after the gunshot rang out, the brown's arc intersected the black's arc, and the two collided in midair.

The brown rammed into the black's left side, its

head lowered. The black uttered a muffled grunt of surprise and sailed away from the collision. It flew, like a wad of paper shot at a wastepaper basket, right at the furnace. Its head and limbs bumped against the edge of the gaping iron mouth, but its momentum was great; they folded and disappeared into the inferno an instant after the torso.

Grace raced around the furnace, slammed the door shut, and latched it. She turned to see the brown beast dodge between the legs of the flabbergasted Leber. Ungodly howls of anguish rose up behind her. They echoed through the metal gullet, through the room, through the soul, as if the pit of hell itself had opened.

Leber, his face almost comically lost, turned on heavy, numb feet, as gracefully and swiftly as a pregnant cow getting up, and stepped into the hallway. Grace followed, too late to keep him from getting off one shot. But it didn't hit its target, anyone could see that. The brown, still racing full tilt, skidded around the corner at the end of the north-south hallway, paws scrambling, and disappeared.

"Don't shoot!" Grace screamed, grabbing Leber's arm.

Stätter came running breathlessly down a side corridor. His gun was drawn and his face was a heart-hammering red. Leber looked at him, then back at Grace, his face wiped clean of all expression.

He shook off her restraining hand. "I'll talk to you later," he managed. Then he motioned to his partner, and he and Stätter went trotting off down the hall.

But they didn't look like they knew what they were doing, and Grace thought there was little to worry about. The brown would find someplace to go to ground in this labyrinth. For that matter, he might already be changing, the curse slipping away into smoke.

She walked back into the furnace room. Behind the glass were flames, engulfing flames. The howling screams had stopped. There was the crackle of hungry fire and a dull thud. Something that might have once been a human foot struck the glass lightly, like a fetus kicking the walls of its womb. Then it fell away again into the flames.

Grace turned and went back into the hall, closing the furnace room door softly behind her.

Epilogue

He slept for forty-eight hours, on and on. Grace woke him at one point, fearing he'd gone into a coma or back into some past domain whence he couldn't return. But he surfaced readily enough when she shook him, thanked her dryly for the interruption, then rolled over and went back to sleep.

The cells of his body were changing in imperceptible ways beneath the sheets.

When he finally got up, Gerde made him breakfast. Grace sat and had tea while he ate, watched him with her steady, almond-shaped eyes. He appeared to be in an almost giddy good humor, humming as he filled his belly. She supposed he had a right to be.

She finally worked up her nerve and spoke. "Now that you're feeling better, I, uh, I suppose I should be getting back to the States."

He sighed and put down his fork, filled his cup from a pitcher of coffee on the table. "I wouldn't mind goin' back to New Orleans myself. Visit for a bit." He took a loud sip. "Maybe we'll find someone there to run the shop."

Grace's lips pressed into a thin line.

"Don't ya think, Gracie?"

"And then you'll come back here?" she asked casually.

"Yup. There's still a bunch of work to be done in the library. And, I confess, I haven't been doin' it."

"I'm sure Gerde can help you get it straightened out," she said, looking down at her cup.

"What about you? You'd be . . . hell, you know that's your thing. If you wanna stay, that is. Or you can go back with me and then come back later. . . ." He put down his cup and stretched his arms in a phony yawn. It was a sure sign of embarrassment.

She felt a deep burn color her throat. She didn't look up. "You didn't want me on this case," she pointed out in a neutral voice.

He let out a long exhale and said nothing for a moment. "I didn't want you in Munich, that's all. I just . . . I was worried about ya, I guess."

She studied him, her lower lip quivering. "You're full of shit."

"I'm serious." He rubbed the growth on his chin, not meeting her eyes. "I remember what happened in New Orleans. I didn't want to put either one of us through that again. I know it was selfish, but that's honestly why I . . . why I didn't have you join me there. Bad reasoning, but it looks like you did better here in Rittersberg anyway."

She scooted back the chair and folded her arms, her face determined. "Look, I appreciate, Gabriel Knight, that you're the strong, silent, independent type."

He made a *brat* sound with his mouth. *"Silent?"*

"And I appreciate your concern for my safety, if that's what you call it. *But* . . . either I'm in or I'm out."

"I realize that."

"I'm *in* or I'm *out*," she repeated, giving him her stubborn chin. "Full partners. Or I'll make other plans."

" 'Full partners'?" He laughed and laughed, bright and joyful. She frowned, hurt at first, but there was no malice in the sound. "God, Gracie, you are *somethin'*!"

"Well?"

He rose and came over to her chair, leaned down until his lips were only centimeters from her tense little neck.

"You're in," he whispered. Then he strolled, with the cocky gait of his, from the room.

Grace said nothing, but her hands trembled as she took another sip of tea.